The Shelter

Andy Mellett-Brown

To my beautiful wife Patricia Anne,
for believing in me always.

CHAPTER ONE

th
Friday, 10   November 1944

A trolleybus stops on Haverstock Hill and a young woman steps from the platform into the darkness, drawing her knee-length woollen coat about her.   The rain, which has been pounding the side of the trolleybus since Euston, is turning to sleet and, as the bus pulls away, she is caught by a swirling gust of wind that is so cold, it leaves her gasping in its wake. She fumbles for her top button but fails, wholly, to prevent water from trickling down her neck with an icy finger. She shudders and utters a silent curse.

There had been little sign of rain when, earlier that day, she had completed her shift, said goodbye to the other girls in the hut and walked the short distance to the station. But as the train had clattered towards Euston, the smog that normally coated the city like a great grey shroud had been washed from the skies by the downpour. She'd watched it from the grimy carriage window, falling in sheets across the London skyline.

She wipes the rain from her face, her cheeks stinging in the cold. As she turns to make her way along Haverstock Hill, a rain-sodden newspaper wraps itself around her leg. She reaches down to untangle it, struggling to maintain her balance on the slippery pavement. She notices the headline before the soaking paper falls to pieces in her hand.

She stands in silence, listening to the familiar sounds of a street that she has known since childhood. She pushes the headline from her mind and is there, for a moment, skipping beside her mother, stepping gingerly from paving stone to paving stone, willing her feet to avoid the cracks.

She sighs. Still, she loves her days off and always looks forward to returning home. She works long hours at the Park and, by the end of each shift, she is usually too tired to socialise with the other girls, preferring to return to her room in the little cottage at Wolverton where she has been billeted.

The cottage, which overlooks the Grand Union Canal is a few yards from *The Galleon*, an old public house beside the canal. The newer girls at the Park, who have to make do with the more basic accommodation in the camp huts, think it a scandal that she has been billeted so close to a public house, yet prefers to spend her evenings in her room, rather than at the bar. They tease her about it endlessly.

She smiles. If the truth be told, she would prefer the camp. Though many of the girls are civilians, it is run along military lines and she likes the discipline. It reminds her of life at home, before the war. Her father had run the house like a military barracks, barely allowing them time to think, let alone to worry. Now, he is away and the world outside is full of nothing but suffering and chaos.

On the camp there is little time for worrying. On Tuesday evenings the day shift girls are confined to barracks and the huts have to be cleaned, the bedding changed and everything polished until it sparkles. Afterwards there is usually a lecture and often there are rehearsals. It seems to her such a shame that while much effort goes into the productions, nobody from the outside is invited in to see them. Still, the internal audience is always appreciative and on occasion the productions turn into quite uproarious affairs.

Unlike many of the girls, she would also prefer the security of camp life. There are sentries posted on the entrance to both the male and female camps and while the men can walk through the women's camp, which they do in order to collect coal or coke from the nearby sheds, they are most certainly not allowed to loiter. Girls have been known to try to sneak a man into one of the female huts but when they are caught there is always hell to pay.

She is no prude but disapproves of such antics and struggles to understand what some girls find so attractive about a brute in a uniform. Not that all of the men at the Park are brutes, by any means. Some of them, especially those who work in decryption, are very well educated indeed. They tend to keep themselves to themselves, pre-occupied as they are with some complex code or mathematical equation. She thinks them almost other-worldly. Not at all the sort of men to be smuggled into to a camp hut in the dark.

She is tired now and stumbles on the slippery pavement as she makes her way along. Last night Elsie, who sits at the desk next to hers and who has been her closest friend since their first days together at Beaumanor, had insisted on joining her at The Galleon for a few drinks before her weekend away. Elsie is from a wealthy family and dresses and speaks well. The other girls say that she looks like Margaret Lockwood. The young woman in the woollen coat supposes that they are right. Elsie is tall and beautiful and always looks a picture.

But while Elsie carries herself like a film star during the day, she has a habit of drinking like a fish at night and last night Elsie had excelled herself. By eight thirty, she had already attracted the attention of a rather handsome but very drunk naval petty officer. When he'd bragged, altogether too loudly for his own good, about a log book that he said he'd liberated from a German U-boat, Elsie had hatched a plot to take it from his kit bag. Talking her out of it had been the devil of a job.

By half past ten, Elsie had been quite unable to walk to the bus stop, let alone make it safely back to her camp hut. The petty officer had offered to accompany her and Elsie would have gone too. The young woman in the woollen coat wonders what would have become of her had she not intervened and insisted that Elsie spend the night at her billet.

Elsie had snored like a train half the night and when, in the small hours of the morning, the young woman in the woollen coat had abandoned any further hope of sleep, she'd discovered the log book poking from Elsie's inside coat pocket.

One of these days, Elsie was going to get herself in to the most terrible trouble. But at least it would not be today.

'I didn't. Oh Lord, please tell me that I didn't take it,' she'd said over breakfast, her head in her hands.

'You did. Earlier this morning, while you were sleeping off last night's excesses, it might interest you to know that I was busily attempting to make amends for your thoroughly reckless behaviour.'

'You returned it.'

Elsie had said it with such relief that she hadn't had the heart to tell her why she had been unable to return the book to the hapless petty officer. The young woman in the woollen coat wonders what she is going to do with it on her return to the Park. She consoles herself with the thought that for now, at least, it is safe.

Elsie had looked like she'd been dragged through a hedge backwards when she finally hauled herself out of bed. But, to her credit, by the time they had left to catch the bus to the Park, Elsie was Margaret Lockwood again. As they queued at the Park's main gate, they had giggled secretly about the look of disappointment on the petty officer's face when, declining his offer to accompany Elsie back to the Park, they had stumbled out of The Galleon, arm-in-arm and grinning like fools.

The young woman in the woollen coat picks up her pace. She wants to be home and out of the freezing rain.

The air raid siren startles her as it wails a sudden warning and her heel slips on the curb. Her ankle twists painfully and she finds herself on one knee. She utters a curse, more for the ladder in her stocking than the discomfort. They cost her a fortune and these are her last pair. She gets to her feet and hobbles to the side of the pavement to sit, for a moment, on a garden wall. The iron railings have been removed to make more Spitfire engines, or some such, and she squeezes, uncomfortably, between the sawn off metal stumps.

As she sits, nursing her ankle, people begin to emerge from their houses like spirits from a mausoleum, floating out into the night. She observes their progress, in silence.

The residents of Haverstock Hill are mostly too elderly to have been called up for national service but there are younger women among them, some on their own and some with small children. Far from being afraid, as they ought to be, the children look excited to be out in the night. They skip along beside their mothers despite the rain, their gas masks bobbing up and down in boxes on strings around their necks.

A woman with a small child stops, the little boy tugging her by the hand, urging her to hurry. 'Shh, Joe. The lady has hurt herself. Are you alright lovey?'

'No, I am not alright. I have twisted my ankle and I am positively soaked,' she snaps. It is most unlike her to be short. Especially with someone who is showing her some consideration, but her ankle is throbbing.

'Well, I wouldn't sit there all night if I were you. God knows what the bloody Krauts are up to. You don't even hear them coming. One hit Islington a few nights back. Arms and legs all over the place, there were. And worse.'

The woman turns and, giving in to her son, hurries away.

The young woman in the woollen coat wonders, with a shudder, what could be worse than arms and legs.

The street is filled with people now, all walking in one direction. This puzzles her until she remembers the shelter on the corner. She has no intention of spending the night there. She detests the underground, with its grimy tunnels and overcrowded platforms. The shelters are worse. Rows and rows of bunk beds, sometimes two or three high, with rubbish strewn floors and, worst of all, the dreadful din. Children crying, people arguing, coughing, laughing, snoring and the Lord knows what else. How anyone actually manages to sleep down there is a mystery to her.

She gets to her feet and limps along with the flow of people. *'Twenty minutes,'* she thinks *'and I'll be home.'*

Shortly, she is able to see the entrance. The shelter is a squat, circular building, with a square tower rising from its centre. She supposes that this is a ventilation duct, drawing stale air from the tunnels many feet below. With its featureless walls, flat roof and tower, the shelter is quite unlike any of the other buildings in the street and she finds herself wondering whether it is as conspicuous from the air as it is from the ground. She is almost past the entrance when she hears someone call out and feels a hand on her shoulder.

CHAPTER TWO

Monday, 24th May 2004

Harry Stammers stretched and reached for his coffee. It was cold. He got up from his desk, walked the few yards to the kitchen, emptied his cup and refilled it from the jug on the percolator. He stood for a few moments, gazing out of the window, across the lake. The spray from the fountain had formed a rainbow in the bright May sunshine. A group of school children were playing beside the water. A small boy broke away from the others, picked up a stone and threw it, hard, out into the middle of the lake. A teacher walked across to him and grabbed him by the arm. Harry remembered seaside holidays, throwing stones into the sea. He had never once managed to out-throw his father. He sighed. He'd loved it when they had all been together and the holidays most of all. Then everything had changed and the holidays had stopped.

The telephone on Harry's desk was ringing. He walked briskly back to his office and picked up the receiver.

'Stammers.'

'Harry, it's Jane. There's some post for you. Can you come and collect it? I'm on my own again this morning.'

'Where's Linda? Not off sick again? When are you going to do something about that bloody woman?'

'Oh dear. Did we get out of bed on the wrong side this morning?'

'Yes, as a matter fact we did.'

Jane Mears was in her early thirties. She was neither a particularly attractive woman, nor was she popular with the majority of her colleagues. Not that this appeared to bother her in any way. She made little or no effort, Harry thought, on either count.

She was impossibly thin and flat chested and always dressed plainly. Harry had only ever seen her in trousers. With a sharp, bird-like face framed by short, jet black hair, the impression was, Harry had to concede, more masculine than feminine. Not that he cared which side Jane batted for. He liked her. She was honest and about as direct as it was possible to be. But more than that, Harry liked her because she was thoroughly committed to her work at the Park. Which, in a sane world, would have won her more admirers there, than it had. But a sharp tongue and an unwillingness to tolerate fools, whether gladly or otherwise, meant that she was never going to win any popularity contest.

'You can tell me all about it at lunch time if you like but, in the meantime, just get your arse up here and collect your damned post,' Jane said.

Harry said that he would and hung up. He put on his jacket and stepped out on to the archive landing. He had opted for an office in the archive as much of his work was there and he needed the peace and quiet. The archive was located on the first floor of a large concrete building at the centre of the Park. It was accessed via a flight of metal steps which, so far as Harry was concerned, made no sense at all. Whenever equipment or documents were donated, they would be brought to the archive for investigation. Lugging boxes of paperwork and heavy equipment up the metal stairs was a distinctly perilous enterprise that Harry could have lived without.

He descended the steps and, at the bottom, lit a cigarette using his hand to shelter the flame from the cool breeze blowing in from the lake. He blew a smoke ring. Jane had been right. He had got out of bed on the wrong side this morning. Although not entirely right. He'd been unable to sleep and had spent much of the night in his arm chair, reading. He must have drifted off at about two in the morning and had woken shortly after five, with the book on his lap and a crick in his neck.

Harry walked the short distance to the bungalow, a small, single story building at the top of the Park. He stubbed his cigarette out on the pavement outside and opened the door. Jane was seated immediately opposite the entrance. Other than her desk, which was always tidy, the office was, as usual, a shambles with papers, files, books and equipment piled everywhere.

'Ah, it's Mr Happy,' she said, with barely a smile.

Harry grunted a retort under his breath.

'Before you say anything, I'm warning you that the Major is looking for you and he is a not a happy bunny.'

'What have I done this time?' Harry asked.

'It is not what you have done, as you well know. It is what you haven't done. He is expecting a progress report, at the very least.'

'Damn it. I'm doing it as quickly as I can. I'm a curator, not a bloody private detective.'

'Hey, don't shoot the messenger. I'm just warning you. He is in his office and I can hear him growling from here,' said Jane.

'Warning noted.'

Harry collected his post from his pigeon hole and beat a hasty retreat. As he closed the door behind him Jane called out 'Give me a ring at lunch time and we'll catch up then.'

Harry walked back to his office and sat down at his desk. He looked at the pile of letters he had collected. Junk, mostly. He went through them, tossing them into the waste paper basket until he got to the final envelope. He opened it, read its contents and reached for the telephone but before he could dial the number he felt his mobile phone vibrating in his pocket. He retrieved the phone and recognised the number flashing on the tiny screen. 'Hi Mike.'

'Hey, hey, Harry. What are you doing at the weekend?'

'Nothing and it is staying that way.'

He had known Mikkel Eglund since their days at University, when Mike had been studying electronic engineering and Harry, social history. Originally from Norway, Mike spoke with a broad accent and this, coupled with a distinctly Scandinavian sense of humour, tended to put off people who didn't know him well. As a consequence, he had a narrow group of friends which happily included Harry.

'Oh, come on. A bunch of us are going to take a look at an old receiving station on Sunday morning and I thought you might be up for it.'

'You did? Well I'm not. I'm still not out of the woods from the last little escapade.'

Harry remembered the local newspaper headlines. How Jane had managed to calm the Major, he would never know.

'Are they still mad with you about that?'

'You are kidding? I am the curator of a museum with a national profile. We have a multi-million pound bid in for a grant from the Heritage Lottery Fund. I cannot get caught breaking into M.O.D. sites. The old boy nearly had my balls for his Christmas tree.'

'Man, it looked like an empty building in a field. How were we to know it was still M.O.D? '

'Well it was.'

'Sure, but in Norway we have soldiers guarding those places. You have sheep?'

'No. We have Securicor. Remember?'

'Hey, but your arse looked great coming over that fence.'

Harry had to laugh. When the security guards had shown up they had made a run for it and Harry had caught his trousers on a piece of barbed wire, going over a fence. It had torn a gaping hole and Mike, half a dozen paces behind and camera in hand, had snapped off a couple of hasty photographs, principally of Harry's backside. The first that Harry had known about them was when, a few days later, they appeared on the internet, much to everyone's amusement.

'Name me another museum curator with his arse plastered all over the net.'

'I don't even want to go there,' Harry said.

There was an easy silence.

'So where is this place you're going on Sunday?' Harry couldn't believe that he was even asking.

'Just north of Hemel Hempstead.'

'Security?'

'Nope. It was decommissioned in the nineties.'

'What's it used for now?'

'Nothing. The land around it is leased out for farming.'

'That's what you said the last time.'

'Come on, man. It'll be cool.'

Harry hesitated. 'It is a shame but I just can't afford to get caught again,' he said.

'Look, if you don't want to come in, you can always handle the radio from the car. We could do with a lookout this time,' Mike said. 'There's a pint in it?'

Incredibly Harry found himself entertaining the idea. He didn't have anything else planned and the chances of getting caught a second time did seem fairly remote.

'Alright but this time, if the enemy shows up, I'm off and to hell with the lot of you.'

'Done.'

Harry thought that he would be, if anything went wrong.

CHAPTER THREE

th
Friday, 10   November 1944

'Excuse me Miss, but you need to come inside.'

'What?' says the young woman in the knee length woollen coat.

'The air raid, Miss. It is not safe,' says a man in a dark uniform. It looks at least one size too small for him.

'We can take a look at that for you,' he says, nodding at her foot. There is a white "W" painted on the front of his tin hat.

'It is quite alright. I am less than twenty minutes away from home,' she says, trying to mask the anxiety she is feeling at the prospect of a night in the shelter.

The warden looks at her. As if to justify his impatience, there is low boom some way off in the distance. Within moments the sky to the southeast has turned orange.

An elderly man standing next to her turns to look, his face glowing faintly in the reflected light. 'The City, I reckon. Aldgate way. Poor sods,' he says, shaking his head.

The warden takes her by the arm.

'Look, my mother will be worried sick if I'm late,' she says, almost casually. She turns, as if to leave but he has a firm grip.

'She'll be a bloody sight more than worried if you are blown to pieces out here,' he says and with that he marches her through the doorway.

Inside, the shelter's upper lobby is a mass of people. A second, unusually tall warden, is attempting to form them into two orderly queues.

'Ron?' calls out the first warden over the din. 'This one's done her leg in. Help her into the lift would you?'

'Yes mate,' the warden named Ron calls back. He sails effortlessly towards them through the waiting mass, like a tall ship in high seas. 'Come on, Miss.'

He says it kindly enough but when she tries to speak her voice is drowned by the noise. Taking her arm, he escorts her to the front of the queue.

An elderly woman with no teeth and a bright pink scarf gives her a withering look. 'What's wrong with 'er then? That she can't wait like the rest of us?'

'Now then Mrs Davies, that's quite enough of that,' says Ron above the din. 'We'll get you all down below in good time but this young lady needs the nurse.'

The young woman in the woollen coat can feel her cheeks burning. As she stands waiting for the lift to arrive from below she can see that the queue on the left is moving more quickly, as people disappear down the stair well, their feet clanking on the metal steps. The stairway coils its way around the lift shaft and disappears out of sight. She cannot imagine how many stairs there are to the bottom.

She doesn't have long to wait for the ascending lift. As soon as it has stopped the warden heaves open the red metal gates and helps her inside. People from the queue follow, including the woman with the pink scarf.

The young woman in the woollen coat is leaning against the metal lift cage when she remembers her bag. Her stomach lurches in momentary panic. She left it by the garden wall. She feels for her purse which is in her pocket. There is nothing of great value in the bag. Just a few clothes, her diary and some fruit for her mother, saved from the canteen that morning. You can't get fresh fruit for love nor money these days and her mother adores an apple in the morning. The knowledge that she has lost the bag leaves her feeling ill at ease. Like she has left part of herself above ground by the garden wall. She dismisses the thought with some effort.

She looks around the lift car and sees that the woman with the pink scarf is wearing a night dress beneath her coat.

The woman notices her staring. 'Bloody Krouts. Just tucked up in bed I was, but I didn't much fancy a visitor from across the water tonight,' she says, grinning. 'Mind you, there's been bugger all else in that bed since my old man joined up, and that's a fact.'

There is a ripple of laughter among the other lift passengers, followed by a dull clunk as the lift stops with a jolt. The gates open and she follows the others out into the lower lobby, at the far end of which is another warden sitting at a desk, taking the names of those entering the shelter and checking their bunk tickets. The young woman in the woollen coat doesn't have a ticket. Nor does she want a damned bunk. The mattresses smell of sweaty old men. She would rather find a corner somewhere where she can sit and wait out the raid.

She waits in the queue for what seems like an age.

The warden has dark bags under his eyes.

'Name?'

She tells him.

He makes an entry in the log, glancing up at a clock on the wall. 'Identity card?'

She fumbles in her pocket and finds her purse. She removes her card and gives it to the warden.

He examines it and hands it back to her. 'You're are a long way from Bletchley aren't you?'

'Yes,' she replies, unable to mask completely the irritation in her voice.

He waits for her to offer further explanation but she says nothing. He sighs. 'Ticket?'

'No, thank you.'

The warden looks up. 'I meant, can I see your ticket?'

'No, you can't. I don't have one.'

'Would you like one?'

'No, thank you,' she says curtly.

The warden studies her for a moment. 'Are you sure? The raid may keep us down here half the night.'

'I don't care. The bunks smell, dreadfully. I will find somewhere else to sit.'

The warden has lost patience. 'Please yourself Miss,' he says, dismissing her with the wave of a hand.

She glowers at him, turns away and follows the others toward the tunnel entrance.

There are signs on the wall giving directions to the tunnel sections: "Godley"; "Baden-Powell"; "Frobisher"; "Ashurst"; "Scott"; "Livingstone"; "Rhodes"; and "Kimberly" but only one of them appears to be in use.

As she edges forward, she thinks about her mother who is probably with her neighbours in the Anderson shelter at the bottom of the garden. Mother always watches the clock when she is expecting her and her non-arrival is bound to have put her in a spin.

The young woman in the woollen coat is suddenly close to tears. Her clothes are soaking wet and her ankle hurts whenever she puts weight on it. *Why tonight, of all nights?*

She thinks of Elsie back at the Park or, more likely, propping up a bar somewhere and curses her luck.

CHAPTER FOUR

Monday, 24th May 2004

At lunchtime Harry called Jane and arranged to meet her for a coffee and something to eat. The canteen was housed in one of the Park's few long wooden huts to have been fully restored. Its exterior had been painted green and inside, the hut had been fitted out as a wartime canteen. Harry had heard countless American visitors comment on how "awesome" it was to be eating where the Park's wartime staff had eaten before them. It always made him smile. Hut Four had, in fact, been occupied by Naval Intelligence, the canteen having been located elsewhere.

Jane was already seated at a table when he arrived. Harry bought a sandwich and a coffee and joined her.

'I hope you're in a better mood than you were this morning,' she said, giving him a disapproving stare.

'I am. I finally got an answer from Elsie Sidthorpe.'

Jane's expression turned to one of puzzlement.

'She is one of the women I've been been trying to track down for the Major's little shindig.'

'Well, thank God you've found one of them. Only several hundred more to go. The Major will be pleased.' She said it in her usual caustic manner.

Harry wasn't taking the bait. 'It was actually quite an intriguing letter.'

'Oh?'

'She says that she has a notebook full of names and other details for me. She also wants to talk to me about one of the women she worked with, but she will only speak to me in person.'

'In person?'

Harry had a mouthful of some indescribable sandwich. He nodded.

'I wonder why?'

'I don't know, but I'm off to see her on Thursday,' he said between mouthfuls.

'Progress at last then. Where does she live?'

'In a nursing home in Suffolk. I'm going to drive over there.'

Jane put her coffee down. 'You are not driving to Suffolk in that old banger of yours?' she spluttered, shaking her head.

'She is not an old banger, she is a classic motor vehicle and we are having a day out at the seaside.'

'Well I hope you'll be very happy together.'

Harry had given up on his sandwich. The canteen deserved its reputation for stale sandwiches and stodgy food. It was probably the only thing about the place that was authentic. But at least the coffee was passable.

'So what was up with you this morning?' Jane asked.

'Nothing much. I just didn't sleep very well again, that's all.'

'The recurring dream?' She gave him one of her knowing looks.

Harry was beginning to wish he'd never told her about it. 'Yes. I wake up at the same point every bloody time. Or at least I think so. I can never quite remember.'

'You're obviously worrying about something. Your mother, maybe? Has anything happened?'

'Jane. She left when I was eight. That was almost twenty-five years ago. If anything was going to happen I rather think it would have happened by now.'

Harry paused. His mother had left home when he was a boy. One moment she'd been there. The next, she'd been gone. Her clothes had still been in the wardrobe. Her shoes in the cupboard under the stairs. She had simply vanished. His father had barely acknowledged to Harry and his sister that she had gone. He had not so much as mentioned her name in all the years since. It had been like she was never there.

'Do you honestly think she is dead?' Jane asked.

'I have no idea but I hope so,' said Harry.

Jane looked shocked. 'Harry Stammers, that is an awful thing to say. You can't possibly mean it.'

'Well, if she is dead at least that would explain why she has never contacted us.'

'That is no reason to wish her dead, Harry. She is still your mother, whatever her reasons.' She said it, with more than a hint of anger.

'Maybe so. But if she is alive, how could she have stayed away for so long? How could she have done that to my father, let alone to two small children?'

'That is all very well. But mothers don't just abandon their children for no reason and nobody just vanishes.'

'Well she did. No postcards from a beach somewhere. No birthday or christmas cards. No phone call. No message in-a-bloody-bottle. Not a word.'

Jane didn't answer. There was an awkward pause.

Harry broke the silence. 'Look, it was a long time ago and we didn't do so bad. It is just always there in the back of my mind. One day I'll find out what happened to her. If I can find the women who worked here sixty years ago, I damn well ought to be able to find out what happened to my own mother.'

'*If* being the operative word,' said Jane.

Harry got off the train at Euston and took the escalator down to the Northern Line platform, as he did every evening. It was unusually quiet and, for once, he didn't have to push his way onto the train. He sat down and picked up a newspaper which had been left on the seat next to his and casually turned the pages. He yawned. He'd dozed on the train from Bletchley. He'd need to be careful not to do the same on the Tube or he'd end up in bloody Edgware.

As he turned the pages of the newspaper his mind drifted to the conversation with Jane. His comments about his mother had evidently touched a nerve. Maybe she had her own demons. Thinking about it, other than that she was single and lived on her own, he knew relatively little about her personal life. Perhaps he should try a little harder. Or perhaps not. Personal lives were a risky business.

Harry's eyelids had become heavy. He detested fighting sleep on the Tube. His head nodded forward and he woke with a jolt. '*Damn it*,' he thought. Or had he said it out loud? Two school children sitting in the seats opposite him whispered to each other and sniggered. He shifted uncomfortably in his seat.

Harry found himself gazing into the darkness through the tube train window. There were cables running along the tunnel walls and lamps that flashed by every few yards. He found himself counting them. Flash. *Twenty-one*. Flash. *Twenty-two*. His eyelids drooped. Flash. *Twenty-three*. A woman's face. *Twenty*... Harry's head came up with a start. A face looking in at him through the window. His bag slipped off his lap and onto the floor, emptying its contents as it fell. The children sitting opposite made no effort to hide their amusement and burst into peels of laughter. Harry barely noticed them. He glanced at the passenger to his right who was reading. To his left, he caught the eye of a middle-aged man in a suit and immediately felt foolish. He coughed nervously. He knelt down and tried to gather his scattered thoughts along with the contents of his bag. The face had been so vivid.

The train came to a halt and the doors opened. Passengers pushed past him. *A woman. Dark, curly hair. Red lipstick.* There had been something familiar about her which Harry could not place. He thought of his mother and tried to picture her in his mind. His father had destroyed all of their photographs of her but he'd seen pictures that his grandmother had shown him. Grainy, black and white pictures of a teenage girl on a park swing. Harry stood up and immediately felt dizzy.

Another passenger pushed past. 'Oh for God's sake,' she muttered.

Flustered and sweating, Harry sat back in his seat clutching his bag to his chest. He swallowed hard. She had looked directly at him. Not an impression, like a picture in a frame or an image on a screen. But a woman who, for a moment, had been there on the other side of the window. And not just looking in, but looking in *at* him. He could not escape the feeling that she'd had something to say. Something to tell him.

Harry realised that the train had begun to move again and wondered where he was. As the train accelerated, he caught sight of a sign on the platform wall as it flashed by. It read "Belsize Park".

CHAPTER FIVE

Thursday, 27 th May 2004

Harry turned the key in the ignition and the Triumph's engine spluttered to life. He looked at his watch. It was six-fifteen in the morning. If he put his foot down he would be past Junction 28 by seven, well before the usual rush hour chaos would turn the M25 into a car park. Then the A12 would take him the remainder of the way and, with any luck, he would make it to Southwold before nine. That would give him an hour to take a look around before his appointment with Elsie Sidthorpe.

It had been an odd few days. Several sleepless nights, the recurring dream and that business on the tube train. He still felt uneasy about it. It had, of course, been a dream, but the lucidity of it had shaken him. He had been so shaken that he had mentioned it to Jane over lunch the following day.

'You need to start taking more care of yourself Harry. Take a break. Maybe go and see your father,' she had said.

He had known what she was thinking. If he was honest, he was thinking it himself. 'Look, I am fine about my mother. It was a long time ago. I am not going to go raking it all up again with Dad,' he had said, perhaps a little too defensively.

'Well maybe you should,' she had responded. 'Maybe your sub-conscious is telling you that it is time to face it with him.'

Maybe it is, Harry thought.

On the face of it, they were on reasonable terms but Harry had no doubt that his father's unwillingness to discuss his mother's disappearance had put a barrier between them. It was, as a consequence, a superficial relationship at best. There were too many things that Harry could not mention. Too many things of which his father simply would not speak. As he manoeuvred the little green sports car out of the garage it occurred to Harry that his father wasn't getting any younger.

Harry stopped the Spitfire, got out and closed the garage door. The issue of his parents had been on hold for much of his childhood and the whole of his adult life. It could wait a little longer. A good run to the coast in the Spitfire was exactly what he needed. Harry smiled, clambered back in to the driver's seat and was away.

The journey to Southwold went without a hitch. The Spitfire had burbled along merrily for once and, as he turned off the A12 onto the Halesworth Road, Harry's spirits had improved. Elsie's nursing home was a few minutes walk from the town centre and, as he was early, he decided on a coffee. He pulled into a parking space in front of *The Crown*, paid at a nearby parking meter and looked around for a cafe.

Harry could smell the aroma of malt and hops in the air from the brewery behind the High Street's northern facade. He lit a cigarette and stood, blowing smoke rings. He was not a fan of seaside towns, with their gaudy arcades and gift shops. Southwold, on the other hand, was an exception with its many pretty shops and restaurants. And, best of all, there was not an arcade in sight. Perhaps it was the lack of a train station that kept the day trippers away. He decided that he liked the place.

Harry found a cafe and ordered a coffee. He paid the waitress at the counter and sat at a sunny table by the window. The coffee was excellent. He leant back in his chair and was gazing out of the window across the town square, enjoying the sunshine, when he noticed a blue Saab reversing into the space next to the Spitfire. It was a tight fit and he flinched as the Saab inched backwards. The car stopped and a woman in black, knee length boots and a burgundy jacket got out and walked across to the parking meter. Even from a distance, Harry could see that she was gorgeous. She had curves in all the right places and her shoulder length brown hair shone in the sunlight. Harry looked at the Saab. She had good taste in cars too. He glanced at the Spitfire. Although not as good as his.

Thinking about women and cars reminded him of his last girlfriend, Rebecca. She had hated the Spitfire, complaining that it was too low, especially on the motorway where lorries would tower above them and buffet the little sports car as they sped by. She had nagged him relentlessly about ditching the car in favour of something bigger and more modern. Ironically, he had ditched Rebecca instead.

He looked at his watch. It was nine forty-five. He got up, left the cafe and worked his way back along the High Street. He stopped for a few moments outside a fishmonger's. He couldn't remember the last time he'd seen a fishmonger's shop in London. They had all succumbed to the onslaught of the supermarket, along with the greengrocers and most of the butchers. *More's the pity,* he thought.

On his arrival at the nursing home, Harry was shown upstairs by a girl who looked no more than sixteen and spoke faltering English with an East European accent. He wondered how the elderly residents, many of whom would surely be hard of hearing, coped with the girl. They stopped outside room seventeen.

The girl knocked and called out 'Mrs Sidthorpe. It is Natalia. You have other visitor.'

If he was the other visitor Harry wondered who else was visiting Mrs Sidthorpe. There was a brief pause and the door was opened by a woman with shoulder length brown hair. She was wearing black knee length boots and Harry could see a burgundy jacket hanging on the back of a chair. She was even more beautiful at close quarters than she had seemed from the cafe window.

'Mr Stammers, welcome. I am Ellen Carmichael. Please come in.'

CHAPTER SIX

Elsie Sidthorpe's room was bright and airy and larger than Harry had expected. There was even space for a dining table and a small kitchenette at one end. The room was tastefully, rather than lavishly decorated and was furnished plainly. Elsie Sidthorpe was sitting in a high backed arm chair next to an open window. As Harry entered, she started to get up.

'No please don't get up.' Harry crossed the room and shook her hand.

'Delighted to meet you Mr Stammers. I trust that you had a good journey?'

'Yes indeed and please call me Harry,' he replied.

'Very well and thank you so much for coming to see us.' She spoke with an impeccable English accent.

Elsie was a particularly slight woman. Though obviously frail, her piercing blue eyes and animated features gave the impression of an intelligent, lively mind.

'Could we offer you some tea Harry?'

He hesitated. 'I'm afraid that I don't really drink tea.'

'Then we will have coffee. I much prefer it myself but English men are usually habitual tea drinkers. Ellen, would you mind awfully?'

Harry laughed. 'Yes, I suppose they are.'

As Ellen got up to make the coffee, he caught her eye and she smiled. The two women were startlingly alike, with the same bright blue eyes and high cheek bones. Harry's eyes flicked from one woman to the other.

Elsie smiled. 'You have noticed the likeness, I see.'

Harry nodded. 'Yes.'

'People assume that we are grandmother and granddaughter.'

'You're not?' He had assumed as much.

'No. Ellen is my great niece. My sister Edith's granddaughter.'

'But she'll always be my Gran,' Ellen called out from the other side of the room.

Elsie dropped her voice to a whisper. 'Edith passed away when Ellen was a child and since then…'

'She has been the best grandmother,' Ellen interrupted, 'that I could possibly have wanted.'

Elsie waved away the compliment with her hand. 'Tush tush.'

'Actually, I was thinking that Ellen probably looks now much as you did when you worked at the Park.'

Elsie smiled. 'She does indeed. A most astute observation. As I would have expected from someone with such an important role at Bletchley Park.'

'Well I don't know about that. The Park cannot afford to employ many staff and so I find myself doing all sorts of things that one wouldn't normally associate with the job of a curator.'

'Like searching for elderly ladies and visiting them in nursing homes?' Elsie said with a smile.

'Yes, exactly,' Harry replied.

'Tell me about what it is like at the Park now. I was last there in nineteen forty-five, although I can remember it as though it were yesterday.'

Harry described the crumbling huts with some embarrassment. One of his reasons for taking the job had been the appalling state of the place. He and Mike had visited the Park the year before he joined, with a view to getting into Block G, which, as far as they knew, had never been opened to the public. The block had collapsed in places and was considered unsafe. They had returned a week later, at the crack of dawn and had extensively photographed the block's interior.

'It is so sad to hear that it has been allowed to fall into such a state of disrepair,' Elsie said.

'It is more than sad. It is a disgrace. Bletchley Park is of national importance. If the Park was in America, it would never have been allowed to decline so badly.'

'I dare say that is true. But then it would probably have been turned into one of those beastly theme parks that they appear so fond of over there.'

Ellen had returned with a jug of coffee and laid out three cups and saucers on a small table beside Elsie's chair.

'Do you take sugar Mr Stammers?' asked Ellen.

'It is Harry. No sugar, thank you.'

Ellen seated herself on the chair next to Harry's. He couldn't help glancing at her legs which were bare above her boots.

'I gather that you are researching the work of Hut Six?' said Elsie.

'Not exactly. Much of that research has been done but we think that the work of the women at Bletchley has tended to be understated. We have been trying to find as many of the A.T.S. women who moved to Bletchley in nineteen forty-two as possible.'

'You mean those of us who worked for the Central Party?'

Harry nodded. 'Yes. We know that this was made up of a number of army men and A.T.S. women and later, a group of men from the U.S. Army.'

'That is correct. I cannot remember when they joined us, exactly, but there were quite a lot of them and they were devilishly handsome. Although, to be frank, I could not abide their ghastly accents,' Elsie smiled.

'You were transferred to Bletchley in 1942?'

'Yes. I was a log reader at Beaumanor when they moved us to the Park. I have written down the names of the other women who transferred to Bletchley with me, although I doubt that I have them all and, of course, several of them may have passed away by now. Ellen would you pass Harry the note book from the sideboard please?'

Ellen retrieved a small note book and handed it to Harry. He leafed through it. The notebook was full of details in Elsie's spidery handwriting. He recognised some of the names but others were new to him.

'This is absolutely wonderful,' he said.

'Good. Please keep it. For your research.'

'Are you sure?'

Elsie nodded.

'Thank you.' Harry picked up his cup and tried the coffee. It was very strong, exactly as he preferred it. 'You said in your letter that you wished to talk to me about one colleague in particular?'

'Yes, I do. Her name was Martha Watts.'

'And that you wanted to speak to me in person about her.'

'Yes.'

'May I ask why?'

'You may. Martha and I were at Beaumanor. We transferred to Bletchley together. She was a charming girl and we were great friends. But in November 1944, she disappeared during a trip to London. I never saw her again.'

Elsie looked away, seemingly lost in thought. Harry and Ellen exchanged glances.

'Do you know what happened to her?' Harry said, addressing Ellen.

'Don't ask me. This is the first I have heard of it,' Ellen answered.

Elsie cleared her throat. 'I am sorry. It still upsets me. At the time, I thought that I had no choice but to put it behind me. But the older I get, the easier it seems to be to remember.'

'I understand.'

'It is kind of you to say so Harry but I am not sure that you do. You see, I have not spoken to another living soul about Martha since a few days after she vanished.'

'Why ever not, Gran?' asked Ellen, sitting forward in her chair.

'Because I was instructed not to.'

There was a pause.

Harry said, 'Perhaps we should start at the beginning.'

Elsie looked at him, with her piercing blue eyes and nodded.

'Would you like some more coffee Harry?' Ellen asked.

'Thank you, yes.'

She re-filled his cup.

'Martha and I worked at Bletchley Park together,' Elsie began. 'Her mother lived in London and, whenever she had a weekend off, Martha liked to visit her. As you know, Bletchley Station is nearby and the train runs straight into London.'

Harry nodded. 'Yes, I use it myself.'

'Do you?' said Elsie.

'Yes. I live in Golders Green and travel back and forth to Bletchley every day, unless of course I have a meeting elsewhere,' Harry said smiling.

'Quite so,' Elsie replied, falling silent again and closing her eyes.

Harry wondered whether she had fallen asleep. He looked at Ellen who shrugged.

'It was Friday, the tenth of November 1944,' Elsie said, opening her eyes and looking directly at Harry. 'Martha caught the six-thirty from Bletchley into London,' she continued. 'I remember walking her to the gate. It was the last time I ever saw her.'

'What happened to her?' asked Harry.

'I wish I knew, Harry. I have spent many years wishing it. When I called the house the following morning to speak to Martha, Mrs Watts told me that she had not arrived. The poor woman was in a dreadful state.'

'How awful,' said Ellen.

31

'Yes it was. There had been the most dreadful air raid. The explanation offered to her poor mother was that Martha had probably been killed in the raid and her body burned in the ensuing fire.'

'A reasonable explanation, perhaps' said Harry.

'Do you think so?' Elsie replied, perhaps a little too sharply. She hesitated. 'I'm sorry. But I knew the route, you see. From the station to her mother's house. She always took the bus because she hated the Underground and then walked the rest of the way.'

'So perhaps she was killed in the bombing as she walked back to the house,' said Ellen.

'No, dear. That was not the case.'

'How can you be certain?' asked Harry.

'Because a few days later I went to see Mrs Watts. I felt terribly sorry for her and so afraid for Martha. I caught the bus from Euston and then walked along the route that Martha would have taken. There was no new bomb damage. None of the buildings along her route had been hit.'

'But there was an air raid?' said Harry.

'Oh yes. I checked with the air raid wardens. I made quite a fuss about it in fact. But the nearest damage was at Aldgate, where many poor souls lost their lives.'

'Then perhaps she took a different route. Perhaps she was at Aldgate for some reason?' said Harry.

'No. I am convinced that something else happened to her.'

'Why?'

'Because when I got back to the Park, I was told, in no uncertain terms, that I was to accept the explanation I had been given for Martha's disappearance. It was made quite clear to me that I was to ask no further questions and that it would better for me if I forgot about Martha altogether.'

'Why would they have said that?' asked Ellen, looking at Harry.

Harry ran his hand through his hair. 'It is difficult to be sure. It may be that they were simply trying to avoid any publicity. Bletchley was a very secret site. Had the Germans discovered that their ciphers were being broken, they would almost certainly have made changes and this could have set back the deciphering process by several months or even permanently. Great efforts were made to maintain secrecy.'

Ellen nodded.

'You say that you were told to accept the explanation and to forget about your friend.'

'Yes, that's right,' Elsie agreed.

'By who?' Harry asked.

'I don't know. I was interviewed as soon as I got back from London. Whoever it was knew that I had spoken to the local wardens. But I'm afraid that he did not give a name.'

'But it was not someone who you recognised?'

'No.'

'So probably not someone from the Park?'

Elsie shook her head. 'No, I do not believe so.'

'And in plain clothes, rather than uniform, I take it?'

'Yes,' Elsie agreed.

Harry pondered her words. 'Probably a security officer of some kind. Possibly police, but I can't be certain.'

'And you haven't spoken to anyone about Martha since that day?' asked Ellen.

'No, I have not. Hardly a day has passed when I have not thought about her, but everyone at Bletchley had secrets Ellen, dear. Secrets that we were required to keep.'

'Yes, indeed,' Harry interjected. 'It is one of the miracles of the war that the Park was never discovered. It is something of which everyone who worked there can be very proud.'

'Thank you Harry, but I do not feel very proud of this particular secret.'

They fell silent.

Harry could hear the clock ticking on the mantel piece. 'Are you absolutely certain that Martha was not at Aldgate that night?' he asked.

Elsie sighed. 'Very well. I cannot be absolutely certain about it. I wish I could because then perhaps I would not have spent every day of the last sixty years wondering what happened to her. But I do not believe, for a minute, that she was there. There was absolutely no reason for her to be there and it was nowhere near the route that she would have taken to her mother's house.'

They were silent again.

'Why me and why now?' Harry said, breaking the silence. 'Why are you telling me about this sixty years later?'

'Because I am old and because I want to know what happened to my friend before I die. Because I am too old to find Martha myself. I should have looked for her sixty years ago.'

'Surely you don't think Martha is still alive?' Ellen said.

'I don't know,' Elsie replied. 'Perhaps she is but I do not expect that to be so. However, if she is dead then her remains are somewhere. That is one fact of which I think we can all be certain.' She looked pointedly at Harry. 'Martha did not burn in a fire that night, Harry. Or if she did, it was not by Herr Hitler's hand.' She paused. 'I want to say goodbye to her. Before I go.'

Harry exchanged glances with Ellen who looked at him hopefully. He turned to Elsie. 'Why are you telling me about this? I am a museum curator, not a private detective.'

He realised, as he said it, that he'd said much the same to Jane Mears a few days earlier.

'Harry. You found me. Is that not so?'

'Yes, but that is hardly the same.'

'Perhaps not. But you are evidently rather good at finding people. You can find Martha for me. I know you can.'

Ellen and Elsie were both looking at him.

'Please.'

'But it was sixty years ago,' he pleaded.

Ellen intervened. 'All of your research at Bletchley relates to events that took place in the past, doesn't it?'

Harry looked at her, opened his mouth to speak and then closed it again.

'Gran is right, Harry. You are precisely the right man for the job.'

CHAPTER SEVEN

Friday, 10**th **November 1944

She spots the woman with the pink scarf as she disappears through a narrow gateway. The metal gates make the tunnel seem more like a prison than a place of refuge. She follows the others and, entering the main shelter, she is struck by its enormous scale. A row of metal bunks stretches out ahead of her along both sides of the tunnel for as far as she can see. People are checking their tickets against the numbers on the bed frames.

She passes along the tunnel but makes slow progress. People are milling about between the bunks, greeting each other and swapping stories. She passes a side passage with stairs leading to the underground station above. Other passages are closed off by locked metal gates. The passageways are in darkness and she occasionally catches sight of a mouse or rat scuttling across the walkway. She shivers. *'Please God let the air raid pass quickly so I can get out and home.'*

She finds an unoccupied corner and sits down on an upturned wooden crate, rubbing her ankle and grimacing at the pain. She leans back against the tunnel wall and closes her eyes. A tear trickles down her cheek. The ladder in her dark stocking makes her pale white flesh glow like the moon in the tunnel light. Her curly brown hair is a complete mess. She takes off her coat and spreads it across her lap to hide the ladder and her knees. She hopes that the coat will dry quickly in the draughty tunnel.

She has been sitting on the crate for ten minutes or so, when a young man passes by. He is dressed in a suit and smart brown leather shoes. Her Mother always says that you can judge a man's character by the shoes that he wears.

The young man stops after a few paces and turns. She catches his eye and he smiles but, as he starts to speak, his voice is drowned out by an announcement over the tannoy. They both listen. The air raid is expected to continue for some hours and shelterers are advised to make themselves comfortable, as an early all-clear is unlikely. The man steps closer.

When the announcement is over, he says 'You look as thrilled as I am to be stuck down here.'

'No, I am most certainly not thrilled. I am completely miserable.'

'At least it is dry. You look positively drenched.'

The man looks to be in his twenties. To say that he is well spoken is an understatement. He sounds like an announcer on the wireless or like one of the senior men at the Park. He is evidently a man of means too. The cut of his suit is impressive and she catches sight of heavy gold cufflinks as he bends forward to shake her hand.

She attempts to stand but sits back down with a start when her ankle gives way. 'I have had quite possibly the worst day ever. I twisted my ankle in the ghastly rain. I must look a dreadful mess. Whatever must you think?'

'Not at all. I think that you are quite possibly the prettiest drowned rat I have seen all day,' he says with a smile. 'May I pull up a crate?'

She smiles and nods. 'You may.'

She is hesitant at first, but he is a charming man and, within minutes, they have struck up an easy conversation.

'A director, you say?'

'Yes.'

She has been watching him intently as he speaks. 'If you don't mind me saying so, you seem terribly young to have such a senior position,' she says.

'No, I don't mind at all. I suppose that I have the war to thank for that, with so many men away fighting.'

'It must have been quite a change. From studying at university, I mean.'

'The war has changed many things for many people.'

She notices that there is more than a hint of regret in his voice. 'You have not been called up for national service?' she asks.

'No. My job is on the reserved list.'

She notices the ring on his finger and wonders about his wife. 'I expect that your wife was relieved?'

'Yes,' he says but offers no more.

They are silent for a moment.

He asks about her work and she recites the cover story that she has been instructed to use when such questions arise. She changes the subject quickly. 'You were already down here when the siren sounded?'

'Yes. I was here for a meeting. My colleague had already left. Unfortunately, I had not.'

She shifts her feet and he notices her flinch.

'Is it terribly painful?' he asks, looking down at her feet.

'Yes it is, rather,' she says bending down to massage her ankle. 'It feels a little swollen too.'

He appears to think for a moment. 'Look here, these crates are terribly uncomfortable and we really ought to get you looked at,' he says.

She remembers the signs for the medical station in the lobby. 'I am sure it will mend. Besides, the nurses will surely have more important matters to attend to.'

He looks at his watch. 'Very well then. I have another suggestion.'

'A suggestion?'

'Yes. We have a room that the labourers use. There is bound to be a first aid kit there and I expect that we will find something with which to strap your ankle. The men are always pulling a muscle or falling off something.'

She looks at him uncertainly.

'It is not very far. We might even find something to drink.'

She remains silent. She doesn't know this man who seems so concerned about her, although there is certainly something about him that she likes. She thinks of Elsie and the petty officer at '*The Galleon*'. Elsie would have left with him had she not intervened and Elsie would certainly not be hesitating now. A wealthy man with an important job, a good suit and brown leather shoes. Elsie was probably taking far bigger risks at this very moment and enjoying them. Besides, he is a respectable married man with an important job. What is she worrying about? Quite suddenly her caution seems absurd and, with that thought, her reluctance evaporates.

She smiles, stands, and tries to catch her balance. When she stumbles, his arm is instantly around her waist and for a moment her heart is in her mouth. He apologises and carefully removes his arm, ensuring that she has her balance before stepping away from her a little.

There is an uncomfortable silence.

'I don't think I'll get very far in these,' she says suddenly, kicking off her shoes.

He bends down and picks them up.

'It is this way,' he says.

CHAPTER EIGHT

Sunday 30th May 2004

Harry woke with a start. He groped for the button to silence the alarm and looked at the time. It was 6.15 A.M. *Shit. Why did I allow Mike to talk me into it?* he thought. He turned over, with every intention of going back to sleep but then he remembered that Mike and the others were picking him up at seven. He groaned, hauled himself out of bed and went to the bathroom. He shaved, showered and walked into the kitchen to make some coffee, drying his hair on a bathroom towel.

Harry's flat was a single storey building. It had been built for his landlord's elderly mother but she had died before she could move in. Jane called it "The Old Folks Home". The flat was joined to the landlord's house via a garage and Harry had initially worried about his privacy but, on being shown around, he had immediately liked the place. It was decorated plainly, which suited Harry's taste. He especially liked the cavernous bathroom with its double width, walk-in shower. Not that he had yet managed to convince any female acquaintance to walk into it with him. In point of fact, Harry had been single when he moved in, was single now and had every intention of remaining that way.

Fortunately the landlord also allowed to him to use the garage which had doors leading into Harry's flat on one side and the main house on the other, It was big enough for the Spitfire and Harry's other passion - a 1964 Lambretta TV175 motor scooter which he was restoring.

Harry put on his walking boots and made a flask of coffee to take with him. He was standing by the back door smoking a cigarette when he heard a car pull into the driveway. He stubbed out the cigarette, put on his jacket and was about to open the door when the car horn sounded. It was not quiet. Harry opened the front door.

'Hey hey, Harry,' called out Mike, leaning from the Hilux's window.

'Thanks for waking the whole bloody neighbourhood.' Harry stomped over to the car, threw his bag in the back and got in.

As well as Mike, there were three others in the car. Tomasz, a skilled computer hacker, was the youngest of the group. Originally from Poland, he could speak perfect English but, unless he had a drink or two inside him, rarely said more than was absolutely necessary. He had long mousy hair, was as skinny as a rake and usually looked like he had been up half the night, which he probably had.

Marcus was an experienced climber and looked the part. Blond haired, blue eyed and with the kind of build that made women go weak at the knees, his climbing expertise had been invaluable to the group. Getting into underground tunnels and bunkers was usually straight forward enough. Getting out again, without someone who could handle ropes, was often another matter entirely.

Harry didn't much like Erik. He was an adrenaline junky who, unlike the others, had no particular interest in the places they visited. As far as Harry was concerned, he took too many risks. He was, however, a professional photographer and had taken, even Harry had to concede, some remarkable pictures of their exploits.

The trouble was that pictures meant publicity and Harry had to be careful. What they were doing was not exactly illegal, providing they did not cause any damage, but it did usually amount to civil trespass. Harry's job meant that he could not afford to have his name associated too closely with a group that was becoming notorious for getting into the most unlikely buildings. Erik, on the other hand, loved the notoriety that publicity brought.

'How long is it going to take us to get there?' asked Harry.

'About an hour and a half,' replied Mike. 'Are you coming in or will you act as lookout?'

'I better stay outside.'

'Wimp,' said Erik.

'Maybe. But I'd rather be a wimp with a job.'

'Oh come on, it'll be a walk in the park,' said Erik.

Harry said nothing.

'What does access look like?' asked Marcus.

'The main building is in the middle of a field. There are two gates onto the site and a public footpath along the site's western boundary. The land is owned by a local farmer. He's called Pickles apparently,' said Mike.

'I wonder if that is what he farms?' said Tomasz.

Everyone turned and looked at him in surprise and they all laughed.

'So no security guards. If the farmer turns up we'll just say we lost the path and decided to look around,' said Mike.

Erik pulled a face, 'Shame. I was hoping for a repeat performance.'

'Well I'm not,' said Harry. 'And you can leave your keys in the car. The first sign of any trouble and I hit the road. That was the deal.'

'There won't be any trouble,' the others said in unison.

'Just try and keep your arse in your trousers this time, Museum Boy,' said Erik and they all laughed again. All except Harry. Erik was already getting to him and they'd barely started.

They pulled off the road shortly before eight-thirty. Erik took the Hilux through a gate and parked it alongside a small copse of horse chestnut trees. It was a good vantage point. Harry could see across the field to the former receiving station. It was a single storey, 'H' shaped building with a wide tower where the two wings of the building joined.

'If we have to, we'll go down the tower. It is bound to be a ventilation shaft. But I'm hoping that there'll be a broken window or something,' said Marcus.

'Bollocks to that. I'm going down the tower anyway,' said Erik.

Harry and Mike exchanged glances.

They all got out of the Hilux and Marcus checked the climbing gear. Harry lit a cigarette and offered one to Tom.

'Thanks,' said Tom taking the cigarette and accepting a light.

Harry knew not to expect any further conversation. They both looked out across the field, Harry blowing smoke rings. It was going to be a warm day. The morning mist was already lifting and, above it, the sky was clear.

Mike called them all together and handed a radio to each.

'Will anyone else be able hear us?' Harry asked.

'Unlikely. We're miles from anywhere and they're very low power.'

The others seemed familiar with the handheld radios. Mike showed Harry how to operate his.

'If you get fed up listening to static, turn this knob clockwise until the squelch closes, like this.' He turned the knob and the radio went quiet. 'Just don't turn it all the way or the signal might not break through the squelch. Got it?'

'I think so. Will they work underground?' he asked.

'Possibly not well enough to get back to you. So two of us will explore the building above ground while the others go below and then we'll swap. Whoever is above ground ought to be able to hear those below, so they can relay anything that you radio to them. If anyone turns up, just call whoever is above ground and we'll make a run for it.'

'Before I drive away, you mean.'

Mike smiled. 'Yes, before you drive away.'

'Have fun guys,' said Harry, as the others headed off across the field. He watched them for a while and then got back into the Hilux and put the handheld radio to his ear. 'This is Harry. Are you receiving me? Over.'

'Is who receiving you?' said a voice which sounded like Mike's.

'Mike. Over.'

'Yes, I am receiving you,' came the reply.

'And you don't need to say "over". This is not the Battle of Britain, arsehole,' said another voice that sounded like Erik.

Harry gritted his teeth. 'I was just checking.'

He put down the radio and poured himself some coffee from his flask. It was going to be a long morning.

Once the group had reached the receiving station Mike called to say that they had found an open window. It had been a bit awkward but Tom, the smallest of the group, had got in and had managed to open an old fire door. Marcus and Erik had found the entrance to the bunker below and were going down while Mike and Tom were exploring above ground.

Harry settled back in his seat and closed his eyes. His mind was just beginning to wander, a certain prelude to sleep, when his mobile phone began to vibrate. He pulled it out but didn't recognise the number.

'Hello?'

'Hi Harry. It's Ellen Carmichael.'

Harry sat up. 'Oh. Ellen, hi. How are you?'

'I'm fine, thanks.' She hesitated. 'I didn't wake you, did I?'

'Erm.. No, not exactly.'

'You sound like you're half asleep.'

'Do I? Sorry. I was, err...' He hesitated.

'Well, anyway. Gran has remembered a box of photographs that she has stored in the loft at home. I'm on my way to collect them. She thinks that, among them, are some pictures from her time at Bletchley Park. If I can find them, I'm going to pop them over to her this afternoon. There's a chance that Martha Watts may appear in one or two of them.'

'Right. That's good.'

'I thought that it might help us, if we could put a face to her name.'

Harry hesitated. He had only agreed reluctantly, and under some duress, to help Elsie in the search for Martha Watts. He'd been half-hoping that he wouldn't hear anything more and would be able to quietly forget about it. On the other hand, if it meant spending more time with Ellen Carmichael, it might just be worth it. 'Yes, I guess it would. If you manage to identify her in the pictures, perhaps you could get them scanned and emailed to me?'

'Actually Harry, I will be in Leighton Buzzard on Monday morning, on business. I could bring them up to you at Bletchley if you are going to be there?'

'Well, yes, I'll certainly be there.'

'Great.' She hesitated. 'Perhaps we could... '

'Harry, this is Mike. Are you there?' The last part of Ellen's sentence was drowned out by the radio.

'Sorry Ellen what was that?' Harry said into the mobile phone.

'I said that per...'

'Harry this is Mike. Are you receiving me?'

'Ellen, I'm sorry, could you hang on a moment?'

Harry put his mobile phone down on the seat next to him and picked up the radio. 'Mike, this is Harry. Over.'

'You should get over here. It's an amazing place. Marcus says that it is huge below ground and Erik has taken some great photographs.'

'Can I call you back in a few minutes? I'm on the phone. Over.'

'OK.'

Harry retrieved his phone. 'Ellen, sorry, are you still there?'

'Yes, I am.' She sounded intrigued. 'Where are you?'

'Actually, I'm sitting in a car, in a field, in the middle of nowhere,' Harry said.

'And what, may I ask, are you doing there?'

'That is a very good question. In fact, it is a question that I have been asking myself all morning.'

'So?' she asked.

'So, what?'

'So, what *are* you doing?'

'You wouldn't believe me if I told you,' Harry answered.

'Harry Stammers. Are you always this evasive?' she said, sounding exasperated.

'No, you really wouldn't believe me if I told you,' Harry persisted.

'We will see about that on Monday.'

'Monday?'

'Oh, do pay attention,' she said.

'Oh, yes, Monday. Right. Good.'

'And if you had been listening instead of doing whatever you are doing in your field-in-the-middle-of-nowhere you would have heard me say,' she took a breath, 'that you can give me a guided tour of Bletchley Park after I have shown you the pictures. I would love to see where Gran worked.'

'Yes, of course. Well, I look forward to seeing you on Monday.'

'I haven't finished yet.'

'Oh. Sorry.'

'And after that, if you are very lucky, I will let you take me to lunch.'

Harry smiled. 'That would be great.'

'My meeting is at 9.30am and should only last an hour. So I can be with you sometime after eleven. How would that be?'

'Sometime after eleven would be fine.'

'Good. See you then. Oh and Harry?'

'Yes?'

'Do people really still say 'over' when they use a radio?'

'Apparently not.'

'I thought not. It's a bit Battle of Britain isn't it? Anyway, see you on Monday,' and with that, she was gone.

Harry put the phone back in his pocket and leant back in the seat with his hands behind his head. *Well that was unexpected*, he thought.

After a few moments, he got out of the Hilux, lit a cigarette and stood blowing smoke rings and thinking about Ellen Carmichael. He was going to have to take the proposed search for Martha Watts more seriously. But where to start? All he knew was that she had gone missing on a Friday evening in November 1944. He knew she had caught the six-thirty from Bletchley but after that, he knew nothing. In fact, he realised, he couldn't even be certain that she had been on the six-thirty. Elsie Sidthorpe had said so, but she hadn't actually seen Martha get on the train. In any event, how on Earth was he going to be able to trace her movements sixty years later?

He finished the cigarette, and got back into the Hilux.

He woke up thirty minutes later to the sound of someone knocking on the driver's window. He wound it down.

'This is private land,' said a red faced man, with thinning, white hair.

'Oh. Is it?, said Harry, trying desperately to gather his thoughts. 'I had no idea. I'm sorry.'

'It has a big metal gate and a fence around it. What does that say to you?'

'Ah yes. Well, I was tired and there was no lay-by. So I thought I better pull in somewhere to take a break and, well, this seemed like a nice spot.'

'I'm not debating that it's a nice spot. The point is that it is my private nice spot. And it is a lot less of a nice spot with this bloody great thing smack bang in the middle of it.'

'Yes, point taken. I'm sorry. I'll go.'

'That you will. But not before you've written down your name, address and registration number. If I see you here again, I'll have you done for trespass. Is that clear?'

'Yes, completely.' Harry opened the glove box and found a pen. He could not find anything to write on. The farmer looked distinctly unimpressed. Harry suddenly remembered the radio. If one of the others called while the farmer was within ear shot, he would know that Harry had lied. Pretending to search for something to write on, Harry leant across the dash board and surreptitiously switched the radio off. As he did so, he noticed a piece of paper in the passenger's foot well. He picked it up and thought for a moment. Then he wrote down a name and address. He hesitated.

'Come on, get on with it. I haven't got all bloody day,' said the farmer.

'I've forgotten the registration number.'

The farmer looked at him. 'This is your car, is it?'

'Yes, of course it is.'

'Bloody townies. Think you're God's gift but not an ounce of common sense between the lot of you. Give it to me,' said the farmer holding out his hand. Harry handed him the slip of paper and the pen. The farmer marched to the front of the Hilux and wrote down the number from the plate. Then he marched back to the driver's window. 'Remember. I see you here again and it'll be the police. Now get off my land and mind you shut the gate.'

'Yes, I will. Look I'm really sorry.'

'Be off with you and...'

Harry didn't wait for him to complete the sentence. He started up the Hilux, did a three point turn and drove back towards the road, stopping at the gate to let himself out.

In the distance, he could see the farmer watching him. Harry waved a farewell. The farmer did not return the gesture. Instead he turned around and marched off toward the building in the middle of the field.

Shit. He reached for the handheld radio and switched it on. 'Mike, are you there? Its Harry.' But there was no reply. 'Mike? Anyone? Its Harry.'

'Mike is down below. It's Marcus. What's up?'

'The bloody farmer turned up. I had to leave. He's heading your way.'

'Oh, fuck. Just a second.'

Harry heard Marcus call Mike on the radio, but he couldn't hear Mike's response.

'Harry, its Marcus. Mike says follow the road round to the other side of the field and pull up by the gate. We'll meet you there in five minutes.'

'Alright, but you had better hurry. I don't think it will take the farmer much longer than that to get to you.'

'Don't worry. We're moving.'

Harry put the Hilux into gear and followed the road, turning left with the field boundary. After a few minutes, he pulled up at the gate. The field boundary, with its chain-linked fence turned left again and ran across the field but there was no road in that direction and Harry guessed, correctly, as it turned out, that this was the gate to which Marcus had referred. He picked up the radio and found himself shouting into it. 'Come on guys. Where are you?'

'Calm down. We're coming,' said a voice over the radio. Looking up Harry saw first Erik, radio in hand, and then the others. They were charging, full pelt, toward him. As they clambered over the gate and threw themselves into the Hilux Harry could see the farmer in the distance. He was shouting something but Harry couldn't hear him above all the commotion. He put the Hilux into gear and his foot down, hard on the accelerator. The Hilux took off.

Harry had no idea what direction they were going in but he didn't slow down until he had put several miles between them and receiving station.

'Slow down Museum Boy,' said Erik. 'A bit of excitement and you're pissing your pants.'

Harry pulled over in a lay-by, red faced and furious. 'I knew this was a bad idea. Erik, I thought you said that it would be a walk in the fucking park and if you call me "museum boy" one more time I'm going to put this car in a fucking ditch and you can all walk home.'

'Calm down Harry,' said Mike, quietly.

'Yeah. For fuck sake,' said Erik. 'It's just a joke. Anyway, what are you sweating about? We got away didn't we? Old Pickles, or whatever his name is, will never find us now.'

'I need a cigarette,' said Harry and got out of the Hilux. He walked a few paces away from the car, lit a cigarette, inhaled deeply and tried to relax. After a few moments Mike joined him.

'You alright, bud?'

Harry sighed, 'Sure. I'm fine.' He took another pull on his cigarette and blew a smoke ring. 'Mind you, Erik was wrong about the farmer.'

Mike looked puzzled. 'Meaning?'

'Meaning, before I left he made me give him a name and address. He won't have much trouble finding Erik,' said Harry and grinned.

Mike looked at him blankly and then the penny dropped. 'Oh no, you didn't?'

'Oh yes I did. I told him that my name was Erik Donaldson and gave him Erik's address. Divine justice I'd say,' Harry said with a satisfied smirk.

Mike took Harry's cigarette from his hand and inhaled deeply. 'Sweet,' he said.

CHAPTER NINE

Friday, 10th November 1944

She puts her arm around his waist and they walk a short distance together, before turning into a passage to the left. As they proceed along the tunnel she finds herself telling him a good deal more about herself than she would normally tell somebody who she has only just met. There is something about him that makes her feel safe.

The staff room is basic but comfortable with a small desk, several stalls, two bunks and a row of lockers. She seats herself on one of the bunks while he opens one locker and then the next, until he finds the first aid kit. It does indeed contain some strapping. He removes his jacket and kneels in front of her. They look at each other.

'What is it?' she asks.

'I'm afraid that you will need to remove your stocking before I can strap your ankle,' he replies apologetically.

She blushes.

'Would you like me to look away?'

'If you wouldn't mind.'

He gets to his feet and turns to face the door.

She slides the laddered stocking down her leg. It feels exciting to be removing it in his presence. She removes the stocking from her other leg. She can hardly turn up at home in one stocking.

'Thank you, I am decent now. You can turn around,'

He kneels in front of her again, taking her foot in his hand and carefully examines her ankle. 'It is badly swollen. You'll be limping for a few days, but the strapping should help with the swelling.'

His hands are warm and he applies the strapping with great care.

'It is hellishly painful,' she says but, in truth, his touch is like electricity. It sends a warm feeling up the inside of her leg.

'I hope that feels a little better,' he says, getting to his feet. He walks across to the lockers and produces a bottle.

'This might help,' he says handing it to her. 'I am afraid that there are no glasses.'

He sits beside her on the bunk. The bottle contains brandy and a reasonably good one at that.

'Would you like me to look the other way again, while you take a swig?' he says smiling.

She laughs, unscrews the top from the bottle, takes two full gulps and coughs as the burning liquid goes down her throat. 'Oh my goodness,' she splutters. 'That was not very lady like and you, the perfect Gentleman.'

They both laugh and she hands him the bottle.

He takes a gulp and puts the bottle on the table. 'Where were you going, when the siren sounded?' he asks.

'I was on my way home. My mother lives a short distance from here.'

'I have my car parked outside. I could drop you home once we get the all clear. Unless of course there is someone at home who would be less than pleased to see you clambering from a Gentleman's car, minus your stockings.'

'That is terribly decent of you,' she replies 'and no, there is nobody else waiting there for me. Mother is always complaining that I should be married by now. She'll probably invite you in for a cup of tea.'

He laughs. 'In that case I had better remove my wedding ring to save her disappointment.'

She has not eaten since lunchtime but it is not just the hunger, or the brandy that is making her feel light-headed. She has to keep reminding herself not to giggle like a child. She reaches for the bottle and takes another gulp.

'I did not have you down as a drinker,' he says, teasing her.

She thinks that he is a fine man. His hands were so gentle on her feet. She wonders how they would feel on her back or on her breasts. The thought both surprises and excites her.

He turns towards her and she leans forward and kisses him on the mouth. He pulls away awkwardly. She flushes.

'I'm terribly sorry. It must be the brandy. You must think me the perfect slut.'

He holds her gaze and says quickly, 'Not at all. It was just a little unexpected.'

He picks up the brandy bottle, takes another gulp and hands her the bottle. She declines.

'If I drink anymore I might do something that I will really regret,' she says.

He replaces the bottle on the table. 'So might I,' he replies.

'Would you?' She hears the sound of her own voice, but feels oddly disconnected from it and from her life outside the shelter.

He looks at her but says nothing.

'Would you regret it?' she repeats. It is as though somebody else is speaking. A woman who she barely recognises.

He holds her gaze for a moment. Then he slowly shakes his head. 'No. No, I don't suppose that I would.'

She cannot deny that she wants him. At that moment, she wants the thrill of his hands on her body more than she had ever wanted the touch of a man. 'What about your wife?' she asks.

He looks up. 'What about her?'

'You love her, surely?'

'Yes.'

She is silent.

'But I cannot deny that I am attracted to you,' he says, reaching across and taking her hand.

Her heart is beating so hard that she wonders if he can see it. She allows him a kiss. The thrill of it makes her tremble.

'She would be hurt,' she says.

He says nothing. He kisses the side of her neck.

'Jealous,' she says.

'Jealous, you say?'

He sits back, resting his head against the wall, sighs and appears lost in thought. 'I doubt that,' he says after a few moments 'Furious, certainly. Perhaps even murderously so, but I doubt very much that she would be jealous.'

She is puzzled. How could his wife not be jealous at the thought of him with another woman? She is certain that, had she been married to him and he had come home smelling of another woman's perfume, she would have been jealous. Insanely so.

'Doesn't she love you?' she asks.

He appears to ponder the question. 'My wife is a woman of great determination. She has planned a life for us. She is determined to... To make it a reality.' He appears about to say more but falls silent.

'But?' she asks.

'She loves me in her way. But...' he hesitates, 'it would take more than a mouthful or two of brandy for her to kiss me like you just kissed me.'

She is startled by the look of emptiness she sees reflected in his eyes. Emptiness and some other emotion that she cannot fathom.

'Then why did you marry her?'

He sits up and reaches for the brandy bottle. 'A very good question. I suppose,' he says after a few moment's reflection, 'that I was impressed by her.'

She thinks it an odd reason to marry a person. 'Impressed?'

'By her strength of character. By the certainty with which she conducts herself. People are drawn to it. Men especially.'

She finds herself bristling. She cannot help but feel a little threatened by this woman who, if what he says is true, can attract a man by force of personality. What is she in comparison?

'And are you still impressed?' she says, failing completely to mask the hint of envy in her voice.

'Not impressed, no.'

'Then what?'

He is silent. 'I suppose that I am a little afraid. Her passion is not for me but for the life she has planned for us. I am, I think, something of a means unto an end.'

He says it with a bitterness that startles her.

'It is not a passion that you share then?' she says, searching his face.

'No it is not.'

'Have you told her that it is not what you want?'

'No.'

'Why ever not?'

He says nothing.

'Surely, she is not so frightening as all that,' she says dismissively.

She sees a flash of irritation in his face and there is awkward silence between them.

'I am sorry. I do not mean to pry.'

She holds out her hand. He takes it and his lips are suddenly on hers. He kisses her with such urgency that she is momentarily lost in the passion of it. His hand slides around her back and then inside her blouse. His touch is exquisite. She can feel her skin bloom under the heat of his hand. She cannot deny that she wants him and yet something about him troubles her.

He pushes her down onto the bunk and undoes the buttons on her blouse. She can feel him, hard on her leg. His hands on her neck. His lips and tongue on her chest. His teeth…

'No.'

His hands are suddenly under her skirt.

'Stop. Please.'

Now he seems more like an animal than a lover, tearing at her clothes. And then it comes to her. Along with the bitterness, she recognises resentment in his eyes. She begins to feel afraid. As he holds her down she knows that she does not want to be taken by him. Here in the shelter on a dirty staff room bunk.

'No!' She shouts and struggles to push him off.

He holds her down with an arm across her chest. She feels his free hand between her legs.

'For God's sake!'

There is anger in his eyes. His hold on her loosens momentarily as he fumbles with his belt buckle.

Fear blossoms in her chest and she feels a sudden rush of adrenaline. She pushes him with all her strength, her finger nails biting into his shoulder. Her strength surprises her and, as he loses his balance, she rolls out from beneath him and staggers to her feet.

She stands for a moment looking at him. Oddly she no longer feels afraid. She feels humiliated by the trust she has put in him.

'How could you?' she yells.

He is red in the face.

'You cannot stand up to your own wife, but you would force yourself on me?'

He has started to clamber to his feet.

'What are you trying to prove?' she hurls.

He takes a step towards her.

'That you are a man?' and she laughs. She doesn't know why she does it. Perhaps it is anger. Perhaps it is pity. But she laughs out loud. At the absurdity of what is happening. At him. And as she hears herself laughing, she knows that it is the worst possible thing she could be doing. But she cannot stop herself.

He springs at her. 'You know nothing about me,' he shouts and with the red fire of fury in his eyes, strikes her full and hard across the face.

CHAPTER TEN

Sunday, 24th May 2004

Harry enjoyed the journey back, secure as he was in the knowledge that, for once, he had got one over on Erik who was oblivious and continued to make jibes, largely at Harry's expense. Harry didn't mind at all. In fact, the jibes served only to improve Harry's spirits. Erik would be laughing on the other side of his face if Pickles made good his threat and passed the details Harry had given him to the police.

It was shortly after midday when the Hilux pulled back into Harry's drive.

'See you, guys. Let me know when the pictures are up on the forum Erik?'

'No sweat, Museum Boy,' said Erik.

God he never stops, thought Harry, winking at Mike as he got out of the car. He closed the door and watched the Hilux reverse out of the drive.

It had been warm all morning and the sun was shining brightly. Harry was looking forward to a shower, a change of clothes and then, as the landlord and his family were away, perhaps he'd sit in the garden with a beer and his book. He put his key in the door and let himself in, throwing his bag through the bedroom doorway. As he did so, he noticed the red light on his answer phone flashing. He walked into his bedroom and pressed the play button.

The first message was from a company selling windows. Harry didn't bother listening to the whole message and pressed the delete button. He sat down on his bed and had begun to unlace his boots as the second message began to play.

'Mr Stammers, this is the Whittington Hospital,' said a female voice.

Harry froze.

'I'm afraid that your father, Edward Stammers, has been taken ill,' continued the message. 'He was admitted to the hospital early this morning. Would you please contact us as soon as possible. The number is…'

Harry jumped to his feet and reached for his bedside cabinet drawer with one hand, while rewinding the answer phone with the other. He rummaged about in the drawer for a pen while the message began to re-play and had only just found it in time to scribble the hospital's telephone number down on the back of his hand. His heart was in his mouth as he dialled the number.

'Hello, my name is Harry Stammers,' he said when the call was answered. 'I got a message to call you. I understand that my father was admitted earlier today.'

'Just a moment caller, I'll put you through to admissions.'

The line clicked and rang several times. Harry sat back down on the edge of his bed. 'Oh, for fuck's sake,' he said out loud as Bohemian Rhapsody began to play through the handset. Harry tucked the receiver between his ear and shoulder while he struggled to remove his boots. It was some minutes before a voice came on the line. Less than an hour later, Harry was standing at his father's bedside.

Ted Stammers was a big man. He'd been an engineer, initially for the Post Office and then for British Telecom and had only recently retired. Much of his working life had been spent climbing telegraph poles and hauling heavy cables. Harry had never seen him smoke and he'd only ever seen him drunk on three occasions. The last time had been at his daughter's wedding. Kate had been furious, Harry recalled. His father, who was normally a quiet man, had been dreading making the speech. By the time he'd lurched to his feet it was all too evident that he'd had a skin full and the speech had caused uproar. His father had started by loudly proclaiming how relieved he was that Kate had at last got "some poor bugger" to take her off his hands. Kate hadn't spoken to him for months.

Harry stood beside the hospital bed looking down at his father. The nurse, who had shown him to the bed, had warned him to expect the worst. 'He's had quite a serious stroke,' she had said but Harry had hardly heard the words let alone taken them in. The man on the bed in front of him didn't look like his father at all. He was lying on his side with his knees tucked up against his chest. Harry noticed the greying stubble on his face and his hair, which was plastered across his forehead with sweat. Harry stood staring, trying to take it in.

He was still standing in silence some minutes later when he heard the curtain behind him being pulled.

'Harry?' said a voice from behind him. He felt Kate's arm on his shoulder. He turned and hugged her.

'What's happened to Dad? Is he alright? Let me see.'

Harry reached for her hand, held it tightly and looked at her for a moment. Then he stepped to the side so that she could see the man on the bed in front of them.

'Oh my God,' she said, all colour draining from her face.

Harry sat, staring into nowhere while Kate got them some coffee. The hospital canteen was enormous but mostly empty. The serving counter ran along one side of the space, behind which could be seen the kitchen. Harry could never understand the modern fad for open plan restaurant kitchens. They were invariably stainless steel affairs, staffed by some spotty teenager with long hair who fancied himself as a bit of a Gordon Ramsey. They were usually anything but. Far better, Harry thought, to secrete the kitchen and its staff away behind solid walls and closed doors.

'Did you want anything to eat? I forgot to ask,' Kate said, putting down the tray with their coffee and seating herself opposite Harry.

'No, thanks. I don't have much of an appetite,' replied Harry.

'Me neither.'

Kate Stammers was Harry's younger sister by two years. They had been close as children, but their adult lives had taken them in different directions and, in the absence of a conventional family to bring them together, at least on birthdays and at Christmas, they had gradually drifted apart. Harry had barely seen her since her wedding, due in large part to her new husband. Jonathan Longhurst was a barrister and Harry couldn't stand him. The problem, so far as Harry was concerned, was that Longhurst did not seem to be able to leave his professional persona behind at court. Whenever they met, he would would delight in engaging Harry in some great debate, usually about "our something for nothing society" or the "failing state education system". Harry did his best to avoid taking the bait but Longhurst seemed to know all the right buttons to press. Having engaged Harry, he would then take huge delight in defeating any argument that Harry could marshall, no matter how vigorously Harry defended his corner. As a consequence, Harry had learned to avoid any and all contact with the man.

'How have you been keeping?' Kate asked.

'Fine. You?' replied Harry.

'Fine.'

'Jonathan?'

'Busy. He's got some big cases at the moment. It just never seems to stop.'

They were silent.

'Do you think Dad's going to recover?' she said, a little hesitantly, as though fearing the answer.

'I don't know Kate. The doctor seemed reasonably optimistic but who knows? It sounds as though it was a pretty serious stroke.'

'What if he can't look after himself? The doctor said that if he recovers, he could be left with some paralysis. How will Dad get by on his own? Can you imagine him living in a care home or something?'

'No. But if that is what it comes to, he'll have to cross that bridge. We all will. Dad has spent a life time avoiding things. Maybe this is something that he will not be able to avoid.'

'What do you mean by that?' Kate said, bristling.

Harry hesitated. 'Nothing. I'm sorry. I guess now is not the time.'

'It wasn't his fault that she left, you know. You've always held it against him,' Kate said angrily.

'I don't blame him for Mum going,' Harry replied. 'I blame him for not finding her. I blame him for not even trying. I blame him for pretending she was never there.'

'You don't know that. We were children. He could have been scouring the streets for all we knew. God knows what he went through.'

A couple of a table by the door noticed her raised voice.

'I hope he does know,' said Harry, leaning forward and lowering his voice. 'Because Dad hasn't said a word to the rest of us in thirty years.'

Kate looked at him furiously. 'That is typical of you. Dad is lying in a fucking hospital bed and all you can think about is a mother who walked away from us and never came back. She's not some saint, you know. She didn't run away to become a missionary. She abandoned her own children and left Dad to pick up the pieces.'

'That's the point Kate. We don't know why she went. We don't know because he won't tell us.'

'Maybe he doesn't know. If you want to be angry with someone, try being angry with her. Dad is seriously ill Harry. He might never wake up.'

'Well if he does, I'm going to have it out with him. I want to know what happened. Why she left. Where she went. Before it is too late.'

CHAPTER ELEVEN

Friday, 10th*** November 1944***

She feels the bridge of her nose crunch and tastes blood in her mouth. Her mind does not register that he has hit her, until her ankle has already given way and she has started to tumble. As she falls, she thinks of her mother in the Anderson shelter at the bottom of the garden, waiting for her and worrying. She thinks of Elsie in the bar at *The Galleon* and the other girls at the Park. She thinks about the bag that she left by the garden wall with the fruit inside, which will spoil and go to waste. There is a momentary flash of light and a sharp piercing pain as the side of her head hits something hard and unyielding, and then there is only darkness.

CHAPTER TWELVE

Monday, 31st May 2004

Harry had been working on the report for the last hour. He had made good progress thanks, in large part, to Elsie Sidthorpe's notebook. It contained a great deal of information that he had been able to use and the report was now looking in reasonable shape. Harry was relieved. It was well overdue.

Jane had called shortly after he had arrived and had told him that the Major wanted to see him in his office at ten-thirty, sharp. Harry printed off two copies of the report, put them in his bag and walked the short distance to the bungalow.

'There you are. The Major is already waiting for you. Go straight in. Oh and Harry?' and said Jane, from behind her desk.

'Yes?'

'Do straighten your tie.'

Harry walked down the corridor, adjusting his collar and knocked on the Major's door.

'Ah Stammers, please come in and take a seat. I won't be a moment.'

The Major got up, as Harry seated himself at the desk, and left the office. Harry smiled. The Major always did this whenever Harry went to see him. He seemed to think that it was good form to leave visitors waiting for at least a few minutes.

Major Sir John Huntley-Gordon was a small, overweight man with a greying moustache and beard. Now in his seventies, he had been at Sandhurst and had retired from the Royal Signals, following a singularly unspectacular career. He was always impeccably well dressed. He wore a silk handkerchief in his top pocket and a matching bow-tie. Despite the fact that he was now a civilian, the Major still liked to be referred to by rank. He could be bombastic at times, but most of the staff respected him, not least for the progress that had been made at the Park under the his stewardship. He was also thoroughly loyal to his staff, many of whom were, like Harry, really quite fond of of the *Old Boy*.

Harry took both copies of the report from his bag and was shuffling his papers when the Major came back into the office.

He sat in the leather seat behind his desk and looked at Harry. 'So, Stammers, what progress?'

'I have printed an update for you, Major,' Harry said, handing him the report.

'Splendid, splendid,' said the Major as he turned the pages. 'We have the reunion pencilled in for August, so we absolutely must get invitations out to all those you have traced very shortly. You do know that we have the Duke of York coming to do the presentations don't you?'

'Yes Major. I am aware of that. It has just been a little more difficult than I anticipated. Of course so many of them have passed away or are just not in the records that we have.'

'A damn shame. But I see here,' he said, looking at the report 'that the list is a good deal longer than it was.'

'Yes, Major. I recently went to see a lady called Elsie Sidthorpe and, very fortunately, she provided me with a lot of new information on the role of the group from Beaumanor, as well as the names of many of its members.'

'Excellent news. I trust that she will be able to attend the reunion?'

'Uncertain due to her health, I'm afraid. She lives in a nursing home in Suffolk. But I certainly hope so.'

'Good. Good.' He paused. 'Who is this?' the Major said pointing to a line that Harry had underlined in the report. He peered at it across the desk.

'Martha Watts. Her case is an interesting one and I would very much like to investigate it further. In fact, I have someone coming to see me shortly with some photographs that may help.'

'What is so interesting about her?'

'Martha Watts came here from Beaumanor with Elsie Sidthorpe. She went missing in November 1944. The official explanation was that she had been killed in an air raid but her body was never found.'

'Would that have been unusual?'

'Possibly not, but following her disappearance, Elise Sidthorpe says that she was told, in no uncertain terms, to stop asking questions. She is convinced that Martha was not killed in the air raid.'

'And who does Mrs Sidthorpe say told her to stop asking questions?' asked the Major.

'She doesn't know, but my guess that it was Intelligence,' Harry replied.

'Do you think that Miss Watts may still be alive?'

'No, I very much doubt that.'

'Then what is in it for the Park, Stammers? We've enough on our plate trying to find the living, let alone a young lady who very well have died in an air raid sixty years ago, whatever Mrs Sidthorpe believes.'

'Yes, I appreciate that Major. But the Martha Watts case is intriguing. Why was Mrs Sidthorpe warned off and what did happen to Miss Watts? It does seem odd that she should disappear so completely. It may turn out to be one of those human stories that bring the people who worked here to life.'

The Major looked at him thoughtfully. 'Yes, I can see that Stammers. We could make quite a story of it, if you do manage to get to the bottom of it.'

'Yes, it could generate quite a lot of public interest.'

'Indeed it might,' the Major said thoughtfully, scratching his beard, before appearing to make up his mind. 'Very well Stammers, but please keep me posted.'

'Yes, Sir.'

With that, Harry's audience with the Major was over. He got up, gathering his papers and left the Major's office.

'How did it go?' Jane whispered, as Harry passed her desk.

'Well. Amazingly well actually,' Harry said with a puzzled expression on his face.

'Bloody hell, that makes a change. You can tell me about it at lunch.'

Harry nodded and then hesitated. 'Oh, I almost forgot. Not today. I have another lunch time appointment.' Harry tried to look mysterious as he walked out of the bungalow but he couldn't help smirking.

At about twenty past eleven the telephone on Harry's desk rang.

'Mr Stammers, it is the Gate. We have a Miss Carmichael to see you.'

'Oh yes, thanks. I'll be down for her in a moment.'

Harry went into the bathroom and looked at himself in the mirror. He checked his teeth and straightened his hair. It was odd, he thought, that he should feel nervous but there was no time to think about it now. He went out on to the landing and looked across to the gate. He could see Ellen Carmichael standing by the gatekeeper's hut. She was wearing sunglasses and was dressed in a pale floral summer dress, with a bag over one arm and a pale blue cardigan over the other. Harry noticed that she was wearing brown boots. He thought that she looked about as good as it was possible for a woman to look. She saw him, waved and started to walk towards him. He met her at the edge of the lake.

'Good morning.' She smiled and kissed him on the cheek.

'Hello Ellen, how are you?'

'I am very well thank you,' she said airily. 'So this is Bletchley Park.'

They stood for a moment looking out across the lake to the fountain and the mansion beyond. The spray from the fountain shimmered in the sunlight.

'What a lovely place,' she said 'and there's the mansion,' Ellen said pointing across the lake.

'Yes, that's it. Bit of a mess architecturally speaking but quite a vision on a morning like this. Would you like to come up to the office? We can have a look at your photographs there.'

'Yes, alright,' she said brightly.

They walked across to the archive and Harry showed her up the steps and into his office.

'Do you work here on your own?' Ellen said, glancing around.

'A lot of the time, yes. Most of the other staff are up in the main office. But sometimes there will be someone sorting through the archive. Can I get you a coffee?'

'Oh, yes please,' she said, smiling.

Harry went to the kitchen and filled two cups with coffee from the jug on the percolator and returned to his office which seemed brighter somehow. It was as though Ellen had brought the sunshine in with her.

He set the coffee cups down on his desk. 'So, you have some photographs for me?'

'Yes, I do.'

She took an envelope from her bag, removed the photographs and spread them out on the desk in front of him. 'Gran has written the names of the women in the pictures on the back of each photograph.'

There were eight black and white photographs in all. Harry examined the first of them. It was of a woman in a pale dress and dark shoes, with her back to the camera, standing in front of one of the Park's Bombe machines. The picture only showed part of the woman's face. Harry turned the photograph over. 'This is Martha Watts?' he said, with some surprise.

'It is a shame that we can't see much of her face in that one. But yes that is Martha,' Ellen replied.

Harry examined the second photograph. It was of a woman in military uniform standing in front of a brick building. 'This looks like the mansion, but it is an odd angle and I'd need to examine it more closely to be sure,' Harry said.

'Her name was Gwen Simpson. Gran says the she died about fifteen years ago.'

Harry examined the third photograph. Three women were pictured very clearly and Harry immediately recognised Elsie Sidthorpe. He turned the photograph over, but was disappointed that Martha's name did not appear. He looked at the fourth and fifth pictures together as they were very similar and could well have been taken on the same day. They were of several women seated at desks. 'I think these were taken in Hut Six. We have some pictures that are very like them in the archive,' he said.

He turned the fifth picture over and saw that Martha Watts was named as the third woman from the left. Again the picture of Martha was not clear enough to be recognisable. 'It is such a shame that they're not clearer. We could possibly scan them and have Martha's image enlarged, but I doubt that it would make much difference,' he said.

'Keep going.' Ellen could not hide the excitement in her voice.

The sixth and seventh pictures were of groups of women sitting on the grass in front of one of the huts, but Harry couldn't identify the hut in question. None of the women were Martha.

He picked up the last of the photographs and caught his breath. It was of two women. Harry could see that on the left was Elsie Sidthorpe. He flipped the photograph over. Written in Elsie's spidery writing was "Me (left) and Martha (right), August 1944". Harry flipped the photograph back and forth, looking at the name, then staring at the woman on the right. He had paled noticeably.

'What is it?' said Ellen, looking puzzled.

'Oh it's nothing really,' he said, flustered.

'What?'

Harry hesitated. 'Martha just looks like somebody I saw on the tube the other day, that's all.' He immediately felt foolish and tried to gather his thoughts. 'So we have a clear photograph of Martha, which is a start.'

'Yes. She's pretty, isn't she?'

'Yes, she is,' Harry said, examining the picture more closely. Martha had a friendly, open face and curly dark hair. She was indeed, an attractive young woman. He tried to avoid comparing her with the face he'd seen momentarily on the tube train but he could not escape the feeling that the face was familiar.

'So where do we go from here?' Ellen asked.

'That is a very good question,' Harry replied.

'I mean, we don't even know for sure that Martha caught the train at Bletchley do we?'

'No, we don't.'

'And even if she did, I cannot imagine how we will trace her movements when she got to London. If she got there. She could, after all, have got off the train anywhere,' said Ellen.

Harry was thoughtful. 'Do we know whether she had any brothers or sisters?'

'No. But I could give Gran a ring and ask her, if you like.'

'Shall I get us some more coffee while you call her?'

Ellen nodded.

Harry returned to the office a few minutes later with two fresh cups of coffee. Ellen was just ending her conversation. 'Good news. Martha had a younger brother and an older sister,' she said passing a note to Harry. 'She also remembers that they lived in Roderick Road.'

'Your grandmother has an excellent memory.'

'Yes, but she can't remember the house number. She only remembers the name of the road because there was a chap she liked at the Park called Roderick. I think they had a bit of a thing going. In fact, I rather get the feeling that Roderick wasn't the only one.' Ellen said grinning.

Harry smiled. 'What about Martha's mother and father?'

'Gran says that her father was in the army and was away when Martha disappeared. But she doesn't know what became of them.'

'It is most unlikely that the family still live in Roderick Road,' Harry said, looking at the names on Ellen's note. 'John and Barbara Watts. Not exactly unusual names and, of course, Barbara is quite likely to have married and taken a different surname.'

They were quiet for a moment.

'Could we have a look in the census records to see how long they remained in Roderick Road?' asked Ellen.

'I'm afraid not. Access to them is restricted by the one hundred years rule. But we might be able to find a set of Kelly's.'

'Kelly's? What are they?'

'They are like the modern Yellow Pages. They mostly list trades people and businesses, but sometimes they contain all of the addresses in a particular street and who lived at each house. I'll talk to the local library and see if they have a set.'

Harry spent the next hour and a half showing Ellen around the Park. She was captivated by the huts but disappointed that not all of them were open to the public. 'It is shocking that so many of them are in such an awful state,' she said.

'I know. Seeing it like this was what made me apply for a job here.'

'You wanted to do something positive about it?'

'Yes,' he smiled.

'And have you?'

'I like to think so. In my own small way.'

Ellen took Harry's arm.

'What do you do? For a living I mean,' Harry asked.

'I have a shop.'

'Really? Where?'

'In Barnet. Do you know it?'

'A bit. I live in Golders Green, so we are almost neighbours. What do you sell in your shop?'

'We paint furniture, mainly.'

'We?' Harry asked it, as casually as he could.

'My business partner Nicky and I. We opened the shop together in two thousand and one.'

Harry couldn't entirely hide his relief.

'What about you?'

'What about me?'

'Are you single, idiot? That was what you were asking, wasn't it?'

'Yes. I suppose it was.' Harry grinned, a little sheepishly.

'Well?'

'Yes, I am single.'

'Good,' she said, squeezing his arm playfully. 'So, single Mr Stammers, where are you taking me for lunch?'

Unbelievably, they had lunch in the Park canteen. Harry had taken Ellen to see the mansion and as they were leaving to walk back to his office, Ellen had noticed the green painted hut.

'Is that the canteen?'

'Yes, but...'

'Let's have lunch there.'

Harry had been thinking of taking her to an out-of-the-way pub he knew in Little Brickhill. It had a beautiful garden full of flowers. 'God, no, you don't want to eat in there. The place will be packed and the food tastes like cardboard.'

'Oh come on. I want to experience the authentic taste of Bletchley Park,' she said laughing and with that she had grabbed his arm and hauled him into the canteen.

Harry had been right. The place was packed.

Ellen looked about at the mock nineteen forties decor. 'It looks just like it must have done when Gran was here. I can see her and Martha, sitting there gossiping, can't you?' she said, wistfully.

'Hardly. I hate to burst your bubble but this is Hut Four. It was used by Naval Intelligence during the war. The canteen was elsewhere.'

'Spoil sport,' she said, pinching him.

They found a vacant table, looked at the menu and Harry went to the counter to order their food.

'You fiend,' said a voice in the queue behind him. Harry turned.

'You absolute fiend,' said Jane, grinning. 'First you blow me out for another woman. Then you have the audacity to bring your fancy woman here. I am distraught.'

'In point of fact, I did not bring her here. She brought me here,' said Harry.

Jane pulled a face. 'Save your lame excuses. You're a cad and a bounder Harry Stammers.'

Harry could see several people in the queue staring at him.

'She's joking,' he announced to the queue.

The queue looked dubious.

'Jane, tell them you're joking, for God's sake.'

Jane had taken out a tissue from her pocket and was blowing her nose. An elderly woman in the queue said 'Men' with considerable disdain.

Jane leant across to whisper in his ear, feigning tears. 'That'll teach you. Who is she?'

Harry gave her his best impression of a withering look.

'Her name is Ellen Carmichael. She's a relative of Elsie Sidthorpe's. Elsie was here in 1944.'

'She is gorgeous,' said Jane, just a little too enthusiastically for Harry's liking.

'Yes, I know,' Harry said, tersely.

'I thought you were staying single.'

'I was.'

'Hmm..' Jane looked dubious.

'I mean, I am.'

'Well I suppose I could forgive you.'

'Thank you.'

'But don't think that you are getting off that lightly.'

Harry looked at her questioningly.

'I see there's a spare seat at your table. You can invite me to join you and I'll vet her for you.'

This is getting better and better, Harry thought.

It turned out that Ellen and Jane had quite a lot in common and the two of them talked, almost without pause, for the next half an hour. Harry sat mostly in silence, listening to their conversation and watching Ellen. The excitement in her voice, when she described their search for Martha Watts was infectious and Jane appeared almost as captivated with her as Harry was.

Jane offered to scan and enlarge the photographs that Ellen had brought with her to the Park. She also offered to speak to the library in London. By the end of lunch Jane and Ellen were exchanging telephone numbers and Jane had promised to drop by Ellen's shop when she was next over that way. Harry's ambitions for a quiet lunch with Ellen were in ashes.

After lunch Harry walked Ellen back to her Saab which was parked in the car park by the lake. She said 'I'll call you tomorrow,' gave him a peck on the cheek and was gone.

Harry stomped back to his office feeling murderous. He was going to kill Jane Mears. He was going to tear off her arms and her legs and throw them into the lake and then he was going to jump up and down on her bleeding remains.

CHAPTER THIRTEEN

At home that evening, Harry's mood had not improved. He'd called the hospital but his father's condition was unchanged. Nor was he feeling optimistic, either about his chances with Ellen Carmichael or their search for Martha Watts. It was bound to end inconclusively. Martha Watts was almost certainly dead and the chances of finding out what had happened to her, beyond the explanation given at the time, seemed remote at best. If the investigation got nowhere, he'd have no reason to maintain contact with Ellen Carmichael and that would be that.

He flicked the remote control from station to station and yawned. Did he want a relationship with her anyway? Jane had been right: - he had wanted to stay single. His last relationship had been a complete disaster. Besides, Harry reflected, he had started to enjoy living on his own. He could watch what he wanted on the television, go where he wished, eat and drink what he liked, go to bed, get up, drop his clothes where he took them off and leave his pants on the bathroom floor without somebody else complaining about it. He yawned again and decided to go to bed. He went into the bathroom to brush his teeth. He removed his clothes and made a point of dropping his pants on the floor.

Harry got into bed and closed his eyes. He thought of the face he had seen on the tube train and of Ellen's photograph of Martha Watts. The face had been in the back of his mind all day. He thought of the grainy black and white photograph of his mother that his own grandmother had shown him. Perhaps Martha Watts had chosen to leave her family and friends like his mother had left Harry and his family. It wasn't right that anyone could just walk away like that. It wasn't fair on the people left behind. He had to do something. He had to find them.

Harry woke with a start. His mobile phone was ringing. It was on the floor beside his bed. He reached out and groped about for the phone. 'Yes?' The call had to be from the hospital.

'Harry?'

'Yes.'

'Did I wake you?'

'Yes. Who is it?' He was still half asleep.

'It is Ellen. I hope you don't mind?'

'Ellen? Ellen.' Harry was instantly awake. 'What? Are you alright? No. I mean, yes.'

'Oh dear. I did wake you, didn't I?'

'I meant yes, you did wake me and no, I don't mind. At all, as it happens.'

'I'm sorry,' said Ellen, giggling.

'No really, it is fine.' Harry said, sitting up and rotating his legs so that he was perched on the side of his bed. 'Are you alright?'

'Yes, I am fine. I just wanted to say thank you.'

'Thank you? Why? For what?'

'For agreeing to look for Martha.'

'You don't need to thank me. It is important. I know that.'

'Yes, it is important. To Gran and to me.'

'And also to me. Nobody should stay lost Ellen. If for no other reason than what it does to the people left behind…' Harry's voiced trailed off into silence.

'I just hope that we can find out what happened to her.'

'We will,' Harry said. 'Somehow.'

In the event, the search for Martha Watts's living relatives was far easier than either Harry or Ellen could have imagined it would be. Harry arrived at the Park at 9.00am the following morning and had just walked into his office when the telephone on his desk rang.

'Good morning Loverboy,' said Jane.

'Hi Jane and what can I do for you this fine morning.'

'Goodness me. We are in a good mood this morning aren't we?' she said, sounding a little surprised.

'Yes, we certainly are.'

'Good night was it?'

'It improved after lights out, put it that way.'

'Too much detail!' screeched Jane.

'No, I didn't mean anything like that.'

'I do not want to hear about your nasty little nocturnal habits, thank you,' Jane said.

'I do not have any nasty little nocturnal habits.'

'Yes, well I am about to make your good morning even better.'

'Really? How are you going to do that?'

'Would you like a list?'

Harry thought for a moment. 'Yes, alright.'

'Fine. First I am going to give you Martha's mother's full address in 1944. Second, the full names and dates of birth of Martha's brother and sister and his late wife. Third, the names of their children. They had three by the way. Fourth, I am going to tell you that John Watts is not only still alive and kicking but he's also living at the same address in Roderick Road. Fifth I will, if you are extremely lucky, give you his telephone number. And lastly I am going to send you my bill and, believe me, I do not come cheap.'

Harry was stunned. 'What? You cannot possibly have discovered all that since yesterday.'

'Oh, can't I?'

'Seriously?' said Harry.

'Oh ye of little faith,' Jane said triumphantly.

'I'm on my way.'

Harry went straight from his office to the bungalow. He found Jane sat behind her desk with her arms folded across her chest and a grin on her face. 'How?' he said, breathlessly.

'Easy. After lunch yesterday, I rang the library in Gospel Oak.'

'Gospel Oak,' Harry repeated.

'They did indeed have a set of Kelly's Directories and the very nice female librarian was happy to look up Roderick Road for me.'

'And?'

'And it turned out that there was a Watts living at a house in Roderick Road in all the editions after the war until the most recent edition they had, which was from 1972.'

'No?'

'Yes. At number seventy-six actually. So it struck me that if they were still there in 1972, they might still be there today. Thirty years is a little more likely than sixty, after all.'

'I guess so,' Harry agreed.

'So I dialled Directory Enquiries and asked for the telephone number of Mrs Watts at 76 Roderick Road, Gospel Oak.'

'And they had it listed?'

'No, of course not. She would be more than a hundred years old by now, idiot. But they did have a Mr John Watts living at that address. He is seventy, by the way.'

'No!'

'So I called him last night when I got home and when I told him that I was from Bletchley Park he was very excited. But the best is yet to come,' she grinned.

'What?'

'He didn't know that his sister, Martha I mean, had worked here.'

Harry thought for a moment. 'Well, no I don't suppose that he would have done.'

'He was absolutely delighted. The poor man got quite emotional. I could not get him off the phone.'

Jane stood up and went over to her bag which was hanging on the coat stand. She took out a sheet of paper in a plastic cover and handed it to Harry. 'Have a look at that.'

On the sheet of paper Jane had drawn out the Watts family tree. Harry examined it for several moments.

'Jane, this is incredible,' he said.

Jane was watching him, a look of smug satisfaction on her face. 'He would be happy for you to go and see him.'

Harry looked up. 'Does Ellen know?'

'No. I was going to call her first thing this morning, but I thought I would let you do it.'

Harry looked at her. Then her circled her desk and put his arms around her. 'Jane Mears. You are a living bloody marvel.'

Harry walked back to his office. He stopped by the lake, slid a cigarette out from the packet and stood, silently blowing smoke rings. Ellen was going to be thrilled and he could not wait to tell her. He stubbed out the cigarette under his foot, returned to his desk and dialled the number that Jane had given him.

Jane had been right. It was difficult to end the conversation with John Watts. But after twenty minutes, Harry had finalised arrangements.

As soon as he had finished the call he dialled Ellen's number.

'Ellen Carmichael Interiors'

'Er.. Is that Ellen?' Harry said.

Ellen laughed. 'Hello Harry Stammers. Yes, it's me.'

'Sorry. Do you mind me calling you at work?'

'Don't be silly.'

'No. Right.'

'You sound excited.'

'What are you doing tomorrow?'

CHAPTER FOURTEEN

Harry had arranged to collect Ellen from her Barnet shop at 1.30 P.M. It was a relatively easy journey from his flat in Golders Green, although the Spitfire had struggled up Barnet Hill. He had reached the summit with some relief and took the right hand fork at the church into the High Street with twenty minutes to spare. *Ellen Carmichael Interiors* was on the right, just before the junction leading up to Hadley. He stopped on double yellow lines outside the shop and sounded the horn.

'You're early,' Ellen said, clambering into the passenger's seat next to him. 'I had forgotten how low these things are.'

'You have been in a Spitfire before?'

'Yes, my father had one when I was little. Carmine red. WYF500G. I loved it when Dad took me out in it. Especially if the weather was good and we could have the roof down.'

The journey from Barnet to Gospel Oak took over an hour. The traffic was awful and Harry was sure that they were going to be late. Ellen looked gorgeous as usual. She was wearing a short, blue skirt and yet another pair of boots. Harry noticed that she wasn't wearing any tights and had a hard time keeping his eyes on the road.

Ellen noticed. 'Shall I wear jeans the next time you take me out in your Spitfire?' she laughed.

Harry flushed. 'I was just admiring your boots,' Harry lied. 'I have seen you three times and you have been wearing a different pair each time. How many pairs of boots do you have, for heaven's sake?'

'I like boots.'

Harry thought that he would like to see her dressed in nothing but a pair of them. 'I am becoming rather fond of them myself,' he admitted.

'I had noticed. Just keep your eyes on the road, buster.'

They arrived fifteen minutes late. 76 Roderick Road was a three-story terraced property with a blue front door and an alley between it and the next house. There was a small front garden with a well tended hedge. As they opened the front gate, Harry noticed the curtain in the window twitch. Mr Watts had evidently been waiting for them.

John Watts showed them into the lounge. 'It is such a pleasure to meet you both. We've been so excited since your call, Mr Stammers.'

Harry looked at Ellen who shook her head. 'We?' he said, glancing about the room for the signs of another occupant.

John Watts looked at Harry blankly for a moment. 'Force of habit,' he said, smiling. 'It's just me, of course. Make yourselves comfortable while I fetch us some tea,' he said disappearing into the hall.

The lounge was full of furniture and the clutter of everyday living. An old leather sofa and two arm chairs arranged around a large coffee table filled the middle of the room. The sofa looked like it had been there for so long that it might have taken root.

At the far end of the room was a large, cast iron fireplace that Harry guessed was Victorian. It had particularly ornate, tiled side panels which Harry bent down to examine.

'Not really my taste,' said Ellen.

'Nor mine. But you've got to admire the craftsmanship that went into this kind of thing. Who could be bothered nowadays? It's all massed produced in bloody Taiwan.'

'That's progress for you,' said Ellen.

An old fashioned sideboard almost filled one wall. It was covered in framed photographs which Harry assumed were of members of the Watts family. Looking at them Harry reckoned that every generation of the last sixty or so years was represented. There were so many pictures that they had overflowed on to all four walls and just about every other surface.

John Watts re-appeared with a tray which he put on the coffee table.

'You have a large family Mr Watts,' said Ellen, seating herself on the sofa.

'Yes, Dora and I have..' He hesitated. 'I mean *had* three children, all grown up now of course. They have given me seven grand children, would you believe? Then there is my sister Barbara's family. She had two daughters and they all had their own children. That is my mother and my father,' he said, pointing to black and white wedding photograph hanging above the fire place. 'And there is Siss.' He walked over to a corner shelf and reached for a framed photograph of a young woman standing in front of seaside hut. The floor board creaked as he reached for it. He handed the photograph to Harry who sat down next to Ellen. They examined the picture together.

'She was a very pretty girl,' Harry said.

'Yes, she was. Clever too. We were devastated when she was killed, particularly mother. She was especially fond of Martha and very proud of her. She would have been prouder still had she known about the work Martha was doing,' he said, seating himself in the armchair opposite them.

'She would have been right to have been proud. Martha had been doing some very important work, both at the Park and at Beaumanor where she was previously stationed,' said Harry.

'When did she start at Bletchley Park?' asked John Watts.

'Martha was part of a team that moved to the Park in May 1942.'

'What did she do, exactly?'

'Well, of course we can't be entirely certain what Martha did, personally. But her group were responsible for integrating the knowledge gleaned from signals intelligence with decodes from cryptography. This was enormously important work, Mr Watts.'

'Mother would have been so proud,' John Watts said with some emotion. He cleared his throat.

'One of my reasons for coming to see you today was to ask whether you and your family would like to come to Bletchley Park so that you can see where Martha worked and talk with some of the people that she worked with. We are holding a reunion in August for veterans and their families. With your permission, I would like to add you to our invitation list. We are not allowed to announce a specific date as yet, for security reasons, as we are expecting a very special visitor but, if you are in agreement, we will write to you shortly.'

John Watts looked like he was going to burst with pride and it took him several moments before he could speak. 'I would be honoured, Mr Stammers. I can't tell you what this means to me and what it will mean to my family. It is almost too much to take in.' John Watts blew his nose into a handkerchief that he produced from his pocket.

Ellen beamed at him. 'I think that we could all do with a cup of tea,' she said. 'Shall I be mum?'

There was a pause in the conversation while Ellen poured the tea and handed around the cups. She made a point of filling Harry's to the brim of the cup.

'Thanks Ellen. I do love a good brew,' he said, turning away from John Watts and pulling the most ridiculous face he could manage.

Ellen looked like she was going to burst but managed to contain herself.

'You said that inviting me to Bletchley Park was one of the reasons for your visit. What was the other?' asked John Watts.

Harry hesitated. He didn't quite know how to frame the question he had in mind. He looked at Ellen.

'It must have been terrible for you all when Martha went missing,' she said.

'Yes it was, although I suppose I was the fortunate one. I had been evacuated to South Wales, so I didn't see, immediately, the impact that losing Martha had on Mother. I certainly saw it, though, when I returned to London in 1945. She was never quite the same again.'

'We wanted to ask you about the circumstances,' said Ellen.

'Do you mean about how Martha died?'

'Yes.'

'She was killed in an air raid. On her way home actually,' said John Watts.

'So we gathered,' Ellen said. 'We understand that her body was never found?'

'No.'

Now Ellen was in the quandary that Harry had been in a few moments before. She looked at Harry helplessly. 'I cannot imagine how your poor mother coped,' she said.

'It was wartime. Many families had far worse to cope with, I suppose.'

'Mr Watts, can we ask whether your mother ever had any doubts about what had happened to Martha?' asked Harry.

'Doubts? No, I don't believe so. We knew what had happened to her. She was killed in an air raid.'

'Yes, but…' Harry hesitated.

'Do you mean, because her body was never found?'

'I'm sorry Mr Watts, I hope you don't mind us asking these questions,' Harry said.

'No, not at all. We were told that poor Siss was probably burned in one the many fires that flared up after the bombing.'

'But nothing was ever found to prove that this was the case?'

'No, but we didn't have any reason to doubt it,' John Watts said, looking a little uncertain. He was quiet for a moment. 'Do you?'

Harry hesitated and looked at Ellen.

'As I think you know,' said Ellen, 'my Great Aunt Elsie and Martha were very close friends. Elsie knew that when Martha travelled home she always took the bus to Haverstock Hill because she hated the Underground. She walked home from there. A few days after Martha went missing Elsie says that she travelled to London to see your mother. They had spoken on the telephone and your Mother had been distraught. Elsie took the bus from Euston to Haverstock Hill, as Martha would have done. She then walked along the route that Martha would have taken. She has told us that none of the streets along the route had suffered any recent bomb damage. None at all,' said Ellen.

'Really?' John Watts was thoughtful for a moment. 'But surely Siss could have gone another way?'

'Possibly, but Elsie says that while she was in London, she checked. The nearest that any bomb fell to Martha's route that night was Aldgate in the City.' Ellen said.

'That's at least five or six miles from here,' said Harry.

They were silent.

'So what do you think happened to Siss?' John Watts asked.

'We don't know, Mr Watts. But what we are saying is that if she took her normal route, then she should have made it home safely,' said Harry.

They were silent again.

'Could she have gone to see somebody else on her way home?' Ellen asked.

The old man was quiet for a few moments, seemingly lost in thought. 'If she did, then Mother certainly didn't know about it. Martha had told her what train she was going to be on. I don't think she would have wanted to worry Mother by arriving late.'

'Of course, we don't know for sure that she even made it to London. She could have got off the train anywhere between Bletchley and Euston.' said Harry.

There was another pause.

'Actually, I think that I may be able to help you there,' said John Watts.

'How so?'

'After Mother died, we found a letter among her papers, along with Martha's diary.'

Harry and Ellen exchanged glances. 'Her diary?' said Ellen.

'Yes. I still have it somewhere,' John Watts got up and, after searching for a few minutes, took a large box from the sideboard. He put it on the coffee table and started to rummage through it.

'Shortly after the war, Mother received a letter addressed to Martha. She didn't tell us about it at the time. Yes, here it is.' He passed Harry a large, tatty brown envelope. 'With the letter, was my sister's diary.'

Harry examined the envelope. It was addressed to Martha Watts at Roderick Road.

'If you read the letter inside, you'll see that the person who sent it… What was her name?'

Harry looked at the letter. 'Mrs Pether. June Pether.'

'Yes, Mrs Pether. Well, you'll see that Mrs Pether found the diary in the street during an air raid,' said John Watts.

'Does the letter say where, exactly, she found it?' asked Ellen.

Harry was already reading the letter. 'She found it in Haverstock Hill, not far from the bus stop, a little up from the Underground station,' he said. 'She says that she had always meant to return it but the following morning she received news about her husband,' Harry said.

'That's right,' said John Watts. 'The poor man had been killed and returning the diary understandably slipped her mind. I suppose that it must have sat in the bottom of a cupboard.'

'Until she moved house in…' said Harry, still reading. 'August 1949. The letter is dated the nineteenth.' Harry handed the letter to Ellen. 'May I examine the diary?' he asked.

'Yes, of course.'

Harry opened the diary, leafed through its pages and stopped at the final entry.

'Look at this,' he said turning to Ellen and showing her the page. 'Thursday, 9th November 1944.'

'The day before she went missing,' said Ellen.

Harry nodded. He read the entry out aloud. "*Elsie promising to come for drinks. She will never speak to me again if I refuse. Do hope we are not up half the night. Positively holding my breath for Friday. Cannot wait to see Mother and to sleep in my own bed.*"

'Oh my goodness,' said Ellen. 'That's my great aunt she is talking about.'

'Yes, that's right,' Harry replied. He continued to examine the diary. 'Martha seems to have written in her diary almost every day. So she probably lost it within a day or so of her last entry.'

'On Friday, the tenth,' said Ellen.

'Yes,' said Harry. 'Very probably.'

'The fact that it was found in Haverstock Hill means that Martha must have been there,' said Ellen, looking at Harry.

'More to the point it means that she was not at Aldgate. Not when she lost it, anyway.'

'Mrs Pether says that she found it in during an air raid,' said Ellen. 'Perhaps Martha panicked when the sirens went off and dropped it.'

'And yet your Aunt says that no bombs fell anywhere near Haverstock Hill?' asked John Watts.

'That's right.'

'Then where did Martha go? Why didn't she come home?' he asked.

CHAPTER FIFTEEN

Harry & Ellen sat outside 76 Roderick Road, both deep in thought.

It was Ellen who broke the silence. 'I wonder why Mrs Watts accepted, so readily, the explanation that the police gave her.'

Harry said nothing.

'And I really don't understand why she didn't tell anyone when Martha's diary turned up.'

'Perhaps she didn't want to think about what else could have happened to her. When you lose somebody like that, uncertainty is the worst feeling of all. Maybe she had her explanation and didn't want to let it go.' He fell silent again.

Ellen turned and looked at him. He appeared lost in thought. She took hold of his hand. 'Come on, lets drive back to Haverstock Hill,' she said. 'Do you have a map? We could try to follow the route that Martha would have taken.'

Harry turned towards her and held her gaze. 'Alright. There's an A to Z in the glove box.'

Ellen opened the glove box, retrieved the A to Z and found the page. 'We know she was in Haverstock Hill because of the diary. Somewhere along here,' she said pointing at the map.

'Show me.' Harry said.

Ellen handed him the A to Z.

'If she got off the bus here,' he said pointing at the map, 'at Belsize Park, then the most direct route would have been left into Downside Crescent, then Lawn Road, Garnett Road, Fleet Road and left into Roderick Road,' he traced the route on the page with his finger. 'I guess it would have taken her, what, fifteen to twenty minutes?'

'OK, lets try that route,' said Ellen.

'Any idea what we're looking for?' asked Harry.

'I don't have the faintest idea,' Ellen replied, smiling.

Harry started the Spitfire, did a three point turn and went right at the bottom of the road. They followed the route Harry had traced on the map. After a short drive, they turned into Downside Crescent.

'Shall we park here and have a look around?' said Harry.

Ellen agreed. They found a parking space, got out and began walking towards Haverstock Hill.

Downside Crescent looked like any other leafy, suburban street. The red-bricked houses were well maintained and all had small tidy front gardens with wide wooden gates.

'I guess it would have looked much the same during the War,' said Ellen.

Harry was quiet.

As they neared the junction with Haverstock Hill, Ellen said 'Harry, what do you think that is?'

On their right, was a round, single storey building with a short square tower rising from its middle. It had been painted white and looked very out of place among the street's houses and other buildings.

'It looks like something to do with the Underground. Maybe a ventilation shaft or something'

They crossed the road. At the side of the building were two windows and a plain white door that was obviously not original. Harry tried to look in through the windows, but both had been blackened on the inside.

'Look, a letter box,' Harry said, walking to the door. 'Not a ventilation shaft then.'

'When do you think it was built?' asked Ellen.

Harry looked up. 'Nineteen thirties or forties?'

'Yes, that is what I was thinking.'

They walked around the building into Haverstock Hill. There was a bus stop a few yards away. Ellen looked at it. 'Do you think that is where Martha got off the bus?'

'I doubt it. The bus stop has probably been moved several times since then. Martha could have got off anywhere along here,' said Harry, looking up and down the main street.

An elderly woman was approaching them, pushing a shopping trolley. Ellen had a flash of inspiration. She walked over to the woman. 'Excuse me, you don't happen to know what this building is, do you?'

'Yes, Love,' said the woman. 'That is the old air-raid shelter. From the war. Don't know what it is used for now, mind you.'

Ellen thanked the woman and turned to Harry. He was already looking at her. They both turned and gazed at the air raid shelter in silence. It was perfectly obvious that they were thinking the same thing.

'You don't suppose,' said Ellen, over her shoulder.

'That Martha went into the shelter?' Harry interrupted her, raising his voice as a lorry thundered past.

'Yes,' said Ellen.

'Maybe,' said Harry.

'I mean, if she got off the bus somewhere along here,' Ellen said, turning and looking northwards along Haverstock Hill, 'and the air raid sirens went off.'

'But Elsie said that she hated the Underground. Isn't it more likely that she would have carried on walking? She didn't have far to go, after all.' Harry said.

Ellen thought for a moment. 'Is there any way that we can find out whether she went into the shelter?'

'Sixty years after the event?' said Harry, doubtfully.

'I mean, did they keep a register or anything?'

'Of people going in and out, you mean?'

'Yes.'

'I don't know,' said Harry, running his hand through his hair. 'But I could try to find out.'

They walked back to the Spitfire in silence.

'Is there anything wrong Harry?' Ellen asked suddenly.

'Wrong?'

'Yes, you seem a bit quiet. Like you've not really here.'

In truth, Harry had been thinking about Mrs Watts's reaction to being sent Martha's diary. What would he have done? What would he do now if, out of the blue, evidence of what had happened to his mother landed on his door mat. Did he really want to know? Or would he put it away in a cupboard and try to forget about it too, as Mrs Watts had done?

'It's nothing.'

'Which means that you don't want to talk about it.'

They got into the Spitfire and Harry started the engine. Ellen was a beautiful woman and he couldn't deny that he was attracted to her. He felt at ease with her. Like he could tell her anything. But then this was how it always began. You tell yourself all these things at the start and before you know it you are arguing about the pants on the bathroom floor. Harry sighed.

'Whatever is on your mind Harry, you know you can always talk to me don't you? Whenever you're ready, I mean.'

'I know. And I will. When I'm ready.' Harry smiled. 'On one proviso.'

Ellen looked at him. 'Erm… OK…'

Harry took a breath. 'I sometimes leave my pants on the bathroom floor. They're my pants and I like them there. If you have a hang up about where I leave my pants, we better end it here.'

Ellen looked at him. 'You are weird, Harry Stammers,' she said, shaking her head. 'Weird.'

CHAPTER SIXTEEN

The M.P. got out of the black BMW and waited impatiently for the driver to retrieve his briefcase from the boot.

'Will that be all, Sir?'

'Yes. I'll call you when I am ready to be collected. I would appreciate it you were here swiftly, Stephens. I'm due back at the constituency office at two and I do not want to be late.'

'Yes, Sir.'

The M.P. turned without further comment and climbed the studio steps. As he reached the door, his mobile phone rang.

'Dennis, where the fuck are you? You were supposed to be briefing me here at eleven.' He waited impatiently for the reply. 'The Daily Mail? Well what the bloody hell are you doing fielding calls? You are paid to keep me briefed. Get some bloody underling to sit in front of the telephone. I expect you here in fifteen minutes.' He ended the call, stuffed the mobile phone back into his pocket and went through the revolving doors.

Inside, the receptionist recognised him instantly. 'Good morning, Sir. Please take a seat. Someone will be down for you shortly,' she said, entering his details on a pad in front of her.

He glanced at her irritably. 'Promptly I trust,' he said, turning away without waiting for a reply.

'Just a moment, Sir,' she said apologetically, tearing a slip from her pad and putting into a plastic holder. 'You'll need this.' She held out the badge. 'It is a pass, Sir. For security.'

'Yes, I do know what it is.' The M.P. took the badge and walked across to the leather seats in the waiting area. He sat down and removed a copy of The Mail from his brief case, flicking through the newspaper until he found the page he was looking for. 'Oh, fucking hell,' he said, under his breath.

'Mr Banks, do you condemn these stories about expensive dinners and weekends away at five star hotels?' said Jim Preston, the BBC's most forthright news presenter.

The MP leant forward in his chair and looked Preston in the eye. *You are not going to intimidate me, you snivelling little bastard.* 'Yes I do condemn them. They did not come from my campaign team, I can assure you of that.'

'But they did come from someone who is sympathetic to you. That is the point. Isn't it?'

'I have no idea where they came from.'

'Well they didn't come from someone who was sympathetic to your opponent, did they?'

'You would have to ask them. I can only reiterate that they did not come from me or from anyone on my campaign team.' *Stick that in your pipe and smoke it,* the M.P. thought, with the barest hint of a smirk.

'Do you agree that such articles bring the campaign for the leadership of your party into disrepute?'

'Look, I have come here today,' said the M.P., putting on the most condescending manner he could muster 'to talk about the real issues confronting my party and our country. I am sure that the British public do not want to hear any more about this unfortunate piece of cheap tabloid journalism.'

Preston sat back in his chair and crossed his legs. *What have you got for me next, you snidey little shit?*

'Mr Banks, you are the person appointed by your party to oversee finance and resources at your party's campaign headquarters, are you not?'

Is that the best you can do? Banks was beginning to relax, despite the heat from the studio lights. *This is too easy. He is no match for me.* 'Yes that is right and I take those responsibilities exceptionally seriously.'

'Simon Frankham was, until recently, one of your senior managers, wasn't he?'

'Yes, he was.'

'Did you or did you not take the decision to dismiss Mr Frankham from his position?'

'The decision to dismiss Mr Frankham was taken in the light of an internal investigation which had come to the conclusion that there were inexcusable failures in the strategic management of that section of the party headquarters. A section for which Mr Frankham was directly responsible.'

'Mr Frankham was not a member of your campaign team was he?'

'That is of no relevance to his dismissal.'

'In fact, Mr Frankham works for the campaign team of one of your opponents, doesn't he?' said Preston.

'That is a matter for Mr Frankham, but look, let me make it absolutely clear that this has nothing whatever to do with his dismissal.' Banks was pleased with the progress of the interview. He was countering Preston with consummate ease.

'Why did you shout down a colleague at the party conference last week, for sending flowers to Mrs Frankham in what she said was a Christian gesture?'

'I didn't, as I believe she has now confirmed,' the M.P. snapped.

'She has confirmed that, has she?'

'She has said that I did not shout her down.'

'She said that you were extremely upset about it.'

'I thought that it was an inappropriate thing to do, given that Mrs Frankham's husband had just been dismissed by the Party, but look, I hope we are not going to spend this interview talking about flowers and other such nonsense.'

93

'Mr Banks, have you ever lied to your party board?'

The M.P. was immediately on his guard. 'Certainly not. I gave a very full account of this matter to the Board yesterday. That decision has been the subject of a great deal of scrutiny but it was a decision that I was required to take. An internal report found that there were serious weaknesses and I acted according to what I believed was right in those circumstances.'

'Is there anything that you would like to change in relation to your statements on this so far?'

What are you up to? What have you got? The M.P. studied Preston carefully. 'No, absolutely nothing. I have given a very full and frank account.'

'Right, well perhaps you could help us with this then could you? In your statement to the Party Board, you are on record as saying that you had not issued any instruction with regard to Mr Frankham prior to publication of the report. But in his evidence Mr Johnson says that before the report was made public, you instructed him to fire Mr Frankham. Are you saying that Mr Johnson is lying?'

Where in God's name did you get that from? If Johnson is leaking to the press, he will regret it, Banks thought. 'I have given a full account of this and the position is exactly as I told the Board.'

'Mr Johnson says that you told him to fire Mr Frankham or you'd have to consider his position. So Mr Johnson was lying, was he?'

No of course he wasn't lying. 'Let me tell you exactly what the position is. I was entitled to express an opinion to Mr Johnson and I did express an opinion to Mr Johnson. But I was not entitled to instruct Mr Johnson to dismiss Mr Frankham and I did not instruct him.'

'Mr Johnson says that he told you that Frankham didn't deserve to be suspended, let alone dismissed. He says that he told you that the failures that you were trying to heap on Frankham, were in fact caused by weaknesses in the oversight of the Campaign Headquarters at the most senior level.'

Yes and Johnson brought about the demise of his own career at that moment, I will make absolutely certain of that, thought the M.P.

'I suppose that means you, doesn't it?' said Preston.

'Mr Johnson was entitled to his view, as I was entitled to mine.'

'Mr Johnson says that you exploded,' said Preston.

If he thinks that was an explosion, Johnson has a surprise coming to him.

'He says that you said that anything less than immediate suspension was not acceptable and that if he didn't suspend Frankham immediately, you would have to think about removing him.'

I'll be doing more than thinking about removing him, I'll be arranging for both his fucking legs to be broken. The M.P. was beginning to lose his temper. 'Look, Mr Johnson was not removed and Mr Frankham was only dismissed after publication of the report. Johnson can say whatever he likes but...'

'Did you threaten to remove Mr Johnson if he did not suspend Mr Frankham?'

'The truth of the matter is...' Now the M.P. was decidedly rattled.

'Did you threaten to remove him?'

Of course I threatened to remove him but if you think that I am going to say that on the lunchtime fucking news, you have another thought coming. 'I did not remove him.'

'But did you threaten to remove him?'

'I took specific advice on what I could and could not do.'

'Did you threaten to remove him?'

I am going to have Dennis's bollocks for this. 'Mr Johnson was not removed.'

'Did you threaten to remove him?'

'I have already given a full account of this.'

'I note that you are refusing to answer the question. Did you, or did you not threaten to remove him?'

Too bloody right I am refusing to answer the question. 'Look, I think we're going around in circles here.'

'Yes, and I am sorry to appear rude but I don't think you are answering the question. It is a very simple one.'

'I expressed my opinion, as I was entitled so to do. I expressed it very strongly. But I did not instruct him because I was not entitled to instruct him.'

'Right, since we are not going to get any further than that, we will leave it there. We will go on to your bid for leadership of the party. How do you intend to unify your party if you can't even unify your own team at party headquarters?'

Impertinent little shit. Banks gathered his thoughts, sat up in his chair and looked to camera. 'Sometimes in politics, you have to take tough decisions. Even when people do not agree. You must have the courage to do the right thing. That is what the British people would expect of any party leader. In this case I was prepared to take a tough decision. Doing the right thing is not always easy, but in this case it was my duty to take that decision in the interests of my party and that is what I did.'

Preston had one more salvo to fire and the M.P. was ready for it.

'Mr Johnson has said that he will not support your leadership bid. If the rest of your team come out and say that they will not support it will you concede that you do not have ability to unify your party?'

Cheap shot, the M.P. thought. *You're losing your touch Preston.* 'Look, I have many supporters at our headquarters, among my parliamentary colleagues and across the party. But I am not complacent. I know that some of my fellow party members are still not entirely certain. I continue to work tirelessly for my party and my country. When the chips are down, people know that they can rely on me to take tough decisions and, most importantly, to do the right thing.'

'Do you seriously expect to become leader of your party?' The contempt in Preston's voice was plain.

'I think that those in my party who see that there are tough decisions to be taken will see that I have taken those tough decisions. I have never shied away from taking responsibility and I think that is something that they will take as being exactly the sort of qualities my party needs when it comes to electing their next leader.' *And if they don't, I will shit on them from a very great height.*

'Max Banks MP, thank you.'

'Thank you,' *and fuck off.*

Stephens held open the door of the black BMW.

'Where the fuck is Dennis? I told him I wanted him here in fifteen minutes and that was over an hour ago. I'll have his balls on a fucking stick.'

'I'm afraid I don't know Sir,' said Stephens closing the door and smiling to himself. He had worked for the MP long enough to know that as long as Dennis remained loyal, his job and his balls were probably both safe. Banks could be ruthless, there was no doubt about that. Stephens had been surprised by his ruthlessness at times. But he also needed allies and Dennis was loyal to the core.

By the time that he had got into the BMW, Banks was already on the phone.

'No, it did not go fucking well,' Stephens heard him say. 'That bastard Preston had me over a fucking barrel. Where is he getting all this stuff? Well, you should know. I pay you to fucking know. He made me look like a complete arse.'

Banks ended the call abruptly. 'Stephens, get me to the constituency office and hurry up,' he said, sinking back in his seat. He let out a long sigh. 'On second thoughts, I've had enough of this circus for one morning. Take me to Wymondley Hall. My bloody constituents can wait.'

The drive to the Banks house took a little over an hour. Stephens drove the BMW up to the gates, buzzed the intercom and the gates opened. He drove down the gravel path. He had been to the house many times but he still couldn't help but be impressed by its grandeur. He got out of the car and held open the passenger door. Banks got out and walked into the house without a word.

Only the rich and powerful leave their front doors open, Stephens thought. *As a dare to the rest of us.*

Max Banks strolled through the hall and into the expansive library. He poured himself a Scotch from a decanter on the sideboard, swallowed it in one and poured himself another. The library door opened.

'Mother Dear,' he said over his shoulder. 'How are you?'

'Do not "Mother Dear" me Maximillian. I have just seen you on the lunchtime news. Are you an imbecile?' She leaned heavily on her walking cane but Banks knew from experience that his mother was anything but frail.

He flinched at the insult. 'I was badly advised, mother. That's all.'

'You are always badly advised,' the old woman scoffed. 'How many times have I told you? That advisor of yours. What is his name, Davis?'

'Dennis.'

'Dennis. Nothing but a liability.'

'Mother, please. Dennis may not be entirely reliable, but he is loyal. In any case, while we may have been discovered throwing dirt, in the long run mud sticks. We have never shied away from a fight for the heart of the party. Dirty or otherwise.'

'Heart of the party,' she scorned. 'Save that rubbish for the fools back at Central Office. You are no more interested in the heart of the party than I am.'

'I have told you, it is not called *Central Office* any more,' he snapped. 'It is *Campaign Headquarters*.'

His mother had reached the high backed, leather chair by her writing desk and sat down, stiffly.

'How is Father?' Banks ventured.

'How should I know? Rather wisely, he gives me a very wide berth. It is probably the only wisdom he has shown in sixty-five years and do stop trying to change the subject.'

'This morning's little episode was nothing but an inconvenience. My support in the Party is holding up rather well, actually. It will take a damn site more than a bit of mud slinging to blow my campaign off track.'

'I despair, Maximillian,' she said.

Banks braced himself. He knew what was coming.

'You are fifty-two. I spent the first twenty-five years of your life ensuring that you received the best education that money could buy. While you were being educated, I built the company into one of Britain's most successful, despite that idiot of a father of yours. For the last ten years I have poured a not inconsiderable sum of money into your political career and, in the last eighteen months, into your campaign for the leadership.'

'Yes I know, Mother and don't think that I am not grateful.'

'Grateful?' she screeched, clambering to her feet. 'It is not gratitude that you owe me. You will repay me by becoming Party Leader and, providing the Party does not tear itself to shreds first, Prime Minister. I will not allow anyone or anything to stand in our way. Do you understand me?'

'Mother, that bastard Preston got one over on me today. But that is the first and last time. It will not happen again. If he thought that "expensive dinners" and "weekends away" business amounted to dirty tricks, he doesn't know his arse from his elbow. I do not intend to simply win the Party leadership, I intend to destroy any and all opposition. When I take over as Party Leader, dissent will not be tolerated.'

CHAPTER SEVENTEEN

Harry steered Ellen toward the bar. He had been hoping for a couple of seats at his normal table by the door but the place was packed and all the tables were taken. He liked the *Horse and Groom*, even when it was busy. Tucked out of the way, it was unlike the ghastly gastro chains on the High Street, with their dreadful themed decor and surf and turf menus. A bit grubby around the edges, but proper ale pulled by hand, pork scratchings and a landlord who had been at the pub for as long as Harry could remember. It was a good, old fashioned London local.

'So what else does a museum curator do in his spare time? Apart from breaking into empty buildings that is,' Ellen said, pulling herself up onto one of the bar stalls. Harry thought that she looked as gorgeous as ever.

'Not a lot. I read a bit.' Harry smiled. 'What do you fancy?'

'Pinot, please.'

'Large?'

'Why not? It's been a long day.'

Harry perched on the stall next to her and tried to catch the landlord's eye. After waiting several minutes he decided on the 'wave the tenner in the air' method. It worked every time. Harry ordered Ellen's wine and a pint of Broadside.

'Plus the Spitfire and the scooter keep me busy.'

'Scooter?'

'Yes. I have a Lambretta. I have been restoring it, on and off, for the last couple of years.'

'Why a scooter and not a proper bike?'

'What do you mean "proper bike"? Bikes are for long haired layabouts. All that greasy hair and clobber. It's diabolical,' Harry said, putting on his best cockney accent.

Ellen looked at him blankly.

Harry laughed. 'It's a quote. From Quadrophenia.'

'Quadrophenia?'

'The film. Don't tell me you've never seen it.'

'I've never seen it.'

Harry shook his head. 'Well I am going to have to put that right.'

They were silent for a moment.

'Are you alright? You seem a little distracted,' Ellen said.

In truth, Harry was not in the best of spirits. It had taken him twenty minutes to get through to his father's ward earlier that afternoon, only to be told next to nothing by a disinterested nurse with an accent he could barely understand.

'Is it that obvious?' he asked, looking down into his pint.

'It's obvious that you have got something on your mind.'

It wasn't that he didn't want to tell her. It was more that he had hoped that an evening out with Ellen Carmicheal would help him to put his father's stroke to the back of his mind, but now he was going to have to explain the whole thing.

'My father was taken ill on Sunday.'

'Oh, no.' Ellen said, looking concerned. 'Is it serious?'

'He had a stroke. He's in hospital.'

'God, that's awful. You poor thing.' She reached for his hand and squeezed it. 'You didn't have to come out tonight, you know.'

'No, I needed to get out. There's nothing I can do about it and sitting at home, twiddling my thumbs wasn't going to help.'

'I guess not.'

They were silent again.

'Are you very close to him?'

It was one of the questions that he had been hoping to avoid. He didn't want to lie to her, but neither did he want to spend the whole evening talking about his relationship with his father and, least of all, the reasons for his complete lack of any relationship with his mother.

Harry chose his words carefully. 'Not very close, no. But we only have one family and I wouldn't want to lose him.'

'I'm sure it won't come to that Harry,' she said, squeezing his hand again. 'People can and do recover from strokes, you know.'

'Well, lets hope that Dad is one of them.' Harry picked up his drink and half drained the glass. 'I'm sorry if I was a bit quiet,' he said. 'I should have told you.'

'Don't be silly. I was just worried about you that's all.'

Harry tried to give her a reassuring smile but it probably looked more like a grimace.

'Oh, I meant to tell you,' he said, trying to lighten the conversation. 'I emailed an old friend of mine at the transport museum this morning, about the shelter at Belsize Park. I thought that if anyone would know whether they kept a register, Simon would.'

'And did he?' said Ellen

'Not exactly. But he is going to talk to a colleague at the London Museum, in the City. Apparently, one of the curators there is a specialist on the Blitz.'

'That sounds positive,' said Ellen.

'Let's hope so, because right now I can't think of another way of finding out whether Martha went into the shelter.'

Ellen picked up her glass. 'Could we go and have a look at the shelter, do you think?' she said, sipping her wine. 'To get a feel for the place.'

'That was one of the reasons I suggested meeting up with the guys. One of them is bound to know what the shelters are used for now.'

Harry reached for his glass but discovered that somebody had mysteriously replaced it with an empty one. He was reaching for his wallet and another tenner when he noticed Mike and Marcus wading their way towards them through the crowd.

'Here they are,' he said, nodding towards them.

'Oh, he's *gorgeous*,' Ellen managed to whisper, before they emerged from the crowd.

'All brawn and no brains I'm afraid,' Harry said.

'Who has?' said Marcus, winking at Ellen.

Ellen giggled.

I don't believe it, Harry thought. Ignoring the question, he introduced them both to Ellen, giving Marcus the evil eye in the process. 'What are you drinking fellas?'

'Well there's a thing,' said Marcus to Mike. 'When was the last time Harry paid for a round?'

Mike scratched his head and looked doubtful.

'Actually, you owe me a pint for the quick getaway at the weekend,' said Harry.

Mike ignored him and Harry ordered their drinks. The landlord lined them up on the bar in front of them.

'So what's the occasion then?' Marcus said, grinning.

'Occasion?' said Harry.

'First, you suggest meeting up a for a pint.' Marcus turned to Ellen. 'He never suggests meeting up for a pint.' He turned back to Harry. 'Then you buy us a drink.'

'He never buys us a drink.' Marcus and Mike said in unison.

'Yes I bloody do,' objected Harry.

'No you bloody don't,' they both said.

They all laughed.

'Alright, cut the double act,' said Harry. 'Do either of you know anything about the air raid shelter at Belsize Park?'

They were thoughtful for a moment.

'It is one of the deep level shelters isn't it?' said Mike.

'Yup. There are half a dozen of them, or thereabouts. They were built beneath the Underground stations, although a couple of them were never completed. St Paul's and the one at The Oval, if I remember rightly.' said Marcus.

'See, I told you that they would know,' Harry said to Ellen.

'Why do you want to know about Belsize Park?' asked Mike.

'Ellen and I are researching one of the women who worked at Bletchley Park. She went missing in 1944 and there is a possibility that she went into the shelter at Belsize Park on the night she disappeared,' said Harry.

'Well it is a bit late to be mounting a search party now, isn't it?' said Marcus.

'We'd just like to take a look, that's all. To get an idea of what the shelters were like,' said Ellen.

'Do you know what they are used for now?' asked Harry.

'Storage, I believe. Mostly documents. Film and video at Goodge Street,' said Marcus.

'Do you reckon we could get access?' Harry asked.

'Official or… um… unofficial,' Mike said, grinning.

'I'd rather do it officially.'

'You could try but I doubt it,' said Marcus. 'The authorities are getting jumpy about public access to anything underground, especially in London. Bloody al-Qaeda. Can't you try to pull a few strings through the museum?'

'Probably,' said Harry.

'We could get Tom to find out who has the lease at Belsize Park if you like. That guy's a genius at finding things out that he shouldn't,' said Mike.

Harry was never certain, afterwards, what had happened next. One moment he was draining his glass and the next, he was sprawled on the floor, with the taste of blood in his mouth and beer all over his shirt.

'You bastard.'

Harry opened his eyes and tried to focus. Ellen had leapt from her stall and was crouched down beside him. Mike and Marcus were struggling to restrain another man, who Harry eventually recognised.

'I'm warning you Stammers,' Erik hurled. 'If I end up in court and lose my job, I'll be naming you and you can join me on the fucking dole queue.'

Ellen was kneeling on the floor beside Harry and was trying to help him up.

'Erik, come on man.' Mike was struggling to hold him.

'That shit can't take a fucking joke.'

By now, the pub landlord had calmly put down the pint that he'd been part-way through pulling and had strolled around the bar. Harry had seen him eject unruly customers before. Harry scrambled to his feet and watched the landlord grab Erik by the scruff of his neck and, single handedly, drag him through the Horse and Groom crowd, which parted like the Red Sea before Moses. With his free hand, he opened the pub door and with the other, threw Erik out into the street. By now the hubbub in the pub had died to little more than a whisper. 'Banned,' the landlord said out loud. He marched back to the bar, without further comment and resumed serving customers. The hubbub returned like someone had thrown a switch.

'Is someone going to tell me what that was all about?' said Ellen, glancing at each of them in turn.

Harry's face hurt. He started to speak but he stopped and groaned.

'He said something about the police turning up at his studio?' said Marcus. 'It must have been that farmer, what was his name? Pickles?'

Oh shit, Harry thought and nodded. 'It was just a joke,' Harry managed to say weakly, through clenched teeth.

'Harry?' said Ellen looking at him like an angry school teacher.

'Just after I spoke to you from the field in the middle of nowhere. Remember?'

'Of course I remember.'

'Well the farmer turned up and demanded my name and address.'

'And?'

'And so I gave him Erik's.'

'No. No you didn't. Seriously?' said Marcus, starting to laugh.

'It was just a joke. I wouldn't have done it had I thought that it was going to cause any real trouble.' said Harry.

Mike was now laughing along with Marcus.

Harry interjected 'Erik's a bloody hooligan,' he said, wiping the blood from his nose on his shirt sleeve.

'Oh man, that is the funniest thing I've heard in ages,' said Marcus, slapping Harry on the back.

Harry flinched. 'He can dish it out, but he can't take it.'

'Sure,' said Mike, 'but I'd watch my back for a while if I were you. Erik was on fire.'

'Great. Bloody great,' said Harry. 'I knew it was going to be a disaster. Why do I let you guys talk me into it?'

'No brawn and not much in the way of brains either,' said Marcus, winking at Ellen again. Harry narrowed his eyes at Marcus and even Ellen had to laugh.

They finished their drinks and Harry decided to head home. His face felt like it had been hit by a small train.

'Thanks for the entertainment mate. It was better than staying in and watching Eastenders,' said Marcus.

'Yes, top evening Harry,' said Mike, patting him on the back.

All four of them left the pub together. The cool air made Harry slightly giddy, as they stepped out into the night.

'We'll have a word with Tom about Belsize Park,' said Mike.

'Great to meet you Ellen. We must do it again, though I have to admit, we're not usually as entertaining.'

'Cheers guys,' said Harry and they were gone.

Harry took a breath and wondered what to do next.

'Are you alright?' said Ellen.

'I've been better, to be honest.' He got his out cigarettes and offered one to Ellen.

'No thanks, I'm trying to stay off them.'

'Oh, sorry.'

'No, don't be silly. It doesn't bother me if you smoke. In fact, I quite like it. Makes you look kind of manly. Especially with that bruise under your eye.'

'Bruise?' said Harry.

Ellen reached out and touched his face. Harry flinched.

'Don't be such a baby.'

Harry lit his cigarette and wondered how to ask her back to his flat without it sounding all wrong.

'So are you going to invite me back for coffee or what?' said Ellen, smiling and taking his arm.

'Sure,' said Harry, suddenly feeling very pleased with himself, despite the ache in his jaw.

Harry woke to the sound of his alarm as usual. He groped for his mobile phone, found it under his bed and silenced the alarm. Then he turned over. Ellen was laying beside him. She was awake and watching him. She had a broad grin.

'Good morning Mr Stammers,' she said, 'and how are we feeling this morning?'

Harry thought that he was feeling very well indeed. Ellen was the only woman ever to have invited herself back to his flat for coffee and to have almost thrown a fit when he had said that he would put the kettle on. She had taken hold of his arm and frogged marched him down the hallway to his bedroom.

Ellen reached across and touched his cheek.

'Ouch. It still hurts,' Harry groaned and started to get out of bed but Ellen grabbed his arm.

'And where do you think you're going,' she said, sliding her other hand toward him under the duvet. 'I haven't finished with you yet.'

'Bathroom. Black eye,' was all that Harry managed before her hand found its target.

Half an hour later Harry made it as far as the lounge, turned on his PC and then went into the kitchen to make some coffee. 'We'll have to get a move on I'm afraid,' he called out, thinking that Ellen was still in bed. 'I've got to be at the station by ten past.'

'Such a shame. I was so enjoying our leisurely morning,' Ellen said from the doorway. She was wearing one of Harry's shirts.

'Me too, but one of us has got to earn a living.'

'Cheeky. Just because I don't need to be in the shop today, doesn't mean that I don't work for a living.'

Harry's PC made the "you have mail" sound.

'It's from Simon,' he said, opening the email.

'Simon?'

'From the transport museum. He's heard back from the Museum of London. Apparently, all the shelters were required to keep logs of people going in and out. I suppose it makes sense. In the event of an emergency, I mean.' He continued to read.

Ellen walked across to him and put her arm around his shoulder and they read the rest of the email together.

'Look at this,' he said and read on. 'They have most of them at the London Museum, including the logs for Belsize Park. I wonder if they'd let me borrow them?'

'Do museums normally lend out historic documents?' Ellen asked.

'Not to members of the public, they don't. But they do loan things to other museums. I'll pop them an email.'

He hit the "reply" button and started to type. 'What are you going to do today? You're welcome to stay here, if you want to, you know,' he said hopefully.

'Thanks, but I better get back. I need to feed my cat.'

'You have a cat?' Harry said over his shoulder, clicking send.

'Yes. Do you like cats?'

'I'm not sure. It's not so much that I don't like them. But I kind of get the feeling that they don't like me. I think I'm more of a dog man.'

'Well I think Jade is going to like you. In fact I am sure of it.'

'Hey, I've got a favour to ask,' said Harry.

'Oh, have you now?' Ellen said suggestively.

'Yes. My walk-in double shower has led a sheltered life. It has only ever had me in it. I was rather hoping that we could educate it a little.'

Ellen giggled. 'Just so long as yesterday's pants are not on the bathroom floor.'

CHAPTER EIGHTEEN

Harry got back to his desk at about one, having spent the morning in one of the Park's disused huts, cataloguing the equipment stored there. It was a task that he had commenced on his appointment but, in truth, there was little sign of it being completed any time soon. Why no real attempt had been made by his predecessors to order the donations made to the park, Harry couldn't guess. But, if he was honest, he was rather glad that they hadn't. The stores contained all sorts of seemingly random paraphernalia and his sessions sorting through it often revealed objects that were both a surprise and a delight.

Harry took a gulp of coffee, hit the space bar on his computer keyboard and typed in his password. He sat for a moment, reading his email. Then he picked up his telephone and dialled Ellen's number.

'Hello?'

'Hi Ellen, it's Harry. I've got some good news for you.'

'You have?'

'Yup. I got a reply from the London Museum.'

'And?'

'And they've agreed to lend the Belsize Park logs to Bletchley Park. All I need to do is arrange a courier and we can collect them straight away.'

'Oh, that is good news,' said Ellen, excitedly.

'I know. Actually, I'm going to need some help going through them,' he said hopefully.

'At the Park?'

'No. I'd like to take them home with me for the weekend, but they're probably going to be too heavy to take on the train.'

'Will you have them this afternoon?'

'Yes, I hope so.'

'How about I pick you up from the Park and we drive back to your place?'

'Are you sure?'

Ellen sighed. 'What do you think?'

Harry couldn't help but grin at the prospect of another night with Ellen Carmichael.

'How's your father?' she asked, changing the subject.

'No different. I spoke to the hospital this morning.'

'I meant to ask how your mother is taking it?'

Harry hesitated. He was going to have to talk to her about it eventually.

'They're no longer together.'

'Oh.'

'It's a long story.'

'Which means that you're still not ready to talk about it?'

Harry thought for a moment. 'It's something that none of us really talk about.'

Ellen said nothing.

'But perhaps it is time we did.'

'I'll bring a bottle of wine,' said Ellen.

'Better make it two,' replied Harry,

The courier delivered the log books just before five. Harry had asked for the log for November 1944 but the Museum had sent three volumes. Covering the latter part of October, the whole of November and part of December. Harry selected the volume that covered the week of the tenth of November and locked the others in his office filing cabinet.

Shortly after five-thirty there was tentative knock on his open office door. Harry looked up to see Ellen standing in the doorway.

'Sorry, did you mind me coming straight up?'

'Of course not,' Harry said, getting to his feet so quickly that he almost fell over.

'Only, the chap on the gate said it would be alright.'

Harry walked across to her. 'You look great.'

'Why thank you Mr Stammers,' she said, grinning. 'You don't look so bad, yourself.'

'Come and see,' he said, taking her hand and leading her to his desk.

'Is that it?' she said, looking at the log book.

'That's it. Do you want to take a look?'

'Not yet. Let's take it back to your place and look at it there.'

'OK.'

'Besides, there is something I want to do first...' and she spun him around and kissed him.

'You taste nice,' he said.

'You smell… mouldy,' she said, wrinkling her nose.

'Ah, yes. Sorry. That'll be the store room. I spent the morning wading through piles of old radio equipment and God knows what else. I'll have a shower when I get home.'

'Sounds good to me,' she said grinning.

'You don't have any regrets then? About last night.'

'Do I look like a woman with regrets?'

'Not exactly.'

'So what are you waiting for?'

'Eh?'

'Oh, for heaven's sake,' she said, reaching for the log book and taking his jacket from the back of his chair.

In the event, Harry found it easier to talk to Ellen about his mother than he had anticipated. She had asked him about it almost as soon as they had settled into the Saab and had listened carefully, without comment, as he explained his mother's disappearance.

It was only after he had finished that she spoke. 'It must have been tough, growing up without your mum.'

'Yes I guess so but what made it really difficult was my father's refusal to talk about it. Or even to allow us to mention her.'

'He's never spoken to you about it? Not at all?'

'No, never.'

'What does he say if you ask him?'

Harry was silent for a moment. 'I don't really ask anymore. I gave up asking a long time ago. In fact, I think we gave up talking about anything important a long time ago.'

Ellen sighed. 'That is so sad. What will you do now?'

'You mean, if he regains consciousness?' said Harry.

'Yes.'

'I don't know.'

Ellen was thoughtful. 'Can I tell you what I think?'

'Yes, of course.'

'I think you should talk to him. I mean, it's not like our search for Martha. Your mother is probably out there Harry, alive. Somewhere.'

'Perhaps.'

'You don't sound very sure.'

Harry sighed. 'I've thought about it a thousand times. But I just can't square it.'

'Square what?'

'Why, if she is out there, she has never made any attempt to contact us?'

'Only she knows that. And maybe your father too. Which is why you should ask him.'

'Before it is too late,' said Harry. It was almost a whisper.

'Yes.'

Ellen fell silent and Harry found his mind wandering back to Martha Watts. Here he was searching for the truth about a complete stranger who had gone missing almost sixty years previously. And yet he was reluctant to ask his father for the truth about his own mother. If his father died, he might never discover it.

'You're right,' he said suddenly, as they turned into the drive in front of Harry's flat. 'Whatever he knows and however difficult it might be to hear it, it is time I found out.' He turned to her and kissed her on the cheek. 'But first, we have to find Martha.'

They got out of the car and Ellen took his hand. 'Are you sure you want to? We can put off the search for Martha until your father is better. You've got an awful lot on your plate already.'

Harry smiled. 'You are joking. We've just got started and who knows where,' he said, opening the Saab's rear door and retrieving the log book from the back seat, 'this little baby is going to take us.'

'So long as you're sure,' Ellen said.

'I am. Positive.'

CHAPTER NINETEEN

Harry sat beside Ellen, looking at the log book on the table in front of them. He glanced sideways at her. 'Ready?'

'It is odd but I feel a bit nervous about this,' said Ellen. 'If Martha's name is in the log then we will know that the explanation the police gave her mother was wrong.'

'I think we already know that, don't we?' replied Harry.

'I guess. But it has all seemed rather abstract up to this point,' said Ellen.

Harry opened the log book. 'Well lets hope that it is about to become a little more real,' he said, turning the pages until he found the first of the entries for the tenth of November.

They both looked at the open log. On each page were recorded the names of the shelterers, a ticket number, and the time of their entry or departure.

Harry noticed immediately that there had been a surge in the number of people entering the shelter after 8.20 P.M. 'Probably when the air raid siren sounded,' Harry observed.

Ellen nodded.

Harry ran his finger down the list of names, with Ellen following his movements, until he got to the bottom of the page. Then he turned over the page and did the same again. He worked his way through all of the records for people entering the shelter. The log book showed that by about 9.30 P.M. the flow of people entering had slowed and then all but stopped. People had started to leave at about 2.30 A.M.

'And there's the 'all clear',' Harry added.

He was surprised to see that many of the shelterers had evidently preferred to spend the night underground, with the bulk of people leaving after six.

Martha's name did not appear anywhere in the log.

'She's not there,' he said gloomily and looked at Ellen.

'Let me try. Maybe we missed her.'

Harry passed the log to Ellen, who repeated the search.

'She's not there is she?'

'Shh,' Ellen continued to scan the entries. On the third page she stopped and turned back a page. 'That's odd,' she said.

'What is?'

'Look at the time of the last entry,' she said, pointing to the entry on the bottom of the left hand page. 'It is given as "20.40". Now look here,' she said pointing, to the top of the page on the right.

Harry looked. 'The next person entered at 20.55.'

'Up to that point, there is a more or less continuous flow of people,' Ellen said. 'Look, sometimes several people are even recorded as having entered at the same time.'

'There is a gap.' Now that Ellen had pointed it out, it was obvious.

'Yes there is. There's a page missing,' said Ellen.

Harry took the book from Ellen and held it open at the spine. 'It has been done very carefully. Look.'

The page had been been cut away close to the binding.

'It must have been done with something like a scalpel.'

'It's extremely neat,' said Harry.

They looked at each other.

'Why would someone do that? If they had made a mistake, why not put a line through it, or just tear the page out. Why go to the trouble of removing it so carefully?' said Ellen.

Harry checked the whole of the remainder of the log. There were no further gaps, or missing pages.

'What do you make of it?' asked Harry, running his hand through his hair.

'Well, somebody obviously went to some trouble to remove it. Why would they do that?'

Harry said nothing.

'Let's just suppose that Martha did go into the shelter. We've got good reason to think that she was in the vicinity. We know that she was not seen again, so it follows that something could have happened to her while she was there,' Ellen reasoned.

'But we can't be certain that she did go into the shelter, Ellen.'

'I know, but think about it. Martha was in Haverstock Hill that evening. We know that much because her diary was found there. We also know that she caught the six-thirty from Bletchley. How long does the journey into Euston take?'

'Today it takes about forty minutes but it would probably have taken longer then.'

'Alright, lets allow an hour. So she gets into Euston at about half past seven. She waits for a bus for, what, ten minutes?'

Harry shrugged. 'Maybe.'

'How long does it take to get to Haverstock Hill by bus?'

'That is much more difficult. The routes were probably different,' Harry replied.

'Alright. But roughly.'

'Say between thirty minutes and an hour?'

'So that would put Martha in Haverstock Hill between eight and half past. Roughly.'

Harry nodded again.

'She gets off the bus and the air raid siren goes off,' said Ellen.

'Which was at twenty past. That's when people start to enter the shelter,' said Harry.

'Exactly. The gap in the log is from 8.40 P.M. to 8.55 P.M. It all fits, Harry.'

He thought for a moment. 'It does. There's no denying that.'

'So we have a missing woman, in the vicinity of the shelter at around the same time that somebody goes to a lot of trouble to very carefully remove a page from the shelter log. A page on which the names of people entering the shelter are recorded.' Ellen paused.

Harry sat back in his chair, with his hands behind his head. 'There's something else,' he said.

'What?'

'There's only one page missing and there's no mention of Martha elsewhere in the log. So if she did enter the shelter, it doesn't look like she came out again.'

They were silent.

'The only thing that is worrying me,' Ellen said, breaking the silence, 'is that removing a page from the log book was a bit obvious. It didn't take us very long to discover it. Surely the police would have discovered it too.'

'Only if they looked,' said Harry. 'People must have gone missing after every air raid. How hard would they have looked for one missing woman? Would they have even made the link to the shelter? After all, at the time there was no particular reason to think that she was there. The trouble is, we still can't prove, positively, that she was.'

'No, we can't,' Ellen said. 'You are right. But something tells me that she was.'

Harry said nothing. Instead, he got up and went to the back door to smoke a cigarette while Ellen continued to examine the log book. She did have a point. They could not be certain, of course, but the evidence did seem to put Ellen at the Belsize Park shelter. He put his cigarette out and returned to the table.

'The whole of the rest of the log seems in order. I can't see any more gaps,' Ellen said.

'Let's say that you are right. Let's say that Martha did enter the shelter and that someone removed the page from the log book to conceal that fact. As you say, we know that she disappeared and was never found. That is not in dispute. So what are we saying happened to her?' said Harry.

'If somebody altered the log to conceal her entry, then they didn't want anyone to know that she was ever there. Which means that something must have happened to her that somebody wished to hide,' said Ellen.

'Are you saying that she was killed?' Harry said, naming the elephant in the room.

'Well, it is a possibility.'

'I don't know. We're making one hell of a leap.'

'Are we?' said Ellen. 'There is no evidence that Martha was killed in the air raid. No witnesses, nothing that puts her in the line of fire, and of course, no body. Admittedly, it could have been burned, but there is no actual evidence of that either. And yet that is the accepted explanation. With no evidence at all to support it. Alternatively, we've got the diary and the details of a journey that are quite likely to have placed her at Belsize Park at about the same time that we know there was an air raid. It is also likely that she would have passed the entrance to the shelter on her way to her mother's house. We know that she went missing after that and we know that a page has been removed from the shelter log. So which is the most likely scenario of the two?'

Harry thought about it. 'There's something else. If she was murdered, then the person who murdered her also entered the shelter and, at some point, must have left it. Unless he came in with Martha and left within the missing fifteen minutes, his name is likely to be in that log, somewhere.'

Ellen looked at him. 'How many people would you say went in?'

'I don't know. Hundreds at least.'

'And how many of them were men.'

'Probably not more than a third,' said Harry.

'Lets focus on them, in the first instance. If the murderer entered with Martha, then his name will be missing from the log along with Martha's. But he might appear in the list of people leaving,' said Ellen.

They made a list of all the men who had entered the shelter on the tenth of November. Then they went through all the people who had left the following morning, checking male names off against the list of entrants. There were nine men recorded as having left who were not in the log as having entered.

'They have to be from the missing page,' said Ellen. 'Are they our first group of suspects?' she asked.

'Only in so far as they are likely to have entered at roughly the same time as Martha. The murderer could have been there already, or he could have entered after Martha.'

'I suppose so,' said Ellen.

They were both silent.

Harry had a thought. 'Pass me the log a moment,' he said. Ellen handed the log to him and Harry flicked through the pages.

'What's this?' Harry said, pointing to an entry in the log.

'Yes, I noticed a couple of entries like that,' said Ellen.

An entry at 23.15 gave the name of the person leaving the shelter as "BELCO Ltd". They looked for the other similar entries together. Someone from BELCO was recorded as having entered the shelter at 16.30 and again at 04.15, the following morning.

'That's odd. There is no exit time for the second entry, the one at 04.15,' said Ellen.

'They were probably maintenance people and left without signing out. Contractors do that up at the Park all the time. It drives our security people nuts,' said Harry.

'Yes I guess so.'

Harry stifled a yawn and stretched. 'My brain hurts. Perhaps we've got far enough with this for one day.'

'Can we eat? I'm starving,' said Ellen.

Within ten minutes Harry was on his way to the *Hong Kong Garden*. He'd been going to the little Chinese restaurant since he had first moved to Golders Green. By all accounts, it had been on the North End Road for ever. Mrs Georgiou, the elderly woman who lived opposite Harry's flat, swore blind that it had been there in 1974, when she and her late husband arrived in Golders Green following the Turkish invasion of Cyprus.

The food at the *Hong Kong Garden* wasn't spectacular but at least it tasted like it had been cooked that day. Which was more than could be said for most of the other local Chinese restaurants. In any case, Harry liked Mr Wu, the restaurant's elderly owner. They had exactly the same conversation whenever Harry visited. It had become something of a ritual.

Harry arrived at the restaurant and stood outside finishing his cigarette. North End Road was almost as busy at night as it was during the day. The difference was that the suited men hurrying to catch a train and mothers dragging their children to school were replaced, at night, by groups of hooded teenage boys and girls in impossibly high heels and short skirts. Watching them made Harry feel old. He stubbed out his cigarette and went in.

'Hello Mr Harry,' called a smiling Mr Wu from across the restaurant, at the top of his voice. The seated customers interrupted their conversations and turned to look at Harry.

Harry smiled to himself. 'Good evening Mr Wu.'

'How's business?' Mr Wu said, rushing over.

'Business is very good.'

'Good. Good. Busy?'

'Yes, very busy.'

'You finish work?'

'Yes, I've finished.'

'You look like you need noodle.'

'That sounds good,' said Harry.

'You eat now. Here or takeaway?' Mr Wu took out a pad from his pocket.

'Takeaway tonight please, Mr Wu.'

'Very good.'

Harry gave him the order and paid for it with his debit card. He looked up at the Chinese God sitting in an alcove above the doorway to the kitchen and wondered how often Mr Wu replaced the apple put there as an offering.

'Twenty minutes OK?'

'Yes, that's fine.'

'You want cracker?'

Harry's stomach rumbled. 'Yes, thanks, some crackers would be great.' He sat down and picked up a motoring magazine. He'd been reading it for a few minutes when somebody sat down next to him and tapped him on the shoulder.

'Hi.'

Harry looked up. 'Oh, Tom, I didn't know you came here?'

'It is on my way home.'

Mr Wu came scuttling across again and took Tom's order.

'I don't suppose you've heard anything from Erik have you?' Harry enquired.

'No.' said Tom.

'Did you hear about what happened the other night?'

'I heard that he put you on the floor.'

'You could say that,' Harry said, touching his face. It was still tender. 'I was just wondering whether anyone had heard from him. I feel pretty bad about it.'

'Not me.'

There was a pause. Conversation was not one of Tom's strengths. 'He's an arsehole. You should have decked him and done us all a favour.'

The comment took Harry by surprise. 'I think that I was the one who ended up looking like the arsehole.'

'Not good. In front of your new girl.' said Tom.

Harry hadn't thought of Ellen as his new anything. 'She's not exactly my new girl.'

'Not what I heard.'

'We're doing some research together, that's all.'

'The Belsize Park thing?'

'Yes, did Mike mention it to you?'

'Yes.'

God this is hard work, thought Harry. He decided to press on. 'Actually, have you ever heard of a company called 'BELCO'?'

'Sure,' said Tomasz.

'You've heard of them?'

'Yes.'

Harry looked at him. 'And?'

'They're a big electrical firm. Mostly industrial.'

'Right,' said Harry. 'I don't suppose that there is any way of finding out what they were doing at the Belsize Park shelter in November 1944, is there?' said Harry.

'There's always a way.'

'Is there?' Harry was surprised.

'Why do you want to know?'

'I'm researching a woman called Martha Watts who used to work at Bletchley Park. She went missing.'

'In 1944?'

'Yes.'

'What has BELCO got to do with it?'

'Probably nothing. We have the shelter log from the night Martha went missing. Someone from BELCO went in and out a couple of times. We'd like to know who they were and what they were doing there.'

'Your food Mr Harry,' said Mr Wu, materialising in front of them like a little Chinese genie.

'Thanks,' Harry took the bags and stood up. 'I guess I better get this back before it gets cold,' he said to Tom.

'Doesn't do to keep a woman waiting,' Tom replied with a grin.

'Help yourself to my prawn crackers,' said Harry.

'I'll see what I can find out.'

'Sorry?'

'About BELCO.'

'Oh yes. Right. Thanks Tom,' Harry said, opening the restaurant door.

'Night Mr Harry.'

'Goodnight Mr Wu.'

CHAPTER TWENTY

Harry made his way up to the archive, his feet clanking on the steel steps. He inserted the key in the door and let himself in, brushing the rain from his coat as he entered. The corridor to his office ran through the centre of the building's upper floor. The only natural light came from the little metal framed windows in the rooms on either side. The rooms were lined with steel shelves, on which were stacked row upon row of box files and donated equipment at various stages of cataloguing and restoration.

The morning's cloud laden skies and heavy rain meant that, as he entered, the corridor was in almost complete darkness. He switched on the light, hung his coat on the little row of hooks behind the door and went into the kitchen to make some coffee.

Harry stood at the window, looking out across the lake, while the percolator began to gurgle. The news from the Whittington, that his father had regained a level of consciousness during the night, ought to have raised his spirits. And for a while it had. Perhaps it was the dreary weather and the lack of progress he and Ellen had made in their search for Martha Watts that had dampened them again.

It had been five days now since they had first examined the shelter log. It had not been difficult to find the telephone number for BELCO. He had found it on the internet and had immediately called them. However, finding anyone at the Company who had even rudimentary knowledge of their wartime activities had proved quite another matter. His final conversation had been with a manager in their human resources department. It had left him in little doubt that, even if they had records dating back as far as 1944, which he thought they probably didn't, they were certainly not going to discuss them with him.

Harry had spent hours mulling over the possible explanations for Martha's disappearance. For five days he had thought of little else. As he stood, looking out across the lake, Harry acknowledged, for the first time, that it was beginning to get to him.

He was not an obsessive. His work often involved hours of painstaking research. He loved nothing more than to bury himself in piles of historic documents or lose himself in one of the store rooms. But, until now, he'd always been able to leave his work behind at the Park gates. To go home and watch television. Or nip out for a pint at the *Horse and Groom*. Or spend an evening in the garage, stripping the Lambretta's engine or rebuilding the carburettor.

Harry poured himself a coffee from the now steaming percolator.

But for the last week, each time he had passed through Belsize Park Underground Station, which he did twice a day, he'd had a growing feeling that Martha was there. It was an odd sensation which, at first, he'd tried to ignore. It was as though, when the train drew to a halt at the station and the doors hissed open, she would be there, waiting for him. Last night, he'd gone as far as getting off the train and walking up and down the platform in frustration. She was there. He could sense it. Harry pulled a face and looked at his reflection in the window. It was crazy and he knew it.

Later that morning Ellen called him on his mobile phone.

'Hi Harry. Any news?'

'No nothing. Maybe Tom will come up with something. I must give him a call.'

There was a pause.

'I meant about your father.'

'Oh. He regained consciousness last night. He hasn't spoken. They're running some tests.'

'That's great. Really great,' Ellen said, sounding like she was thinking something but not saying it.

'I'm going to drop in to see him after work.'

'Harry, are you alright?'

'Yes, of course.'

'I'm worried about you.'

'I'm fine.'

'No, Harry. You're not. You're stressed. I can tell.'

'Ellen, I'm fine.'

'You must be worried sick about your father.'

Harry said nothing.

'Anybody would be.'

'No, it's not that.' He said it in an almost-whisper. 'Well, of course I'm worried about Dad,' he corrected himself.

'But?'

Harry was silent.

'Is it me?' said Ellen quietly.

'No. Absolutely not. You're fantastic. Please don't think that it is about you, Ellen.'

'Then what is it?'

'It's hard to explain. I'm not even sure myself.'

'Harry, talk to me.'

'It's just… You're going to think I'm nuts.'

'No, I'm not.'

Harry hesitated.

'Please tell me?'

'It is just that I go through Belsize Park station twice a day and, every time I do, I can't help feeling that she is down there Ellen. It's nuts.'

'No, its not nuts. I think she is probably down there too.'

'No, but I don't just think it. I kind off... well, *feel* it. It's the oddest thing.'

Ellen was silent for a moment. 'What time are you going to see your father?'

'I was thinking of going straight from here.'

'How about I meet you at the hospital? If you are up to it, perhaps we could go for something to eat. It might do us both good to relax a little?'

'That sounds great.' It did. Harry could already feel himself beginning to relax.

'I'll book us a table. I can always cancel it if you decide that you'd rather go home. Say for nine o'clock?'

'Fine.'

'What time do you want me to get to the hospital?'

'I don't know. Eight-ish?'

'OK'

'I'll meet you at the main entrance.'

The hospital canteen was full of people. Harry found a table, in a corner by the window and sat down. He stared past the coffee cup in front of him, oblivious to the noise and the people on the next table. It hadn't been his father's sagging face or the saliva that had dribbled from the corner of his mouth that had shocked him. He'd seen stroke victims before. Neither was it the wires or tubes attached to him or the elderly man in the next bed who had called out in distress, his voice so slurred that the words had been unintelligible. It had been his father's vacant eyes and the thought that the man who had once looked out through them might already be gone.

It was true that his father had refused to speak of his mother. That he would fly into a rage at the mere mention of her name. But it had been Harry who had allowed it to continue. And Kate. Rather than confront him, they had allowed him to silence the questions. They had allowed her to be erased from their lives, so that it was as if she had never existed. Sitting by the hospital bed, looking into his father's vacant eyes, what had shocked Harry more than anything was the thought that his father's stroke might now erase her forever.

He rubbed his eyes and glanced up at a television screen on the canteen wall. It was tuned to the news channel. One of the candidates in the contest for the Tory Party leadership had been caught playing dirty tricks and was trying, desperately, to parry questions from an outraged interviewer. *And they wonder why so few people bother voting,* Harry thought. He looked down at his watch.

He had promised Kate that he would call her from the hospital but the noise in the canteen was going to make an awkward conversation more difficult still. He dialled the number.

'Kate? It's Harry.'

'Harry? How is he?'

Harry took a deep breath. 'He's conscious, but sleeping most of the time.'

'Has he spoken?'

'No. He...' Harry hesitated.

'What?'

'He's not communicating at all, Kate. I was with him for about an hour, but I don't think he even knew that I was there.'

There was a long silence.

'Did you speak to a doctor?'

'Only briefly.'

'What did he say?'

Harry swallowed. 'There has been some damage Kate. You can see it when you look at him. But they are saying that it is too early to be sure about the extent of it.'

'Yes, but what are they saying about the chances of recovery?'

'All they will say is that we should be prepared for the worst.'

'What the fuck does that mean?'

It was Harry's turn to be silent.

'Harry?'

'Look, I'm in the canteen and its pretty noisy. Are you still coming up in the morning?'

'Yes.'

128

'Can we talk again then?'

'Sure.'

Harry suddenly felt sorry for his sister. 'Try not to worry. At least he's awake. It's a start. We are just going to have to be patient.'

'I know that.'

'I'll talk to you tomorrow,' he said and ended the call.

He picked up his coffee, drained the cup and walked back through the hospital towards the main entrance.

Ellen was waiting for him by the main doors. 'How is he?' she said, hugging him.

'He's awake. If you can call it that.'

Ellen held him at arms length and looked at him. 'You look terrible.'

'You look gorgeous,' Harry said. 'And you're not wearing boots for once.'

'I fancied a change.'

'Come on, let's get out of here. Bloody hospitals. I hate them.' Harry took her hand and led her through the automatic doors.

'Does anyone actually like them?'

Harry doubted it. 'Where are you taking me?' he said.

'Are you sure that you are up to it?'

They had set off across the hospital car park.

'Absolutely. In fact, I'm starving. I haven't eaten since lunchtime.'

'I thought you might fancy hot and spicy?' she said with just the hint of a smile.

'Always,' he said with a wolfish grin.

'Behave yourself. There's a great Indian in Barnet. We sometimes go there after work.'

'Sounds good to me.'

They found the Saab and got in. Ellen started the engine and reversed out of the parking space. As she did so, Harry's felt his mobile phone vibrate.

'It's a text message,' he said pulling the phone from his pocket. 'Oh great.'

'What is it?' said Ellen.

'It's from Mike.'

'And?'

Harry read the message out loud.

'SPOKE TO ERIK. HE'S LOST IT BIG TIME. I'D STAY WELL AWAY FROM THE HORSE AND GROOM IF I WERE YOU. ERIK STILL PRETTY WOUND UP. MIKE.'

'He'll get over it... won't he?' said Ellen.

'You don't know Erik. He's always had it in for me and now this. I should have kept my mouth shut.'

CHAPTER TWENTY-ONE

'I needed that,' Harry, said pushing the plate away and picking up his glass. They had managed to get through the whole meal without talking about Martha Watts but they both knew that the subject was going to come up sooner or later.

'I've been thinking about what you were saying earlier,' ventured Ellen.

'About what?' Harry asked, draining his glass and knowing exactly what she was referring to.

'About your feeling that Martha is down there. At Belsize Park, I mean.'

'I knew you'd think I was nuts.'

'I don't think you're nuts. But its obviously bothering you Harry. Why?'

Harry thought for a long moment. 'Because it's just not like me.'

Ellen frowned. 'In what way?'

Harry tried again. 'I research things for a living. Important things. I can spend days, sometimes weeks studying some distant historical event, piecing together all of the available evidence before I even try to come to a view. It's a logical process and if, at the end of it, the evidence is inconclusive, then the outcome is inconclusive. That's how it works. That's how I work.'

'So what is bothering you?'

'What is bothering me is where the hell this *feeling* is coming from. Ellen, last night I got off the bloody train and walked up and down the platform, like some lunatic. What was I doing? Waiting for her ghost to pop up and say "Over here!"?'

Ellen laughed.

'It's not bloody funny,' Harry said, pulling a face,

'Harry, its called intuition. Something is telling you that she is down there. Some piece of evidence that maybe we missed, or an idea that hasn't made its way to the surface yet. Something in your subconscious mind.'

'Mumbo jumbo.'

'And you've been under a lot of pressure. Your father's illness and the issues that has raised about your mother.' Ellen paused, as if she had said something that she didn't mean to say. She was silent for a moment.

Harry waited.

'Maybe, our search for Martha and your search for your mother have become a little muddled. Maybe searching for a missing young woman is all a bit too close for comfort, you know?'

'I'm not searching for my mother.'

'Aren't you? Are you sure?'

Harry frowned and ordered another beer from a passing waiter.

'Not for me,' Ellen said, anticipating his question and waving the waiter away. 'Look, Harry, give yourself a break. They're real people, Martha and your mother. Not some distant event or machine that you're researching. It's different. You saw how much finding Martha means to Gran and I can only imagine how it must have felt to lose your mother when you did. So you've got feelings about it. Something has made a connection for you. There's nothing wrong with that. Stop beating yourself up about it.'

'Maybe.'

'Come here,' and she leant across the table and kissed him. 'Perhaps you are human, after all. With emotions and instincts, like the rest of us.'

Harry laughed. 'Alright. I never claimed to be anything else.'

Ellen smiled. 'I know you didn't. But I really think that you've been worrying about nothing. If your intuition tells you that Martha Watts went into that shelter, then maybe she did. If it's any consolation, my intuition tells me that too and I can't really explain it either.'

Harry finished his beer, they paid the bill and got up to leave.

'Are you coming back to my place?' said Harry hopefully.

Ellen grinned. 'Wild horses wouldn't stop me.'

They arrived back at Harry's Golders Green flat a little after eleven. Ellen turned the Saab onto the driveway and pulled up in front the garage, the car's headlights flooding the building with light.

'Hmm… that's odd,' Harry said, more to himself than to Ellen.

'What is?'

'The garage door. It's not shut properly.'

He got out, walked around to the front of the car and tried the door handle. It wouldn't turn. He reached into his pocket for the key and tried it in the lock but the key wouldn't turn either. He took the key out, put it back in and tried it again but the lock wouldn't budge.

Ellen had turned off the Saab's ignition and got out of the car.

'What's up?' she said.

'The lock. It's stuck,' Harry said. 'I must have jammed it when I closed it. Don't worry. I'll sort it out in the morning.'

'Let me have a go,' Ellen said, walking toward him.

'Oh, don't worry, honestly,' said Harry.

'Come on, let me have a go,' she said, holding out her hand.

As Harry handed her the keys she froze and the keys tumbled to the ground. She was looking over his shoulder. Harry turned around. 'What is it?'

'There was somebody there,' she whispered. She had hold of his arm.

'Where?'

133

'Over there, by the alleyway,' Ellen hissed.

'I can't see anyone.'

'It was a man. He stepped out of the shadows as you handed me the keys and disappeared into the alley. I'd swear that he was watching us.'

'Why would he be watching us?'

Ellen turned and looked at him furiously. 'How would I know why he was watching us? I'm not making it up,' she said between gritted teeth.

'Alright. I'm sorry. Let's just get inside. Have you locked the car?'

'Yes.'

Harry bent down to pick up his keys. He walked Ellen to his front door, let them in and closed the door. He turned on the light. Ellen was as white as a sheet.

'Harry, call the police.'

'Why?'

Ellen looked at him. 'Why do you think?' she barked. 'Someone was over there. I saw him.'

'Alright, calm down. Standing across the street at the bottom of the alley isn't a crime. It was probably a neighbour having a cigarette.'

'He was probably trying to work out which house to break into. Harry, call the bloody police.'

Harry looked at Ellen but said nothing.

'Alright, I'll call the bloody police. Where's the phone?'

'There's one in the bedroom, on the cabinet in the corner. I'll make us some coffee.'

Harry walked along the hallway to the kitchen. What the hell was going on? Whoever it was that Ellen had seen, had obviously tried to break into the garage. That much had been clear from the angle of the garage door and the seized lock. But what were they after? The Lambretta? Who even knew that it was there? He hadn't had the scooter out for months. Harry unlocked the door into the garage, turned on the light and went in. The Spitfire was untouched and the scooter was on its stand. Nothing had been disturbed. He made his way around the Spitfire and inspected the garage door. It looked like somebody had attempted to lever it open from the outside and in the process had bent the locking bar. He checked the door into the landlord's house. It was secure which was just as well. The Landlord and his family were still away on holiday.

Harry went back into his flat. Ellen was waiting for him. She did not look any calmer.

'Well?' she said.

'I must have jammed it. The locking bar is bent. Are the police coming out?'

'Probably not.'

'Why not?'

'Because I made the mistake of telling them that you were with me.'

'What has that got to do with it?'

'If I had been on my own, they would have sent someone. As it was, they said that, since no crime had been committed, they didn't have sufficient personnel for a courtesy visit.'

'Great. What about the man across the road?' Harry asked.

Ellen crossed her arms and looked at him. 'They said that standing across the street at the bottom of an alley isn't a crime and it was probably a neighbour having a cigarette or something.'

Harry gave her a superior look. 'Told you,' he said smugly.

'Smart-arse,' said Ellen.

Harry stood, naked, at his open back door, blowing smoke rings and wondering about Ellen's reaction to the watcher in the alley. It had rattled her, for sure, but she was evidently not the kind of woman to remain cowered for long. On the contrary, she'd dragged Harry to the bedroom, pushed him onto the bed, removed first his clothes, then hers and proceeded to burn enough energy to power a small village. If that was how Ellen reacted to a little drama, he'd have to find the guy's telephone number and book him for a repeat performance.

His thoughts turned to the garage door and the watcher across the road. Somebody had clearly tried to break in to the garage. Why? And having failed to get in, why wait across the road to be spotted by Ellen on their arrival home? It didn't add up.

He scratched himself, yawned and thought about the warm body, curled up in his bed. He could still smell her on his face. He smiled, stubbed his cigarette out on the wall beside the door, sending a shower of tiny sparks onto the grass, and went back to bed.

The following morning, he was making coffee and toast when he heard the "you have mail" sound from his PC in the lounge. The email was from an address that he didn't recognise. He was about to dismiss it as junk when the contents caught his eye.

He read the email several times before the contents registered. So it had been Erik watching them from across the road. But the garage door? What the hell that all about?

'What an arsehole,' Harry said out loud.

'Who is?' said Ellen from the doorway.

Harry turned and looked at her. 'Oh, it's nothing.' She had her head buried in a towel and was wearing nothing but her knickers.

'What is?' She threw the towel on the back of a chair and crossed the room toward him.

Harry clicked on the close button. 'Just junk mail. Unbelievable, some of the rubbish people send you.'

She stood in front of him with her hands on her hips. Harry wanted to bury his face between her legs.

'Harry Stammers, are you ogling me?' she said.

Harry flushed. 'Yes.'

'Good.'

CHAPTER TWENTY-TWO

Tomasz Dabrowski sat at his iMac G4 and rubbed his eyes. The security at BELCO was good and had kept him out for most of the night. But now that he had access to outgoing email from the Company's I.T. Help desk, it was just a question of waiting for the inevitable password reset request. He sat, watching a stream of email. It never ceased to amaze him how sloppy help desk staff could be.

Twenty minutes later he had the new password of an administrator in the Human Resources Department. As his email address was john.plant@belco.co.uk, Tomasz guessed correctly, at the second attempt, that his login ID was 'plantj' and not 'jplant' which had been his first attempt. He entered the password, supplied by the help desk and hit return. He was then asked for a four digit passcode and guessed, correctly again, the numbers '1234'. He smiled to himself.

He looked at the menu. As a relatively junior member of staff, 'plantj' did not have unrestricted access to the system. However, since he worked for the HR Department, he could view the personnel records of the Company's employees. He also had access to the Company's archived records, presumably so that he could retrieve the details of former employees for reference purposes.

Tomasz initiated a search for the keyword "director" and was presented with a list of the company's directors. He printed the full list, noting one in particular. It was a name he recognised. He brought up the full record for this person and several of the other directors and printed them off. They made interesting reading.

Next he selected the Company's archive. He was astonished to find that the archive included details of contracts stretching back to the Company's foundation. He initiated an advanced search for the keywords "shelter" and "belsize park". The system showed thirty-seven records. Tomasz selected each of the records, one by one. He viewed and saved each one.

Next he tried search on the keywords "Martha" and "Watts". This resulted in the message "The system found 0 results". He also tried "Bletchley" and "Park", again with no result.

His telephone rang. It was his mother.

'Hello mama,' he said in Polish.

'Tomasz, you promised to call me yesterday. Your brother called. Your sister called. But you? No. You do not call your own mother. You never call your own mother.'

'Mama, you know how busy I am. I'm sorry OK? How are you?'

'How am I? Now you are asking?'

'Yes, now I am asking.'

'It is not for me that you should be asking.'

'How is papa?'

'Your papa is a sick man Tomasz and he asks for you.'

'Mama, you know that I cannot afford to come home. Not yet. I would if I could.'

'Yes, yes I know that. But soon he will be gone and it will be too late.'

'We have talked about this before. I will come as soon as I can.'

'You have work there in England?'

'Yes, you know I do. But it is expensive living here. You think it is bad in Poland? It's not so easy over here you know.'

'I know, your sister says the same.'

'You have spoken to Monika?'

Tomasz glanced at his screen. The system had timed out.

'Mama, I have to go. I'll call you tomorrow. Give my love to Papa and Jakub when you speak to them. I love you.' He put down the phone.

Tomasz clicked the login button and entered 'plantj' and the help desk password at the prompts. The system flashed "Your login ID or password was not recognised". *Damn it.* He picked up his telephone and dialled the help desk number.

'Banks IT Help desk. Can I take your name please?'

'John Plant.'

'Your login ID?'

'plantj.'

'How can I help you Mr Plant?'

'You reset my password earlier, but I've just been logged out and the password no longer works.'

'Just a moment and I'll check your account status.'

Tomasz waited, while the help desk played "House of the Rising Sun".

'Caller, can you confirm your name please?'

'I told you. John Plant.'

'And your date of birth Mr Plant?'

Tomasz hung up. *Shit.*

Max Banks walked up the steps and into the foyer.

'Good morning Mr Banks,' said the pretty receptionist.

He ignored her and walked to the escalator. He pressed the "call" button and waited for the lift to arrive. Inside he looked at himself in the full height mirror and straightened his collar.

The lift stopped at the fourth floor. He exited and strode purposefully through the open plan office, ignoring the nods and greetings from the few staff who looked up. He made a mental note of the names of those who did not bother.

He entered his office, sat at his desk and booted his PC. He picked up his phone and dialled "0".

'Good morning Mr Banks.'

'Coffee, Joan.'

'Yes, Mr Banks.'

'Any messages?'

'Yes, Mr Banks. Dennis at your constituency office called. He wants you to call him back.'

'Well he can wait.'

'I think it was urgent.'

'I said he can wait. Anything else?'

'Yes Mr Banks. IT security called. Somebody called Slater?'

'Don't know him. What did he want?'

'He said that there was a breach of security this morning, on one of our email servers.'

'Get him on the line for me. Now.'

'Yes, Mr Banks.'

He hung up. The bloody press had been hounding him since the Preston interview. Now they were hacking into his email system. He would find out who it was and they would regret it.

The phone on his desk rang.

'Mr Banks, I have Slater on the line for you.'

'Put him through.'

The line clicked.

'What's this all about Slater?'

Slater hesitated. 'Err.. This morning, we noticed some unusual activity on one of the email servers, following a password reset.'

'Unusual activity. What does that mean? Spit it out man.'

'Yes, Mr Banks. Well, it turns out that an intruder had access to the system for about twenty-five minutes.'

'And why are you telling me this?'

'It is procedure, Mr Banks. When certain keyword are used or records…'

'Yes I know that you idiot. Which keywords were used?'

'I have just emailed you a complete list of the man's activities, Sir. It is all there.'

'Man? How do you know that it was a man?'

'When we locked him out, he was foolish enough to telephone into the help desk. We recorded the call. Would you like me to play it back to you.'

'Yes.'

There were several clicks and the man's voice came on the line. Banks listened. The call ended.

'Have we any idea who he is?'

'Yes we do. He didn't bar his number and so we were able to do a reverse look-up. We have his address and, assuming it was the account holder, his name. It is at the bottom of the email we sent you.'

'Anything else?'

'No, Sir.'

He put the phone down, opened the email and read its contents. He sat back in his chair and looked at the list of records accessed by the intruder. The current directors. That didn't concern him. Neither, in normal circumstances, would the list of archived documents he'd accessed. But a line in Slater's email stood out. He reached for the phone on his desk.

CHAPTER TWENTY-THREE

The North End Road was as busy as ever. A constant stream of cars and vans passed by in front of Harry, their headlights glittering in the pouring rain. He had stayed on at the Park for the volunteers meeting but it had dragged on. The Major's ability to waffle endlessly was legendary but tonight the Major had been in exceptional form and, by eight, Harry had been losing the will to live. Taking his chances during a lull in the proceedings, he had finally slipped away. Hopefully un-noticed or he'd be sure to get it in the neck the following morning.

Harry stood at the curb side, willing the stick-man on the crossing sign to change to green but the little red bastard refused to budge. Sometimes, Harry regretted his decision to stay in London. He could have moved to any number of leafy villages, closer to the Park. Fuck it, he still could. But in the end... Actually, what *had* stopped him? He'd told everyone that he loved living in the Capital, with its proximity to the West End, the shops, restaurants, pubs, clubs and all the rest of it. But that wasn't really true and Harry knew it. If he was honest, there had been one reason and only one reason.

After what seemed like an age, the lights finally changed but as Harry stepped forwards, a number eighty-three thundered past like some great red, lumbering whale, sending a sheet of dirty water across the curb. *Oh great,* Harry thought. *Fucking great.* He stepped onto the crossing and sloshed across the road in his now water-logged shoes.

Reaching the far side, Harry happened to glance over his shoulder. A man in a khaki raincoat was a dozen paces behind him. He was a big man, with wide shoulders, a shaved head and a goatee beard. The same man had been on the tube train, sitting a few seats further along on the opposite side of the carriage. Harry looked away. Come to think of it, hadn't the same man been on the train from Bletchley? It was difficult to be certain in the darkness. Was he following him? Harry dismissed the thought but picked up his pace nonetheless, more to reach home and escape the rain, Harry told himself, than to escape his imagined pursuer.

Harry remembered that he needed milk and, spotting a gap in the traffic, sprinted across the Finchley Road and into the little grocery shop on the opposite side. He stood for a few moments, brushing rain from his coat and wondering whether the man in the khaki coat would be waiting for him outside.

'Hi Mo,' Harry said to the man behind the counter.

'Oh, hello. Is it raining?'

Harry had been visiting the shop since he first moved to Golders Green but could never tell whether Mohammed, who ran the place with his daughters, was being serious. Mo was friendly enough but rarely, if ever, smiled.

'You could say that.'

Mohammed nodded.

Harry picked up a newspaper, collected his milk from the fridge and stood behind a middle aged woman who was paying for beer and cigarettes.

'Do you have any brandy,' she said in a broad Irish accent.

Mohammed reached up and selected a bottle from the shelf behind him. The woman paid and left. Harry heard the bell on the door tinkle as she opened it. He put the newspaper and milk on the counter. He didn't hear the door close again and turned to see two young men enter the shop followed by the man in the khaki coat. He was wearing dark leather gloves, which Harry thought odd for the time of year. Harry looked at Mohammed. The man went to the magazine section and stood with his back to them browsing the magazines.

'Mo,' Harry whispered, 'the guy over there by the magazines...'

Mohammed leant forward.

'Do you know him?' asked Harry.

'No,'

'I think he's following me.'

Mo looked at the man and then back at Harry. 'Following you?'

'Yes.'

'Why would he be following you?'

'I don't know,' Harry whispered.

Mohammed appeared to consider Harry carefully. 'Over there,' he said, glancing to his right. 'The back door.'

'Thanks Mo,' Harry said. He stepped away from the counter and walked toward the rear exit, browsing the shelves as casually as he could.

The two young men who had entered the shop with the man in the khaki coat had now moved to the counter, blocking Harry's view of the man and, more importantly, the man's view of Harry. He slipped out of the back door, into the little yard behind. He found the gate, opened it and stepped into the alley behind the row of shops. Harry ran down the alley, as fast as he could and out into the street beyond. It might be paranoia but he didn't much fancy finding out in some dimly lit back alley.

Harry didn't stop running until he'd reached home, gasping for breath and fumbling for his keys. He looked over his shoulder. There was no sign of the man. He found the key, let himself in and was soon inside with his back to the closed door.

Jesus, Harry thought. First Erik had tried to knock his head off, then the watcher in the alley and the attempted garage break-in, the crazy email and now somebody had followed him home. *What the hell is going on?*

Harry went in to his bedroom without turning on the light. The curtains were open and Harry edged to the window and peered out cautiously so as to avoid being observed. The street outside was empty.

Mike had said that Erik had lost the plot. He wasn't wrong.

The rest of the evening passed without incident. After making himself something to eat, Harry sat down with the log book on his lap, leafing through its pages, one after the other. The truth was in front of him, somewhere. Harry was sure of it. But where?

Harry looked at the shortlist that he and Ellen had made and wondered, not for the first time, whether one of the men had followed Martha into the shelter. He opened the log again and found the first of the nine names.

Their oversight hit him like a thunderbolt. "Ronald Wiggins" had lift the shelter with "Jane Wiggins". Probably a mother and child, but certainly related. How could they have missed it? Ronald could hardly have murdered Martha if he was a child and even if he was an adult, the fact that he had been accompanied made it much less likely.

Harry cross checked the other names on the list and found that six of them had left the shelter at the same time as women with the same surname. Sometimes, they had left with two or three others - presumably a family, taking shelter underground, together. Harry put a line through the six names and looked at the three remaining. They had each left and, very likely, entered the shelter unaccompanied. Could one of them be Martha's killer?

Harry took the list and log book and sat in front of his PC. Without any real hope of finding a link, he spent the next hour trawling the internet for any reference to the three names, wartime crimes and Belsize Park. He found precisely nothing.

He got up and was walking into the kitchen to make some coffee, when he heard the "you have mail" sound from his PC. *More bloody junk mail*, he thought. Harry finished making his coffee and returned to his PC. He sighed wearily. *No, I do not need my penis enlarging*, he thought and dragged the offending email to the junk folder. As he released it, the folder popped open and a name caught his eye. It was an email from Tomasz Dobrowski. Harry looked at the date. The email had been sent four days earlier. He opened it and read its contents. Then he opened the attachments, one at a time, read them and saved them to his hard drive.

Saving the last of the documents, Harry reached for his mobile and dialled Tom. There was no reply. Then he tried Ellen. Again without response. *Damn it,* he cursed. He looked at his watch. It was well after midnight.

He got up, found his cigarettes and went to his back door. Lighting a cigarette from the packet he stood, gazing out into the darkness. Two bright specks of light moved across the garden and froze, blinking at him. Harry blew a smoke ring. How did Tom do it? He stood, turning the information over in his head. Then he returned to his PC and spent the next two hours reading everything he could find on the tunnels at Belsize Park. Just before three in the morning, he stopped, yawned and leant back in his chair. In spite of the time, he smiled broadly to himself. He had just found the perfect hiding place for a body.

The following morning Harry arrived at his desk feeling like death warmed up. After clambering into bed at half past three he'd been unable to sleep. Lying on his back in the darkness, staring at his ceiling, he had tried to imagine himself as the murderer. What would he have done with the body? Would he have tried to remove it from the shelter? What would he have done with it then? The trouble was that if the murderer had hidden it in the abandoned tunnel then it had lain there, undiscovered for sixty years. Was that really feasible?

By half past six, as the alarm on his mobile phone had sounded, Harry had made a decision. Whatever else, he needed to see the deep shelter at Belsize Park for himself.

He ran his fingers through his hair and picked up the phone.

'An abandoned tunnel? Are you sure?' asked Ellen.

'Yes, absolutely. They broke into an underground stream while they were digging it. They were going to try to re-route the water via a series of pipes, but it proved too costly and the tunnel was closed. As far as I can tell, it has never been re-opened.'

Ellen was silent.

'There's something else. Are you sitting down?' said Harry.

'Yes. What?'

'Among the documents that Tom sent me are the notes from a meeting at Belsize Park between BELCO Limited and the Ministry of Works. Have a guess at the date?'

'The date of the meeting?'

'Yes, the date of the meeting.' Harry couldn't hide his excitement.

Ellen was silent again.

'The tenth of November 1944.'

'The day that Martha went missing?' Ellen exclaimed.

'Yes, exactly.'

'The meeting took place on the day that Martha went missing? What do the notes say?'

'It's not what they say, Ellen. It's who they say was present. The notes give the names of the people who were present from BELCO. Remember the log entries?'

'Yes.'

'There were two BELCO employees at the meeting. The foreman. His name is in the log, both in and out.'

'And the other one?'

'Arthur Wallington. He was a company director until he retired in nineteen eighty-seven. His name doesn't appear anywhere in the log book.'

'So he must have been the one who signed in and out as "BELCO Ltd".'

'Yes.'

'Is he still alive?'

'I don't know. I didn't find much about him on the internet and nothing after his retirement. But the important thing is that if he is the BELCO employee referred to in the log, then he left the shelter in the middle of the air raid on the tenth, went back in early on the morning on the eleventh and left it again, without signing out. Why would anyone do that, least of all a company director?'

'Hmm…'

Harry could almost hear Ellen thinking.

'Maybe he just forgot something and went back to retrieve it?' she said.

'At four-fifteen in the morning? And why is there no exit time? Remember, this is the day when we're pretty certain Martha went into the shelter. It is also the day that a page was removed from the log, very possibly to hide her entry.'

'OK. But if it was Wallington and he did hide her body in the abandoned tunnel, wasn't he taking a huge risk leaving it down there?'

'Not if he knew that the abandoned tunnel was unlikely to be re-opened. Wallington was their Technical Director, Ellen. The BELCO people would have been working with the tunnel engineers. Wallington would have known that the body was unlikely to be discovered.'

'He would still have been taking a risk.' Ellen sounded dubious.

'Yes he would. But, knowing what he did about the tunnel, it would have been a far greater risk to have attempted to bring her body out, for disposal above ground. After all, a body is a difficult thing to move in secret. And to hide. '

Ellen was silent.

'There's one more thing. The Company that run the document store at Belsize Park now are called "Safe House Limited". I'm going to give them a call later to see if they'll let us visit the shelter.'

'Do you think they will?'

'Mike and Marcus didn't think so, but we'll see. I'll tell them that I'm researching the history of the shelter as part of my work here at the Park.'

'Which is the truth… kind of,' Ellen said.

'Exactly.'

Harry's final meeting of the day finished at half past four. When it was over, he returned to his office, dialled Directory Enquiries and, armed with their telephone number, made a call to Safe House Limited.

To say that the they were obstructive would be an understatement. Under no circumstances did the company allow visitors to the Belsize Park "vaults". They handled sensitive and confidential records and did not allow access by non-Company personnel. Harry asked to speak to a senior manager and then insisted on it. The senior manager was equally intransigent and Harry took exception to the man's tone. 'What is it, exactly, that you have stacked under the beds down there anyway?' He said it just to wind the man up and succeeded. After a brief pause, the line had gone dead.

Harry sat brooding at his desk. There had to be a way to gain access to the underground shelter. He pulled his mobile phone from his pocket and dialled Tomasz's number. There was no reply. Come to think of it, he hadn't spoken to Tom since they had bumped into each other at the Hong Kong Garden. Tom had obviously gone to some effort to get the information on BELCO. It seemed odd that he hadn't answered any of Harry's calls since.

The telephone on Harry's desk rang. It was Jane. He listened to her and put the phone down. 'Shit,' he said out loud.

Harry lit a cigarette on his way up to the bungalow and blew a defiant smoke ring, before stubbing the cigarette out on the path outside.

'Now here is a rare sight,' said Jane sarcastically as he entered. 'I haven't seen hide nor hair of you for days. Where have you been and who are *Safe House Limited* pray tell? The Major is in a right old pickle.'

'Yes I am sorry, I've been a bit…'

'Tied up with a certain Miss Carmichael?' Jane finished his sentence for him. 'Quite literally, no doubt.'

Harry grinned sheepishly. 'You might say that.'

'I do say that and you can take that smirk off your face.'

Harry decided to change the subject. 'They're a document storage company.'

'And?'

'They have the lease on the Belsize Park shelter.'

'Which you think Martha Watts entered but never left?'

Harry was surprised and his expression must have shown it.

Jane pulled a superior face. 'You are not the only one with a private channel to Ellen, you know. She and I have got a bit of a thing going actually.'

'Oh yeah? Well hands off. She's mine,' Harry said, with a little more force than was strictly necessary.

Their conversation was interrupted by a blast of hot air from the direction of the Major's office. 'Stammers? Is that you? My office. At the double!'

Harry pulled a face and Jane sniggered. 'Don't mention the war,' she said.

Harry knocked on the Major's door.

'In,' said the Major.

Harry entered and sat down. He half expected the Major's usual disappearing act but on this occasion it did not materialise. The Major looked like he was about to explode.

'Stammers, please explain to me why I have just had the Managing Director of one of the country's leading security companies on the telephone, asking me why my curator is poking his nose into matters which are, and I quote "none of his damn business".'

'I was not poking my nose into anything, Major. I was just asking whether I could take a look around the tunnels at Belsize Park. For research purposes of course.'

'And what research purposes would those be... No, on second thoughts,' the Major said, holding up his hand 'I don't care what your bloody purpose was. Safe House are in the business of storing highly confidential records for some very important organisations.'

'I know that but...'

'Including,' the Major said, interrupting, 'for Her Majesty's Government. Do you really think they're going to be doing guided tours anytime soon?'

Harry was silent for a moment. 'No, I suppose not.'

'There is no suppose about it,' the Major barked.

'No, Major.'

'And for the record, Stammers, they do not have anything stacked under the bloody beds. Is that clear?'

'Yes, sir.' Harry flushed.

'Good God man, given our history here, I would have thought that you might have understood the sensitivities of operations like Safe House, a point which was made rather forcefully by their M.D. just now.'

Harry was silent again.

The Major glared at him, somewhat alarmingly.

'I'm sorry, Sir,' Harry muttered, looking into his lap.

The Major looked at Harry and sighed. 'He also reminded me that they have a rather influential MP on their Board.'

'Do they?' Harry said, looking up. A bell was ringing in the back of Harry's head but he was struggling to make the connection.

'Yes, they bloody well do,' thundered the Major. Harry felt the blast of hot air from across the desk. 'He's on the Culture, Media and Sport Committee and, as such, wields a certain amount of influence when it comes to funding matters. Am I making myself clear?'

He was making himself abundantly clear. 'Yes, Major.'

'Get out Stammers. And if I hear another whisper from Safe House Limited, I will have you hung, drawn and bloody quartered, is that understood?'

'Yes, Major.'

Harry beat a hasty retreat along the corridor.

'Well done,' whispered Jane as Harry approached her desk. 'That was very entertaining. Can we do it again sometime soon?' she said, grinning.

'Not bloody likely,' said Harry, already at the door.

CHAPTER TWENTY-FOUR

The 17.27 to London Euston was delayed. Harry stood on the platform and listened to the automated announcement. Overhead line problems at Harrow and Wealdstone. *There are always overhead line problems at Harrow and bloody Wealdstone.* Harry looked down at his watch. He had agreed to meet Ellen at eight, for supper at his flat. He tried to work out how late he could afford to be before he'd have to call her.

A high speed train passed through the station, buffeting the people on the platform as it roared past. Harry put his back to the oncoming carriages to avoid the turbulence and watched the train until it was no more than a tiny speck in the distance. He looked up and down the platform. There was no sign of the man who had followed him, if indeed he had been followed. Perhaps he had over-reacted. The whole thing seemed surreal and completely out of proportion to the joke he had played on Erik.

The little coffee bar on the platform was closed, so he bought a Coke from a vending machine, found a platform bench and sat down. The southbound platform was now quiet, as it was most evenings. Travelling into the city at the end of the day, had its advantages. Harry glanced up at the arrivals board. His train was now due at 18.06. If it arrived when it was due, he ought to make it home in time.

Harry pulled his mobile phone from his pocket and dialled Kate's number. 'Hi, Kate, it's Harry.'

'Hi, Harry.'

'Have you been to see Dad today?'

'Yes, I was at the hospital this afternoon.'

He could hear the sadness in her voice. 'And?'

'And nothing. He's the same. He just stares. When he is not sleeping.'

Harry was silent.

'Are you going to see him later?' Kate asked.

'No. I thought I'd go tomorrow. I'm stuck at Bletchley. The trains are running late.'

'So go later. We need to keep talking to him.'

'I know that, Kate, but I have to work and I can't always get away early enough to make it to the hospital in time.' He knew how it sounded.

'That's just an excuse and you know it,' she said, her voice prickling.

Harry sighed. 'That is not fair.'

'Isn't it? He's your father, Harry and he needs you. He's the only family we've got.'

Harry could feel his temper rising. 'And you know that, do you?' He said it and immediately wished that he hadn't.

'Meaning?'

'Forget it.'

'I don't believe you.' she said angrily.

'Look, I didn't call you to fight. I just wanted to know how Dad was. That's all.'

'Yeah? Well then go and see him for yourself.'

'Fine. I will. Tomorrow.'

Harry put the phone back in his pocket. It was Kate's way of coping. It always had been. If reality becomes too difficult, create an alternative, hold to it and if anyone interferes, use any and all means necessary to force them into retreat. Kate's weapon of choice was usually guilt and on this occasion, Harry had to concede, she had used it to some effect.

The southbound train finally arrived at 18.12. At least it was a fast train, stopping at Leighton Buzzard and London Euston only. Harry settled back into his seat and closed his eyes. *Why does life have to be such a bloody trial?*

He came-to with a start, brought back to his senses by his mobile phone vibrating in his pocket. He managed to pull it out in time to answer it.

'Harry? It's Tom.'

'Tom, I've been trying to get hold of you,' he said, trying to reclaim his thoughts from the junk yard to which twenty minutes sleep on the train had consigned them. 'I wanted to thank you for the stuff you sent me on BELCO.'

'No problem,' came the reply.

'No, really, Tom. It has been a great help. How the hell did you manage it?'

Tom was silent for a moment. 'It was not so hard. People are careless.'

'Well however you did it, I am very glad that you did,' said Harry.

'Sure,' Tom said and added hesitantly 'How's it going, your search for the woman?'

Harry heard the hesitation in his voice and wondered about it, then dismissed the thought. Exchange more than two sentences with Tom and he usually did sound hesitant.

He outlined their progress. Tom listened in silence. When Harry was finished, Tom said 'How can you be so sure that she was at Belsize Park?'

Harry told him about the diary.

'And you have seen this diary yourself?'

'Yes, John Watts, Martha's brother, has it.'

'And the log?'

'I borrowed it from the London Museum.'

They discussed the entries in the log.

'Arthur Wallington. What have you found out about him?'

'Only that he was a Technical Director at BELCO and is now retired. He's probably dead. There's nothing about him on the net, after his retirement.'

Tom was silent.

'I think we're going to have to go and have a look at Belsize Park Deep Shelter, Tom,' Harry said.

'No,' Tom said forcefully and then hesitated. 'It would be very difficult.'

Harry was surprised by his response. It was unlike him to be negative in principle, no matter how difficult an explore might prove to be.

'But you and the others have been into secure buildings before?'

Tom was silent. 'Of course. But at Belsize Park there will be too much security.'

'Yes, well I was hoping that you might be able to find out about that.'

Tom was silent again.

'Well, look, lets see what the others think. Perhaps they'll come up with something,' Harry said hopefully.

'OK. I will think about it. I'll call you.' Tom ended the call.

Harry leant back in his seat. He had imagined Marcus being the more reluctant of the group and Ellen was going to throw a fit, but Tomasz? He had not expected that. He yawned. On the other hand, in the short time that Harry had known him, Tom had never been predictable. Harry's thoughts began to wander.

He was woken by the jolting of the train as it crossed the points on the run-in to Euston. Harry opened his eyes, stretched his arms and got off the train to the sound of hissing air-brakes. He inserted his ticket in the barrier, walked through the automatic gates and up the ramp toward the station concourse, intending to smoke a cigarette on the forecourt outside before catching a Northern Line train to Golders Green. As he reached the top of the ramp, the station tannoy announced that "the train at Platform ten is the 19.27 to Birmingham New Street" and a tidal wave of bodies surged towards him. He looked at his watch. It was seven-fifteen. He had forty-five minutes to make it home. Harry stood aside and waited for the flow of people to subside. Then he headed for the escalators to the Underground Station.

At Belsize Park, a little more than ten minutes later, Harry looked out of the tube train window. There was that feeling again. He could almost feel her eyes watching him. The platform was full of people, pushing to board the train. Others, who had alighted, were shoving their way toward the tunnels that led to the up escalators. People of all ages, sizes and colours. Harry could feel the hairs on the back his neck standing on end. It was surreal that they could be going about their business unaware that a young woman lay hidden, probably within a few hundred yards of them. But it had been this way for a long time. For sixty years. How many lives had passed through the station in that time, unaware of her presence?

Harry crossed the road at the crossing opposite Golders Green station. As he stepped onto the curb, he found himself looking over his shoulder but there was nobody there. He slipped a cigarette out of its packet, lit it and blew a smoke ring. Perhaps it had been nothing more than his imagination.

Harry walked up to his front door and inserted his key in the lock and pushed open the door. As he did, he knew that that something was not right. He could sense it. He stepped into the flat and looked to his right. Two drawers lay upside down, their contents scattered about on the bedroom floor. He walked down the corridor, checking the bathroom and kitchen as he went. Nothing.

'Hello? Is there anybody there?' he called out. Suddenly aware that the intruder might still be there, he could feel his heart pounding and his stomach in his mouth.

He looked at the door into the garage and could see that it had been broken open, the wood around the lock having splintered in the process. He continued into the lounge. The room had been turned upside down. His belongings were spread across the floor. Every drawer and cupboard had been emptied. His PC lay was on its side with the panel off. Harry bent down to inspect it and then stood up and looked around the room.

'Harry? What's going on? Harry?' Ellen had let herself in through the open front door.

'In here,' Harry called out.

'Oh my God!' Ellen was at the entrance to his lounge, clutching a bottle of wine and looking ashen.

Harry was surrounded by chaos. The place didn't look like his flat and it didn't feel like his flat.

Ellen was watching him. She made no move to enter further into the room. 'Are you alright?'

Harry said nothing. He stepped around his upturned coffee table and made his way towards her, avoiding the broken glass from a picture that had been hanging on the wall above his sofa. They held each other in silence.

Finally, Harry said 'It is gone.'

She looked at him, with a question in her eyes.

'The log book. It's gone.'

CHAPTER TWENTY-FIVE

Harry and Ellen stood in the kitchen waiting for the police to arrive. The operator had told him not to touch anything and they had moved into the kitchen where Ellen was making coffee.

'It just doesn't make any sense, Harry. So Erik was angry but why would he break into your flat and take the log book?'

'I don't know. I really don't.'

'Tell me again what was in the email. The one you didn't want to worry me about.' There was more than a hint of sarcasm in her voice.

Harry ran his fingers through his hair. 'He said that I was going to have to pay and that he'd be watching me.'

'So it was him who I saw across the road the other night.'

'Maybe.' Harry hesitated. He was thinking about the man in the khaki coat.

'What?' Ellen said, holding his gaze.

'I'm not sure. But I might have been followed the other night.'

'You might have been followed? By who?'

'I don't know. But it certainly wasn't Erik.'

'When?'

'On my way home from work on Monday. He got off the tube with me and was behind me as far as Mo's.'

Ellen looked at him blankly.

'It's a paper shop on the Finchley Road. I don't know, Ellen. I'm really not sure. It's just that with all this,' Harry said, waving towards the living room, 'I just can't help wondering whether Erik is trying to put the frighteners on me.'

'Alright. But why would Erik take the log book? Did he even know about it?'

'If he did, I certainly didn't tell him.'

'So why take it? It doesn't make sense.'

Ellen was right. It didn't make sense. None of it did.

A thought struck Harry and he groaned.

'What?' said Ellen anxiously.

'What the hell am I going to tell the police?'

'What do you mean?'

'They are bound to ask whether I have any idea who might have done this. If I tell them about Erik, then he'll get another visit. He already blames me for losing the contract.'

'You have got to tell them Harry. He's attacked you once and, if he is behind all this, then it has gone too far. Much too far.'

Harry knew that she was right. 'And if he isn't?'

'I'd let the police be the judge of that,' Ellen said, shaking her head.

'I should speak to him. If I apologised, in person, maybe that would make a difference.'

'And maybe it would make it worse.'

It took a little over thirty minutes for the police to arrive. They had pulled into the drive outside Harry's flat, with the police car's blue lights flashing, which Harry could not help but find irritating. The burglar had long since gone and they had not exactly rushed to the scene.

The two officers asked Harry to list what was missing.

'Was this book very valuable,Sir?' said the eldest of the two officers.

'No, I wouldn't have thought so. It was of historical interest, but I doubt that it has any particular financial value.'

'And you say that your computer hard drive is missing?'

159

Harry looked at the remains of his PC. 'Isn't that fairly obvious?'

'It seems a little strange that someone would have gone to the trouble of removing the hard drive from your computer, Mr....'

Harry sighed. 'Stammers. Yes, it does seem strange.'

'Was there anything on this hard drive?' the older officer said, exchanging a knowing glance with the younger officer.

'Yes, of course there was. There was about three years worth of data on it.'

'I meant was there anything on the drive that could be of any value or interest to anyone else?'

Harry was beginning to lose patience. 'Not unless the burglar plays Football Manager. Getting Barnet F.C. to the Premier League was bloody priceless,' Harry said but his sarcasm was evidently lost on the two officers who looked at each other blankly.

'If the book was of no financial value, can you think of anyone who might have wanted the book for any other reason?' asked the younger officer.

'No. As I said, the book is of historic interest. It would only be of use to someone who was doing similar research to mine, in which case they would hardly have needed to steal it. They could have borrowed it, as I did.'

Then came the obvious question. Harry hesitated but Ellen, who was standing next to him, nudged him with her elbow. Harry told them about his disagreement with Erik.

'Could we see this threatening email? Asked the older officer.

'No. You can't.' Harry really was losing patience.

'Why is that?'

'Because somebody has stolen my bloody hard drive.'

'Ah, yes.'

They had to wait another hour for the scene of crime officer to arrive to look for finger prints before they could begin to tidy up.   The two officers had left by the time that he arrived. The only finger prints in the flat belonged to Harry and Ellen. Evidently, whoever had broken in to Harry's flat had worn gloves.

Harry closed the door after the SOCO had left, went into his bedroom and threw himself face down on his bed.

'Hey, you. No slacking, you've got a lot of clearing up to do,' said Ellen from the doorway.

Harry groaned and rolled over onto his back. Then he put his hands behind his head. 'All work and no play makes Jack a dull boy,' he said grinning.

'And all play and no work makes Jack a mere toy,' replied Ellen.

'You know, I've been thinking,' said Harry. 'It is time I took this thing with Erik by the horns. I'm going to call him. If I don't and it wasn't him who broke in, then the first he will know about all this is when the police knock on his door. Again. If he is innocent, that will really piss him off and who could blame him?'

To his surprise Ellen agreed. 'But, either way, he is not entirely innocent Harry. He did hit you and he did send you that email. I just don't think he did this. I don't think he stole the log book or took your hard drive. I think you should try and sort it out with him. And then we need to start thinking about who did.'

Harry pulled his mobile phone out of his pocket. 'It's now or never,' he said, dialling the number. 'Erik, it's Harry.'

The conversation with Erik did not get off on a high note. Erik was still furious about losing the contract and he was unapologetic for the assault in the pub. So far as he was concerned, Harry had deserved it.

Harry had activated the speaker phone so that Ellen, who was sitting beside him on the bed, could hear what was being said. He was already regretting it. Within seconds, she had grabbed a notepad and pen and was frantically scribbling him instructions. Why did women do that?

Listening to Erik, Harry quickly decided that arguing with him was not going to get him anywhere. Erik was not the sort of man who was ever going to back down. But Harry was. He waited for Erik to finish speaking and then he apologised. The joke had been exactly that, but he saw now that it had been in poor taste and Harry sincerely regretted it.

Harry's unreserved apology seemed to do the trick, at least in part. Erik thawed, slightly. Now for the difficult part. Harry took a breath.

'Erik, there is something else I need to tell you. My flat was broken into earlier today.'

'Yeah? What's that got to do with me?'

'Somebody attempted to break in a few days ago. We saw them watching us from across the street. I was also followed home from work.'

'And?'

'I have to ask you. Was any of that your doing?' Harry held his breath.

'Why would I follow you home or break into your flat?'

'That email you sent me.'

'What about it? I was just trying to rattle you, that's all.'

'Yeah, well you succeeded,' Harry bit his tongue.

Erik said nothing.

'Look, I'm sorry. But you hit me in the pub, then send me a threatening email, then I am followed and somebody breaks into my flat. What would you think?'

'I'd think I had something that somebody else wanted,' Erik replied. 'Believe me, you've got nothing that I want.'

'Are you saying that it wasn't you?'

'I don't see why I need to say anything to you Stammers.'

Harry thought that Erik might need to say it to the police.

'Erik, please. I need to know who is doing this and why. If it is you, I'd rather the two of us sorted it out now. If it is not you, then I want to make sure that the police know it is not you.'

'You spoke to the police?'

'Yes I spoke to the police. My flat was broken into. Whoever it was, trashed the place.'

Erik was silent.

'The police wanted to know whether anyone had threatened me.'

'And you told them that I had?'

'Yes, I did.'

'For fuck's sake.'

'If you are telling me that you have had nothing to do with anyone following me or breaking into my flat, then that is what I will tell the police. But for the record, Erik, I did not tell them that I thought you were behind it. OK? They asked me whether anyone had threatened me recently. Whether I could think of anyone who might want to harm me in any way.'

Erik was silent for a moment.

'It wasn't me. OK? I had nothing to do with it. I was pissed off about what you did. I'm still pissed off about it. It lost me a fucking good contract. I went off at the deep end with you at the pub the other night. The email was a stupid idea. I'd had a few too many, you know what I'm saying? But that is all. Why the fuck would I break into your flat?'

'Thank you. That is all I needed to know,' said Harry feeling relieved.

Erik said nothing. After a few moments, the line went dead. Erik had hung up.

Harry looked at Ellen. 'So what do you think?'

'I think he's telling the truth.'

Harry nodded. 'So do I.'

'Which means that somebody else has been following you and that, whoever it is, also broke in and took the log.'

They looked at each other.

'Harry, whoever it was, knew what they were looking for. They took the log and sabotaged your computer and nothing else.'

'I know.'

For the first time Ellen looked scared. Harry put his arms around her.

'Somebody knows don't they?' she said. 'Somebody knows and somebody wants to stop us.'

'Yes, I think they do,' Harry agreed.

Harry called Mike from his desk the following morning and told him about the burglary at his flat.

'They stole nothing but the log from Belsize Park?'

'That and the hard drive from my PC.'

'What was on it?'

'All my research and of course, the documents Tom sent me from BELCO.'

'So someone knows about your search for the woman from Bletchley Park?'

'Evidently.'

'Any idea who?'

'Not a clue. But I reckon we must be on the right track. Otherwise, why would someone go to the trouble of stealing the log book?'

Mike was silent. 'Are you sure that you want to go further with this Harry. I mean, it is starting to get heavy.'

'I know. But we've come too far to give it up now. That log book was stolen for a reason, Mike. I'm pretty certain that it is all tied up with what happened to Martha Watts.'

'Man. Do you have any definite idea about what did happen to her?'

'Not exactly. Ellen and I both think that she went into the shelter. We have got an approximate time for that because of the missing page from the log. And there's nothing in the log to say that she came out again.'

'Perhaps there was an accident?'

'No, I don't think that it was an accident. If it had been, she would have eventually been found. In any case why would someone be trying to cover it up all these years later?'

Mike was quiet. 'If it wasn't an accident, then what?'

Harry hesitated. He knew how it would sound, but there was no other way of saying it.

'Everyone who went in to the shelter is recorded in that log, apart from the people listed on the missing page and one other.'

'One other?'

'Yes. According to the records that Tom unearthed, someone from BELCO attended a meeting in the shelter on the afternoon of the tenth. He went in and out twice, without his name appearing in the log at all and the second time he entered in the small hours of the following morning.'

'You think he killed her?'

'Well she was never seen again.'

Mike was silent.

'Yes, I think she was killed and I think that her body was hidden in the flooded tunnel.'

'Man…'

'Which is why I want to go and have a look,' Harry said, hesitantly.

'Oh fuck, I knew that's where this was heading.'

'I know. It's not going to be easy.'

Mike was silent.

'But I need to see it for myself. Do you think it can be done?'

'I don't know. After you mentioned it the other night at the pub, I made some enquiries. You can't get into the shelters. The company that leases them has them sewn up.'

'They're called "Safe House Limited" and you're right, they don't allow access. I almost caused an international incident just by asking. They were straight on to the Major and I was told, in no uncertain terms, to drop it.'

'Shit.'

'But I'm not going to drop it Mike. If she is down there, then she deserves to be found. Its important to Ellen and to her great aunt, for one thing. Besides, somebody trashed my flat.'

'Yeah, I get that. Makes it kind of personal.'

'Yes it does. But that is my problem, not yours. If you'd rather not get involved…' Harry held his breath. Without Mike he knew he was all at sea.

'Man, I like a challenge. You know I do. But this one could land us all in a heap of shit if we get caught.'

'True. So we better make sure that we don't get caught.'

Mike was quiet for a moment. 'Who do you want on the explore with us. If we can work out a way to get in. Not Erik after what happened the other night? I wouldn't even tell him, if I were you.'

Harry breathed out.

'I don't intend to. No, not Erik. I was hoping for you, me, Marcus and Tom.'

'Have you spoken to them?'

'Only to Tom. I was going to discuss it with Ellen too, but the break in at the flat has rattled her. It might be better if I didn't tell her. It will just freak her out.'

'Sure. I'll talk to Marcus and we can catch up for a pint later in the week?'

'OK, but we'd better make it somewhere other than the *Horse and Groom.*'

'Hell, yes,' said Mike.

'What about the *Bull and Bush* in Hampstead? Do you know it?'

'Sure.'

'Shall we say Friday?'

'OK.'

Harry ended the call and thought about Ellen. They had worked on finding Martha together. It felt like a betrayal just to be thinking about doing it without telling her. But he was pretty certain about how she would react if he told her and it wasn't good.

CHAPTER TWENTY-SIX

John Watts folded the newspaper he'd been reading and tucked it down the side of his leather sofa, as he always did. It was a habit that had driven Dora to despair. She would find it there every morning and complain about it bitterly over breakfast. 'John, you lazy bugger,' she would berate him, 'why can't you put your paper in the bin when you've finished with it?' and she'd swipe him across the back of the head with it. He smiled to himself. He'd say 'Sorry, Love. Give it here,' but she never would. She would sigh and say 'I'll do it,' and take it out to the bin for him. It was one of their many rituals.

The old man sat for a moment and closed his eyes. He could remember her every detail. The way she dressed. The way she spoke. The scent of her hair. The mannerisms that only he noticed. Her 'foibles', he called them. It had always delighted her that he knew her well enough to notice them. The sound of her laughter echoed in his mind.

He remembered how difficult it had been when she went. His life had felt completely empty. For months on end, he had shambled around the house, going through the motions. He remembered how everything had seemed so grey, like all the colour had been drained away with her passing. He was ashamed to admit it now, but there had been mornings when he had lain in bed, praying to be allowed to find sleep and to never wake up.

Then one morning, he had opened his eyes and she had been there. He had been unable to explain it, even to himself. The crushing sense of loss that he had been living with had simply gone. In its place was the certain knowledge that he wasn't alone. She was present, as if she had never gone away. If it was madness or just old age, he didn't care.

He had got out of bed, that first morning, fully expecting to find her making breakfast in the kitchen. When he had found the kitchen empty he had simply closed his eyes and there she was. She had been with him ever since. Nowadays, if he didn't try too hard, he could see her without closing his eyes. When he wasn't expecting it, he would catch a glimpse of her. Sitting in her chair or pottering about the kitchen or standing by the bedroom window.

'Come on my lovely. It is time we got to bed,' he said out loud 'it has been a long day.'

John and Dora climbed the stairs together. He got changed, went to the bathroom, then turned out the lamp by the side of his bed and, in minutes, they were asleep in each other's arms.

Outside, a man waited in the shadows. He watched as the light on the landing came on and the downstairs light went out. Then an upstairs light came on and, a few minutes later, off again so that the whole house was in darkness. The man waited. Then he slipped across the road, a dog barking in the distance. He found the alley between the houses and made his way, in silence, to the back of the property.

The man tried the back door. It was locked. He tried the windows. They were closed, but he noticed that the latch was up on the fanlight above the kitchen sink. He climbed onto the sill, lifted the fanlight and reached inside. After a few moments his hand found the main window latch. He lifted it and opened the window.

The man climbed inside, being careful not to disturb the plates and pots on the draining board. He closed the window behind him and let himself down onto the floor. He stood in silence for a moment, listening. Then he removed a small flashlight from his pocket and switched it on. He went to the kitchen door and looked across the hallway. The house was silent. He returned to the kitchen and opened each cupboard and drawer, one after the other. Then he went back to the kitchen door and walked across the hallway to the lounge. He began opening cupboards and drawers and searching through the piles of books on the coffee table and on the bookshelf beside the window.

'Wake up.' John heard Dora's voice and turned over. 'Wake up, you dozy old bugger. There's someone downstairs.'

John opened his eyes and listened. His hearing wasn't as good as it used to be. 'Don't be daft. It's just the central heating pipes,' he closed his eyes. Then he heard a floorboard creak. It was the one in the lounge, by the window. It creaked when you stood on it, to reach for a book from the shelf beside the window. He had done it himself a thousand times.

'There. I told you. Call the police,' Dora's voice was urgent.

'Stop worrying, Love, it is probably nothing,' he said, getting up and putting on his slippers. He knelt down and fumbled under the bed. After a few moments he removed the cricket bat and stood up, listening intently. He could hear nothing.

The man was kneeling in front of the side board. He removed a box, put it on the floor in front of him and started to look through its contents. Finally he stopped and removed a small leather bound book. It had the year "1944" embossed in gold on the front cover. He removed his glove, opened the diary and used the flashlight to read the first few lines. He smiled and put the diary in his coat pocket. Then he put his glove back on, carefully replaced the box and closed the sideboard door.

The man stood and froze. He could hear the sound of slippered feet on the floor above. He extinguished the flashlight and moved swiftly, across the hall into the kitchen. He stepped behind the kitchen door and put his hand in his inside pocket. He withdrew a knife, flicked it and the blade extended.

John Watts stood at the top of the stairs, listening as hard as he could but he could hear nothing. The street lamp across the road shone through the landing window, throwing an orange light across the upstairs hallway and part-way down the stairs. He peered down the stair well but could see nothing in the gloom. He cursed the old age that made him afraid in his own house.

John held the cricket bat in front of him. His palms were sweating and he could feel his legs shaking. He took a deep breath. 'Who's there?' he called out. Silence. 'I said who's there?' he called again and immediately felt foolish. There was nobody there. He looked at the cricket bat in his hand. He was just a foolish old man.

'Now I'm up, Love, I may as well make a cup of tea,' he said out loud. He stepped forward, feeling for the top stair with his foot. Normally he would have held the bannister but the cricket bat was in his right hand. As he swapped hands, his foot found space instead of the expected stair and he felt his body begin to topple.

'Don't be long John,' he heard her call from the bedroom. 'It is cold here without you.'

The man waited for the avalanche of sound to stop, refolded the knife, put it back into his pocket and stepped around the door into the hallway. He smiled. John Watts lay in a twisted heap at the bottom of the stairs. Even in the half-light the man could see the pool of blood spreading out beneath his head. He stood still for a moment. Then he walked back into the kitchen. He found a disposable cloth by the sink and wiped the surfaces he had stood on as he had entered through the window. He made sure that the main and fanlight windows were closed and secured their latches. He walked back into the hallway and unlocked the front door's mortice lock using the key that had been left in place. He slowly opened the front door, peering out into the night. Then he stepped outside, eased the front door closed and used the key to lock the door. He put the key in his pocket. It was a risk, but the old man was certain to have a spare set in the house somewhere. Old people were always anxious about losing keys. He glanced up and, for a split second, thought he saw a woman standing at the bedroom window, peering out at him. But as he looked more closely he saw that it was the shadow thrown by the orange street light on the bedroom curtains. He smiled and disappeared, silently into the night.

CHAPTER TWENTY-SEVEN

It was the heat and the smell of disinfected plastic that he detested more than anything else. Harry couldn't decide which was worse.   Perhaps if they turned the heating down and opened some windows, people might be more inclined to get up out of their beds or their chairs, which were arranged around the walls like a waiting room. Harry glanced at the few elderly patients who had made it as far as the day room and wondered what they were supposed to be waiting for.

He got up and opened the window behind his father's wheelchair, feeling the fresh air on his arms as it flooded in through the opening.   The leaves on the Horse Chestnut tree outside were flickering gently in the breeze. A young couple passed by on the footpath below. Outside, life continued as normal but, in here, it had been all but drowned in a sea of polished linoleum and washable plastic arm chairs.

Harry returned to his seat and sat watching his father. He'd aged. For the first time in Harry's life, his father looked like an old man. In fact, Harry reflected, the blank face staring back at him through empty eyes hardly looked like his father at all. And yet, he was undeniably Edward Stammers. The same Edward Stammers who had thrown stones into the sea, played football with him in the park and ran along behind his bike as Harry had peddled like crazy, trying to stay upright.

Harry moved his chair closer, so that he was looking directly at him. This was also the same Edward Stammers who had shown the police officer into their front room and closed the door, leaving the eight year old Harry and his sister Kate standing outside, without explanation. The same man who had emerged in stoney faced silence and who had never spoken of his wife again. The man who had shut her out of their lives so that it was as though she had never existed. The man who sat in front of him now, with her memory locked away, perhaps forever.

'I won't let you do it, you know,' Harry said hoarsely.

His father said nothing.

'Do you hear me?'

Nothing.

'She went away, for a reason. I know she did.'

Not a flinch.

'But it was you who tried to erase her from our memories, wasn't it?'

Edward Stammers stared back at him blankly.

'Eight years old, Dad. I was eight fucking years old. I couldn't even grieve. You took that away from me too.' Harry gritted his teeth against the tide of bitterness rising from the pit of his stomach.

'You know what happened to her, don't you?' Harry leant forward and stared into his father's face, following his eye movements.

Nothing.

'You've always known, you selfish bastard.'

And there it was. The tiniest hint of a twitch.

Harry took hold of his father's shoulders.

'I will find her, you know. One day. With or without your help.'

Father and son stared at each other in bitter silence. Then a single tear trickled, slowly down his father's left cheek.

Harry's mobile phone rang as he walked back across the hospital car park.

'Harry, it's Tom.'

'Tom, I'm glad you called. We're going to meet at the *Old Bull* in Hampstead on Friday. Do you know it?'

'Sure.'

'About eight?'

'I'll be there.'

'Great.'

Tom was silent.

'Sorry, you called me didn't you. What's up?'

'I think I may have found a way.'

'A way?'

'A way to get into the shelter.'

Harry stopped walking. 'Are you serious?' It was a stupid question. Tom was always serious.

'Yes.'

'How?'

'I have been looking at their security. It is not so good.'

'You think you can get us inside?'

'Yes. That is the easy part.'

'What is the not so easy part?'

'Getting down to the tunnels. That is the not so easy part. There are video cameras on the stair well and the lift would make too much noise.'

'And security guards?'

'Of course. Two. They sit in a small control room, watching the CCTV cameras.'

'So how will we do it?'

'The day shift hand over to the night shift at ten o'clock. When the night shift arrive all four guards go into the staff room. They are there between ten and fifteen minutes. Then the day guards leave and the night guards return to the control room.'

'How do you know?'

'I have been watching them. They do the same every day.'

'Now I am lost,' said Harry bewildered.

'The CCTV system is controlled via the internet. It is not very secure.'

'You have hacked their CCTV system?'

'Yes.'

'Jesus.'

'While the guards are in the staff room, there is nobody watching the cameras.'

'OK, but how will we get in?'

'Through the main door. Entry is controlled by a combination pad.'

'And you have the combination?'

'No. But I will have it.'

'How? No, on second thoughts, I can guess,' Harry said.

'Once we are inside, we go to the lift.'

'I thought you said that it would be too noisy to use the lift?'

'We will not use the lift. We will abseil down the lift shaft.'

Harry's jaw dropped. 'Abseil.'

'Yes.'

'What about the cameras?'

'There is no camera inside the lift shaft.'

Harry tried to grasp the implications. 'You're saying that we're going to abseil one hundred feet down a lift shaft in the pitch black?'

'No.'

Harry was confused. 'But you said…'

'There are lights in the stair well. You will not be in the dark'

Harry put the drinks down in front of the others and sat at the table. 'So let's go over this again,' he said. 'Tom, you will set Mike's PC up so that he can view and control the Belsize Park cameras from his place.'

Tom nodded.

'Marcus, Tom and I will arrive at Belsize Park, in Marcus's van, at 21.30. We will park in Downside Crescent and wait for the night guards to arrive, at which point I will call Mike.'

They all nodded.

'Mike, you will pick up the night guards on the camera in the entrance lobby and will tell us as soon as all four guards are in the staff room. The three of of us will then enter through the main door, using the combination that Tom will obtain for us.'

They all looked at Tomasz.

'You are certain that you will be able to obtain the combination?' asked Marcus.

'Yes. It is changed every twenty-four hours. The new combination is sent by text to the guards,' replied Tom.

They all looked at him.

'Text is not so easy to intercept. It is a good system.'

'Then how will you get it?' asked Marcus.

'They also record the new combination on their computer system. That is not a good system,' Tom said.

They all looked at each other.

'Once we are in,' Harry said, 'Marcus and I will go to the lift. Tom will go to the control room and disable the camera controls.'

Tom nodded.

'Will Mike still be able to control them?' asked Marcus.

Tom nodded. 'Yes. I will disable the console in the control room only.'

'You will then join us at the lift. You won't have long Tom. Are you sure you can do it?' asked Harry.

'Yes I am sure. It will be easy.'

'Mike, you will point the cameras away from the lift entrance. If the night guard manages to reactivate the controls and attempts to point them back again, you will prevent him. But try to be subtle about it. If it comes to it, we want him to think that there is a fault and nothing else.'

Mike nodded.

'We cannot use the lift. It would make too much noise. So, we will climb out of the lift through the hatch in the ceiling,' said Harry.

'Correct,' said Tom.

'Once we are on top of the lift, we will be invisible from the entrance. But we will need to be quiet. If the guard makes in inspection, we don't want him to hear us. Marcus will arrange the climbing gear. Tom is going to stay on top of the lift and will maintain contact with Mike. We will be using handheld radios to keep in touch with you as we descend Tom, like we did at the receiving station. Once we are down, Marcus will remain at the bottom of the lift shaft, while I explore the shelter. Marcus will be able to relay messages from Mike via Tom, if need be.'

'What about getting out again?' asked Mike.

'We will have to climb back up using ascenders,' said Marcus. 'Harry, you've done some rope work before, but I can take you through the technique again before we go. It will be quite a tough climb, so we'll need to take our time.'

'Wouldn't it be easier to just disable the cameras on the stair well and make a run for it?' asked Mike.

'It is one hundred feet up to the surface. The guards would almost certainly notice the blank camera feed. It would be too risky to rely on them staying in the control room long enough for us to get to the top. They'd catch us on the stairs,' said Harry.

Marcus agreed.

'Once we are back on top of the lift, Mike you will disable the cameras in the lobby. From there it will take us less than a minute to get to the door. If we are lucky, the guard won't even notice the blank camera feed. If he does, then hopefully he will spend several minutes trying to work out why the camera has gone off line while we make out escape. But we will need to be quick and stay quiet. Any noise and the guard will be on to us.'

They were silent for a moment. Harry emptied his pint glass.

'What are you going to be looking for down there?' Tom asked, looking at Harry.

Harry hesitated. 'First, I will be looking for the abandoned tunnel. I know roughly where the entrance should be. I just hope that it hasn't been bricked up. If I find it, I'd like to know how feasible it would have been to have hidden a body there and for it to have remained undiscovered all this time.' Harry paused. 'And third, I guess I'll be looking for any sign that she was there.'

They were silent.

'Are there any other questions?'
They all shook their heads.

CHAPTER TWENTY-EIGHT

Ellen Carmichael tapped out the last of the figures from the stock take onto the computer at Carmichael Interiors and clicked "Update".

'Thank God for that,' she said, stretching and stifling a yawn. She was dead on her feet.

'Amen to that,' replied Nicky. 'Will you cash up or shall I do it before I go?' Nicky gulped the last of her coffee.

'Oh God. I had forgotten. No, don't worry, I'll do it,' Ellen said, reaching for the till key. 'Got anything planned for later on?'

'Yes. A long bath and an early night.'

'Not going round to Harry's then?'

'He's having a boys night out, apparently,' Ellen said pulling a face.

'What do museum curators do in their spare time?' asked Nicky.

'I didn't ask. I don't think I want to know,' replied Ellen and they both laughed. 'What about you?'

'A takeaway and a DVD. Tim's mum and dad invited us over, but I said that I was working late,' Nicky said, looking at her watch 'Which is the truth. It's gone nine.'

Nicky picked up her bag and went into the back of the shop. Ellen tallied the card machine and printed the till reading. After a few moments, Nicky reappeared with her coat on.

'I'll see you in the morning then.'

'Thank you, darling,' said Ellen, leaning across the counter and kissing Nicky on the cheek.

'Will you lock me out?' Nicky asked.

'No, just close the door over. I'll only be a few minutes.'

Nicky left and the shop was quiet for the first time all day.

Ellen finished cashing up, switched off the computer monitor and walked through to the back of the shop, turning lights off as she went. She found her coat and bag and went out into the yard at the back of the shop, closing the door behind her. As she turned the key in the lock, she glanced at the CCTV monitor through the window in the door and caught a movement. Ellen peered at the monitor. She could see the outline of a man in the darkness. He was looking in to the shop through the front window.

When they had first opened the shop, they had been so careful about security. Ellen watched the man as he moved off to the right. Toward the alley that led to the back of the shop. 'Shit,' she said under her breath.

She turned and hurriedly got into the car, glancing over her shoulder along the alley. She threw her bag on the back seat, put the key in the ignition and was about to close the car door when a gloved hand reached in from behind her and removed the key. Ellen gasped and struggled to close the car door but the man held it.

'Look, if you want the takings, they're in the back.'

'Sit still and don't turn around. I don't want your money.'

Ellen felt her stomach lurch in panic. She looked across toward the passenger door. Sat in the car she was vulnerable, but out of it she'd stand a chance. 'Then what do you want?' she said, trying to sound calm.

As if he was reading her mind, the man operated the car's central locking from the key fob and the locks on the three closed doors engaged with a clunk.

'Remain seated.'

Ellen's mind was racing but the panic was already turning to anger. She was not about to become this man's victim.

'Who are you?' she said through gritted teeth. 'What do you want?'

She wanted to see his face.

The man slammed his hand down, hard on the car roof.

The sound brought tears welling into her eyes. She wiped them away with the back of her hand.

'I said, do not turn around Miss Carmichael.'

Ellen gripped the steering wheel. 'How do you know my name?'

'I know a lot about you. I know about what you do, where you go and where you live. I know about Nicky, your partner, and your sister and her family. But they do not concern me. It is you who concerns me.'

'What are you talking about?'

'You know exactly what I am talking about. Your search has come to an end Miss Carmichael.'

'Search? What search?'

The man laughed. 'Very well. Let me spell it out for you. The woman you are looking for was killed in an air raid sixty years ago. Her mother accepted that and you will accept it now. Do you understand?'

Ellen's mind was running at a hundred miles an hour.

'If you do not, then she will not be the only one who is never seen again.'

'Are you threatening me?'

'Yes and believe me, I am not in the habit of making idle threats.'

'I'll call the police,' she said, her voice breaking. 'You have no right.'

'No, you will not. If you do, then right or no right, I will begin with your sister and her family. You are interfering in something that you do not understand. But enough. You will cease interfering from this point onwards. Do you understand?'

Ellen could not control the tears. 'Yes.'

'Good. I will now place the keys on the roof of your car. You will wait until I am gone before retrieving them,' the man paused 'Treat this as a friendly warning Miss Carmichael. I will be watching you. End the search for the woman. If you do as I say, then this will be the last time you will hear from me. The next time, if there is a next time, I will not be so friendly. Do I make myself clear?'

'Yes.'

Ellen heard him put the keys on the roof. She sat still and tried to stop herself shaking. She took several breaths and slowly looked over her shoulder. The man had gone. She retrieved the keys, closed the car door, pressed the central locking button and reached for her mobile phone.

Harry had finished his drink and was debating whether to have another, which would mean leaving the Spitfire outside and getting a cab home, when he felt his mobile phone vibrate in his pocket. He recognised the caller from the number displayed on the tiny screen.

'Hi Ellen. How did the stock take go?'

'Harry,' as soon she spoke Ellen found that she could not control herself and burst into tears.

'Ellen, what's wrong?'

'He was here Harry. The man who broke into your flat. He was here.'

'What? What do you mean he was there?'

'He was waiting for me when I left the shop.'

'Shit. Are you alright? Did he hurt you?'

'No. No. I am fine. He didn't touch me.'

'Where are you exactly?'

'I'm sitting in my car in the yard at the back of the shop.'

'Ellen, get out of the car and go back into the shop and lock yourself in. I'll call the police.'

'No! Don't do that. He knows where I live Harry. He knows where my sister lives. If we contact the police…'

'He threatened them?' Harry broke in.

'Yes. If we go to the police.'

'Ellen, listen to me. Get out of your car. Do it now. While you are in the phone to me. Go into the shop and lock yourself in.'

'I can't.' She was still shaking.

182

'Yes, you can. You'll be safer inside. If the man re-appears, dial 999. I don't care what he said. Just call them.'

'Alright. Stay on the phone.'

'I will. Don't worry.'

Harry heard her unlock her car door and close it again. 'Just a minute, I need to unlock the door.'

'OK.'

He heard the sound of her keys.

'Are you inside?' Harry asked.

'Yes.'

'Right. Now lock yourself in. Put all the lights on. Make yourself a cup of tea. I'll be there in less than thirty minutes. Remember, if he shows up again, call the police immediately.'

'I will.'

Harry was already heading for the door. Marcus and Mike had overheard most of Harry's conversion and had followed him to the door.

'Do you want me to come with you?' asked Mike.

'No, I'll handle this. I'll give you a ring later,' he shouted over his shoulder.

Once outside the pub, Harry sprinted across the road and ran down the side street, people scattering as he passed. The Spitfire started first time. He reached for a cigarette and lit it. Harry couldn't remember the last time he'd smoked in the car. He didn't like it, even with the hood down.

The drive to Barnet was a blur. Harry only slowed down when he rounded a bend and a police car pulled out behind him. Harry prayed that they were not on their way to Barnet. His prayer was answered when the police car turned left after a few minutes and Harry put his foot down again.

Finally, he pulled up outside the shop and called Ellen on his mobile. She answered straight away.

'I'm outside. Are you OK?'

'Yes. Yes I'm fine. Come round the back and I'll let you in.'

Harry was shocked at the state of her when she opened the door. She was as white as a sheet and her eye liner had run, leaving dark smears on her cheeks. As soon as he was inside, she was in his arms and hugging him tightly.

'It's alright. You are safe now,' he said soothingly.

'I was so frightened,' was all she could say.

After several minutes, they went into the workshop at the back of the shop and sat down.

'What are we going to do Harry?'

'Tell me exactly what he said.'

'He said that Martha was killed in an air raid sixty years ago. That her mother accepted that and that I must accept it now. He said that he knew where Nicky and my sister lives and that he'd be watching me. That if I continue the search for Martha, he would start with my sister and her family.'

'Jesus.' Harry fell silent.

Ellen looked at him. 'Why me Harry? Why not you?'

'I don't know. Maybe he saw you as a soft target. Maybe he thought that he could get at me through you.' Harry hesitated. 'Did he say anything about Belsize Park?'

'No. Why would he have?'

Harry hesitated. 'I wasn't going to tell you. I didn't want you worrying.'

'Worrying? About what?'

'I was with Mike, Marcus and Tom earlier. We are going into Belsize Park next week.'

Ellen looked aghast. 'What?'

'Tom has found a way to get into the shelter.'

'And you were not going to tell me?'

'I didn't want to worry you. Not after the break in. It frightened you Ellen, I know it did.'

'Of course it frightened me and I'm even more afraid now. That man, whoever he is, means it Harry. Do you understand? If he had wanted to, he could have taken me tonight and then you'd be looking for another missing woman.'

Harry paled. 'Ellen, this man, whoever he is, cannot possibly know about our plans for Belsize Park. We can be in and out in one evening. If we're careful, he won't even know that we were there.'

'I cannot believe that you are even thinking about it,' Ellen said, furiously.

'Which is why you should stay out of it. If he's watching you, then he'll think we've dropped it.'

'Harry, you cannot go into Belsize Park. Not after tonight. It is too dangerous.'

'But think about it. We must be getting close. Why else would he have taken the log? Why the threats?'

'Harry, for God's sake. Listen to yourself. We can't even prove that she was there.'

'Yes we can. We can find out what they did with her.'

'But we don't even know who "they" are,' Ellen pleaded.

'Whoever they are, and whoever he is, he won't be expecting us to go into the shelter.'

Ellen was quiet for a moment. 'Harry please. There must be some other way. Don't go down there.'

'I have come this far. I am going into the shelter and I am going to find out what happened to Martha.'

Ellen was ashen again. '*You* have come this far. *You* are going to find out what happened to Martha. When did this stop being about us and start being about you Harry?'

'I didn't mean it like that. You know I didn't.'

'Do I?' Ellen stood up and put her coat on. 'For God's sake Harry. People are at risk here. Real people. This isn't some bloody research project.'

'I can't give up now Ellen. We're too close.'

She opened the back door open and looked at him.

'Come back to my place. I don't want you to be on your own tonight. I'm worried about you.'

'You could have fooled me. Go home Harry,' Ellen answered. Her eyes were as cold as he had ever seen them.

Harry got into the Spitfire and started the engine with every intention of driving off into the night. How could she even think of giving it up when they were at last making progress? Real progress or why had the man broken into his flat and why had he threatened her? They were so close. Harry thumped his hands on the steering wheel. 'Damn it and damn him.'

He'd hardly noticed the two middle aged women, weaving their way toward him, but they'd noticed him. Startled momentarily by the noise of his hands hitting the steering wheel, the taller of the two tottered towards him. She was wearing impossibly high heels and a ridiculously short skirt. She tapped on the Spitfire's window, giggling and waving toward her friend. Harry tried to ignore her but she carried on knocking. He wound down the window.

'Bad night sweetheart? We'll cheer you up, won't we Linda?'

Harry was dizzy just breathing in the alcohol on her breath.

'I'm waiting for someone. My girlfriend. She'll be out in a moment.'

'We don't mind sharing, do we Linda?' she said, calling to her friend over her shoulder.

'Sorry ladies.'

'Spoil sport,' and she tottered back to Linda who was holding on to a street lamp in order to avoid falling over. Harry watched them stagger off into the distance, their bottoms wiggling in their skirts.

He sighed. Ellen was right, of course. The search for Martha Watts was about the two of them. It had always been about the two of them.

He got out of the car and walked around to the back of the shop. Ellen was standing at the back door, apparently deep in thought.

'Ellen, I'm sorry. You are right. Finding Martha… well, it is important. But you are more important.' He looked at her and held her gaze. 'It has always been about you.' He coughed and ran his fingers through his hair.

'You always do that. When you're nervous.'

'What?' said Harry.

'Cough and that thing with your hair.'

'Do I?'

'Yes you do.'

Harry put his hands in his pocket. 'Do you remember when I came to meet Elsie? I saw you getting out of your car. In the town square. I was watching you from a cafe across the road. I had no idea who you were. But I thought that you were the most beautiful woman I had ever seen. I was right. You are.'

Ellen pulled a face. 'Cut the crap, Stammers.'

Harry tried to look hurt.

'I'm coming with you,' she said.

'What?' Harry could not hide his surprise.

'I'm coming with you. To the shelter.'

Harry didn't know what he had expected her to say, but it certainly hadn't been that.

'Are you serious? You said yourself that its going to be dangerous.'

'I know and I was right. I'm always right, by the way.'

She said it with a straight face and for a moment Harry wondered whether she was actually serious.

'Finding Martha is important to both of us and it is something we need to do together,' she said.

'But we are going to be abseiling one hundred down a lift shaft. I'm wetting myself, just thinking about it and I have done quite a bit of abseiling before.'

'Abseiling?'

'Yes and if you've not done it before, you'll never manage it.'

'In which case it is a good job that I have done it before. As a matter of fact,' she said smiling and folding her arms, 'I rather suspect that I have done a good deal more abseiling than you have.'

Harry didn't know how to answer that. Instead, he grinned. 'I wondered how you got those muscles.'

'And which muscles might those be,' she said taking him in her arms and kissing him.

CHAPTER TWENTY-NINE

The tow path was in near darkness. What little light there was shone down onto the canal from the street lamps above and shimmered on the rippling water. The air temperature had dropped by several degrees as Tomasz made his way down the steps. A light breeze was blowing along the canal, but he was already sweating as he stepped on to the tow path and turned to pass under the bridge. The walls on either side were covered in graffiti. The pungent smell of urine filled his nostrils. He could almost taste it. This place reminded him of the slums in Kraków where he grew up. The places where the homeless now lived. They smelt like this.

As he passed under the bridge he heard a grunt and then a cough. Tomasz stood still. He knew what kind of people used these places. Whether you were in London or Kraków. He saw a movement and peered into the darkness. A man was sitting in the shadows, against the wall on the opposite bank. Tomasz could see what looked like a bottle in his hand. Or perhaps it was a beer can. Tomasz spat, even though his mouth was dry.

A few dozen paces further on, he stopped again. He could turn around now. He could go back the way he had come. Move to another city. Manchester or maybe Leeds. Perhaps he could take his sister with him. They could start again. With his talents, it would not be so difficult.

Tomasz thought, seriously for the first time, about running. He had met people like this man before. In Poland, there were many such men, controlling the lives of the ordinary people. In some places you could not work, or get a place to live, or borrow money without their say so. He had come to England to escape them and yet here he was. It was the same wherever you went.

'Out late, Dabrowski?' said the man, stepping out from the shadows. 'You should be more careful. You never know who you might meet down here, wandering about like you own the fucking place.'

Tomasz looked at the man, his thoughts of running evaporating in the breeze. 'You told me to come. So I have come.'

'I can see that. Obedient lot, you Poles. Fucking stupid but at least you do as you're told.'

Tomasz felt the insult in the pit of his stomach. 'What do you want?'

'You know what I want.'

He did know. He thought again about running. The man was too big to tackle directly. He would be too strong. But big men generally could not run and perhaps Tomasz could outpace him.

As if he had heard Tomasz's thoughts, the man stepped to the side.

'Thinking about running Dabrowski?'

Tomasz said nothing.

'Go ahead. Run all the way back to Warsaw if you like and take that whore of a sister with you. Perhaps our friends in Warsaw will take her in payment for what we will ask them to do to you.' The man hesitated. 'Second thought, better make that part-payment. Your sister is an ugly bitch.'

Tomasz felt bitterness rising in his throat. 'Kraków. I come from Kraków.'

Tomasz didn't see the blow coming until it was too late. The back of the man's hand struck him on the side of his face with such force that he was knocked several feet backwards. He stood swaying, the taste of blood in his mouth.

'Stop wasting my fucking time,' the man spat. 'Did Stammers swallow the bait?'

'Yes.'

'When?'

'Next week. Friday.' Tomasz spat the blood from his mouth onto the tow path.

'Good. He believed your story?'

Tomasz nodded.

'Idiot. He does not suspect?'

'No. I am his friend. What is there to suspect?'

The man ignored his question. 'How many of them?'

'Two. I will stay on top of the lift. The fourth man will be watching the cameras.'

'Excellent. The fewer people in the lift shaft, the less likely that you will be discovered.'

Tomasz looked at the ground. How could he go through with it? He would be sending Harry to an almost certain death.

'I hope you are not having second thoughts Dabrowski.'

'What you are asking…' Tomasz hesitated. 'The fall. It will kill him.'

The man stepped forward and suddenly his hand was around Tomasz's throat. His face came close. Even with his breathing restricted, Tomasz could smell the alcohol and cigarettes.

'Listen to me you shit. I am not asking. I am telling. You will follow my instructions to the letter. You do that and we will consider your debt paid. You can fuck off back to Poland and your sister and little Dita can get on with their lives. You fuck up, and believe me, when I have finished with Dita, she will be lucky to have any fucking life at all. She certainly won't be having any children of her own. Do you know what I mean?' The man leered in Tomasz's face.

Tomasz's head was swimming and the man's voice had begun to sound muzzled.

'But, Ellen. She knows as much as he knows,' Tomasz choked.

'I will deal with her. In fact I have already introduced myself. I didn't even have to touch her and she was shitting her knickers. I will enjoy convincing her to forget all about it. If you are very lucky, I might even let you watch.'

The man released his grip and Tomasz fell to the ground. He lay there panting.

'Get up.'

Tomasz tried to scramble to his feet but was too dizzy. He knelt on all fours panting.

'Fucking Polaks. Not a fucking man among you. At least your women know how to have a good time.' The man grinned broadly. 'Just make sure you do it right or you'll be hearing Dita's screams from whatever hole you try to hide in. Got it?' and with that the man pushed Tomasz to the ground with his foot.

'I said, got it?'

'Yes,' Tomasz coughed. And the man was gone.

CHAPTER THIRTY

Max Banks put the phone down and leaned back in the leather library chair.

'Well?' asked his mother.

'It is arranged.'

'And you will dispose of the Pole once Stammers is dealt with?'

'Mother, for heaven's sake. Stephens will ensure that Dabrowski keeps his mouth shut. Be assured of that.'

His mother turned to face him, leaning heavily on her stick. 'I have told you. I want the Pole removed,' she said. 'We cannot risk him talking.'

'Dabrowski will not talk. Stephens will make certain of that. In any case, when Dabrowski does as he has been instructed he will implicate himself. From that point on he will have a better reason than anyone to keep his mouth shut. Unless, of course, he wishes to spend the rest of his life in prison.'

'What part of "I want him removed" did you not understand? Stammers must be dealt with and the Pole removed.'

Banks got up from his chair and reached for the decanter on the sideboard. 'I do not have time for this, Mother. I am trying to run a leadership campaign,' he said, pouring himself a drink.

His mother brought up her stick and slammed it hard on the desk, knocking her own glass onto the floor. 'Do not defy me Maximillian. If Stammers succeeds in uncovering our little secret then your career will be over, along with everything that I have worked for all these years. You're just like your father. No backbone. I want the Pole removed. Is that clear?'

He banged his glass down. 'Do not compare me to Father. He had neither the acumen nor the ambition to run a business like ours. While he was a director he was a liability. Since his retirement, he has been nothing but an embarrassment. I have never understood why you did not dispense with him years ago.'

'You know full well why I did not dispense with him.'

He picked up his drink and drained the glass. He did know. It was by keeping his father by her side that the secret had endured. Away from her influence, his father's resolve would have weakened long ago.

He had always despised him. What little personality his father must have had as a young man had evidently withered under his mother's onslaught, because his earliest memories were of a father who could not make a decision without deference to her. By the time that he had hit thirteen, his father had retreated altogether to his study.

He remembered his thirteenth birthday. Mother had announced at dinner that she had secured a place for him at Eton. He would start there in September. Hastings and several of the other boys had already told him that they were going to Harrow and he had complained bitterly to his mother. But she had dismissed him with a wave of her hand. After dinner, he had knocked at his father's study door and begged him to intervene. 'Your mother has made up her mind,' had been the inevitable response.

'But father, I will never see Hastings again.'

His father had looked up from his papers and observed him blankly. 'Who?'

Hastings had been his closest friend since his first days at school. They had spent repeated summers together. He had been on holiday with the Hastings family on several occasions. How could his father not even know who Hastings was?

'You're just scared of her. You're a bloody coward,' he had shouted. Then he'd turned and run from the room, slamming the door as hard as he could as he left. As he ran up the stairs, he had half hoped that his father would erupt from his study in anger. But the door had remained closed.

'What about the Carmichael woman?'

Banks hesitated. Dealing with Ellen Carmichael was going to be more awkward. 'Stephens has already paid Miss Carmichael a visit. He is in no doubt that with Stammers out of the way and the Pole silenced, we will have no further trouble from her.'

'It is so typical of you to underestimate the female. Miss Carmichael has proven, thus far, to be a woman of some resolve. That does not surprise me. She comes from a good family.'

Banks almost choked. 'A good family? How in God's name do you know that?'

'I have been making my own enquiries Maximilian. Her father was Thomas Carmichael QC.'

'Was?'

'Yes. He died in 1997 of cancer of the bowel, after a long and rather unpleasant illness. Indeed, Miss Carmichael comes from a long and rather distinguished line of lawyers but, apparently, was determined to make her own way in life. A most admirable attitude, wouldn't you say?'

Banks sighed. 'We will deal with her. I would rather not have to risk another accident. But if we have to, be assured mother that we will.'

'Yes, you will. If you had any sense you would have dealt with her already.'

Banks decided to remain silent. This was not an argument that he was going to win.

'What have you done with the diary and the book from Belsize Park?'

'They are quite safe, Mother.'

She turned and looked at him. 'I did not ask whether they were safe. I asked what you have done with them.'

'They are in my bag.'

'Give them to me.'

'You want them now?'

'That is what I said.'

Banks walked across to the desk and took the two books from his bag and handed them to her. She took them and, without so much as glancing at them, locked them in a desk drawer, putting the drawer key in her pocket.

'And Mr Watts?'

'In hospital.'

'Do the police realise that the diary was taken?'

'No. Stephens left no trace. Mr Watts was discovered by a neighbour who called an ambulance. He had fallen down the stairs of his own accord, albeit with a cricket bat in his hand.'

'And that didn't raise a suspicion?'

'Apparently not. Stephens was very careful.'

'But Mr Watts will know when he cannot locate the diary.'

'I doubt that. The old man was already senile. Stephens said that he heard him talking to himself. Fortunately, he received a nasty head injury from the fall and is not expected to regain consciousness.'

'That is fortunate indeed,' she said, walking to the window. Let us hope that Friday will bring an end to the matter.'

'There is no need to trust in fate, Mother. Mr Stammers has been so keen to find a body at Belsize Park. It is almost poetic that it will be his that is retrieved and nobody else's.'

CHAPTER THIRTY-ONE

Friday came more quickly than Harry had anticipated. Ellen collected him from his flat and they drove to Mike's house in the Saab.

'You've got good taste so far as cars are concerned, I'll give you that,' he said.

'I've had a Saab ever since I got my licence. This is my third one actually.'

Harry put his hand on Ellen's thigh and squeezed it. She was wearing black climbing trousers and shoes. 'I've never seen you in trousers,' he grinned. 'You look pretty good.'

'Thanks.' She hesitated. 'You're nervous aren't you? I can tell.'

'A bit.'

'Me too. But once we're in, the adrenaline will kick in. That should take care of any nerves. It usually does.'

Harry nodded. Ellen appeared confident and unflustered by what they were about to do. This was a new side to her character that he had not seen before. He liked it.

'Did you remember your camera?' she asked.

'Yes, it is in my back pack.'

'I brought one too. If we do find anything, then we should take as many photographs as possible.'

They pulled up in front of Mike's house. Marcus's van was already parked outside. They got out, took their bags from the boot and Harry knocked on the door. Mike opened it and they went inside. Harry glanced at his watch. It was a few minutes after eight.

Mike showed them through to the dining room. Marcus was seated at the breakfast bar drinking coffee. Tomasz was sat at a table in the corner. Mike had set up a temporary workstation, a network cable stretching across the room and out into the hallway. Tomasz and Marcus were both dressed, head to toe, in black.

'Jesus, we look like a gathering of bank robbers. Marcus, have you got the sawn-off?'

They all laughed, except Tomasz who was concentrating on the monitor screen. Harry glanced across at him.

'I usually use wireless, but Tom reckons that a wireless connection might not have been man enough for the job, so he's rigged me up a cable,' Mike said.

Harry walked across to Tom and stood, looking over his shoulder. On the monitor screen Harry could see the feeds from six of the cameras at the Belsize Park shelter.

'That's incredible. There is no way that they can tell we are watching?'

'The guards, no,' Tom replied. 'The IT company, maybe. If they bother to check the log. Then they will see an unusual IP address.'

'Can't they trace our location from that?'

'No. We are using a proxy. So all they will find is the proxy's address in California. Besides, why would they check? It is Friday. They will have all gone home for the weekend.'

'Are there just six cameras?' Harry asked.

'No. There are twelve,' Tomasz said. He clicked on an icon and the screen changed to cameras seven to twelve.

'There are cameras in the entrance lobby, the stair well, the lobby at the bottom of the lift shaft, the shelter itself and look,' he clicked on camera twelve and the image filled the screen.

'The control room?' said Harry, peering at the monitor.

'Yes.'

Harry could see the two guards seated at a desk. On the desk were two monitor screens. One of the guards was reading a newspaper. The other was eating what appeared to be a sandwich.

'The guards can view both sets of cameras. Two banks of six, one on each monitor,' said Tom.

'The cameras in the lobby and the shelter tunnels are going to be a problem. Can't we turn them off or something,' said Harry.

'If we do, we risk the guards investigating,' said Mike from behind them. 'But we can do better than that. Show them, Tom.'

Tom clicked on an icon and the view reverted to a panel of six pictures. He clicked on camera five. The dimly lit lobby at the bottom of the lift shaft filled the screen. Then he clicked on an icon in the corner of the image that looked like a joystick. 'Watch,' he said. He manipulated the joystick and the camera view moved. 'Slowly, slowly,' said Tom. 'We don't want the guards to notice. If we point the camera away from the lift, it won't be as easy for them to see you as you leave the lift shaft.'

'Can't they move it back?' asked Ellen.

'Yes, normally. But I am going to disable their controls.'

'What about the cameras in the shelter tunnels?'

'There are four. Cameras nine to twelve,' Tom said clicking on their views, one after the other.

Harry looked closely. 'They look pretty dim and there is no colour.'

'They have night vision when the main lights are out. Mike will need to watch them carefully and point them away if you come into view. You will need to dim your torches too. Otherwise the guard may see the beam.'

'How we will do that? My torch doesn't have a dimmer,' said Harry.

'We've thought of that,' replied Mike. He put his hand in his pocket and pulled out a pair of socks. 'Put these over your torches,' he handed one each to Ellen and Harry. 'That should give you just enough light to make your way along without the guards spotting you.'

'Pure genius,' said Harry, grinning.

'Once you are in the service tunnel, you can remove the socks. There are no cameras down there. But be careful not to point your torches back towards the main tunnel. There is a camera at the far end and any reflections will show up like a beacon,' said Mike.

'OK, that is all looking good,' said Harry. 'Marcus, what about the climbing gear?'

'It is all in the van.'

'Another thought,' said Mike. 'When we are in the lift shaft, try to keep away from the sides of the shaft if you can. They are steel mesh. I will point the cameras in the stair well at the stairs or the outer wall, but there are points at which the mesh of the shaft is in view. Thankfully the main stair lights will be off and the emergency lighting is fairly dim, so even if you come into view it may not be obvious to the guards. But we don't want any movement catching their eye.'

Harry nodded. 'Mike have you got the radios?'

'Yes, just a moment.' He retrieved them from his bag and handed one each to Ellen, Harry, Marcus and Tom. 'Tom, is your mobile charged?'

'Yes,' replied Tom.

'Does anyone have any questions?' asked Harry.

'Yes. I do,' said Mike.

They all turned towards him.

'What happens if you get caught?'

They were silent for a moment.

'If we get caught, then everybody sticks to the line that it was my idea,' said Harry. 'We were there to find and photograph the discussed tunnel. It should be really easy to stick to that. It is, after all, the truth.'

'OK but how are you going to explain your method of entry?' asked Mike.

'I don't know, but we must not reveal that Tom obtained the combination by hacking into their system. If we do, then we could all be in deep water. Using a combination number that we have obtained through hacking almost certainly amounts to breaking and entering.'

'So how are you going to explain it?' asked Mike.

'Do we have to explain it?' said Ellen.

They all looked at her.

'I mean, I have never done anything like this before, but surely if we get caught and the police want to charge us, then the onus will be on them to prove, beyond reasonable doubt, that we committed an offence. It will be undeniable that that we went in through the main door because that will be on the camera in the lobby, but it will also be evident that we got in without causing any damage.'

They were all silent.

'Unless anyone can think of anything better, I think Ellen is right. If we get caught then we tell the truth:- the door was unlocked when we went in. Let them prove that we had the combination. Remember, this is simply a contingency. We are not going to get caught, are we?'

'Let's hope not,' said Ellen.

Harry looked at his watch. It was just after eight thirty. 'Mike, can we get a coffee and go over the plan, once more?'

Harry, Ellen, Marcus and Tom sat in the van, Harry in the front with Marcus.

'Are you alright back there?' Harry called through the hatch.

'It is not exactly comfortable,' replied Ellen 'but we're fine.'

'Good job your windscreen is tinted,' said Harry.

'Yes, why is your windscreen tinted?' called Ellen from behind them.

'You don't want to know,' grinned Marcus. 'This van has seen more than its fair share of action,' he said winking at Harry.

'Oh God,' said Ellen from behind.

Harry laughed. He looked at his watch. It was 21.52.

'Better be quiet now. They are due at any moment,' Harry said and, as if on cue, a red Ford Mondeo pulled up and parked opposite them. Marcus picked up his mobile and dialled Mike's number. Two uniformed security guards, each carrying a bag over their shoulder, got out of the Mondeo and made their way toward the shelter.

'Mike?' Marcus whispered. 'They've arrived. You should have them in view in a few moments,' he said, pressing the speaker phone button.

The security guard stopped and punched a number into the lock. He opened the door and went inside.

'Got him,' said Mike.

'Is everybody ready?' asked Harry.

They each said that they were.

'As soon as they are in the staff room, we go,' said Harry, sounding tense.

'They're walking down the corridor to the control room,' said Mike. 'They're inside. Talking.'

They waited. Harry was holding his breath. Minutes passed.

'Shit. Why aren't they moving?' Harry said out loud.

'They're still talking.'

'Shit.'

'It's alright, they're moving,' said Mike's voice over the speakerphone. 'They're walking further down the corridor. Just a second.'

'What?' they all said at once.

'Its alright. I was just moving the camera. The entrance to the staff room at the end of the corridor was barely visible so I moved it. I can see them now. They're going in,' he paused for a moment. 'That's it. They're inside. Good luck guys… and girl.'

Harry wound down the window and looked both ways. The street was empty. 'OK. Let's go.' Harry hissed.

CHAPTER THIRTY-TWO

Marcus and Harry got out and Marcus slid the van's side door open. Ellen and Tomasz clambered out. Ellen passed Harry his back pack and slung hers across her shoulder.

Marcus picked up a large bag with the ropes and other abseiling gear inside. He shut the van door.

'Hurry,' whispered Harry. 'We don't to be seen by the neighbours.'

They ran across the road to the shelter door.

'All clear inside?' Marcus said into the phone and nodded.

Tomasz punched the number into the lock and the door buzzed. The buzzer sounded like the loudest burglar alarm Harry had ever heard.

'Shit,' Harry whispered, through clenched teeth.

They hesitated.

'Mike, is there any movement inside?' Marcus spoke into his mobile. 'Thank Christ for that.' He shook his head. 'Nothing.'

They opened the door. Marcus, Harry and Ellen ran across to the lift. Tomasz made his way down the corridor and disappeared into the control room.

Harry eased the lift gates open, trying to make as little noise as possible. He caught Ellen's eye. 'How the hell did they miss that?' he said glancing towards the main door. Ellen shrugged. 'I don't know and right now, I don't care.'

Marcus was the first into the lift, followed by Harry. Marcus bent down onto all fours and Harry went to clamber on his back.

Ellen put her hand on Harry's shoulder. 'I'll go first,' she whispered. 'I'm lighter. I can pull up the bags.' She clambered into Marcus's back and reached up to the hatch. She pushed and the hatch door swung upwards. She hauled herself up onto the lift roof. Marcus stood up.

'What a woman,' he said grinning.

'Marcus!' came Ellen's voice from above them. 'The climbing gear?'

Marcus retrieved the bags and passed then up to Ellen, one at a time.

'You go next Marcus. I'll wait for Tom.' Harry bent over and Marcus climbed on to his back and hauled himself through the open hatch.

Harry looked at his watch. Three minutes had passed. 'Come on Tom,' he said peering out of the lift toward the control room. Several more minutes passed. 'Come on,' he said through gritted teeth. After a few moments Tomasz appeared. Harry breathed out. Tom ran down the corridor and into the lift.

'Jesus, Tom. You took your time.'

'Sorry.'

'You next.' Harry bent over and Tom clambered up to the hatch.

'Harry! The lift gate!' hissed Marcus.

Harry turned and began to close the lift gate. It was then that he heard voices. 'Mike says the guards are moving,' whispered Ellen from above.

Harry eased the lift gate closed as silently as he could. He was sweating profusely.

Marcus had let a rope down from above. Harry grabbed it and shimmied his way up far enough to grab the loft hatch. 'Hurry,' whispered Ellen.

Harry was struggling to pull himself through the hatch door. Suddenly Marcus put his hand under Harry's arm pit and hauled him up.

'The rope,' hissed Marcus.

Harry dragged the rope up, just as the day guard came within sight of the lift car. Ellen, who had the phone in one hand, put the finger of her free hand to her lips. 'Shh,' she mouthed silently.

Harry could barely see her in the half light.

The four of them stood in a tight huddle, holding their breath. After what seemed like an age, they heard the retreating footsteps of the guard as he made his way back to the control room.

'That was close,' said Ellen. 'Mike says that the guard stopped about twelve feet form the lift gate and looked around, as though he had heard something.'

'Good job he didn't notice that,' said Marcus pointing to the open hatch.

Harry bent down and closed the hatch door.

There wasn't a great deal of space on top of the lift car. Several greasy black steel cables ran from its centre up to the top of the shaft. Harry could see the running gear up above them. On the roof of the lift car was a metal box. It was padlocked shut and, presumably bolted to the roof of the lift car. Harry wondered what it contained, but gave it little thought.

The lift car itself was tight against the shaft on three sides. But at the rear was a narrow void, just wide enough to provide access to the shaft below. Harry peered over the edge. His eyes had already adjusted to the low light and the lift shaft appeared reasonably well lit by the emergency lights in the adjoining stair well. But still, it looked one hell of a drop. He could barely make out the bottom of the shaft.

Marcus was busy preparing the ropes and tackle. 'We'll use this,' he said, pointing to an anchor point in the centre of the lift car roof. 'Once I have attached the rope, be careful not to trip over it.'

'What are the guards doing?' said Ellen into the phone. She paused while she listened to Mike's reply. Then she relayed back, 'They're reading. They haven't even noticed that they've can't control the cameras.'

'Excellent,' replied Harry.

'We're ready,' said Marcus.

They all looked at each other.

'I'll go first,' said Harry.

'I thought Marcus was going first. Then Ellen. Then you Harry,' said Tomasz.

'Did we agree that?' replied Harry, a puzzled expression on his face.

'Yes, we did,' said Tomasz.

'Well it doesn't really matter,' offered Ellen.

'We should stick to the plan. Harry last down and first up.' Tomasz was insistent.

Harry looked at Ellen questioningly. He really couldn't remember agreeing a climbing order.

Ellen shrugged.

'How about I go down first and come up first. Ellen second. Marcus third?' Harry suggested.

'That's a deal,' said Ellen.

Tomasz didn't answer.

Marcus took three hard hats from his bag and handed one each to Harry and Ellen. 'I don't want any accidents,' he said. They put them on. Then he reached down and handed them each a harness. 'It looks like a reasonably straight forward decent, but remember to try to stay off the lift shaft wall.'

Harry put on his harness and secured it to the rope.

'Harry?' said Ellen.

He looked at her.

'Go carefully,' she said, kissing him lightly on the cheek.

'I will.'

Harry let himself over the side and stepped down the side of the car. He reached the bottom and manoeuvred himself so that he could let himself down into the void beneath. There was no room to jump out in the conventional manner, so he had to let himself down slowly. He was soon swinging in free air, letting the rope out, one arm at a time. It took some minutes to reach the bottom. Harry stepped on to the ground and took the radio out of his jacket pocket.

'I'm down. Ellen next and tell her to be careful.' He looked up but it was some minutes before Ellen came into view, out of the gloom. He watched her as she let out the rope and descended. Her movements were smooth and confident. She stepped down and smiled. 'That was fun,' she said, disconnecting her harness from the rope.

After a few minutes, the radio crackled 'Marcus is on his way.'

Ellen and Harry stood at the bottom of the lift shaft.

'Has Mike pointed the camera away from the lift gate?' Harry radio'd to Tomasz on top of the lift car.

'Wait,' came Tomasz's reply.

A few moments later the radio crackled 'Yes, the camera is pointing at the far side of the lobby. If you keep to the same side of the lobby as the lift, Mike says that you will be obscured.'

Marcus had soon joined them. He disconnected himself from the rope. 'All set?' he said.

Ellen and Harry nodded.

'Socks on then,' he said grinning.

Harry and Ellen retrieved their torches from their backpacks and slid the socks from their pockets over the lenses.

'Go carefully and call if you need anything. I should be able to hear you but, if we lose contact, don't panic. Once you turn the corner into the service tunnel, the signal may begin to break up.'

They both stepped out of the lift shaft. Harry swept the lower lobby with his eyes and gestured toward the camera. It was high up to their left, pointing across the lobby to the opposite wall. 'Follow me.'

Ellen nodded.

They approached the entrance gate to the shelter. They opened it and walked through, closing the gate behind them.

'Marcus, do you copy?' Harry spoke into the radio.

'Yup.'

'Could you ask Tom to check with Mike where the camera above the shelter entrance is pointing. I think it was camera nine.'

Tomasz interrupted. 'I can still hear you Harry. Just a minute.'

They waited.

'Mike says that he has pointed camera nine at the tunnel floor. If you are quick you will only be in view for a second or two. Mike is watching the guards. They're still reading. So you are good to go.'

Harry looked at Ellen. 'Ready?'

Ellen nodded.

'On the count of three. One, two, three,' and they ran into the shelter. After five or six yards they stopped and looked back. They could see the camera above the entrance way, pointing downwards.

'All clear?' Harry said into the portable radio.

Marcus relayed the answer. 'The guards didn't even glance up. Mike says your socks look good though.'

'Good. I'll call you every ten minutes or so, Marcus.'

'Roger that.'

Ellen giggled. 'Roger that,' she mimicked.

Harry and Ellen looked around. They could not see much. While the lobby at the bottom of the lift had been illuminated by the emergency lighting, the same could not be said for the main tunnel. Other than a series of tiny red lights, spaced at regular intervals along the tunnel's ceiling, the shelter was in complete darkness.

Harry pointed at the nearest of the lights. 'Smoke detectors?'

'Probably. And maybe a sprinkler system.' She had walked across to a row of shelves. 'With all this paper down here,' she said, reaching for a pile of dusty documents, 'and a gentle breeze, any fire and the place would go up like an inferno.'

Harry walked past her and shone his torch ahead of them. He turned and they stared at each other. 'Bunks,' he said. 'Thousands of them probably.'

'It is amazing that they are still down here,' Ellen observed.

'I don't suppose they could easily get them out.'

The bunks ran along the left hand side of the tunnel. They were dusty but there was little sign of rust. 'I guess with no real dampness down here, everything has stayed pretty much as it was,' Harry said.

The right side of tunnel was lined with more modern shelving, stacked with box files, but as they progressed along the tunnel, the shelves gave way to more steel bunks, two high. The mattresses had been removed, leaving the steel mesh on which they would have sat, exposed. The only sound in the tunnel was the occasional rumble of an underground train, passing through the station above.

As they made progress they came across occasional gated side passages and, after twenty minutes or so, a partition wall. Harry disappeared behind it and, after a few seconds re-emerged. 'Nothing very exciting, I'm afraid,' he said. 'Its a toilet.'

'How far before we get to the service passage through to the disused tunnel?' Ellen asked.

'According to the plans, it is at the far end, on the left. I better radio Marcus.'

'Marcus, its Harry, do you copy?'

'Yes, loud and clear. Is everything alright?'

'Yes, just checking in. No problems this end.'

'Good. All quiet here too.'

'Is Tomasz alright?'

'Hang on. Tomasz how are you doing up there?'

Harry couldn't hear the response.

'He says he's fine,' Marcus relayed.

'Great, we're nearing the end of the main tunnel. We may lose you when we turn left, but I'll give you a shout once we are inside.'

'No worries.'

Ellen spotted the camera on the wall, just before the tunnel's end. It was pointing downwards, away from the service passage to their left.

'If we keep to the left, we will be out of the view,' said Harry.

They skirted the camera's field of vision, turned left into the service passage and were immediately confronted by a steel gate. A wide wooden sign, attached to the gate, ordered "NO PUBLIC ACCESS. KEEP OUT." The gate itself was chained and padlocked.

'Shit,' Ellen hissed.

Harry calmly took off his back pack. 'Good job I bought these,' he said, removing a pair of bolt cutters from the bag.

'God above, they look heavy. How did you manage that?'

'I was a boy scout,' Harry lied. He never was.

'You are going to struggle to get back up the rope with that in your bag.'

'So I'll leave them behind,' Harry replied, grinning.

The bolt cutters made short work of the chain and they were soon through the gate.

Unlike the shelter's main tunnel, the service passage beyond the gate was covered in black grime.

'It doesn't look like anyone has been down here in a very long time,' Ellen observed, shining torch into the passage.

A few yards ahead of them, Harry spotted a wooden box. He knelt down beside it and, from beneath, produced an old newspaper. 'Look at this.'

Ellen joined him. '17th of August 1947,' she read out loud.

The paper crumbled in Harry's hands as he turned the pages. 'I think you're right. I don't think this tunnel has been used in quite a while.'

They discovered occasional rooms to their left and right as they made their way along the passage. They entered each room and searched it in turn, taking occasional photographs with the cameras they had each brought with them. Most of the rooms were empty. One was full of filthy grey blankets, piled in heaps. Another had several mattresses stacked against the far wall. But there was nothing of great interest.

'We turn left at the bottom of this passage to get to the disused tunnel. I hope it has not been bricked up. Bolt cutters were one thing. But a sledge hammer was beyond even my limits.' Harry said, as they neared the intersection.

'I guess we'll find out soon enough. Hey, we can remove our socks,' Ellen added, pulling the sock from her flashlight and tucking it in her pocket.

'Yes, I had completely forgotten.' His laughter turned into a sneezing fit. 'The dust down here. Its awful.'

The additional light from their torches flooded the way ahead, enabling swifter progress. The passage soon came to an end at a tee-junction. A sign in front of them directed "MAINTENANCE STAFF" to the right. Ellen looked left, shining her torch ahead, into the darkness. 'Look,' she said.

Visible in the distance ahead of them was another steel gate. 'Can you read what the sign says?' Harry asked, peering into the tunnel.

'I think it says "no access", but I can't quite make it out. That's it isn't it? The disused tunnel,' she said.

'Right where the plans said it would be,' Harry replied.

Ellen turned and was about to make her way toward the gate. Harry took hold of her arm. 'I'd like to try the other way first,' he said, glancing to their right.

'Why?'

Harry shrugged. 'I don't know. For completeness?' In truth he didn't know. But something, at the back of his mind, was telling him that there was something they needed to see. A nagging voice.

Ellen stared at him. 'Okay.'

'We better try Marcus again first.' Harry pulled the radio from his pocket. 'Marcus, it's Harry. Do you copy?'

The reply was weak but still audible.

'We're at the end of the service tunnel. We may lose you from here,' Harry said into the radio.

'No worries. Take care you two.'

Harry stashed the radio back in his pocket and they set off.

The tunnel turned gently and, after a few minutes, ended suddenly, with a door way marked "STAFF". Harry put his hand on the door handle and froze.

'What is it?' Ellen asked.

'Nothing,' he said casually but he let go of the handle without opening the door.

'Harry?' She shone the torch into his face. He looked deathly pale in the torchlight. 'What's wrong?'

'I don't know. I had an odd feeling that's all.'

'Odd? What do you mean?'

'Nothing.' He took a step backward, rubbing his hands together.

'You felt something?'

Harry hesitated. 'It's ridiculous.'

'No, its not. What did you feel?'

'I don't know.' He was struggling for words. 'A sort of feeling of deja-vu?'

'Like you were here before?'

'Sort of.' Harry shivered. 'Maybe the atmosphere of the place is getting to me.' He smiled, trying to make light of a strange feeling of ill ease that had settled into the pit of his stomach.

'Let me,' she said reaching for the door handle. She opened the door and stepped into the room.

Harry stood in the doorway, peering into the gloom.

'It's fine,' she said, turning to face him, her face illuminated by the torch light. 'Come on.'

They explored the room together. Against the far wall, were arranged two bunk frames that, like those in the main tunnel, had been stripped of their mattresses. A small wooden table stood in one corner and a row of metal lockers were lined up along one wall.

Harry approached the lockers and began searching each in turn. They were mostly empty. 'Not much in these,' he said, reaching for another locker door. As his fingers touched the grey metal, he felt a surge of anxiety that was so intense that it almost hurt. It was though someone had grabbed him and was squeezing his rib cage, forcing the air from his chest. He snatched his hand away and took a lung-full of air. But he said nothing.

He glanced at Ellen but she was absorbed with the contents of the desk draw.

'Look at this,' she called out.

Harry was happy to join her.

She had unfolded a set of tunnel drawings. 'Look at the stamp.'

'"BELCO London",' Harry read out loud.

They stood staring at the plans.

'We are getting close aren't we?' she said, reaching for his hand.

'I think so. If only we could find some sign that she was here.'

'Do you really think she was?'

He didn't think it. He knew it. But he could not explain how and was not about to try. 'Do you?'

Ellen looked around, gripping his hand tightly. She shone her torch into each corner of the room. 'I wish I knew, Harry.'

Harry returned his attention to the plans. He found the room where they were and then traced his finger along the route of the disused tunnel.

'It doesn't seem to go very far,' Ellen observed.

'I guess that's as far as they got before the tunnel flooded.'

'Maybe.'

'Let's go and find out,' he said pulling her by the hand.

'You really don't like it in here, do you?'

He stared at her. 'No. I don't,' he said, blinking in the torchlight.

She squeezed his hand.

'Let's take these with us,' he said, releasing her hand and reaching for the plans.

'Do you think we should?'

'No, of course we shouldn't. First rule of urban exploration. Or maybe it is the second rule. I can't remember. "Break nothing. Take nothing". Or something like that. But they are more detailed than the plans I found on the net and far too good to leave behind.' He folded the plans and handed them to Ellen. She put them in her backpack.

They left the staff room together. As soon as they were outside, Harry took a deep breath.

'Come on,' Ellen said, reaching for his arm.

They walked along the passage, passed the intersection, and approached the gate to the disused tunnel. It was heavily chained and padlocked.

Harry shone his torch at a pile of bricks that had been stacked against the tunnel wall. 'I wonder why they didn't brick it up?'

'Who knows? But I'm glad they didn't.'

Harry removed the bolt cutters from his back pack and cut through the rusty chains.

Ellen opened the gate and they walked several yards into the tunnel. 'There might not be any water, but it certainly smells damp,' she said. 'Kind of earthy. More so than the other tunnels.'

Harry agreed. This tunnel had a different atmosphere altogether and the darkness seemed more intense. More oppressive. He didn't think he had ever been anywhere as dark. To make the point, Harry asked Ellen to extinguish her torch. Then he did the same.

'OH MY GOD,' Ellen exclaimed. 'Can you even tell whether your eyes are open or closed?'

'No. I can't see a damned thing.'

'Neither can I.'

Ellen switched her torch back on. Light flooded the tunnel. It was so bright that Harry had to shield his eyes. When they had re-adjusted, Harry switched on his torch and they set off down the tunnel, exploring and taking photographs as they went.

'Look,' said Harry, pointing at the tunnel wall. 'There's a tide mark here. It may not be wet now, but it was, at some point.'

The tunnel sloped gently downwards. As they made their way along, Harry thought that he could hear the faint sound of dripping water. They encountered no rooms as such, although part-built spaces opened on each side. They searched each one but they were empty, save for the occasional pile of rubble, bricks and old tools. It was Harry who detected the first sign of water. It was trickling down the left hand tunnel wall. A little further on, they found a puddle.

Ellen was ahead of him by several yards. She called out. 'My torch is getting dim.'

'Damn it. They were supposed to last for at least four hours. Let's stick together and use one at a time,' he said, approaching her. Ellen switched off her torch and handed it to Harry. He stowed it in her backpack.

'Here,' he said, handing her his. 'You're in front, you better take mine.'

They had continued for only a few more yards, when Ellen stopped suddenly, shining her torch at a large steel door in the right hand tunnel wall. 'Look at this.'

Harry stepped forward and, as he did so, caught his foot and fell forward, knocking Ellen off balance. They both tumbled to the floor, the torch slipping from Ellen's hand. It hit the tunnel wall beside the steel door and went out.

They were plunged into complete darkness.

CHAPTER THIRTY-THREE

'Harry?'

Harry had hit the floor, hard. Had he not been wearing the hard hat he'd probably have been out for the count. As it was, it took him a few seconds to gather his thoughts, disorientated as he was in the darkness.

'Harry?'

'Its OK. Don't panic. I'm alright,' he coughed.

'Thank God. It is so dark. I can't find the torch.'

He could hear her moving about but could see absolutely nothing. He clambered onto all fours.

'Harry?'

'Its alright. Stay still. I'll see if I can find it.' He had found the tunnel wall and a gully at its base.

'Idiot,' said Ellen, 'I'm an idiot. The other torch is in my bag. Hang on.'

At that moment, Harry's hand closed around something soft in the darkness. Ellen's flashlight suddenly illuminated the tunnel and Harry was momentarily blinded.

'What's that?' said Ellen.

'What?' said Harry. He had brought the object up to shield his eyes.

'In your hand,' she said, crawling over to him.

Harry held the object in front of his face and tried to focus.

'Its a purse,' said Ellen.

Harry focussed. He was holding a small brown leather purse. It was unfastened.

'What's inside?'

'A few old coins, look,' he said emptying the coins into his hand.

'Try the side pocket. It is still closed.'

Harry undid the catch and opened the pocket. 'I can't see. Here, shine the torch.' Inside, there were two, folded yellow/brown bank notes. He took them out gently and unfolded them. 'Ten Shilling notes. Pre-decimalisation.'

'What's that?'

A small slip of brown paper had slid out from between the notes. Harry put the notes back in the purse and held the slip of paper under the torchlight.

'I don't believe it,' Ellen gasped.

Harry stared, open mouthed.

Ellen read aloud "Third class. British Railways. Number 16425. 10th November 1944. Bletchley to London. Single Only."

Harry was, for once, lost for words. After a few moments, he managed 'It's hers. I don't believe it.'

'Show me,' Ellen said excitedly.

Harry handed her the ticket and Ellen read it again. 'This is it, Harry. Proof that she was here.'

Ellen stood up and was using her torch to search the ground around them. Harry joined her. They found several more coins and, finally, Ellen reached down and picked up a small key. It was rusty and covered in grime. 'It's an unusual shape. I don't think I've ever seen one quite like it. Do you think it was Martha's?'

'Who knows?' Harry said, examining the key more closely. 'But there's a good chance that it was in the purse when she dropped it.

They stared at each other. 'Bletchley to London,' he said, shaking his head. 'I still can't quite believe it.'

'You were right. That intuition of your was spot on.'

Harry hugged her, their helmets clanking together.

'I'd better see if I can get the other torch working.' Harry retrieved the parts and put them back together but, when he operated the switch, nothing happened. 'Damn it. I'll take out the batteries, in case yours go,' he said unscrewing the base.

'What do we do now?', Ellen asked. 'She was here. But where did she go?'

'Lets look a little further down the tunnel.'

They walked along the tunnel, Ellen shining the torch back and forth. The floor descended gradually, getting steadily damper until eventually they were walking in standing water which gradually rose, covering first the toes of their boots and then lapping against their ankles.

'Harry, we ought to stop soon. The water is getting deeper and we shouldn't chance it with the torch. If this one fails we might have trouble finding our way out.'

Harry took some more photographs before they recounted their steps back to the steel door. They were about to leave when Harry turned and approached the door. He tried the handle, but it was locked firm. 'You don't suppose…'

'What?'

Harry stared at her.

'That she is in there?' Ellen said.

'Well she certainly wasn't brought down here for a picnic. She may have already been dead. Whoever brought her here would have wanted to hide her. If it was Wallington, then he might have had the keys to this. It could well be some kind of electrical installation and that is what BELCO were working on.'

Ellen examined the lock. 'Let me try the key.'

Harry retrieved it from his pocket.

'It doesn't fit,' Ellen said. 'Nowhere near.' She handed the key back to him. 'Do you really think that her body could have been hidden inside?'

'Where better?'

'Well there's no way we're going to be able to open it now,' she said.

'I know. We need to think about where we go from here. Let's get back to Marcus.'

Harry and Ellen made their way back through the tunnels, calling Marcus as soon as they had a signal. Sitting on top of the lift, Tomasz paid close attention to the conversation. If they had found evidence that the woman was in the tunnels, the man from the tow path would certainly want to know about it. If he could obtain the purse, it might even give him some bargaining power. It certainly wasn't going to be a lot of use to Harry.

While Harry and Ellen had been away, Tomasz had taken a key from his back pocket and had opened the box that was bolted to the top of the lift car. Inside had been a knife and a file. The instructions he had been given were to file part way through the rope where it ran over the side the lift car, to give appearance that the rope had frayed of its own accord. He was careful. He didn't want Marcus to notice any unusual movement, but fortunately there was a slight breeze in the lift shaft which made the rope sway. He had filed through roughly two thirds of its diameter. Once Harry was on the rope, he would file away what remained or cut it if he had to. After the fall, he had been told to put the key inside the box with the file and knife and to snap the lock shut, in case he was subsequently searched. They would be disposed of later.

Harry and Ellen had arrived at the bottom of the lift shaft. Marcus used the radio to call Tomasz. 'We are about to start the ascent. Is everything OK up there?'

'Yes. Is Harry coming up first as agreed?'

'Yes, alright.'

Tomasz was sweating.

Down below, Marcus, Harry and Ellen were exchanging glances.

'What is it with him?' said Marcus.

'I don't know. He's being a bit anal isn't he?' said Harry.

'Typical geek. Clever with a PC, but too far up his own backside. No sense of humour either,' Marcus joked.

'Come on guys, give him a break. He has done a great job with the cameras,' said Ellen putting her arm around Harry and kissing him on the cheek.

'I'm not looking forward to the climb, to be honest,' said Harry, gazing up the lift shaft.

'I tell you what. I'll go first,' said Marcus. 'I'll show you how its done,' he said, patting Harry on the shoulder. 'Just don't tell old brains up there. It will freak him out when I climb over the side and not you, Harry.'

'Good idea,' replied Harry, smiling broadly.

'Well, I think you are both being very unkind,' scolded Ellen.

Marcus made ready to climb the rope. When his gear was in place, he nodded to Harry.

Harry spoke into the radio. 'I'm on my way Tom.'

Marcus started to climb, jerking the ascender and stepping up the rope, one arm-length at a time. 'See, its simple,' he said. 'Just take it easy.'

Up above, Tomasz watched the rope go taught against the edge of the lift car. It started to fray, where he had applied the file, almost immediately. He waited. After several minutes, he looked over the edge and could just about make out a shape on the rope, hauling itself up.

Tomasz knelt down and used the file to accelerate the fraying. His instruction was to allow Harry to get at least two thirds up the rope before severing the rope entirely. He waited.

Harry and Ellen sat on the floor, leaning against the side of the lift shaft.

'I wonder what did happen to Martha down here, Harry. I mean, will we ever really know?'

'There's only one person who can tell us that. If he's still alive and we can find him.'

'But why would anyone do such a thing? That's what I don't understand.'

Harry was silent for a moment. 'People do terrible things, Ellen.'

'I know, but why her?'

'She was probably in the wrong place at the wrong time. She was here by chance, after all. I suppose Wallington, if it was him, could have had it in his mind to take a woman. But, more likely, something happened. Something that triggered it.' Harry mused.

They were both silent. Harry glanced up at the rope. 'He must be getting near the top.'

Ellen looked upwards. She could barely make out Marcus, hauling himself up the rope in the gloom.

'We need to find Wallington,' Harry said.

Ellen shuddered. 'We need to stay safe Harry. The man who threatened me and who probably broke into your flat, is dangerous. There was something about him.'

'What do you mean?'

Ellen thought for a moment. 'He enjoyed it. He was enjoying his power over me.'

Harry put his arm around her.

'I think he would have enjoyed hurting me, if he hadn't just wanted to scare me half to death.'

Suddenly, from above, Harry heard a muffled shout. He glanced upwards and as he did, he saw the rope beginning to descend. It took less than a second for his brain to register what was happening, but in his mind time had slowed. He caught Ellen's eyes. There was a look of confusion on her face. Marcus was falling. The thought registered suddenly. A scream. The rope coiling in a heap in front of them. Marcus's body hurtling towards them, arms flapping. Downwards. Towards Ellen.

She was leaning on the post beside the lift shaft gate. He had only seconds to shove her out of the way. He levered his legs beneath him and pushed her as hard as he could. The gate swung open and she slumped sideways and rolled, face downwards with Harry on top of her. There was a sickening crash and a sudden dead weight across Harry's legs. Ellen screamed. The sound of it echoed away into the tunnel. And then there was silence.

Harry hauled his legs out from under the ropes and staggered to his feet. Ellen cried out in pain. Harry glanced over his shoulder. He held on to the lift shaft fence.

'My ankle,' Ellen moaned.

He knelt down beside her. 'Try not to move,' he said, pulling up the left leg of her trousers. He grimaced. Ellen's foot was at a peculiar angle. 'Stay still. It looks like you've broken your ankle,' he said stroking her shoulder.

Ellen had pushed herself up on her elbows and was trying to turn around. 'Marcus? Oh my God. Marcus.'

'Don't look Ellen. Just lay still.'

Harry got up and went to the broken climber's side. His arms and legs were twisted beneath him and there was blood trickling from his mouth.

'Jesus Christ. Marcus?' Harry put his ear to Marcus's mouth. He could hear a gurgling breath. 'Jesus, he's alive.'

'What?' called Ellen. She had turned herself over and was sitting up. 'Oh God. Marcus,' she sobbed.

CHAPTER THIRTY-FOUR

Harry sat at the table in the interview room, with a cup of coffee in his hand. The door opened and a police officer entered.

'Mr Stammers, I am Sergeant John McPherson,' he said, sitting down on the chair opposite.

'Is there any news? About Marcus I mean,' Harry asked.

'Mr Dawson is alive, Mr Stammers. But he is in intensive care. All the hospital will say at this stage is that he has been very seriously injured.'

Harry tried to swallow. 'What about Ellen?'

'Miss Carmichael?'

'Yes.'

'Well it looked like a broken ankle to me.'

'Yes, but have you heard anything from the hospital?'

'No. Now if I can ask you a few questions?'

'Yes, of course.'

'Your full name, Mr Stammers?'

'Harry. It's Harry Stammers.'

'No middle name?'

'No.'

The sergeant took down his date of birth and address.

'And what do you do for a living, Mr Stammers.'

'I work at a museum.'

'Which museum would that be?'

'Bletchley Park.'

Sergeant McPherson leant back in his chair. 'What do you do at Bletchley Park?'

'I am a curator. Well *the* curator actually. There is only one.'

'Thank you. Now I would like you to tell me exactly what you were doing in the tunnels at Belsize Park.'

Harry took a deep breath. 'Research. I was doing some research.'

'For Bletchley Park?'

'No,' Harry hesitated. 'Yes. Well no, not really.'

The police officer looked at him and waited. Harry shifted uncomfortably in his seat.

'Well, was it for Bletchley Park, or wasn't it?' McPherson said after a few moments.

'No, it wasn't. I came across the tunnels as a result of my work at Bletchley, but I was exploring them for myself.'

'Exploring? I thought you said "researching"?'

'Researching then.'

'Really. And what were Miss Carmichael, Mr Dabrowski and Mr Dawson doing there with you?'

'They were helping me.'

The police officer hesitated. 'What were they helping you research or explore, exactly.'

'There is a deserted tunnel. When the tunnels were being constructed, they broke into an underground stream and that section of tunnels was flooded and later, abandoned. There has been very little written about it.'

'So you decided to find this deserted tunnel?'

'Yes, that is correct. I wanted to find the tunnel and to photograph it.'

Sergeant McPherson was taking notes. 'Did you find the tunnel you were looking for?'

'Yes, as a matter of fact we did,' said Harry.

'And did you photograph it?'

'Yes I did.'

'Is this your camera?' he said, bending down and removing Harry's camera from a bag on the floor. 'We will want to examine the pictures you took. Do you have any objection to that?'

'No. None at all.' Harry hesitated. 'I will get them back won't I?'

'I rather suspect that depends on what, exactly, it was that you photographed. What else did you do while you were down there?'

'Nothing.'

'You found the tunnel, photographed it and that was all?'

'Yes.'

'You were on your way out, when the incident happened?'

'Yes. Look,' Harry hesitated. 'How long is this going to take? I'm not under arrest or anything am I? I am worried about Ellen and Marcus.'

'No, Mr Stammers, you are not under arrest. I am trying to ascertain whether a crime has been committed. If I conclude that it has, then I may very well arrest you. I will certainly caution you and we will have to do this all over again. Until then, I cannot prevent you from leaving, but I would prefer you to answer my questions.'

'I'm sorry. I am just worried about them, that's all.'

'Well, I'm sorry to say it, but it might have been better had you worried a little more before asking them to climb one hundred feet of rope, suspended in an underground lift shaft.'

Harry grimaced.

'Now, can I ask you how you got in. To the premises I mean.'

Harry swallowed. 'Through the main door.'

'The one with the combination lock.'

'Yes.'

'So, how did you get in?'

'The door was not locked.'

'Are you saying that it was left unlocked?'

'I am saying that it was unlocked when I entered.'

'How did you obtain the combination?'

'I did not obtain the combination,' Harry replied, honestly. He hadn't.

Sergeant McPherson looked at him steadily and sighed. 'Mr Stammers, we have examined the door and it was undamaged. Nor was the look faulty in any way. So, if you went in through the door, one of you must have had the combination.'

Harry was sweating. 'I did not have the combination.'

'But one of you did?'

'You'd have to ask them. All I can say is that I did not.'

Sergeant McPherson stared at him. 'Alright, lets try another tack shall we? Can you tell me why there is a pair of bolt cutters in your bag?'

'They are there in case we found ourselves trapped. I was aware that the tunnel we were looking for was likely to be flooded. I did not want to find myself trapped in running water behind a locked gate.'

'Did you use the bolt cutters, while you were in the tunnels?'

'No,' said Harry, trying to hide the lie.

'Did you take anything from the tunnels?'

'No.' Harry could feel his face flushing.

'Nothing at all?'

'No.' Harry was determined not to reveal that the plans from the rest room and Martha's purse were in Ellen's bag. It was possible that the police had not yet searched it. He had placed it in the ambulance with Ellen before she had been taken to hospital.

'Did you photograph or examine any documents while you were underground?'

'Documents? What documents?'

'It is a simple question, Mr Stammers. Did you photograph or look at any documents?'

'I found an old newspaper. From 1947. But other than that, no.'

'Are you certain?'

'Yes, quite certain.'

Harry had finished his coffee and was dying for a cigarette. 'Am I allowed to smoke?' he asked.

Sergeant McPherson was beginning to look irritated. 'This is not *Z-Cars* Mr Stammers. We are in a modern, public building. Smoking is not allowed. Now can we turn to the incident itself?'

'Sure.'

'Why did you not just use the stairs?'

'Because there are a number of CCTV cameras in the stair well. The guards would have seen us.'

'I can't quite understand how the guards managed to miss you.'

'We were careful to avoid the cameras.'

'I see. So you decided to use the lift shaft?'

'Yes.'

'Are any of you experienced climbers?'

'Yes. Ellen, Marcus and I have all done quite a bit of climbing.'

'Who rigged the ropes?'

'Marcus did.'

'Whose gear was it?'

'It belonged... belongs,' Harry corrected himself, 'to Marcus.'

'And Mr Dawson went first?'

'Yes, on the way up.'

'Whose idea was it that he go first?'

Harry thought for a moment. 'It was Marcus's actually. It was originally going to be me, but Marcus wanted to surprise Tom at the top.'

'This is Tomasz Dabrowski?'

'Yes. That's right.'

'Did you inspect the ropes before you used them?'

'No. Why would I have inspected them?'

'I would have thought that would be glaringly obvious. Are you in the habit of dangling one hundred feet above a lift shaft on a rope without ensuring that it is safe?'

'No, of course not. But it was a team effort and I trusted Marcus's judgement.'

'The rope appears to have frayed on the edge of the lift car. Did it not occur to any of you that this might happen?'

Harry sighed. 'Look, I'm not stupid. Do you think that we would have used the rope had we thought that it was likely to break?'

Sergeant McPherson looked at him steadily. 'No, I suppose not.'

'So you were sitting at the bottom of the lift shaft with Miss Carmichael when Mr Dawson started to climb the rope?'

'Yes.'

'Could you tell me what happened after that?'

Harry described hearing a shout and the rope beginning to coil onto the floor in front of him. He described pushing Ellen out of the way of the falling climber and the sound of him hitting the ground.

'It was very noble of you to think of Miss Carmichael,' observed Sergeant McPherson.

'Thank you. I didn't really think about it. It was pure instinct,' replied Harry.

'I imagine so. So to recap, you say that you got in to the building through an open door.'

'Yes.'

'You lowered yourself down the lift shaft on ropes supplied by Mr Dawson.'

'Yes.'

'This was for the purpose of looking for and photographing an abandoned tunnel, which you say you subsequently found and photographed?'

'Yes, I did.'

'You didn't take anything from the tunnels and you didn't examine any documents while you were down there?'

'No, absolutely not.'

'And you were attempting to leave by the same method when the incident happened.'

'Yes, exactly.'

McPherson shuffled his notes. 'I am going to ask you once more. How did you get in through a locked door.'

'I've told you. It wasn't locked when we entered.'

'Mr Stammers, sticking to such an implausible story is not helping your cause. One of your friends is in hospital with very serious injuries.'

'I know that. But the fact is that the door was open when I entered and that is the truth.'

There was silence.

227

'Very well, Mr Stammers. That will be all for now but we may very well need to talk to you again.'

'I can go?'

The policeman nodded.

'Will there be any charges?'

Sergeant McPherson looked at him searchingly. 'As I imagine you are well aware, entering the premises uninvited amounts to trespass. That is a civil matter. Whether the owners will pursue this with you is a matter for them. You say that you did not break-in or damage or remove anything while you were there. If that proves to be the case, then it is unlikely that criminal charges will follow. Between you and me, Mr Stammers, I don't think the owners want any publicity. The security breach is of acute embarrassment to them. The last thing they want is this all over the papers. They have some important clients who would be less than impressed. Quite apart from that, they do not want to spend the next six months fending off hoards of 'urban explorers'. Is that what you call yourselves?'

Harry shrugged. He couldn't help but feel relieved that the policeman had appeared to accept that they were not there for any other reason.

'I'd say that makes you a very fortunate man. I wish that the same could be said for Mr Dawson.'

Harry's stomach turned at the mention of his friend's name.

CHAPTER THIRTY-FIVE

Harry descended the steps and stood for a moment on the pavement outside the police station, wondering what to do. Marcus was fighting for his life, Ellen had been taken to hospital and he hadn't seen Tomasz since since the police had driven him away from Belsize Park. The whole thing was a complete mess.

He found a bus shelter and lit a cigarette. He looked at his watch. It was one thirty in the morning. He fished around in his pocket for his mobile phone. He could see from the display that there had been several missed calls. He dialled Mike's number.

'Harry? Is that you? What the fuck happened? I've been trying to get hold of you for hours.' Mike's voice was full of tension.

'Sorry Mike. I've been at Barnet Police Station. Its not good.'

'I know that. I watched the medics arriving on the cameras, but I couldn't work out what had happened, exactly. Was that Marcus they took out on a stretcher?'

'Yes. He fell, something like seventy or eighty feet down the lift shaft.'

'Fuck. How the hell did that happen?'

'I don't know, Mike. I keep asking myself the same question.'

'Do you know what shape he's in?'

'I know he's in intensive care. But that's all I know.'

'What about Ellen?'

'Broken ankle.'

'Where are you?'

'I'm outside Barnet Police Station.'

'I'll come and get you.'

'No, I'm going to walk to the hospital to see if I can find out any more.'

'Not a problem. I'll meet you there.'

'I take it that you've had no contact from the police?' asked Harry.

'No. I don't think anyone knew that I was watching.'

'Well that is one piece of good luck. I'll meet you at Barnet General?'

'Sure. Where?'

'Casualty. I guess.'

'Fine, give me thirty to forty minutes.'

Harry ended the call and dialled Ellen's number but it was unobtainable. He dialled Tomasz's number. There was no answer. He put his cigarette out and started to walk up Barnet Hill, crossing just before the church.

What the hell was going on? It seemed as though everything had spun out of control since he had obtained the shelter log. But who even knew that he had it? If Wallington had killed Martha Watts, he'd be well into his eighties by now. Perhaps they had got the whole thing wrong.

Harry's thoughts turned to the man who had threatened Ellen. Discovering his identity was the key. Harry knew it. If they could discover that, then the whole thing might unravel.

Harry turned left into Wellhouse Lane. The Hospital loomed up in front of him. He followed the signs for Casualty and went in through the automatic doors. The streets outside had been empty. He had expected the hospital to be empty also but the waiting room was packed. Harry looked around. A young woman sat with her head in her partner's lap. She looked very drunk. Two young men were arguing by the coffee machine and a security guard was trying to calm them, evidently with little success. An elderly woman sat in a wheel chair with a blanket over her knees. She was singing softly to herself.

Harry walked across to the reception desk.

'Name?' said the female receptionist.

'I'm here to see Ellen Carmichael. She would have been admitted about two hours ago?'

The woman looked up from her keyboard.

'And you are?'

'Harry Stammers.'

'Your relationship to Mrs Carmichael?'

'Miss Carmichael. I'm her boyfriend.'

The receptionist tapped away on the computer keyboard.

'What is Ellen's date of birth?'

'I don't know.'

The receptionist stopped typing and looked up at him. 'I'm afraid we can't give out any details unless you are a relative.'

'Shit.' Harry suddenly felt enormously tired. He ran his hands through his hair. 'Look, its been one hell of a night. Ellen and I were involved in an accident. One of my best friends was very badly injured. I don't even know if he's alive. I just want to know where Ellen is. Can you help me? Please?'

The receptionist looked at him sympathetically. 'This friend of yours who was badly injured. What is his name?'

'Marcus. Marcus Dawson.'

'The young man who fell down the lift shaft?'

'Yes. That's him.'

'Just a moment,' she said, tapping away at the keyboard.

'Mr Dawson is in Intensive Care. I'm afraid that you won't be able to see him tonight.'

'And Ellen?'

'What was her injury?'

'How should I know. I am not a bloody Doctor,' Harry snapped.

'Mr Stammers, I am trying to help you. If you can tell me what the injury was, I might be able to confirm it for you.'

Harry took a breath. 'I'm sorry. I appreciate your help. It was her ankle. I think she had broken it?'

'Yes that's right. A lateral malleolus fracture actually.'

'She has been admitted?'

'Yes she has.'

'Is she alright?'

'I'm really not allowed to tell you that,' the receptionist hesitated and looked at him. 'It says here that she was in theatre. A minor procedure. Try not to worry. She was in recovery and then they took her to, let me see,' the receptionist looked at the terminal. 'Cedar Ward.'

'Thank you.' He turned and began to walk away.

'But I doubt that you'll get to see her tonight Mr Stammers,' the receptionist called out after him.

Harry continued towards the exit.

As he reached the doors, Mike appeared in the doorway. 'Harry. Man. You look like shit.'

'Thanks. I feel like shit.'

'Any news?'

'Let's get outside. I need a cigarette.'

They went outside. Harry lit a cigarette and offered one to Mike.

'No I don't,' he hesitated. 'Oh fuck it, I think I do tonight,' he said, sliding a cigarette from Harry's packet and accepting a light from Harry's lighter.

'Marcus is still in intensive care. I can't get any more out of them than that. Ellen's in recovery. They operated on her ankle. A lateral something fracture. They're admitting her to Cedar Ward.'

'Do you want to try to find her?'

'Yes. I need to see her. If only for a few minutes.'

'Come on then.'

They climbed the stairs to Cedar Ward and went in through the double doors. A   nurse was sitting behind the nurses' station, drinking a cup of tea.   Harry approached her hopefully.

'We're here to see Ellen Carmichael.'

'What? You can't visit this time of night,' the nurse said with a broad African accent.

'We were both involved in a serious accident. I just want to see her for a few minutes. To see that she is alright.'

'What is your name.'

'Harry,'

'Carmichael,' Mike interrupted. 'He's Ellen's brother.'

'Just a moment,' the Nurse said. She got up and walked down the corridor. A few moments later, she returned. 'Ellen will see you. She is in the day room. That way,' she said, pointing. 'She is still feeling a little bit sick from the anaesthetic. So five minutes only and then you must go.'

Harry thanked the nurse. They walked along the corridor and into the dayroom. Ellen was sitting in a wheelchair. She was wearing a white gown and had her foot in plaster.

'Harry! Thank God,' Ellen said and burst into tears.

Harry walked over, bent down and hugged her. 'Are you alright?'

'No. I am not. What about Marcus?'

'Intensive Care. I don't know any more.'

'Thank God he's still alive. I thought he was dead.'

'So did I,' admitted Harry. 'Have the police interviewed you?'

'No, not yet. They're coming to see me in the morning. Have they interviewed you?'

'Yes. I just got out of the station.'

'What did they say? What did you tell them?'

Harry recounted the interview with Sergeant McPherson.

'Isn't it a bit odd that Safe House aren't pressing charges?'

'Maybe. But, look we can talk about that tomorrow. Just so long as you are alright.'

'I'll survive.'

'What about the purse and the map?' asked Harry.

'What purse? What map?' asked Mike.

'Oh hello Mike. I'm sorry.' She beckoned him over.

He bent down and kissed her on the cheek.

'Have you still got them?' asked Harry.

'Yes, they are in my bag. I haven't let it out of my sight,' she said, pointing over her shoulder. 'You'd better take them. In case the police want to search it.'

'Good idea. They took my bloody bolt cutters,' he said, looking at Ellen.

She held his gaze. 'Are you alright Harry?'

He smiled weakly. 'I've had better nights,' he said, retrieving the bag.

'We found these while we were in the tunnels,' he said, removing the map and purse from the bag and handing them to Mike. 'Hold on to them would you? I'll tell you about them later.'

Mike put them in his inside pocket.

'Does your ankle hurt much?' Harry asked.

'No. I just feel sick. The anaesthetic. I think.'

'Do you know when you are going to be discharged?'

'Tomorrow afternoon they reckon. I mean this afternoon. I just have to keep off the ankle as much as possible. But it wasn't a terribly serious fracture.'

'Thank God for that.'

'Harry, will you come and get me? Can I stay with you for a few days? My neighbour will fetch my clothes. I just,' she hesitated and her eyes filled with tears. 'Look, I hate playing the helpless female but I just don't want to be on my own.'

'Don't be silly. Of course you can.' He bent over and kissed her.

'But what about Marcus? It was awful, Mike. Just awful.'

'I know,' said Mike grimly.

Ellen turned to Harry. 'What happened? Marcus knew what he was doing. How could he fall like that?'

'The police said that the rope frayed on the edge of the lift car. It must have been sharper than it looked.'

'But they were good quality ropes, Harry. Ropes like that don't just fray on a sharp edge. I don't understand it.'

'Neither do I.'

'Mr Carmichael, you must go now,' said the Nurse with the African accent from the doorway. 'It is the middle of the night and Ellen must sleep. You can come back tomorrow.'

'Thank you Nurse. We're just going.'

'Harry?' said Ellen.

'Please take care. You look awful.'

'Don't worry about him Ellen. I'll look after him,' said Mike.

Harry pulled a face.

Ellen mouthed the words 'Thank you.'

Mike winked. 'Cool.'

Ellen looked at Harry. 'I'm just praying that Marcus will make it.'

'We all are,' said Harry.

CHAPTER THIRTY-SIX

Harry opened his eyes and, for a moment, wondered where he was. Then it came back to him in a rush. He sat up and swivelled his legs so that he was sitting on the edge of the sofa. He stretched out his arms, yawned and rubbed his face.

He could hear Mike in the kitchen, making coffee. 'Morning,' he said appearing in the door way. 'Man, you look rough. How did you sleep?'

'I slept. That is about the best that can be said about it,' Harry replied. 'Any news?'

'No, I tried Tom but there's still no reply. I haven't tried the hospital yet,' Mike said, handing him a cup of coffee.

Harry noticed a cable running out into the hall. 'You're not still connected to the cameras are you?' Harry asked.

'No, I disconnected it when I left to pick you up from the hospital. I probably should have disconnected it earlier, but I was desperate to know what was happening.'

'It's a shame you didn't record it,' Harry said. 'It all happened so quickly.'

Mike grinned. 'Actually, I did. Well, some of it anyway. I figured out how to do it while you and Ellen were in the tunnels.'

'You're kidding?' Harry said, opened mouthed.

Mike shook his head. 'Of course, it doesn't show the accident,' he added. 'It's just the stream from the upper lobby.'

'Can I see it?'

'Sure.'

Mike walked across to the PC. 'Just a second…', he said, searching for the file. 'Here you go.'

Harry seated himself in front of the screen and clicked "play".

'I started recording just before Tom came out of the lift. I thought that something might have gone wrong when I lost the mobile phone connection.'

'You lost your connection?' asked Harry, without taking his eyes from the screen.

'Yup.'

'Hmm… That's odd. Did Tom say anything?'

'Nope. The line just went dead.'

Harry watched the recording and then scratched his head. 'I don't get it.'

'What?'

'His reaction.'

'What about it?' said Mike.

'Can we watch it again?' asked Harry.

'Sure,' Mike replied, leaning across him and clicking on the re-wind icon.

Harry watched the scene unfold again. 'Look how he reacts. Someone has just fallen down the lift shaft. For all Tom knows, I am lying in a pool of blood at the bottom.'

'And?'

'Well, he doesn't seem in much of a hurry, does he? And why go to the control room, rather than down the stair well?'

Mike said nothing.

'There's something else,' said Harry, rewinding the clip a second time. 'Watch the way the first guard greets Tom.'

Both men watched the recording in silence.

'There,' Harry said, hitting pause.

'What?' said Mike.

'Does the guard look very surprised to you?' Harry asked.

'Well, no. Not really. But he obviously saw Tom coming down the corridor on the camera feed. The same camera feed we're watching now in fact.'

Harry shook his head. 'But Tom is an intruder, Mike. The guards have been relaxing, reading the paper or whatever and suddenly there is an intruder coming down the corridor toward them. Don't you think that they ought to have been a bit more animated than that?'

'I don't know. I guess so,' Mike said doubtfully.

Harry clicked on "play".

The recording showed Tom emerge with one of the guards and the two of them disappear down the stair well.

'Nothing much happens until the paramedics turn up. Watch.'

The lobby had remained empty for some minutes. Then the guard from the control room had emerged to admit the first team of paramedics. Shortly after that, two police officers had entered. Blue flashing lights were visible from outside when the guard opened the door. Then several firemen and three further ambulance staff. Harry continued to watch intently.

Ellen had been the first out, carried on an evacuation chair up the stairs by two burly looking firemen. Then Harry and Tomasz, accompanied by the police officers. Finally, Marcus surrounded by a team of firemen and medics, one holding a saline bottle up in the air as they walked briskly across the lobby.

'God, that must been one heck of a climb,' said Mike, shaking his head. 'More coffee?'

'Please. Yes, it was bad enough just walking up. The firemen who brought Marcus up hardly broke into a sweat.'

Harry had his back to the screen. 'I wonder how Marcus is doing. And Ellen. I must call the hospital,' he said, glancing at his watch. 'Then I better call work to tell them that I won't be in. It's nearly nine thirty.'

Harry, stood up and, as he did so, glanced back at the computer screen. 'Hey,' he said, reaching for the mouse. 'I recognise him.'

Mike came over with two cups of coffee and handed one to Harry. 'Which one?'

'That one,' Harry replied, pointing at a figure who had entered the lobby.

'The guy with the beard?'

'Yes.'

Harry rewound the recording. They both watched the man approach one of the guards. After a short, heated conversation, the man had pulled a mobile phone from his pocket and walked away to make a call. When he had finished, he returned to the guard, exchanged a few words and left, apparently in a hurry.

Harry was about to rewind the recording again when he heard his mobile phone ringing in the lounge. He walked briskly into the lounge to retrieve it.

'Ellen?' he said, without looking at the display.

'No. Harry, it's Jane,' said a whispered voice on the phone.

'Oh, I'm sorry Jane. I'm waiting for a call from Ellen.'

'What, in God's name is going on Harry? The Major got a call first thing this morning.'

Harry hesitated. 'There's been an accident.'

'Oh God. Is Ellen alright?'

'Yes. Well no, she has broken her ankle.'

'What about you?'

'I'm fine.'

'Harry, listen. I can't stay on the phone for very long. But there is a letter on its way to you. The Major is suspending you.'

'Oh for fuck's sake…' But, in truth, he had been expecting it.

'He wouldn't tell me why. But he looked absolutely grim when he told me.'

'Great. That is all I need.'

Jane said nothing.

Harry waited. He knew there was more.

'There's something else.'

'More good news?'

Jane ignored the quip. 'It's John Watts. He's in hospital.'

'What?' Harry had not been expecting that.

'Apparently, he had a fall.'

'Is he alright?'

'No. He fell down the stairs. He hasn't regained consciousness.'

'Shit.'

'The odd thing was, he had a cricket bat in his hand.'

'A what?'

'Look, I've got to go. What hospital is Ellen in?'

'Barnet General, but she should be out this afternoon. She's going to be staying at mine for a few days.'

'OK. I'll call you later. Take care Harry and give my love to Ellen.'

Harry's phone went dead.

'Bad news?' asked Mike.

'Yes, you could say that,' said Harry.

CHAPTER THIRTY-SEVEN

Tomasz stood at the bus stop, waiting for the night bus. It was almost three in the morning and a bus wasn't due for another hour. There was a cab office across the road with a sign which said "24 Hour Service". The office was in darkness but there was a telephone number on the hoarding. He pulled out his wallet. He didn't have enough money for a cab. He put his wallet and phone back in his pocket and zipped up his jacket.

They had thought that it was a joke to swap places on the rope but the man with the goatee beard wasn't going to find it funny that it had been Marcus who had fallen, rather than Harry. Tomasz had only discovered the mistake when he had reached the bottom of the stair well with the guard. He had known, from the moment that he saw Harry kneeling beside Marcus, that he was going to have to run.

How would he break the news to Monika? She and Dita would not be safe. He would have to run and they would have to run with him. Maybe to Manchester. Or maybe back to Poland. If Marcus didn't make it, he could end up being wanted by the police for murder, as well living in fear of the man with the goatee beard.

They had come to England full of optimism, he and Monika. He'd found work almost straight away and Monika had found a young man. A year later, little Dita had been born. Their life had been good. Then Dita's father had left, suddenly. It had taken Monika many months to get over it. Now, she would be uprooted and, if they stayed in England, they would spend their life looking over their shoulder. If the man's threats were to be believed, they wouldn't be entirely safe, even in Poland.

He had thought about telling the police the truth. He had come close to it. But the policeman had said that Marcus might not make it through the night. If Marcus died, he'd have been confessing to murder. He would spend many years in prison. He could not have faced that and so he had lied and now he would have to run. He shivered.

A black BMW with tinted windows pulled up at the bus stop. It remained there. Nobody got out. It occurred to Tomasz that the bus might pass by the stop if the car didn't move away. He looked along the High Street anxiously.

Tomasz heard the buzz of the car's window being lowered and the click of the doors unlocking. 'Get in Dobrowski,' said a voice from inside.

Tomasz didn't hesitate. He ran. As fast as he could and in the opposite direction to that faced by the car. As he ran, he glanced left and right, looking desperately for an alley or a hiding place. Behind him, he heard the squeal of the BMW's tyres as it turned in the empty High Street and the roar of the engine.

He turned right and ran across the road. The BMW was not yet at the junction. If we was quick, he might lose it. There were some advantages to being on foot. He ran across a car park and crashed through an open wooden gate and slammed it shut behind him, panting. He heard the BMW's engine. The yard in which he found himself was briefly flooded with light. Then there was silence.

Tomasz looked up. A steel stair case ran up the back of the building and onto a flat roof. He crept up the stairs trying not to make any sound. As soon as he was level with the top of the fence he spotted the BMW. It had pulled up about thirty metres from the gate. Tomasz stood as still as he could and scanned the car park and surrounding buildings. Nothing moved. All he could hear was the rustle of leaves in the trees and a dog barking in the distance.

From inside his jacket pocket, he felt his phone vibrate. Thank God he'd put it on mute while he had been in the police station or the man would have heard it now. He pulled out the phone and looked at the name flashing on the display. He pressed the red button on the keypad and put the phone back in his pocket.

He could feel the adrenaline flushing his cheeks but he was strangely calm. He was not going to be caught by this man. If he had to, he would take Monika and Dita far away and they would start over again. The man was not going to hurt little Dita. He would not let that happen.

Tomasz continued up the stairs, watching the car park for any sign of movement but there was none. He ran across the flat roof and crouched next to a low partition wall. He waited, his eyes wide in the darkness. A cat appeared on the flat roof and sat watching him, its tail wrapped around its legs. He put his hand to his forehead and found it wet with sweat.

After several minutes, he eased himself over the wall and ran along the adjoining flat roof and flattened himself against the wall of the next building. He looked in through a window. The room was completely empty. The window frame was rotting and the glass looked like it had not been cleaned for a long time. It was one of the empty flats above the shops in the High Street. He tried the sash window but it wouldn't budge. He made his way along the wall until he found another window. This one made a grinding noise as it slid upwards. He stood still again and waited in silence, checking for signs of movement, but again there were none.

He could see the black BMW. As Tomasz stood at the window, wondering whether it was safe to move, the BMW's engine flared to life and the headlights came on. Tomasz crouched as low as he could. He heard the car's wheel spin in the car park's gravel. When, a few moments later, he risked another look, the car was gone.

Tomasz climbed in through the window, gently closed it behind him and stood with his back to the wall, breathing heavily. After a few moments he slid down onto the floor. It had been a close call but he was more certain than ever that he, Monika and Dita would have to run. And he had to move quickly. The BMW might already be on its way. He retrieved his mobile phone from his pocket and dialled the number.

'Monika?' It is Tomasz....' He said in Polish. 'No I'm not alright. We are in trouble. There is no time. You are in danger.'

He listened to her panic stricken voice.

'I'm sorry. I want you to take Dita, right now, to your friend's place in Market Street... Yes, right now. There is no time to explain, but you must go...'

He listened to the stream of questions.

'Monika, listen to me. There is no time. You've got less than fifteen minutes. Get Dita and go. Right now Monika. Promise me?'

He listened to her response.

'Stay there OK? I will come as soon as I can. I love you.'

He ended the call.

He walked across to the front window and looked out. The flat was no more than half a dozen doors up from the bus stop. He could see the cab office across the road but couldn't make out the telephone number in the darkness.

'Shit,' he said in Polish.

He found the flat's front door, opened it and walked down the stairs to the street door. He opened the door, cautiously and peered left and right. Outside, the street was empty and completely silent. He looked across at the cab office. Then he closed the door and dialled the number.

About twenty minutes later he heard the sound of a car pull up outside. The mini cab. He stood up, brushing the dust from his jacket and opened the door.

In the man's hand was a gun which he was pointing directly at the centre of his chest. 'I hope you can drive Dobrowski,' the man said, grinning.

The man with the goatee beard frog marched him to the car, the barrel of the gun poking in his back. He opened the driver's door. 'Get in. Make one move that I am not expecting and I'll blow your head off. Do you understand?'

'Yes,' replied Tomasz. He got into the car.

Stephens got into the passenger seat behind him. Tomasz felt the barrel of the gun in the nape of his neck. 'Now start the car and drive. Left at the church and keep going. Remember, one move Dabrowski. Just one. And it will be your last.'

'Where are you taking me?'

'My employer wishes to speak with you.'

'Why?'

'Just shut up and drive.'

Desperate thoughts were running through his head. He could crash the car. He would only need a few seconds to open the driver's door and run for it. But, as if the man could read his thoughts, he felt the gun barrel pushed hard into the back of his neck. 'Straight over the roundabout, then first left.'

It was hopeless. His only hope was to escape when they got to wherever the man was taking him. Tomasz felt his hands beginning to shake. The adrenaline that had coursed through his veins earlier was ebbing away.

'Straight over the next junction, then we turn left. I'll tell you when.'

Tomasz took the next junction a little too quickly.

'Slow down Dobrowski. We're turning left just after that tree up ahead.'

Tomasz turned off the road and drove down a gravel track. The wheels vibrated as they went over a cattle grid.

'Pull up over there on the right. Along side the other car and be careful. You would not want to scratch it.'

Tomasz stopped the car beside a Jaguar. He couldn't tell what colour it was in the darkness.

'Now get out. Slowly. And walk around to the back of the car.'

Tomasz got out and stood still. They were in a clearing, surrounded by trees. The moon was hidden by low cloud. The man pushed the gun barrel into his side. Escape was, for now, out of the question. He walked around to the back of the car. One of the Jaguar's doors opened and a man got out. He was tall and was wearing a wide brimmed hat which had pulled down over his forehead so that his eyes were in shadows.

'Good evening Mr Dobrowski.'

Tomasz said nothing.

Stephens pushed the gun barrel into the side of Tomasz's head. 'Squeak piggy, squeak.'

'Why? You are going to kill me.'

The man in the hat laughed. 'Whatever gave you that idea. We wouldn't dream of doing such a thing, would we Stephens?' the man said.

Tomasz registered the name in his mind. 'Then why have you brought me here?' he said.

'I have some questions, Mr Dobrowski. You will answer them fully, leaving nothing out and then Stephens here will send you on your way, won't you Stephens?'

'Yes, Sir,' said Stephens.

'Tonight's events, Mr Dobrowski, at Belsize Park were most unfortunate,' said the man with the hat.

'It was not my fault. They told me that it was Harry on the rope. I had no way of knowing that it was Marcus.'

'Indeed. It would be unreasonable to hold you responsible for their little joke. We are not unreasonable men, are we Stephens?'

'No, Sir,' said Stephens.

'So tell me, Mr Dobrowski, Stammers and Carmichael found something in the tunnel did they not?'

'Yes. Yes, they did,' Tomasz replied his voice shaking.

'What was it?'

'A purse. They found a woman's purse.'

This information appeared to surprise the man and he was silent for a moment.

'A purse, you say?'

'Yes,' replied Tomasz.

'Where did they find this purse, exactly?'

'In the abandoned tunnel. I don't know where exactly. I only heard what they said on the radio once they were back in the main tunnel.'

'And what, did they say, was in this purse?'

'They did not say. They just said that it was a purse.'

'Oh come now, Mr Dobrowski, they were clearly excited.'

'Harry spoke to Marcus on the radio. I heard him. They just said that it was a purse. Her purse.'

'Whose purse did they say that it was?'

Tomasz hesitated. If he told them everything he knew, perhaps there was a slim chance that they would let him go. But if they thought that he knew too much, they might be more likely to kill him.

The blow was not wholly unexpected. Tomasz had been bracing himself for it, since the moment he had stepped out of the car. Stephens had lowered the gun, swapped hands, and had hit him with his right fist. The pain exploded in his chest and Tomasz staggered and fell to his knees, gasping for air.

'Whose purse did they say it was?'

'The woman's. The one they are looking for,' Tomasz coughed.

There was another silence.

'I can get it for you. I can get it for you. I know where it is,' Tomasz sobbed, kneeling in the mud.

'Where is the purse now Mr Dobrowski?' asked the man in the hat.

'Ellen has it. It is in her bag.'

'Are you sure?'

'Yes.'

'Did they find anything else?'

'No. No nothing.'

'Are you absolutely certain?'

'Yes. That is all they said,' Tomasz said, saliva dribbling from his mouth.

'Thank you and goodnight Mr Dobrowski.'

Tomasz looked up at the man. A gap had appeared in the clouds overhead and the moon momentarily lit the man's face. 'Who are you?' Tomasz said.

'You are looking at Britain's next Prime Minister, Mr Dobrowski. Not that this will interest you much, being an immigrant. Stephens, I think I would like to watch, if you will?'

Stephens put the gun barrel to the side of Tomasz Dobrowski's head.

'No, please,' Tomasz sobbed.

Stephens pulled the trigger. Pieces of brain sprayed from the opposite side of the Pole's head, followed by a fine mist, pink in the moonlight. Tomasz Dobrowski slumped to the ground and died, face down in the mud.

Max Banks stood for a moment, looking at the body. 'Dispose of it. Then watch her. I want that bag. When she leaves the hospital, remove it from her and bring it to me.'

'Yes, Sir,' said Stephens.

Max Banks turned, got into the Jaguar and drove away.

CHAPTER THIRTY-EIGHT

Friday, 10 th *November 1944*

He stares at the woman on the floor. The wave of fury that had filled him is ebbing away and, as it departs, he stands, frozen, panting, unable to move or to look away.

He watches the trickle of blood from her nose, running down the side of her face, forming a little pool on the floor beside her cheek. He sees the short, red gash, just below her right ear.

Then the next wave begins to gather in his chest. He recognises it as a mixture of panic and despair. He sinks to his knees beside her.

He says her name out loud. He shakes her but she does not stir. He puts his ear to her mouth. He cannot hear her breath. He reaches for her arm but he can find no pulse. He pulls her up and holds her against his chest as the wave breaks and he begins to tremble.

The panic comes suddenly. 'Help!' he calls out. 'For God's sake. Somebody, help!'

But nobody answers. Nobody can hear.

He releases her and staggers to his feet. She is dead. He stumbles backwards. He has killed her. He turns and vomits a pool of green bile onto the floor, the taste of brandy and acid in his mouth.

'Dead,' he whispers. 'Dear God. What have I done?' He slumps down onto the bunk.

The reality of what he has done hits him like a hammer blow to the chest and he struggles for air. Murder. It doesn't matter that he did not intend it. She is dead. It will all end now. He will be discovered and he will hang.

He thinks of his wife. She will know, instantly. She always does. He can never keep anything from her. All their plans. Her plans. The business. Their future. All in ashes. She will never forgive him.

As the wave of panic breaks, the next gathers. Flight. He cannot be found here with her. He staggers to his feet and retrieves his jacket. All he can think of is escape.

He leaves the staff room and closes the door. He runs back the way they had come together. He reaches the gate into the main shelter. He has the foresight to fasten the buttons on his jacket and to straighten his hair.

The tunnel is full of people, many of them sleeping or resting on their bunks. Some are gathered together in small groups, talking. He walks along the tunnel, trying to ignore them and to look as he did before he found her, but it is as though a thousand pairs of eyes are on him.

He passes through the entrance into the lower lobby and walks straight to the lift.

'Oi! We haven't had the all clear yet, mate.'

The warden.

'I know, but I must be away. I have an important meeting tomorrow for which I must prepare. Ministry business,' he says. He fumbles in his pocket for his identity card and waves it at the warden.

'Yes, of course. Sorry, Sir.'

'That is quite alright. But if you can open the lift gate, I would be grateful.' He ignores the voices in his head telling him to run.

'Haven't you forgotten something?' says the warden.

His heart is instantly in his mouth. He glances at the stairs.

'The log, Sir. I need your name for the log.'

'Yes, of course,' he says, feeling foolish. He looks at the man and hesitates. 'I entered as "BELCO". I was here for a meeting with the Ministry. I suppose you should mark me out as the same.'

'Thank you Sir. BELCO it is.' The Warden enters it in the log. 'Just a moment Sir and I will let you into the lift.'

He can feel himself sweating. His hands are trembling and he clasps them together so that the warden will not notice. But he fails.

The Warden looks at him oddly. 'Are you alright, Sir? You seem to be sweating.'

'Yes. Yes, I'm fine. I am just not terribly fond of tunnels. I suffer from a little claustrophobia. Another reason for wanting to leave,' he lies.

'Very good, Sir,' the Warden says, making his way around his desk and walking across to the lift. He opens the gate. 'You will be alright in the lift, Sir?'

'Yes. Yes, perfectly alright.'

'That's what they call irony, that is. You working for the lot doing the electrics down here and being afraid of… If you don't mind me saying so.'

'If we can just get on with it,' he replies impatiently.

The warden closes the gate and presses a button on the wall. The lift begins to ascend. 'Good night, Sir.'

'Good night.'

The lift takes several minutes to reach the upper lobby. While the lift car ascends, he leans against the side of the car trying to calm himself and to think. He has to escape. But he knows that there can be no escape. The body will be discovered when the labourers arrive for work in the morning. There will be an investigation and it will be all too obvious that he was with her. He knows how it will look. He tore her blouse. His name will be all over the newspapers.

The lift comes to a halt with a shudder and he opens the gate. He walks across the entrance hall to the main doors. After the warmth of the tunnels, walking out into the cool air of the street is like entering a refrigerator. The street is deserted and in complete darkness. The street lamps have been extinguished and the houses around the shelter have black out sheets at their windows. He catches the smell of burning timber on the air and looks southwards. The sky in that direction is glowing orange and he can hear the faint sound of ringing bells. He wonders how many buildings are alight. He makes his away to his car and gets in.

He knows that it is hopeless and, for the first time, considers driving to the nearest police station to hand himself in. What else can he do? Run? Where would he go? The mere fact that he would be missing would only add to the suspicion. The alternative is to return home and to say nothing. His thoughts turn to his wife. She will know, whether he tells her or not. She always knows. He can feel himself shaking. He has to stay calm.

He starts the car and reverses out on to the street, leaving the headlamps off to avoid the attention of the air raid wardens. He drives home. There is nothing else to be done. He has to tell her and then go to the police.

He pulls up outside the house. He realises that he has no idea of the time and looks at his watch. It is after midnight. She will probably be asleep. She refuses to use the Anderson shelter in the back garden. She says that she was born in a house and would rather die in one, than in some blasted pig sty in the garden, cooped up like a common beast.

He gets out of the car and lets himself into the house. It is dark inside. He makes his way to the lounge and opens the lounge door. A pool of dim light floods the hall. She is asleep on a chair by the fire, which is no more than a few glowing embers. There is a single lamp on the table and black out curtains are blocking any light from reaching the street outside.

As he enters the room, she stirs and opens her eyes. 'Where in God's name have you been?'

'There was an air raid,' he whispers. He takes his jacket off and hangs it over a chair.

'I know that you bloody fool.' She sits up and looks at him. 'Look at the state of you. What is that on your shirt?'

He looks down at the front of his shirt. It is smeared with blood from Martha's nose and his own vomit.

She gets up and walks across to him. 'What is this?' she says, reaching for his shirt and pulling a face. 'You have been sick and this is blood. Are you hurt?'

'No. It is…' he stammers.

'Oh, for God's sake, pull yourself together,' she says with obvious distain. 'You are shaking like a baby.'

'I was sick.'

'And the blood?' She looks at him. He can see nothing but suspicion in her eyes. She knows. He knew she would. He says nothing.

'The blood. Is it yours?'

He shakes his head.

'Then whose is it?'

He says nothing.

'Was somebody hurt in the raid? You stopped to help. You bloody fool. Why must you always get involved? If you have have spoiled that suit...'

'No,' he interrupts her. He looks at her and can see nothing but steel in her eyes.

'Whose blood is this,' she says, tugging the front of his shirt.

He opens his mouth but the words won't come.

'I will ask you one more time. Whose blood is this?'

'Her name was Martha,' he says blankly. 'I am sorry, but I am afraid that there was an accident. She is dead.'

CHAPTER THIRTY-NINE

Saturday, 3rd July 2004

Harry got out of the Saab, closed the door and bought a ticket at the parking meter. He had opted for Ellen's car on the grounds that she would have struggled to climb into the Spitfire with her foot in plaster. It was getting dark as he walked across the car park toward the hospital main building.

Ellen had been waiting to be discharged all afternoon. Harry found her sitting in wheelchair at the main entrance, talking to a small, stocky man in a porter's uniform. She beamed when she saw him. Ellen thanked the Porter. 'You'll need this,' he said, handing her bag to Harry who slung it over the back of the wheelchair.

'Where to, m'lady?' he said with a grin.

'Any news about Marcus?' she asked, as Harry began wheeling her back toward the Saab.

'A little. I spoke to the hospital this morning. He has multiple fractures but they're mostly concerned about the injuries to his head. He fractured his skull and there is some swelling, apparently.'

'Is he conscious?'

'No,' said Harry, hesitating.

'What?'

'Do you know, it is really odd. I haven't been able to get hold of Tom since the accident. Have you heard from him at all?'

'Hardly. I've been stuck in here.'

'I wondered whether he might have been to see you?'

'No, not a word.'

Harry was struggling to manoeuvre the wheelchair between cars as they made their way back across the car park. 'Something is not quite right there,' he said.

'What do you mean?' asked Ellen.

'With Tom. I've been watching the playback from the cameras.'

'Play back?'

'Mike recorded what happened at the shelter. Not the whole thing, but from the point just after Marcus fell.'

They were almost back at the car when Harry suddenly had the feeling that someone was behind them. As he turned to look over his shoulder, a man stepped out from between two vans. Harry recognised him instantly but had barely registered the thought before the man had pushed him, hard, in the small of the back. Harry slumped sideways and found himself sprawled across the bonnet of a green Vauxhall Calibra. He could hear Ellen screaming. Harry struggled to regain his feet and turned. The man was nowhere to be seen. Ellen was trying to stand up.

'No, don't. Your foot.' said Harry. 'Are you alright?'

'Just a bit shaken,' said Ellen, slumping back down into the wheelchair.

'What the hell was that all about?' said Harry, glancing around.

'The bag. He took it.'

'Shit. I'll go and get someone from the hospital. They're bound to have security.'

'Harry, no,' she said grabbing his hand. 'There was hardly anything in it.' She lowered her voice. 'You took the purse and the map last night.'

Harry looked at her. 'I recognised him.'

'You did?'

'Yes. Didn't you?'

'No, I didn't see his face. It happened so quickly.'

255

'Well I did. He was at Belsize Park. After we left. I saw him on the camera feed.'

'Are you sure?'

'Yes and that wasn't the first time. He's the man who followed me. Before the burglary.'

'Harry, lets just go,' Ellen said, glancing around tensely. 'In case he comes back. He won't find whatever he wants in that bag.'

Harry wheeled Ellen alongside the Saab, opened the door and helped her in to the passenger seat.

'Yes?' said Max Banks, making his way out of the restaurant. 'Just a moment.' He opened the door and stepped out into the evening air, glancing back into the restaurant. He could see his mother who was talking animatedly to the group of men and women seated at the table.

'What? But Dabrowski was adamant.' He listened again. 'Follow them. I want that purse. At all costs. Stay with them. Do you understand?'

Max Banks ended the call, re-entered the restaurant and seated himself next to his mother. He waited for her to fall silent and leant across and whispered in her ear. 'We have a problem, Mother.'

She listened carefully to his whispered explanation, without comment. After he had finished, she looked at the other guests. 'I'm afraid that we are going to have excuse ourselves. An urgent matter has arisen that we must attend to. Please excuse us,' she said standing up.

'We must speak in the morning, Max,' said Alistair Calvern.

'Certainly Alistair. You know that I value your input to my restructuring plans for Campaign Headquarters, above all others.'

'Thank you Max, I very much appreciate that,' said the Party Chairman shaking him by the hand.

'Good night Judith, my dear,' Banks said, turning to Calvern's wife. 'I am so sorry that we must, on this occasion, leave so early.' He kissed her on each cheek. He noticed her perfume. She was, he had to concede, an unusually attractive woman. He caught her eye as she pulled away and held her gaze for a moment. Quite why she had married such a stuffed shirt was beyond him. Banks noticed the slight flush spreading across her cheek. 'It would be splendid to see you again quite soon,' he said quietly.

Max could tell, by the way his mother walked across the restaurant, that she was furious. He braced himself.

Harry pulled into the drive in front of his flat and helped Ellen from the car.

'Put your arm around my shoulder,' he said.

Ellen limped to the front door, her arm around him. Harry let them in.

'I'm fine,' said Ellen, limping down the hallway. 'Make sure that the front door is locked and bolted.'

Harry returned to the front door and looked out into the street. It was now dark. The street was quiet and there was no sign of any pursuer. He closed the door, turned the key in the lock and bolted the door.

As Harry closed the door, a black BMW with tinted windows pulled up on the far side of the street. Its head lights were off. The driver cut the ignition and waited.

Harry walked along the hallway and found Ellen in the living room. She had seated herself on the sofa, her plastered foot resting on the cushion next to her.

'Are you OK?' he said.

She looked at him.

'Alright. Stupid question,' he said. 'I'll make some coffee.'

While he was in the kitchen, she called out. 'What have you done with the purse? Is it here?'

'No, it is at Mike's. Given the break in, I thought that it would be better to leave it there,' he replied.

'Good idea,' she called out.

Harry brought the coffee in and seated himself opposite her. They were silent for a moment.

'I've been thinking,' she said. 'The man who took my bag. He is the key to this. Isn't he?'

'Yes he is,' Harry agreed.

'If we knew who he is or, more likely, who he is working for, then I suspect the rest of it would fall into place,' said Ellen, pausing for a moment. 'You are sure that he followed you from Bletchley?'

'Yes, I am. I recognised him as soon as I saw him on the camera feed.'

'Well if it was the same man, then it is fairly obvious that he is the man who broke into your flat and who threatened me at the shop.'

'Yes, I think that we can be almost certain about that,' said Harry.

Ellen thought for a moment. 'Could he have had anything to do with the accident last night?'

'I don't see how.'

'You said that Tomasz reacted oddly.' said Ellen.

'Yes and it has been on my mind all day.'

'What was odd about it?'

'After the accident happened, Tom came out of the lift and went to the guardroom. He didn't run. He walked. Given that one of his friends had just fallen eighty feet down a lift shaft I would have expected him to have run and possibly down the stairs rather than to the guards.' He was quiet for a moment. 'Also, their reaction when Tomasz appeared in the corridor outside the guardroom. They had obviously spotted him on the camera because one of the guards came out. But again, he didn't rush out and the second guard stayed inside. They just didn't react like they were very surprised.'

'There is also Tom's rather odd behaviour on top of the lift. Has it occurred to you that it was you who were meant to be on that rope Harry, rather than Marcus?' Ellen said.

Harry said nothing. In truth, Ellen had voiced what he had been thinking.

'How long have you known Tom?' she asked.

'I'm not sure. A couple of years. I don't know him that well. He mostly keeps himself to himself. But it was Tom who hacked into BELCO and got us the information about Arthur Wallington. Without him, I'm not sure that we would have ever got into Belsize Park.'

Ellen, wriggled uncomfortably on the sofa and re-positioned her leg. 'So where is he Harry? Have you tried him again?'

'Yes, I tried his number just before I left to collect you from the hospital. Unobtainable.'

They were both silent.

'Alright. Let's go back to the man who took my bag. What was he doing at Belsize Park?'

'He looked like he belonged. He came in, spoke to a guard, made a telephone call and left in a hurry,' said Harry.

'Did he show any ID?'

Harry thought for a moment. 'No, I don't think so. It looked to me like the guard knew who he was.'

'In which case, he is very probably an employee of Safe House or perhaps has some other connection to them.' She thought for a moment. 'What do we know about them?'

'Not a lot. Other than that they store Government records down there, amongst other things and have an influential MP on their board.'

'How do you know that?'

'The Major told me. I called Safe House from Bletchley Park to see whether they would allow me to visit the shelter. Within minutes I had the Major on my back, screaming blue murder. I was told, in no uncertain terms, to stay away from Safe House and from Belsize Park.'

'Who is the MP?' asked Ellen.

'I don't know, but he is on one of the committees that deals with museum funding.' said Harry.

'Ouch,' said Ellen.

'Exactly,' said Harry. 'The old boy was not pleased. And it gets worse. I have been meaning to tell you. They're suspending me.'

'Yes, I know.'

Harry was surprised. 'How do you know?'

'Jane told me. I spoke to her this afternoon.'

'She's been to see you?'

'No, I called her. I was meant to be going out for a drink with her over the weekend.'

'Jesus. I wonder who else she has told.'

'Harry. She wouldn't tell anybody else. She is worried about you, that's all.'

Harry was silent for a moment. 'Did she tell you about John Watts?'

'Yes.'

'Did she say whether there was any sign of a break in?'

'No,' replied Ellen.

'Or whether anything is missing from the house?'

'Like what?'

'Like the diary.'

'Do you think it may have been taken?'

'I don't know. I guess we won't know until he wakes up,' said Harry.

'If he wakes up. He's an old man.'

Harry was silent.

'We have got to find out who the man who took my bag is and what connection there is between him, Safe House, BELCO and Arthur Wallington. There has to be one. We've got to find it and quickly. Then, I think, it will be time to go to the police,' said Ellen.

'I don't think we should do that unless we can put the whole thing in front of them. Otherwise, I just can't see them being interested in a woman who went missing in 1944,' said Harry.

'Well we're both going to have plenty of time on our hands,' said Ellen. 'So first thing in the morning we start on Safe House, BELCO and Arthur Wallington. There is a link, Harry. I know there is.'

They were both quiet for a moment.

'Are you hungry?' said Harry, suddenly.

'Starving. Do you have any food in?'

'Not much and its too late to get anything delivered, but there's a twenty-four hour place near the station. I can be there and back in fifteen minutes. Will you be alright on your own?'

Ellen crossed her arms. 'I might have a broken foot, but I am not completely helpless.'

Harry looked at her lying on the sofa and grinned. 'Actually, I was just wondering how you are going to manage getting out of those trousers, unless you were planning on sleeping in them.'

Ellen picked up a cushion and threw it at him. 'Typical man. One track mind.'

CHAPTER FORTY

The walk to the takeaway had taken Harry less than ten minutes but he had still not liked leaving Ellen on her own. He had almost run the last fifty yards.

'Eating in or taking away?' said the girl behind the counter.

'Taking away,' replied Harry.

'Eight pounds seventy, please.'

Harry paid the girl and waited impatiently for the food. As she was handing it him, his mobile phone rang. Harry pulled it from his pocket and answered it in a hurry.

'Are you OK?' he said.

'I'm fine,' said Mike 'but nice of you to ask.'

'Oh, Mike. I thought you were Ellen.'

'How is she?'

'She's fine. I've just come out for some food but I'm worried about leaving her on her own. Her bag was stollen outside the hospital. It was the man at Belsize Park, Mike. The one I thought I recognised.'

'Are you sure?'

'Yes. I am positive.'

'Actually, that's why I called you. I know who he is.'

'What?' Harry almost shouted.

'Well, not who he is. But who he works for.'

'How?'

'Were you watching the news tonight?'

'No. We haven't had the television on.'

'Well I have. There was a piece on the Six O'clock News about the Tory Party leadership contest. The camera showed one of the candidates getting out of a chauffeur driven car. I recognised him straight away. The chauffeur that is. But, to make absolutely certain, I waited until they re-ran the item on the News at Ten and recorded it, so that I could compare him with the guy on the footage from Belsize Park.'

'And?' Harry could not keep the excitement from his voice.

'It is him Harry. The same man. No doubt. Come over and take a look yourself if you don't believe me.'

Harry stood outside the takeaway, thoughts crowding his head. 'Which candidate was he chaffering?'

'Max Banks. You know, the front runner? He's a total slime bag, but it looks like he has already got the leadership in the bag.'

Harry's mouth fell open. 'He works for Max Banks MP?'

'Yup. Well, he was chauffeuring for him.'

Harry started to walk. 'Jesus, Mike. Banks. He's the MP on the board of Safe House.' Harry quickened his pace.

'It gets better Harry. What was the name of the man from BELCO who you said went into the shelter? The one you suspect of being behind the woman's disappearance.'

'Arthur Wallington.'

'I thought so. You might want to sit down for this.'

'I can't. I've got to get back to Ellen.'

'Well don't say I didn't warn you.'

'What?'

'Max Banks is Arthur Wallington's son.'

Harry stopped in his tracks. 'How can he be? They've got different surnames.'

'Arthur Wallington married Hilary Banks, the daughter of the owner of BELCO. BELCO is short for The Banks Electrical Company Limited.'

'Shit,' said Harry, starting to run.

'Hilary Banks didn't take Wallington's name. Or rather she hyphenated it. Hilary Banks-Wallington. I guess so as not to lose the family name. Bank's full name is Maximillian Banks-Wallington, but somewhere along the line he dropped Wallington.'

Harry was struggling with the implications of what Mike had just told him.

'Fucking hell. That's it, Mike. Martha, Wallington, Banks, BELCO, the man in the car park. That's it.'

'Harry, don't you think you should go to the police. This is big. Too big for us. These are powerful people. Max Banks could be our next Prime Minister for fuck's sake. Can you imagine what will happen if it comes out that his father murdered a woman and hid her body in an air raid shelter?'

'It will be even bigger if we can prove that Max Banks has been trying to stop us finding out.'

'It is massive Harry. It will be the headline for weeks.'

'Look, I'm two minutes from home. Let me to speak to Ellen and I'll call you back.'

Harry ended the call as he turned into his street. He ran the last few yards to his door at full pelt. He fumbled for his key.

From behind him, a voice said 'Stand quite still Mr Stammers.'

Harry whirled around. The man had a gun in his hand. Harry had never seen a real gun up close, but he recognised the silencer attached to the barrel. The man brought the gun up, level with Harry's face and pointed it at his forehead.

'I said, stand still.'

'You?'

'Good evening. Your mobile phone please,' he said, holding out his hand.

Harry hesitated.

'Mr Stammers, either you do exactly as I say or I will spray your brains across your front door and then I will enter your flat and do the same, possibly with some embellishments,' he said grinning 'to Miss Carmichael. Do you understand?'

Harry said nothing. He handed the man his phone.

'Good. Now, you are going to open your front door. You will call out your normal greeting to Miss Carmichael and we will both enter. You will take me to her. If you say or do anything to raise the alarm I will shoot you both. Is that clear?'

'Yes,' said Harry.

'Excellent. Now get on with it.'

Harry opened the door. 'Ellen, it's me. I'm back.'

The man pushed the barrel of the gun into the space between Harry's shoulders. They walked down the corridor, Harry still holding the takeaway in his hand. They entered the lounge.

'Good evening, Miss Carmichael,' said the man, stepping out from behind Harry.

Ellen gasped and struggled to get to her feet.

'Stay seated Miss Carmichael. Unless of course you would like me to shoot Mr Stammers.'

Ellen slumped back into her seat, holding her hand to her mouth. The man walked across the room and stood behind Ellen, pointing the gun at the back of her head.

'Now, Mr Stammers, the purse that you stole from the tunnel. My employer wishes to have it. You will give it to me.'

'I can't. It is not here,' said Harry.

'That is unfortunate. Where is it?'

Harry hesitated. The man flipped the gun in his hand and struck Ellen on the side of her head with the butt. She screamed and slumped sideways.

'No!' Harry shouted, stepping forward toward Ellen.

The man pointed the gun at him.

'Do not fuck me about Mr Stammers. My employer has lost patience with you and I have instructions to kill you both, if necessary, to recover the purse. Now where is it?'

'I told you, we don't have it.'

Ellen was crying and holding the side of her face.

'I will ask you one last time. If I have to ask again, I will put a bullet into Miss Carmichael's right knee. Then her left. I have plenty of bullets in here,' he said, waving the gun. 'I am sure that I will be able to think of some rather more interesting places to insert them, before she loses consciousness. Now where is the purse?'

'I gave it to a friend for safe keeping,' said Harry.

'His name?'

Harry swallowed. 'Mike. Mike Eglund.'

'Thank you. And where is Mr Eglund now?'

Harry told him.

The man was thoughtful for a moment. 'You will take me to him. Both of you. Get up, Miss Carmichael,' he said pointing the gun at her.

'I can't,' she said, still sobbing.

'Help her to her feet,' he said, waving the gun at Harry.

Harry walked across to Ellen and helped her up. He hugged her for a few moments 'I'm sorry Ellen,' he said.

'Do you have any parcel tape Mr Stammers?'

'Yes, it is the draw over there,' Harry replied, pointing to his computer desk.

'You will get it now and you will tape Miss Carmichael's wrists together behind her back.'

Harry did as he was instructed.

'Good. You will take her to the front door. We will walk across the street and get into the black BMW parked across the road. Mr Stammers, you are going to drive. Be aware, both of you, that since, apparently, you do not have the purse, your usefulness to me is rapidly declining. I will have little reason not to shoot you if you do not do exactly as you are told. Do you both understand?'

'Yes,' they answered in unison.

Ellen hobbled along the corridor, with Harry's arm around her.

'Stop,' said the man when they were a few feet from the door. 'Stand against the wall.'

They did so. The man walked past them, pointing the gun at them as he passed. He opened the door and glanced out into the night, the gun still pointed in their direction. 'Good. Now Mr Stammers, you will walk across to the car and open the rear door facing us. Miss Carmichael and I will follow and Miss Carmichael will then get in. You, Mr Stammers, will then walk around to the other rear door and open it. I will get in next to Miss Carmichael. You will get into the driver's seat. Neither of you will speak. Is that understood.'

They both nodded.

'Good, let us proceed.'

Harry gave Ellen's hand a squeeze and looked at her. He had never seen anyone look so terrified. He opened the front door and stepped outside. He walked across to the BMW, glancing over his shoulder as he went. Ellen had stepped out through the door with the man immediately behind her. He waited for them to approach and opened the passenger door. Ellen struggled to get in. The man waved at Harry with the gun and Harry helped her in and closed the door. Then he walked around to the driver's side and held the passenger door open. The man pointed the gun directly at him as he got into the car.

Harry saw his opportunity. Perhaps their only opportunity. He did not hesitate. He slammed the door with all of his strength. It hit the man's wrist. Harry heard the crunch. The gun flew out of his hand and spun across the pavement, coming to rest on a grass verge. Harry estimated that it was about twelve feet from him. He had barely turned to run for the gun when the man exploded from the rear of the car. Harry felt the man's arms encircle his waist and they both collapsed onto the ground. Harry kicked and struggled but the man was too heavy. He was trying to wrestle Harry onto his back. Harry reached out and caught hold of a hard, cold object. As the man hauled him over, Harry brought the object up fast and struck the man across the front of his face. The man howled and slumped sideways, releasing his grip. Harry got to his feet. The man was struggling to stand up. Harry could see a smear of dark red across his face. Harry ran for the gun. He was so focussed on reaching it that he paid little attention to the man behind him. He dived onto the verge and, as his hands closed around the butt, he heard the car door close and the engine roar into life. He turned as quickly as he could but it was too late. The black BMW was already moving, its tyres spinning and squealing on the tar mac.

CHAPTER FORTY-ONE

Saturday, 11th November 1944

'Dead? Don't be ridiculous. Who is this woman? What are you talking about?'

He pulls away from her. She grabs him by the arm.

'Do not turn your back on me. Tell me.'

He looks away. 'I killed her. It was an accident. But I killed her.'

'Tell me. Now.'

He tells her, leaving out the kiss and that he would have made love to her had she allowed it. But she knows.

'You expect me to believe that you took this girl to a private room to dress her swollen ankle?'

'That is the truth.'

'Liar! It is perfectly plain what you had in mind.'

He says nothing.

'You struck her. You actually struck her?'

'Yes. But I did not mean to hit her. I was angry. I did not mean to kill her!'

'Bastard. I am not a fool. You have put everything at risk for this… this slut.'

He says nothing.

She walks to the window, pulls the black out curtain aside and glances left and right.

'I must go to the police and hand myself in. It is all that I can do. It was an accident. They have to believe me.'

She turns to face him. 'Believe you? Are you a complete imbecile? No, I do not need to ask that. You would have taken this woman had she let you, that much is perfectly obvious. And when she had the good sense to deny you, you struck her, knocking her to the floor. Was there a struggle?'

He says nothing.

'Was there?'

'Yes.'

'Idiot!'

She marches across the room and strikes him across the side of his face. He is knocked backwards with the force of the blow.

'You have put everything at risk. Your hanging would be justified but think of the scandal. Think of the ruination. I stand to inherit one of the most important companies in Britain and you have put it all at risk, for a sake of five minutes with a slut on an underground bunk?'

He clutches the side of his face. 'It wasn't like that.'

'Imbecile.' She strikes him again. He feels his teeth cut into the side of his mouth and tastes blood. He coughs and the blood from his mouth mingles with Martha's blood on his shirt.

'You will not go to the police. You are not going to take my inheritance away from me.'

'For God's sake. She is down there and they will find her and when they do, it will not take them long to find me.'

'Then you will go back and hide her body.'

He looks at her, dumbfounded. 'Are you mad? I will go to the police. I will tell them that it was an accident. It was an accident.'

She stares at him. 'No you will not,' she says icily 'If you do, I will tell them that you are a violent man. I will tell them that you have beaten me. I will tell them that you have forced yourself on me.' She looks at him triumphantly. 'I will tell them that you confessed to her murder.'

He stares at her aghast. 'But that is not true. I have never laid a hand on you.'

'I will not have you destroy my future. One day, I will inherit my father's company and I will not see you drag my company into the gutter. God knows why I chose you but I did. I will not be remembered as the wife of a murderer. As the wife of a man who lured a young woman into an empty room and, when she resisted him, beat her to the ground and left her for dead on a dirty floor. You are not going to do that to me. I will not allow it. Do you hear me?'

He looks at her, his face still stinging.

'She will disappear. We are in the middle of the blitz. People go missing every day.'

He watches her speak but he doesn't hear her words. All he can see is Martha's face and her body lying on the shelter floor.

'Did she enter the shelter alone?'

'What?'

'Did she enter the shelter alone?'

'Yes. That is what she told me.'

'Did you speak to anyone while you were with her?'

'No.'

'Are you sure?'

'Yes.'

'Did she say that she had seen anyone she knew?'

'No. She did not say so.'

'Then it will be as though she was never there.'

He stares at her. Unable to comprehend the implications of what she is saying. Then he remembers the log.

'Her name will be in the log. The wardens take the name of everyone entering the shelter.'

She turns away from him and walks to the window, glancing out between the curtains again. She stands there for a moment with her back to him.

'You will remove the page on which her name appears.'

'But the log is held by the wardens.'

'Then you will distract them.' She almost screams it.

'They will notice that the log has been tampered with.'

'Then do it carefully, you idiot,' she says, whirling around to face him. 'Take one of your razor blades and remove it as close to the spine as you can.'

He looks at her. 'I can't.'

'You can and you will.'

'Please. I beg you. Do not make me do this.'

She laughs. 'You are pathetic. Do you know that? I am sick of your cowardice. Behave like a man, for once.'

He feels anger boiling within him and takes a step toward her.

'Go ahead. Strike me down, like you struck that slut. You will hand me the rope by which you will swing,' she spat at him defiantly.

He knew that he was beaten. He knew that she would never let him escape. He had known it all along.

CHAPTER FORTY-TWO

Monday, 5 th ***July 2004***

Harry Stammers stood on the grass verge, clutching the gun and staring at the space where the BMW had been. Ellen. He had taken Ellen. Then it hit him like a bolt of lightning. He had told the man that Mike had the purse and had given him the address. It would take them no more than twenty minutes to reach Mike's house, maybe less with the streets empty of traffic. Harry had to warn him. He ran. Across the road and into his flat.

He dived into his bedroom and reached for the phone. Mike's number. It was on his mobile phone. Harry stood still, frantically trying to remember the number. 'Shit. Shit. Shit,' he shouted out loud. Then it came to him.

Harry dialled. 'Mike, its Harry. You've got to get out.'

'What?'

'Banks's driver. He was waiting for me when I got back. He has taken Ellen. He's coming for the purse.'

'What?' You told him where I live?'

'I'm sorry. He had a gun. He hit Ellen. He would have killed her, probably both of us if I hadn't told him.'

'Fucking hell.'

'Mike he'll be there in ten minutes. Get the purse. You've got to get out.'

'Where am I going to go?'

'I don't know.' Harry thought for a moment. 'It's not safe here. If he finds you gone, he may come back. Golders Green Station. I'll meet you there. As soon as you can. And don't call me on my mobile phone. He took it.'

'Shit. OK. I'm on my way.'

Harry ended the call and went in to the bathroom. He went to the sink, turned on the cold tap and splashed water on to his face. As he reached for a towel, he caught sight of his face in the mirror. Harry stood staring at himself. They had Ellen. It was all he could think of. He would hurt her. He'd already hit her. Harry had to find her. He went back to the lounge. The gun was lying on the table by the telephone. He picked it up and slid it into his inside jacket pocket. Then he picked up his cigarettes and left.

He'd been waiting outside Golders Green Station for ten minutes, smoking one cigarette after another when Mike pulled up in his blue Honda. Harry walked across to the car and got in.

'What are you going to do Harry? You've got to go to the police.'

'I don't know Mike. He's got Ellen. Whatever I do is going to put her at risk.'

'We could just give him the bloody purse.'

'Have you got it?'

'Yes,' Mike said, patting his inside pocket.

'But are they going to be satisfied with that? We know too much Mike.'

'Maybe. But what else can we do? It is too dangerous.'

Mike's mobile phone rang. He pulled it from his pocket and looked at the flashing screen. 'It is him. Look,' he said, handing it to Harry.

Harry activated the speaker phone.

'Hello?' he said, tentatively.

'Harry is that you?'

'Ellen?'

'Harry,' Ellen cried. Her voice was interrupted.

'Mr Stammers, I thought I made it clear that unless you did exactly as I instructed, I would put a bullet through Miss Carmichael's knee cap.'

'If you hurt her, you bastard, I'll find you. I know who you are,' Harry said between gritted teeth. 'If it takes me a lifetime, I'll find you and when I do, I'll kill you.'

The man laughed. 'You have no idea. This was always bigger than you could ever have imagined. You have stumbled from one error to another.'

'What do you want?'

'What do I want?' laughed the voice. 'I want my gun back for one thing. I want that purse and I want you, Mr Stammers. You are going to pay for slamming that door on my hand.'

'Fuck you. I know who you work for and I know who killed Martha Watts. When I go to the police, the whole thing will be blown open and you will all end up in prison.'

'Well said, Mr Stammers. You are showing some balls at last. However, you will not go to the police. If you do, you will never see Miss Carmichael alive again and believe me, when I have done what I have in mind, you will certainly not want to see her dead body.'

Harry paled.

'However, my employer is a kind hearted man.'

'Cut the crap,' Harry interrupted. 'We're talking about Banks. Max fucking Banks.'

The man was silent. 'Very well, Mr Stammers, Mr Banks is a kind hearted man. You have twenty-four hours. In that time, you will gather up everything you have on Martha Watts, especially the purse and, of course, the map from the tunnel. Miss Carmichael has told me all about that, haven't you darling?'

There was a pause. Harry could hear Ellen whimpering in the background. Tears filled his eyes.

'You will bring it and my gun, to a place of our choosing. We will be back in touch with you shortly to see how you are doing and to give you further instruction. But let me be absolutely clear, Mr Stammers, we will be watching and listening. We have many contacts. If you have any doubt about our capabilities, you may or may not have noticed that we have already dealt with Mr Dabrowski, Mr Watts and Mr Dawson, albeit that splashing him across the bottom of a lift shaft was not in our original plan. You will also have noticed that we have done so with impunity. Rest assured that the hand of the law does not extend to my employer. In point of fact and in case you have not been watching the news, he is about to become the law. But to spell it out for you: - If you go anywhere near the police, then not only will we kill Miss Carmichael in a most enjoyable fashion, but we will also deal with Mr Eglund. He is there with you, I take it?'

Harry looked at Mike. 'Yes,' he choked.

'Excellent. I will see you in twenty-four hours Mr Stammers. Until then.'

The line went dead.

Harry sat staring at the mobile phone.

'It is my fault,' he said after a few minutes.

Mike was silent.

'The whole thing.'

'Oh come on Harry. Ellen was just as determined to do this as you were,' said Mike.

'Maybe.'

'What do you think he meant when he said that they had dealt with Tom?'

'God knows. But if what happened at the shelter was not an accident, then Tomasz must have been helping them,' said Harry.

'You think?'

'Yes. It was too easy. Getting into the shelter. The business with the cameras. It was all too easy.'

'Man, and now they've got Ellen,' said Mike.

'God knows what that bastard will do to her.'

They were silent again.

It was Harry who broke the silence. 'I've got to find her Mike. You heard what he said. One whiff of the police and they'll shoot her. So it is down to me.'

'He's bluffing, Harry.'

'Maybe he is. But I can't take the risk.'

Mike hesitated. 'You could just hand it all over to them.'

'I could, yes. But do you think they'll be satisfied with that? Because I don't. Once they have all of the evidence, and they've already got most of it, what's to stop them putting a bullet in both our heads? Are they really just going to let us walk away?'

'Man, this is a nightmare. What are you going to do?'

'I'm going to go back to my flat and find out where Banks lives. Maybe that's where they will take her.'

'Are you crazy?'

'What choice do I have? Don't you get it? They've got Ellen.'

'And how, exactly, are you going to find Banks?'

'Google? I don't know. I've got to find her.'

'I thought your PC got trashed?'

'I've got an old laptop. It's was in a suitcase in the garage. That was the one place he didn't trash.'

Mike was quiet.

'What do you want me to do?'

'I want you to find somewhere safe for tonight. Somewhere you can go with the purse. Somewhere away from here, in case he comes back. That purse is all we've got.'

'Sure.'

Mike started the car and they drove the short distance back to Harry's flat.

'I'll call you in the morning,' said Mike. 'Don't do anything on your own Harry. It is too dangerous. We'll meet up tomorrow.'

'OK. Thanks Mike.'

'Sure.'

Harry got out of the car and went into his flat. He found the laptop and stood at his back door, smoking while he waited for it to boot. It was pitch black outside and Harry stood staring into the night. He thought of Ellen. He wondered where she was and in what circumstances. He wondered what she was thinking at this precise moment. She would be afraid. He had twenty-four hours to find her. He went back to the laptop and began the search.

CHAPTER FORTY-THREE

Ellen had no idea where they were. During the struggle with Harry she had been frantic to free herself from the BMW but the combination of her injured ankle and taped wrists had made escape impossible. She had tried again outside Mike's house but to no avail. Now her eyes were covered and she could see nothing.

Instead she listened. For the first twenty minutes or so there had been traffic noise and plenty of it. But this had gradually declined and now the road was mainly quiet. Perhaps a motorway or an A-road. She guessed that they were heading into the countryside.

She had hoped to glean a sense of direction somehow, but while she could tell that the road was mainly straight, she had finally to concede that trying to guess the direction was fruitless.

They had probably been in the car for about an hour and a half, when they had taken a sharp left turn and driven down a gravel track. Ellen's heart was in her mouth when, finally, they came to a halt. She heard the man get out and open the passenger door. 'Get out,' he said.

Ellen swivelled her legs around and made an effort to get out of the car, but with her wrists taped, she was unable to do so. She felt the man grab the front of her blouse.

'I said get out.'

'I can't,' she said through clenched teeth.

The man hauled her up and she felt several of the buttons on her blouse snap off. She struggled to her feet. The man took her by the arm and she was dragged along a gravel path, up three stairs and into a building which, by the sound of her feet on wooden flooring, Ellen guessed was a house. She had the distinct feeling that there were several other pairs of eyes watching her.

They walked across what Ellen guessed was a hallway.

'Stop,' the man said.

He opened a door and she was pushed inside.

'There is a chair,' he said pushing her to it and spinning her round.

'Sit.'

She sat down carefully. He ankle was throbbing.

'Do not make any attempt to move from here Miss Carmichael. If you do, there is every possibility that you will be shot. Do you understand?'

Ellen nodded.

The man left, closing and the locking the door behind him.

'Wait. My wrists. The blindfold,' she called out. But he did not return.

'Shit,' she said through gritted teeth. 'Think for God's sake. Think. What the fuck is going on?'

Ellen tried to be calm. She told herself that she was not in imminent danger. Had the man intended to kill her, he'd probably have done so by now. Whoever he was. Whoever he was working for.

'Banks.' She said under her breath. During his conversation with Harry the man had mentioned 'Mr Banks' and what had he meant when he said that Banks was about to become the law? *Is he a policeman? What the hell is going on?* Had they been wrong about Arthur Wallington? The harder she tried to think about it, the more jumbled her thoughts became. Whoever

Banks was, he was evidently willing to go to extraordinary lengths to stop them. All she had to do was figure out why. Her mind began to wander.

Ellen woke with a start. Somebody had opened the door and entered the room.

'Who's there?' she said, her voice trembling.

There was only silence.

'Who's there?'

She turned her head from side to side, but could see nothing through the blindfold. She could hear him, though. Breathing. She knew, somehow, that it was a man. She could sense it.

'What do you want?'

He moved slowly to her left.

'I said, what do you want?'

She also knew that this was not the man who had brought her here.

She heard him move back towards the door.

'Wait.'

Nothing.

'Release me. Please. I've done nothing.' She began to cry.

The room was silent, save for his breathing.

'Leave me alone,' she said. 'Leave me alone, you bastard.'

She heard the man move. His footsteps on the wooden floor and something else. A tapping sound. Then she heard the door open, then close and the click of the lock.

CHAPTER FORTY-FOUR

Saturday, 11th November 1944

He is sitting in his car in Downside Crescent. He looks at his watch: - it is five minutes to four in the morning. He can see the doorway into the shelter. A trickle of people emerge in twos and threes. They say their goodbyes and shuffle away into the darkness.

He looks at his hands and steels himself for the task ahead. He knows what he has to do.

He gets out of his car. Sunrise is some way off and the sky is still inky black. He can smell woodsmoke in the air, but the orange glow from the fires of a few hours before has gone. It is bitterly cold and, while he is shivering almost uncontrollably, beneath his coat, he is also sweating.

He walks the few yards to the shelter entrance and opens the door. Inside a warden is helping an elderly man and woman from the lift and directing them to the exit.

He walks across to the lift.

'The all clear sounded a couple of hours ago, Guvner,' says the warden.

'I am aware of that,' he replies, showing the warden his identity card. 'I inadvertently left some documents down below, when I was here earlier. I need to retrieve them.'

'Very good, Sir. Would you like a warden to go with you.'

'No.' He says it with more urgency than is required. 'No.' He calms himself. 'That will not be necessary. I will retrieve them myself.'

'Yes, Sir. I'm sending the lift down again in a few moments, if you don't mind waiting.'

'Actually, if it is all the same to you, I will take the stairs.'

'Oh right, Sir. In that case, please go ahead.'

'Thank you.'

He enters the spiral stair well that winds its way down around the lift shaft. A cold breeze is blowing from behind him. The stairs are deserted but the lift, which is visible through the red steel mesh, passes him several times as he makes his way downwards.

His feet feel like lead. The sound of them clanking on the steps appears to him to grow louder as he descends until he can stand it no longer. He stops, sweating and gasping for breath.

He closes his eyes but all he can see is her body laying on the dirty staff room floor. The thought of it makes his stomach turn and a sense of nausea threatens to overwhelm him. He tells himself that he has no choice. That she is dead and that it cannot be reversed.

After ten minutes, he reaches the bottom of the stair well and stumbles out into the lower lobby. Another warden is seated at the desk, taking the names of the people leaving. The warden looks up.

'Are you alright Sir?' He gets to his feet, scraping the chair behind him. 'Aren't you the chap who doesn't like tunnels?'

'Yes, that's right.'

'Would you like a seat, Sir? You're looking rather queer, if you don't mind me saying so.'

'No, it's quite alright. In my haste to leave earlier, I left some papers in the staff room. I need them for an important meeting later this morning.'

'Well the all clear sounded at half past two but most of them will stay until six, so you'll find the tunnels mostly still occupied.'

'I'll try not to disturb those who are sleeping.'

The warden sits back down. 'Much obliged, Sir. "BELCO", wasn't it?'

'Yes, that's right.'

The warden makes an entry in the log.

'And you are sure that you're alright?'

'Yes. Quite sure, thank you.'

He makes his way through the gateway, into the tunnel.

About half the bunks are still occupied. The shelter is filled with the eery sound of so many pairs of lungs breathing, broken by the occasional cough, whisper or child crying out. He retraces his steps. As he passes by, he notices the upturned crates on which they sat several hours before. He tries to swallow, but his throat is so dry that all he can do is cough.

A woman nursing a baby, looks up. 'Shh…'

'Sorry,' he whispers and continues on.

He reaches the end of the shelter tunnel at last and, turning left, passes through a gate into the service passage. He notices the piles of tools and materials stacked against the tunnel walls and the rubbish blowing around in the breeze.

The services tunnel ends at a t-junction. He peers into the tunnel to the left. In the distance, he can just about make out a set of steel gates in the gloom. He knows they are padlocked. He turns right and approaches the staff room door. He hesitates. He grasps the handle, opens the door and switches on the light.

Her body is in the same place on the floor. He cannot bring himself to look at her face. He walks across to a locker from which he removes a canvas shoulder bag. He returns to the body and, gritting his teeth, he kneels beside her, slides a hand under her neck and, with his other hand slips the bag over her head. That done he lowers her back to the floor and tightens the bag's draw strings.

He was expecting her body to have stiffened. But, evidently, rigor mortis has not yet set in. He returns to the lockers and removes a pair of workmen's boots, a tin hat with a lamp attached and another canvas bag. He sits on one of the bunks, removes his shoes and puts on the boots. He picks up her coat, bundles it into the second canvas bag and puts the bag over his shoulder. Then he switches on the lamp and puts the tin hat on his head.

He walks across to a small cupboard by the door, removes a large set of keys and puts them in his trouser pocket. He opens the staff room door and listens intently. The tunnel is completely silent. He uses one of his shoes to wedge the door open and kneels down beside the body, sliding an arm underneath. But he cannot lift her. He curses and lays her back down. He removes her shoes and stuffs them in his bag. He notices her small, delicate feet and the strapping on her ankle. He feels nausea rising in his chest and swallows hard. He gets to his feet and begins dragging the body toward the door.

As he pulls her through the doorway, her skirt is dragged up around her waist so that he can see her underwear and the mound between her legs. He stops and retches.

He drags her, feet first, to the intersection with the service tunnel that runs back to the shelter. He stops and lets go of her feet. Her legs hit the floor with a sickening thud and he retches again. He turns off his lamp and looks up the passage way toward the shelter. The way is clear but he is aware that he might be seen by anyone looking through the gates. He relights his lamp briefly and looks at his watch. It is 4.45am. At 6.30am the Banks workers will come on duty. Their work is largely finished, but a resident crew has remained to complete maintenance tasks. They will certainly use the staff room. He must act quickly.

He drags the body across the intersection and down the left hand corridor toward the gates to the disused tunnel. As he proceeds the tunnel becomes darker and he stops to turn on his lamp. At the gate he fumbles for the keys, this time placing her legs onto the ground more carefully. He finds the key, releases the pad lock and opens the gate. Then he drags the body through the gateway, closing the gates behind him.

It is not long before the floor of the tunnel becomes wet. A few yards further on and there is an inch of standing water. He shines the beam of the lamp at the body. To his horror he sees that her clothes and hair have become soaked by the water. Her skirt has been dragged up to the lower part of her chest, revealing her bare stomach which glints pink in the lamp light. It is a gruesome sight that he knows he will never forget.

He begins to weep, quietly. He sinks to his knees, sobbing as silently as he can, the water soaking into his trousers. 'Dear Lord, forgive me,' he whispers between sobs. 'I didn't mean to kill her. You know that I did not mean it.'

He kneels in the water for several minutes until the sobbing abates. Then he gets to his feet and continues to pull her along, the water becoming deeper as he progresses. Finally he stops at a wide steel door in the tunnel wall.

He examines the keys on the bunch and tries each one in the lock until he finds the correct key. He turns the lock mechanism and opens the door. Inside, the room, which is about eight feet square, is completely dry and empty, apart from several cables ending abruptly in a tangle of coloured wires. He removes the canvas bag from his shoulder and tosses it inside.

He begins to haul her body into the room. The lip at the bottom of the doorway, which has held back the water, hampers his efforts. Half way through, the body becomes snagged. He pulls, but whatever has caught on her clothing will not release its hold. He grits his teeth, rolls up his shirt sleeves and reaches behind her naked back. The waste band of her skirt has wedged itself around a catch at the bottom of the doorway and try as he might, he cannot release it. He begins to sob again.

After a few moments, he reaches for the hem of her skirt and, with his remaining strength, tears open the skirt and pulls it from the body. As he does so, something flies from her skirt pocket, scattering its contents in all directions. He curses and fishes around in the water. He finds several coins, a lipstick and her identity card. He throws them into the room, along with the remains of her soaking wet skirt. Then he summons the last of his energy and drags her body inside. When he has finished he closes and locks the steel door, removes the key from the keyring and puts it into his pocket. He staggers back along the tunnel, closing the gate and locking it behind him.

Returning to the staff room, he slumps down on the bunk, with his head in his hands. The first part of his grim task is complete. He rests for a few minutes then looks at his watch. It is 5.25am. He has no more than an hour to return the staff room to order, create the diversion, remove the log page and leave.

He removes the boots and tin hat, returns them to their respective lockers, collects his shoes and puts them back on. He stands and scans the room carefully. He notices a puddle of congealing blood and a pool of vomit from his earlier sickness. He finds several rags and, with the remainder of the brandy does his best to wipe up the mess.

When he is done, he surveys the room again and nods to himself. Then he takes another key from the bunch in his pocket and returns the remaining keys to the little   cupboard by the door.

He puts on his coat and stuffs the rags and the empty brandy bottle into his pockets. He takes one last look around the room and leaves, turning the light out and closing the door behind him.

CHAPTER FORTY-FIVE

Sunday, 4th July 2004

Harry was woken by the sound of the telephone ringing. He lurched to his feet, disorientated. For a moment he had no recollection of the events of the night before but, as he rubbed his neck, it returned to him.

'Yes?' he blurted into the phone.

'Harry, it's Jane.'

'Jane.' Harry sat down.

'Harry, is something wrong?'

'What time is it?'

'Just after half nine.'

Harry hesitated. He knew what he had to do.

'Harry? What's wrong? Where is Ellen? I've been calling her mobile but she is not answering. Is she there with you? Is she alright?'

Harry looked across at the gun on the coffee table.

'Last night. After we got back from the hospital. I went out to get some food and when I got back, he was waiting for us, Jane.'

'Who was?'

Harry took a deep breath.

'Harry?'

He told her. When he had finished Jane was silent.

Finally she said 'What are you going to do?'

'I am going to find her.'

'I knew you were going to say that. Harry, you said that this man was armed.'

'He *was* armed, yes.'

'Meaning?'

'Meaning, last night he was able to take Ellen because he had a gun. But I have it now. It is lying on my coffee table. I'd say that evens the odds a little, wouldn't you?'

'Harry, are you mad? There will be more guns where that one came from and he will be a damn sight more experienced than you are at using one. I bet you have never even held a gun before, let alone fired one.'

Harry could feel his temper fraying.

'So what would you have me do?' he shouted. 'Sit here and twiddle my thumbs while they do whatever they want with Ellen? Jump when they say jump? Give them the purse and everything else?'

'I don't know Harry. I need to think.'

'Well, while you are working it out, perhaps you can think about what would happen if I did handover the purse.'

Jane did not reply.

'They know that I have got it Jane. They know that it is the only evidence in existence that Martha Watts was in the tunnel at Belsize Park. Right now, the fact that I have got it is probably the only thing preventing them putting a bullet through Ellen's head.'

Jane remained silent.

'If I hand it to them on a plate, what would be stopping them from shooting us both? They've already tried to have me dropped one hundred feet down a fucking lift shaft. God knows what they did to Tom. John Watts is in hospital. Marcus is in a bloody coma. Do you seriously think that if I hand over the purse, they'll let Ellen and me go skipping off into the sunset?'

'Harry, listen to me. You cannot do this on your own. You work at a museum. You're not some hired hit man.' Jane hesitated. 'If you go looking for Ellen with a gun in your hand, you could get yourself and Ellen both killed.'

It was Harry's turn to remain silent.

'What is Mike's number?' Jane asked.

Harry didn't answer.

'For God's sake Harry. Give me Mike's number. We'll meet you there. Then all three of us can work this thing out, together.'

'I don't have my mobile. It was taken. Along with Ellen,' Harry said bitterly.

'Harry…'

'Alright,' he interrupted her. He recited the number.

'Just stay there. I can be there in an hour. Please?'

Harry hesitated. 'Alright,' he said and pressed the red button on the phone.

Jane was wrong. He'd got enough people into trouble. He was not going to expose Jane and Mike to any more. Saying it out loud had cemented it in his mind. He had to find Ellen. Nothing else mattered and nothing was going to stop him.

Little more than an hour later, Jane and Mike pulled onto the drive outside Harry's flat. They got out from the car and Jane rang the door bell. There was no reply. Jane looked at Mike with a worried expression. Mike looked in through Harry's bedroom window.

'Nothing,' he said.

Jane walked across to the garage door and tried the handle.

'It is unlocked,' she said, heaving the garage door up.

'Shit,' said Mike as the garage came into view.

Harry's Lambretta was on its stand. Otherwise the garage was empty.

Jane tried the door leading into Harry's flat. It was unlocked.

'He must have left in a hurry,' she said.

They went into the flat.

'He said that he was going to find Ellen. We need to find out where he has gone,' said Jane, rifling through a pile of papers on the coffee table.

'I'll have a look in the bedroom,' said Mike.

A few moments later, he returned to the lounge. 'Nothing. You?' he asked Jane.

'Only this,' she said, handing him a note book. 'There are several pages of notes on Max Banks MP.'

Mike opened the notebook and leafed through the pages.

'Look at this,' he said, holding out the pad.

'Safe House Limited is a subsidiary of BELCO. Max Banks is on the boards of both companies.'

'Yes, I saw that,' Jane said, searching through a pile of loose papers on Harry's desk. 'Where the hell has he gone Mike? Not back to Belsize Park, surely?'

Mike was silent for a moment.

'No. Not back to Belsize Park,' said Mike.

Jane turned around.

'He's gone to find Max Banks. Look,' said Mike.

Mike had opened the browser on Harry's laptop and had used the browser's history to list the last few pages viewed by Harry.

'He looked at it at 9.48am, this morning.'

'Right after I spoke to him,' said Jane.

'Where is Little Wymondley?' said Mike.

'It is between Hitchin and Stevenage I think,' said Jane. 'In Hertfordshire. I went to a pub there once. Tiny little place with some very grand houses.'

'I bet Wymondley Hall is one of them. How long will it take us to get there?'

'An hour. Maybe an hour and a half.'

'Which means that Harry could be there already,' said Mike looking at his watch. 'Come on.'

Without thinking, he reached for Jane's hand. 'Oh, sorry,' he said, snatching it back, his face flushing.

'The last man who grabbed me by the hand got a fat lip,' she said.

'I'm sorry. I wasn't thinking.'

Jane looked at him. 'I think I can make an exception on this occasion,' she said, holding out her hand.

Mike grinned. 'Cool.'

Harry pulled into the hedge-lined lane that led to Wymondley Hall, glancing from side to side for signs of an entrance. Shortly, he passed a wide gateway, with high black metal gates. Some yards further was a small lay-by. He pulled over and parked the Spitfire. He walked back along the lane and approached the black gates. On a brick pillar, beside the gates, was the sign for Wymondley Hall. It had been all but invisible from the lane. Harry looked through the gates. The house was a large Georgian building, with a wide gravel driveway leading from the house to the gate. Parked outside the house was a green Jaguar. The was no sign of movement, but it was difficult to see from the distance.

Harry walked back towards the Spitfire, looking for a suitable vantage point from which to observe the house and preferably, somewhere to hide the Spitfire. The man who had broken into his garage would recognise it and Harry did not want to prompt a confrontation until he was sure of Ellen's whereabouts.

Passing the Spitfire, he spotted a gate leading from the road into a dense standing of oak trees. He climbed over the gate and followed a wide pathway, covered in leaves, into the woods. He guessed that it was wide enough for the Spitfire. The pathway led to a small clearing and, beyond that, another pathway ran on, presumably to the far side of the woods. Harry returned to the gate and opened it. He then walked back along the lane and retrieved the Spitfire which he drove through the gateway, getting out to close the gate behind him, and then on into the woods. He parked the Spitfire in the clearing, got out and followed the pathway into the woods, in the rough direction of Wymondley Hall. Apart from the sound of the wind in the leaves above him, the woods were eerily silent.

After five minutes, Harry had reached the edge of the woods. The house was visible to his left, across an open field. From this view point, he could see both the Jaguar and the side of the building. There were several open windows, from which he deduced that somebody, at least, was at home.

He found a log, sat down, lit a cigarette and waited, watching the house for any sign of movement.

Had he arrived in the woods thirty minutes earlier Harry would have seen a black BMW parked beside the Jaguar. He would have seen a woman, with dishevelled hair, being dragged across the gravel to the BMW by a large man, with a shaved head and a goatee beard. He would have seen her bundled into the car's rear compartment and the BMW drive away at speed. Had he looked up he might have seen an elderly man at an upstairs window, a look of resigned sadness on his face, who continued to stare toward the gate, long after the BMW had disappeared down the lane which, only a few minutes later was occupied by Harry's Spitfire.

CHAPTER FORTY-SIX

Saturday, 11th November 1944

As he enters the main tunnel, two women are sitting on a bunk having a whispered discussion. He avoids their eyes as he passes by. He makes his way along as quietly as he can, but the tunnel is beginning to come to life as people wake and begin to prepare for the day ahead. When he finally reaches the lower lobby, he finds the warden still at his disk.

'Did you find your documents, Sir?' says the warden, glancing up.

'Yes, thank you,' he says, patting his inside pocket. 'But I'm afraid that there is quite an argument going on at the far end of the tunnel. I think you had better come.'

The warden looks alarmed. 'Bugger. Are they at it again? Bloody women I expect. You'd think they'd behave themselves down here at least. There is a war on you know.'

'I think they have been drinking. I tried to quieten them but they were having none of it.'

'Well I cannot leave my station. I'll have to call Joe upstairs. He can relieve me.'

'I wouldn't leave it that long if I were you. They were creating quite a commotion. If you don't hurry, you could have a riot on your hands.'

'Oh Gawd blimey,' the warden says looking flustered.

'Look, why don't you call your colleague... Joe was it? And I'll man the station until he gets here. It will only take a few minutes for him to come down in the lift.'

'Well I shouldn't but I suppose I could. It is very good of you, Sir. Are you sure you don't mind?'

'No, not at all. But I think you'd better hurry.'

'Yes, quite so,' the warden says lifting the telephone receiver and dialling the number.

'Joe, its Fred. There's trouble in the shelter again. I bet its those bloody women from Garnett Road.... Yes, would you? There's a chap here from BELCO who says he will hold the fort until you get down here... Yes please, if you would.'

Fred puts the phone down. 'Right. Joe will be down as soon as he can. Are you sure you don't mind?'

'No. Not in the slightest.'

'Righto. Tell Joe I'll be back as soon as I have shut them up.'

'I will.'

Fred gets up from his desk.

'They're right at the end. On the left,' he calls after the warden.

'Right you are. Leave them to me,' he says, passing into the shelter.

As soon as Fred is out of view he walks around the desk and opens the log book. He guesses that she entered the shelter sometime after eight o'clock. He is right. He finds her name almost immediately.

At that moment, he hears the lift come to life. He will have to be quick. Joe will be down in a matter of minutes and Fred will return shortly after that, puzzled at the lack of trouble.

He takes out his wallet from his inside coat pocket, opens it and removes a razor blade. He runs the blade along the page with her name, as close to the spine as he can. When he has finished he removes the page, folds it and puts it in his wallet with the razor blade. He flicks through the log book, letting the pages play through his fingers. He has done an excellent job. It will be far from obvious that a page has been removed.

He hears the lift lurch as it nears the bottom of the shaft. He closes the log and walks across to the lift. Within seconds it has arrived at the bottom of the shaft and the warden called Joe steps out. 'You must be the chap from BELCO.'

'Yes I am.'

'It was very good of you to wait.'

'Not at all. But would you mind awfully if I leave now. I am afraid I am in something of a hurry.'

'No, of course not. Thank you, Sir.'

He steps into the lift and pulls the gate closed. 'Would you?'

'Yes Sir and thank you again. I hope Fred's alright. They can be real so and sos.'

'I imagine that they can.'

Joe presses the lift button and the lift begins to ascend. 'Good night, Sir. Or should I say morning?' Joe calls out.

'Good morning,' he replies. He leans on the side of the lift.

'Thank God' he whispers and closes his eyes. But, with his eyes closed, he can still see her body. Her naked stomach. Her soaking wet knickers. Her bare legs, scratched and grazed from the tunnel floor. Her face. Blood spattered from her nose. Her dark wet hair. He tears open his eyes, sweating and vomits on the lift floor.

CHAPTER FORTY-SEVEN

Sunday, 4th July 2004

Sunday, 4 th July 2004

Harry lit another cigarette. In the hours since his arrival, he'd seen very little movement in the house but the back door, which had been open when he had arrived, was now closed. Quite how he had missed it, Harry didn't know. But he was now certain that the house was occupied, so any thought of breaking-in would have to wait. He glanced at his watch. It was after midday.

Harry got to his feet to stretch his legs, when he heard the sound of a car. He looked back at the house. The Jaguar was still on the gravel drive. It was difficult to work out from which direction the sound of the car's engine was coming. He listened carefully. The thought occurred to him that it might be coming from behind him, back through the woods. If the Spitfire had been discovered, his vantage point would be found with ease. It was only a few yards from the end of the path leading from the clearing.

Harry put his hand in his pocket and pulled out the gun. He ran back along the pathway, as silently as he could, crouching as he went. The noise of the car's engine stopped and Harry darted off the pathway and crouched down behind a tree. He listened intently but could hear nothing. After a few minutes he continued cautiously along the pathway until the clearing and the Spitfire came into view. Nothing else in the clearing moved. Harry waited until a movement caught his eye through the trees. He dodged behind a tree and held his breath.

Harry heard the sound of a man's voice which could only mean that there was more than one of them. He looked at the gun and wondered if he would be able to use it. He could hear the sound of footsteps in the leaves. He moved further behind the tree. If they passed him without spotting him, perhaps he would be able to run back towards the car. Harry dismissed the idea after only a moment's consideration. If the approaching men included Ellen's kidnapper, then this would be an opportunity, perhaps the only opportunity he would get, to discover where he had taken her.

The footsteps became louder. He held his breath until they were level with his tree. Harry raised the gun and held it in both hands pointing it straight out in front of him. As they passed, he took a breath and stepped out behind them. At the sound of his movement, they both turned and Harry saw Jane reach for Mike's arm. He noticed it before he noticed anything else. Before he saw the look of fury on her face.

'For fuck's sake Harry. Point that fucking thing somewhere else,' she said.

Mike grinned. 'Man, oh man. You've been watching the Professionals again.'

'Sorry,' said Harry pointing the gun towards the floor.

Jane stared at him. 'You said that you'd wait for us.'

'I know.'

'So why didn't you?'

'Because I knew that you would try to stop me.'

'Well, congratulations for getting that right,' Jane said, plainly furious.

'How the hell did you find me?'

'Your PC,' said Mike. 'Try wiping your browser history next time.'

Harry looked at them.

'And next time you leave in a hurry, try locking the bloody garage door. Unless, of course, you want another burglary,' said Jane.

'Right,' said Harry.

'Well, is she here?' asked Jane.

'I can't be sure. There is very little movement in the house but enough to tell that somebody is at home,' replied Harry, sliding the gun back into his inside pocket. 'Come and have a look.'

Harry guided them back down the path to the vantage point. The three of them looked at the house.

'Harry, this is bloody madness,' said Jane.

Harry didn't answer.

'Nice place,' said Mike.

Jane glared at him. 'I'm serious. You can't just go bowling in there, even with that thing in your pocket. You'll get yourself killed and quite possibly Ellen too.'

'I didn't ask you to come Jane. Either of you. In fact, I'd rather that you left right now.'

'No can do, man. We discussed it in the car on the way here. I'm in this up to my neck. The guy who took Ellen knows all about me, remember?'

Harry looked at him. 'I'm sorry Mike. I had no choice but to give him your address. He had a gun to Ellen's head.'

'The gun that is now in your pocket, in point of fact,' said Jane.

'Look Jane, I didn't ask you to become involved. You're here because you chose to come here.'

Jane stared at him. 'I am here because for some God-alone-known reason I care about you and Ellen. We both do. We want to find her as much as you do.'

Harry sighed.

At that moment their attention was caught by the sound of another vehicle. This time, the sound of its tyres on the gravel was unmistakeable. It was heading towards the house. They all dropped down onto one knee. As they did so, a car came into view. It drove onto the forecourt and parked beside the Jaguar. It was a black BMW. Even from the distance, Harry could see that the windows were tinted.

'It's the BMW. The one used by the man who took Ellen,' Harry whispered hoarsely.

On the forecourt the driver's door opened and a large man with a shaved head got out.

'It's him.'

'Are you certain?' whispered Jane.

'Absolutely,' Harry answered.

The man walked across to the door of the house and disappeared inside.

'Are you absolutely certain that it is him, Harry?'

'Yes. There is no doubt.'

'So either Ellen is here, or he is holding her somewhere else,' said Jane.

They looked at each other.

'If he leaves again, one of us should follow him,' Harry said looking at Mike. 'We've got to find out where he's holding her.'

'Agreed,' said Mike. 'I'll do it. My car is out on the road. Besides, that heap of yours will never be able to keep up with a seven series.'

'Are you sure?' said Harry.

'Sure thing,' said Mike.

'Jane, you can go with Mike if you want.'

'No. I am not leaving you alone in a clearing in the woods with a gun in your pocket. I'll stay with you.'

Harry smiled. 'Good, I was hoping you were going to say that.'

'Have you got a phone?' asked Mike.

'No,' replied Harry.

'I have,' said Jane.

'Good. If I have to go, we'll need them. What's your number?'

Jane told him and Mike entered the number into his phone.

They sat and watched the house in silence. After about thirty minutes the man came out. He was accompanied by a second

299

man and an elderly woman. They were both dressed in formal evening wear.

'That's Banks. I recognise him,' whispered Harry.

'Me too,' whispered Jane.

'Who's the older woman?' asked Mike.

Neither Harry nor Jane recognised her. They both shrugged.

The man who had taken Ellen opened the rear door of the car and the woman got in, followed by Banks. The man then got into the driver's position and the BMW drove away.

Harry looked at Mike. 'Are you sure?'

'No problem, man,' Mike replied and he was off, running through the woods back towards the clearing.

Harry looked at Jane.

'Not yet. We should wait to hear from Mike and, in any case, I think we should watch the house for at least thirty minutes to make sure that it is empty. They could easily have security guards.'

'I haven't seen any,' said Harry.

'Which is odd, don't you think? He's probably our next prime minister and not a security guard in sight.'

Harry thought for a moment. 'Yes, but until and unless he wins the party leadership, he's just a regular M.P. Do they assign security to every member of parliament?'

'I've no idea but I think that we should wait in any case and for once, Harry Stammers, you are going to do as I say, if I have to tie you to that bloody tree,' she said, glancing at the ash tree behind him.

Harry grinned. After a few moments he turned to her. 'Jane?'

'What?'

'I'm glad you found me.'

Jane grunted something unintelligible.

'Yes. And I am sorry. There is nobody I'd rather have by my side right now,' he said awkwardly.

'Well make the most of it. This is the first and last time I am ever going to contemplate going anywhere with a gun wielding maniac. Got it?'

'Got it,' Harry replied grinning broadly.

Mike ran as quickly as he could. As he approached the gate he saw the black seven series approaching at speed. He dropped onto the ground and lay still until the car had passed. Then he leapt up and vaulted the gate, and ran back along the road. Reaching the car, he fumbled for the keys and unlocked the driver's door. The BMW had already disappeared around a bend in the lane. Mike leapt into the car, started the engine and put his foot down hard.

After several minutes he saw the BMW in the distance ahead of him. After a half a mile he had gained on the car ahead. He slowed. The BMW turned onto roundabout and, as Mike turned into the traffic, he saw the BMW indicating left to turn off, onto the A1. He followed, keeping his distance. Once he was on the A1 he called Jane. 'He's on the A1, heading south, towards London.'

He could hear Jane relaying the message to Harry.

'Stay with him Mike. Let us know if he turns off.'

'Sure thing.'

'And be careful.'

'I will.' He hung up.

Their journey continued southwards. After about twenty minutes they passed under the M25. Mike reported his position to Jane. Then he turned on the radio. Concentrating, as he was, on the black BMW ahead of him, he almost missed it, but the newsreader's mention of the name caught his attention. He listened to the piece and when it was over, dialled Jane again.

'I think I know where he's going,' he said into the mobile phone. 'It has been on the radio. The result of the leadership election is going to be announced at five. He's going to Westminster.'

'He needs to stay with him,' said Harry. 'He may go elsewhere once he's dropped Banks and the woman off.'

Jane relayed the message and ended the call. 'Well at least we know where Banks is heading.'

'I reckon that the old lady was his mother. No wonder they were dressed like that.'

They had been watching the house since Mike's departure. There had been no discernible movement.

'I think it's time we made our move, Jane.'

Jane looked at him and nodded. 'Please keep that gun in your pocket unless it is absolutely necessary to get it out.'

'Understood.'

They made their way through the undergrowth until they reached a wire fence.

'You don't suppose that it's electric do you?' said Jane looking at the fence dubiously.

'Only one way to find out,' replied Harry, stretching out his hand and gently touching the wire. Nothing happened. He lifted the wire and stepped through the gap. 'Come on,' he said, holding the wire so that Jane could follow.

She stepped through gingerly.

'We'll make our way around the side of the building to the back. With a bit of luck, there'll be an open window. Once we're inside, we'll need to search the whole place. If they're in London we'll have plenty of time, so no rush. If we don't find Ellen, we may find something that points to wherever they're holding her.'

Jane nodded.

They ran across the grass towards the house and stopped when they reached the side of the building. They both listened.

'Nothing. Come on,' said Harry.

They crept to the back of the house, trying windows as they went, without any luck.

Finally Harry approached the back door and tried the handle.

'Damn. It is locked,' said Harry.

'Did you really think that they were going to leave it open for us?'

Harry looked through one of the door's small, rectangle window panes. Inside, the doorway led to a wood panelled hallway which ran towards the front of the house. The light from the door at which Harry stood, did little to illuminate the interior.

Harry looked downwards, turned towards Jane and smiled. 'Maybe not. But it was good of them to leave the key in the door,' he said pointing toward the lock.

'If you're going to break a window pane, we'd better be sure there's nobody inside.'

'And how do you propose that we do that?' he said, staring at her.

She shrugged. 'Just do it quietly.'

'Don't worry. If anyone was at home, there'd be a window open. Bound to be.'

Harry looked around and picked up a large stone. He gave the pane nearest the lock one sharp tap and the glass shattered, fragments tinkling onto the hallway floor. They both stood in silence.

'Anything?' said Harry.

'Nothing,' replied Jane, shaking her head.

He removed the larger shards of glass from the frame carefully, before reaching through to unlock the door. The key turned easily.

'Let's hope it's not alarmed,' said Jane, tensely.

'Ever the optimist,' Harry replied, trying the handle. The door opened soundlessly. They stepped into the house, closing the door behind them.

'Do we stay together, or split up? It is a big house,' said Jane.

'I guess it would be quicker if we took a room each. If you finish first, wait for me in the hallway. Remember, apart from the obvious, we're looking for anything that might indicate where they're keeping Ellen.'

'OK,' whispered Jane. She turned and entered what turned out to be the kitchen. It ran along one side of the back of the house. It was the biggest kitchen she'd ever seen.

They met in the hall way outside after several minutes.

'The Kitchen leads to an old fashioned pantry and a laundry. I checked everything.'

'That's the dining room, Harry reported, gesturing at the door from which he had just emerged. 'Very grand. More wooden panelling. How the other half live.'

'Shall we try the next two rooms?'

Jane went into the lounge and Harry entered a room which turned out to be the library. He stood looking at the thousands of books that lined the walls. He approached the shelves with reverence, pulling out the occasional volume and studying the cover. 'Incredible,' he said under his breath. In other circumstances he would have happily lost himself in the collection but they were here for a reason, he reminded himself.

He turned and approached a large mahogany writing desk above which was hung a large portrait of a balding, elderly man in a dark blue suit. He was wearing a row of medals which included, Harry noted, a Victoria Cross. He examined the name plate. It read "Stanley Banks, 1890-1965". Harry looked up at the portrait. Banks had been an imposing man. If he'd been awarded the medal during the First World War, which Harry guessed that he probably had, he'd been a brave young man in his day.

Harry sat at the desk and looked through a stack of papers that he pulled from a filing tray. They were mostly private letters addressed to Hilary Banks-Wallington. He tried the desk drawers. They were locked. He got up and searched the rest of room as best he could. There were several other portraits and photographs but, as far as he could tell, not a single picture of Arthur Wallington, Max Banks's father. Harry left the library and closed the door behind him.

'Anything?' asked Jane.

'It's a library. There's a desk but the drawers are locked. If we don't find anything else, I'd like to break the drawers open before we leave. What about you?'

'The lounge. Nothing.'

'Were there any family photographs or paintings?' Harry asked.

'Yes, lots. Why?'

'Any of Arthur Wallington?'

'If there were, I didn't notice them. Mostly pictures of Max Banks, at various stages of his upbringing I think, and his mother.'

'Same in the library.'

They checked several more rooms together but found little of any interest, noting again the complete absence of any pictures or, indeed, any sign at all of Arthur Wallington. The final room on the ground floor was off the hallway, opposite the front door.

Harry opened the door. 'It looks like a cloak room,' he said, stepping inside. It was a small, square room with hooks on the walls and several built in cupboards. Harry checked each one. They contained mostly shoes and boots. The room was otherwise empty, except for a small arm chair in one corner. Harry went across to the chair and sat down. He put his head back and closed his eyes.

'Come on Harry, we haven't got all day,' whispered Jane.

Harry suddenly opened his eyes. He could feel the hair on his arms standing on end.

'What is it?' asked Jane looking at him.

'Jesus. She was here, Jane.'

'What?'

'She was here.'

'And how the hell can you tell that?'

Harry closed his eyes and inhaled through his nose.

'I can smell her.'

'What?' said Jane walking across to him.

'On the chair. I can smell her perfume. She always wears it,' he said getting to his feet. 'Here.'

Jane bent leant over the chair.

'It is very faint,' she said. 'Are you sure it is hers?'

'It is her perfume. I can't think what it is called. She did tell me. Jesus, Jane. She was here. Maybe she still is. Come on.'

They almost ran up the central staircase.

Before they had reached the top, Jane's mobile phone rang. 'Shit,' she said, snatching the phone from her pocket. 'Mike?' she whispered and listened to his response. 'OK. Keep us posted and please be careful,' she said and hung up. 'The driver dropped Max and Hilary Banks off at the Conservative Party building. There were a lot of press and cameras there. The chauffeur left straight away and Mike said he's heading back towards the A1.'

'Do you think he's coming back this way?'

'I don't know, but we need to hurry.'

'We'd better take a room each,' said Harry, disappearing into a bedroom.

They searched several rooms before Harry heard Jane call out. He left the room he had been searching and ran across the hallway to the room he'd seen Jane enter. He snatched open the door and went in. It was a large, well lived in room, with a sofa, a television and a wide desk. Jane was standing by the side of a large bed. She looked across at Harry.

'What the devil are you doing in my room, young woman?' said a voice from the bed.

CHAPTER FORTY-EIGHT

Harry strode across the room, his hand reaching for the gun in his inside pocket.

Jane looked at him and shook her head. Harry removed his hand.

An old man was sat, propped against a large heap of pillows. He was a small, frail looking man with wisps of white-grey hair on either side of a broad forehead. His resemblance to the pictures of Max Banks that adorned the house was obvious. His eyes were alert, as though at any moment he might spring at them from the bed.

All three of the room's occupants looked at each other in silence.

'Well? If you have come to rob me, you will find nothing here.'

'We have not come to rob you Mr Wallington. It is Mr Wallington isn't it? Arthur Wallington?' Jane said.

'What business is it of yours who I am?' said the old man.

'Mr Wallington, we are sorry to disturb you like this, but please be assured that we are certainly not here to rob you.'

'Then why are you here and what do you want?' the old man said, trying to pull himself upright.

'We are looking for someone. A young woman who we think might have been brought here,' said Jane.

The old man's face appeared to cloud over. 'A young woman? What young woman? There is no young woman here.'

Harry noticed that, as he said it, Arthur Wallington looked away and Harry thought he heard a tremor in the old man's voice.

'Where is she? We know she was here,' Harry said, reaching again for his inside pocket.

Jane frowned at him and shook her head.

'Her name is Ellen Carmichael, Mr Wallington. She was taken by a man who we think works for your son.'

'My son?'

'Yes,' said Jane. 'A man who works for Max. Max Banks.'

'I do not have son called Max Banks. His name is Maximillian.'

Jane sat down on the chair next to Arthur Wallington's bed.

'Mr Wallington, we think that this man...'

'Stephens,' interrupted the old man. 'Damn him. Stephens. Nothing but a common thug.'

Jane glanced at Harry. 'Stephens?' she said, turning her attention back to the old man. 'Is he the man who works for your son?'

'Yes, of course he is. Common thug. Why Maximillian took him on, I will never know.'

'Mr Wallington, we think that this Stephens...' began Jane.

'We don't think it, we know it,' snapped Harry.

Jane gave him a withering look. 'This man Stephens. He has taken our friend and we are afraid for her life. Do you know where he has taken her?'

'Afraid for her life? Why would you be afraid for her life?' he said.

'She was looking for someone. Someone who also disappeared. Many years ago. We think this Stephens is trying to prevent Ellen from finding her,' Jane corrected herself. 'We know that he was trying to stop her. He has taken Ellen, Mr Wallington, and he says that he will hurt her unless we do what he wants.'

'Looking for someone? Taken her? I don't know what you're talking about,' he said looking increasingly agitated. 'Now please, leave me alone.'

Harry was not going to put up with any more. He stepped forward and leant over the bed. 'I've had enough of this, Wallington. You know exactly what we're   talking about. If Stephens harms Ellen in any way, rest assured he will regret it and so will you. Now where is she?'

Arthur Wallington shrank back against his pillow and closed his eyes.

'Harry, for God's sake. He's an old man,' said Jane. 'Mr Wallington? Are you alright?'

After a few moments Arthur Wallington opened his eyes. 'This woman, who your friend was looking for. Who disappeared many years ago. What was her name?' He stared, first at Jane and then at Harry.

'Her name was Martha. Martha Watts. I believe you knew her?' said Harry.

Arthur Wallington stared at Harry, his mouth half open, his eyes slowly filling with tears.

'Mr Wallington, you know what happened to Martha, don't you?' said Jane, calmly.

Tears rolled down his cheeks. 'No. No. I don't know what you're talking about.'

'You're lying, Wallington. Where has he taken her?'

Jane reached for the old man's hand. 'Look, our friend. Ellen Carmichael. She was looking for Martha because her great aunt was a friend of Martha's during the war. Ellen is a good woman, Mr Wallington. A beautiful young woman with her whole life ahead of her. Just like Martha was in 1944. Do you know where Ellen is?' she pleaded, squeezing the old man's hand.

Arthur Wallington looked at her. 'He took her,' he croaked.

'Where?' both Harry and Jane said in unison.

Arthur Wallington was silent.

'Mr Wallington, where has Stephens taken our friend Ellen?'

'To the shelter,' said Arthur Wallington. 'To Belsize Park.'

CHAPTER FORTY-NINE

Mike followed the black BMW until it turned onto the A1. Then he dialled Jane.

'Jane, I think he's heading back to Wymondley,' he said.

He listened to the reply. 'I don't know. I'd say twenty five minutes. Maybe half an hour, max. You had better hurry.'

They passed under a bridge. Then, unexpectedly, the BMW took a sharp left, up a slip road. Mike followed. At the top, he saw the BMW take the first exit and, as he turned off, he saw the BMW's brake lights come on and the car turn sharp left again.

Damn it. Where the hell is he going?

He put his foot down, to keep up and, turning left, found himself on a single track, country lane. There was no sign of the BMW.

He accelerated, watching the road ahead but there were no turnings on either side and no buildings. The lane twisted and turned through open country side and then entered an area of woodland. The road suddenly veered to the right. He turned hard and was immediately confronted by the BMW, which was slewed across the road in front of him. He hit the brakes, the car swerved and came to a screeching halt. The driver's door was flung open.

'Mr Eglund, I take it,' said the man from the BMW. 'Get out.'

Mike clambered from the car, his eyes fixed on the man's gun. 'Into the woods, Mr Eglund. Now.'

Mikkel Eglund looked at him, slowly turned and walked into the woods.

When they were out of sight of the road, the man told him to stop. 'Now, you are going to tell me why you were following me?'

Mike was silent. The man pointed the gun towards his knees.

'Ten seconds, Mr Eglund.'

He remained silent.

The blast from the gun was surprisingly quiet. Mike felt pain explode in his foot. He collapsed to the ground.

'I am feeling charitable Mr Eglund. Knees are such important joints and such a devil to repair. You really can't do much without them.'

He writhed on the ground clutching his left foot. The man knelt beside him and pointed the gun at his head. 'Why were you following me?'

'We wanted to know where you had taken her.'

'We?'

'Harry and I,' he said between clenched teeth.

'And where is Stammers now?' said the man.

Mike was silent.

The man got to his feet. 'Is that a Norwegian accent Mr Eglund? Or Swedish? Such a lyrical language. I wonder what you Scandinavians sound like when you scream,' he said and he stamped, hard on Mike's left foot.

The pain was excruciating and Mike screamed until he had no voice.

'Last chance, Mr Eglund. Where is Stammers?'

'At the house,' Mike croaked.

The man knelt down beside him, grabbed him by the collar and pulled him up so that his face was just a few inches from Mike's.

'The house? Which house?'

'The Banks house,' Mike choked and as he did so he brought his hand up and stuck his fingers into the man's face, trying with all his strength to gauge out his eyes. The man fell backwards, holding his face. Mike leapt to his feet, ignoring the pain in his foot and limped away into the woods as fast as he could go, stumbling as he went.

He heard a single gun shot and felt the bullet enter his back. It was like someone had punched him, but there was little pain. The thud, however, knocked him off his feet. He was already losing consciousness as he fell.

Stephens wiped the blood from his face and put the gun back into his pocket. He walked over to the body of Mikkel Eglund which was lying face down on the leafy woodland floor. A large red stain was spreading across the back of his shirt. Stephens turned him over with his foot. More blood formed a wide, red circle across the front of his shirt. Stephens grinned.

He felt for his mobile phone and dialled a number. 'Get me Mr Banks,' he said and listened to the response.

'I don't fucking care if he's kissing the Queen's arse. Get me Mr Banks or the next time I see you Dennis, I'll break your fucking legs.'

Stephens waited.

'I'm sorry to disturb you Mr Banks, but there has been an incident.'

Jane ended the call to Mike and turned to Arthur Wallington.

'Mr Wallington, we don't have much time. Stephens is on his way here. We have to leave.'

Arthur Wallington had heaved himself up and was sitting on the side of the bed facing them.

'I am coming with you,' he said.

Jane and Harry exchanged glances.

'There is no time. He'll be here in less than thirty minutes and we have to get back to our car,' said Jane.

Harry had gone to the window. 'Where are the keys to the Jaguar?' he said, turning back towards Arthur Wallington.

'There is a set in the key cupboard by the front door.'

'Good. Jane let's go.'

'Wait,' said the old man.

They both looked at him.

'I did not mean to kill her,' he hesitated. 'Martha. I did not mean to kill her. It was an accident. She fell and hit her head.'

'Save it for the police,' said Harry.

'Please. I did not mean to kill her, I tell you.'

'We don't have time for this,' said Harry, walking towards the door.

'Harry,' said Jane. 'Wait. How are we going to get into the shelter?'

'I can get you in. I am a director of the company that runs the place.'

She turned towards him. 'What?'

'They are called *Safe House* or some such nonsense.'

'And you are a director?'

'Yes. I don't attend meetings. She only keeps me on the board, so that we have a majority. But I am a director nevertheless.'

Jane stared at him.

Harry turned towards the old man. 'Martha's body. It is in a room with a heavy metal door, isn't it?'

Arthur Wallington's eyes filled with tears again but he said nothing.

'Is that where Stephens has taken Ellen?' asked Jane.

The old man nodded.

'How do you know?'

'I heard her discussing it with him.'

'Her?'

'My wife,' the old man spat. 'She was adamant, just like she was sixty years ago. I wanted to tell the police. I would have done, too. I wanted to hand myself in, but she simply would not hear of it.'

'Mr Wallington. How are we going to get into the room with the steel door. It is locked.'

'She keeps a key in a drawer in her desk.'

Jane looked at Harry and then turned back to the old man. 'Can you get dressed in five minutes?'

313

'Young lady,' said the old man, wiping his face on his sleeve. 'I may be eighty-seven, but I am not completely decrepit.'

'Good. But hurry,' Jane said turning towards the door.

'Just a moment,' he said, getting slowly to his feet.

Harry looked at his watch anxiously.

Arthur Wallington walked slowly across the room and took a small box from a desk drawer. He opened it and handed Jane a key.

'It is the key to her desk. Second drawer down on the left. In it you will find two keys. Take them both,' he said.

Jane and Harry ran down the stairs and into the library.

'How long have we got?' said Harry.

'Twenty minutes at best,' Jane replied. She went to the desk, inserted the key and opened the draw. Inside two silver-grey keys were resting on a leather bound book which Harry immediately recognised. 'The logbook,' he said.

Jane took the keys and lifted out the log book. Underneath it was another book. 'And Martha's diary.'

'Take them to the car. Wait, I'll get the car key.'

Harry went to the key-safe by the front door. It was no more than a little wooden cupboard from which Harry removed the keys to the Jaguar. He opened the front door and ran to the Jaguar. Jane followed and put the books on the Jaguar's back seat. Harry got in to the driver's seat.

'Harry wait,' said Jane.

'Jane, he's a murderer. A cold-blooded murderer. Whatever he says now, he killed her and he hid her body.'

'I know that. But he can help us get in to the shelter.'

'We don't need any help,' said Harry patting his inside pocket.

'Harry listen. He's a frail old man. You saw the look on his face. Whatever he did, he's had a life time living with the consequences. He wants to do the right thing.'

'It is a bit bloody late for that now,' Harry said bitterly.

She caught his eye and held his gaze. 'Harry, please. Let him come with us.'

At that moment, Arthur Wallington appeared in the door way to the house. He was wearing dark trousers and a tweed jacket and was leaning on a walking stick. Jane ran towards him.

'You found the keys?' he asked.

'Yes we found them,' said Jane.

Jane helped him into the Jaguar and then got in next to Harry who looked at his watch. 'Ten minutes.'

'Turn left, when you get out onto the road. If Stephens is coming up from the A1. He'll come from the right,' said Jane.

'Have you checked your phone. We haven't heard from Mike in a while.'

Jane pulled the phone from her pocket. 'Nothing.'

Harry stopped in front of the gates which had begun to open as he approached. As soon as they were wide enough, he moved forward, turned left into the lane and sped away as fast as he dare on the narrow road.

CHAPTER FIFTY

Precisely seven minutes after Harry, Jane and Arthur Wallington had left Wymondley Hall, Stephens turned left and stopped the BMW in front of the gates. He reached out and pressed a button under the intercom. The gates opened. As he drove up the gravel driveway, he noticed that the Jaguar had gone. He stopped the BMW, got out and pulled a gun from his jacket pocket. He ran to the door and opened it, slowly. The house was silent. He checked the key safe. Then he walked through the house, checking rooms as he went. At the end of the hallway he noted the broken glass at the back door. He walked back through the hallway and climbed the stair case. At the top he immediately noticed the door to the old man's room. It was open. He ran to the room and looked inside.

He dialled a number on his mobile phone. 'Mr Banks, I'm at the house,' he said and listened to the response.

'Somebody has been here,' said Stephens. 'Through the back door, Sir. They broke a small window. The Jaguar is missing and your father is not in his room.' He listened again. 'Just a moment, Sir.'

Stephens ran back along the first floor hallway and down the stairs. He opened the door to the library and approached the desk. 'It is empty, Sir.'

He listened to the response.

'What do you want me to do about Eglund's body? I moved the car, but the body is still in the woods.'

Stephens listened carefully.

'Yes, Sir,' he said and hung up.

He left the house and ran to the car, placing his gun in the glove compartment. The car's wheels squealed on the gravel as he pulled away at speed.

In the Woods to the south of Wymondley, a fox sniffed at a pile of leaves and startled by a slight movement, bolted into the trees. Out of the leaves, a hand appeared. Mikkel Eglund coughed. His mouth filled with leaf litter. He waved his free hand and, clearing the leaves above him, struggled to push his face free of the brown mass covering him. Finding free air, he spat the leaves from his mouth and groaned. There was a dull ache in his left foot and he couldn't feel his left arm at all.

He lay still, panting and trying to collect his thoughts. He remembered the gun shot and brought his right hand across to his left shoulder. His shirt and the leaves around it were wet with a thick, sticky substance. As his hand made contact with his shoulder, he gasped in pain and for a moment lost consciousness.

He lay still and tried to breath more easily. As he did so, the full recollection of what had happened came to him. He gritted his teeth. He'd been shot. Once in the foot and once in the shoulder. His mind reeled. He felt around with the arm that still worked. The whole of his shirt was covered in blood. He guessed that he'd lost a great deal. He had to get help or he was not going to survive. He already felt a weakness spreading up his legs which felt heavy and numb.

Mike used his right hand to heave himself up out of the leaf pile. He looked around the clearing. There was no sign of the man. He had to get help and he had to warn Harry and Jane, if it was not already too late. He dragged himself across to a tree and pushed himself up the trunk with his good leg. The pain in his shoulder was now throbbing mercilessly. He struggled to think.

317

The car. He had to get back to the car. He knew that to do this he would have to walk. They had not come far into the woods. Still, he was not certain that he could.

Mikkel Eglund took several large breaths and heaved himself up onto his good foot. He gasped in pain and stood, leaning heavily against the tree trunk. Sunlight glimmered through the leaves above and he could hear a Chaffinch singing. Mike thought that the woods were so peaceful. He had an overwhelming urge to lay down to sleep. He gritted his teeth and with immense effort limped forward, first one pace and then another.

It took him what seemed like an age to make it back out onto the road. As he stumbled out of the woods, he was almost oblivious to the fact that his car was gone. The thought came to him slowly, as though submerged in a foggy haze. He looked around and slumped to his knees, panting heavily. He was not going to make it. He would die here by the side of the road. Harry and Jane would be caught by the man who had shot him. The desire to lay down and sleep became overwhelming. He slumped sideways and collapsed onto the ground.

CHAPTER FIFTY-ONE

Harry, Jane and Arthur Wallington turned into Downside Crescent. Harry looked at his watch. It was six-thirty.

'I'm really concerned about Mike. I can't understand why he isn't answering his phone,' Jane worried.

'I know. I hope to God he's alright,' replied Harry.

They got out of the Jaguar. Jane walked around to the passenger door and helped Arthur Wallington out of the car. She took him by the arm. He looked tired and frail. 'Come on,' she said and gave his arm a squeeze.

They walked to the shelter entrance. As they approached it the old man hesitated. 'It has been many years since I was here,' he said.

Harry pressed a buzzer above the combination pad at the side of the door. The intercom crackled.

'Safe House. Can I help you?'

'We are here with Mr Wallington, from Safe House. Please open the door,' said Harry hopefully.

'Mr who?' said the voice.

The old man pushed Harry aside with his stick.

'I am Arthur Wallington. I am a director of Safe House Limited. I am also the father of Maximillian Banks-Wallington who I expect you will know. Now open this door immediately,' Wallington said with surprising force.

There was a pause and then then the intercom buzzed. Harry pushed the door open and they went inside. They were met by two security guards.

'Good afternoon,' said the first guard. 'Will you tell me again, who you are and what you want?'

'Young man, I have already told you who I am. May I remind you that, as a director of Safe House, I am your superior. I do not need to explain my presence here.'

The security guard looked at the old man uncertainly and then at his colleague who shook his head. 'I am sorry Sir, but your name does not appear on the allowed list. We have strict instructions only to allow access to people whose names appear on the list.'

'We don't have time for this,' said Harry, stepping forward and pulling the gun from his inside pocket.

Both security guards took a step backwards. 'What's going on? Who are you?' said the first guard, glancing up a camera on the wall. 'There are cameras and they are monitored. Our people back at headquarters will have already seen that,' he said eyeing the gun, nervously.

'Then we had better hurry up,' said Harry waving the gun toward the lift. 'Are either of you armed?'

They both shook the heads.

'Jane, check them,' Harry said.

'What?' Jane replied.

'Check them. For weapons.'

She walked across to the guards and searched them, one at a time. When she had finished she looked at Harry and shook her head.

'Your radios,' Harry said holding out his hand.

Both guards removed the radios that were clipped to their lapels and handed them to him. He threw them to the far side of the lobby.

'We will need torches and the keys to the tunnel gates.'

'In the control room,' said one of the guards, pointing down the corridor.

'Take me to them. Quickly,' Harry said, waving the gun. 'Wait here,' he said to Jane. He followed the guards to the control room.

'Sit down, both of you,' he said as they entered.

They sat.

Harry pointed the gun at the first guard. 'Where are the keys?'

'In the wall cupboard behind you. The large bunch with the red fob.'

'And the torches?'

'In the desk drawer. Over there,' the first guard said pointing to his right.

Harry retrieved two torches from the drawer. Then he opened the cupboard and removed a large bunch of keys with a red fob.

'What's your name?' he said, looking at the first guard.

'Jackson. Alan Jackson.'

'OK. Jackson. Where is the staff room key?'

Jackson looked at him blankly.

'The room where you make your tea.'

'I have it,' said the other guard.

'Give it to me,' said Harry.

The other guard took a small bunch of keys from his pocket and handed it to him.

'Right. Both of you. Get up. Jackson, you are coming with us. You,' Harry said pointing at the other guard. 'Into the staff room. Now.'

They both got up and Harry followed them out of the control room. They walked along the corridor and stopped at the door to the staff room.

'Inside,' Harry said and waved the second guard forward. He opened the door and went inside. Harry turned to the guard called Jackson and handed him the keys. 'Lock him in.'

Jackson turned the key in the lock.

'Right, now back to the others.'

They returned to the lobby.

Harry handed a torch to Jane.

'Now Jackson, you're going to take us down to the shelter and remember, I will use this thing if I have to.'

Jackson looked at the gun, then walked across to the lift and opened the gates.

Max Banks stood up and gave a wave of thanks to the cheering meeting, before turning to his mother and kissing her on the cheek to dozens of flashing cameras. They retreated from the stage and entered a small room at the rear of the conference hall.

'Well done Sir,' said Dennis, grinning broadly.

'I want everybody out,' said Hilary Banks, the smile on her face for the cameras, turning to a scowl as she entered the room.

'That means you,' she said, turning to Dennis. 'Get back out there and deal with any questions.'

Dennis left and closed the door.

'Call him. Now.'

Max Banks dialled the number.

'Put it on speaker phone,' said Hilary Banks-Wallington.

'Stephens, where are you?'

'I'm on the A1. I'll be at Belsize Park in twenty minutes.'

Max looked at his watch.

'Too late. You'll be too late. Hurry, you fool. They must be stopped. At all costs, do you hear me?' screeched Hilary Banks-Wallington.

'I'm sorry Mrs Banks, I'm going as fast as I can.'

Hilary Banks-Wallington snatched the phone from her son's hand and pressed the red button.

'Do you think that Father is with them?'

'Of course he is with them. He will help them free the Carmichael woman and, if they do, there will be nothing stopping them from calling the police. Get your coat.'

'What?' said Banks.

'I said get your your fucking coat, you imbecile. If you think I'm staying here to exchange meaningless pleasantries with that rabble out there, while that idiot of a father of yours betrays us all, you are mistaken.'

'But Mother, I have more interviews to do. Stephens will take care of Stammers.'

'What? Like he took care of the Norwegian?' she spat.

'I have told him to deal with Stammers first. He will go back and remove the Norwegian later.'

'Shut up Maximillian,' she said spinning to face him. 'I have left this to you until now and that has brought us to the brink of ruination. You are no better than your damned father. Stammers should have died in that lift shaft, but you couldn't even get that right.'

'Mother, please,' said Banks.

She raised her hand and slapped him hard across the face.

'Show some backbone you spineless bastard. Without me, you would have nothing, do you hear me?' she shouted. 'Without me there would be nothing. Your father would have gone to the gallows. Do you think I am going to allow him to take us all there again?'

Banks took a step backwards.

'Now call us a cab.'

'What? Where are we going?'

'Just call us a damned cab,' she said, picking up her bag. 'I have a score to settle with Harry Stammers.'

She put her hand into the bag and when she withdrew it, she was holding a small, silver pistol.

Banks gaped at her. 'You can't be serious.'

'I have a score to settle and this time, I am going to settle it personally.'

CHAPTER FIFTY-TWO

The lift car lurched to a stop at the bottom of the shaft.

'Open the gate,' said Harry pointing the gun at Jackson.

He pulled the red metal gates open and stepped out into the lower lobby.

'The lights. Where are they?' said Harry.

'Over there. The bank of switches by the gate.'

Jane walked across to the gate and operated the switch. There was a buzzing sound. Through the gate, she could see that the tunnel was illuminated.

'You go first,' Harry said 'I will be behind you.'

The guard led the way along the tunnel. They made slow progress due to Arthur Wallington. He moved slowly, even with Jane holding his arm. Finally they had to stop to allow him to rest. Jane looked at the old man with concern. He looked almost skeletal in the tunnel light.

She turned toward Harry and shook her head, and then back at Wallington. 'Are you alright, Mr Wallington?'

'Yes. Do not worry about me. I should have done this sixty years ago.'

It took them some minutes more to reach the entrance to the service tunnel. Harry handed the keys to Jackson who opened the gates. They stepped into the passage.

Arthur Wallington stood at the gate, trembling. 'A few moments,' he said, panting and leaning heavily on his stick.

Harry stepped back through the gates and peered anxiously along the tunnel, toward the lobby and the lift.

'She was sitting on a wooden crate when I found her,' said the old man. 'She'd hurt her ankle. She been wearing ridiculously high heels.'

'What were you doing down here?' Jane asked, quietly.

'I'd been meeting with the foreman and someone from the ministry to sign off the works that we'd been doing. There was an air raid and we got stuck down here. She just wanted to get home to her mother,' he said and swallowed. 'I brought her down here,' he said, waving his stick along the passage.

'Why?'

'The staff room. There was a first aid kit in one of the lockers and somewhere to sit.'

'You took her to the staff room?' said Harry, exchanging glances with Jane. 'Down there, on the right?' he said, pointing.

'Yes. I bound her ankle,' he said and paused, looking at the floor. 'I just wanted to help her.'

'But you didn't help her did you?' Harry said with undisguised loathing. 'You didn't help her. You killed her.'

The old man lurched. Jane held onto his arm.

'She kissed me. We'd found some brandy and I…'

'Save it,' said Harry, turning away.

'She kissed me. She was such a beautiful young woman. I…'

Harry and Jane were both silent.

'I was a hot blooded young man. I went too far.'

Jane gasped. 'You didn't…'

'No, no…' he said. 'But she was angry and…' He hesitated. 'I hit her,' he said, wiping tears from his eyes. 'I don't know why. I have thought about it over and over again. Every time I close my eyes to sleep, I see her.'

They were silent.

'She fell,' he said. 'She fell and hit her head on the corner of one of the bunks.'

'That is how she died?' said Jane.

'Yes.'

Harry snorted. 'How bloody convenient.'

'Then why didn't you call the police?' Jane said. 'You could have told them what you have just told us.'

A sound from the far end of the tunnel interrupted them.

'The lift,' said Harry. 'Somebody is using the lift. Come on!'

They hurried down the tunnel. Jane had given Jackson her torch. He led the way, shining the beam ahead of them.

At the bottom of the tunnel they turned left.

'You won't be able to use the key to open that one,' said the guard, as they approached the second gate.

'What?' shouted Harry, grabbing him by the arm and pointing the gun at his chest.

'Harry, for God's sake,' said Jane.

'I'm sorry, but there are no keys to the flooded tunnel. It was closed many years ago and access is prohibited.'

'And you didn't think to tell us?' said Harry through gritted teeth.

'How was I supposed to know that this is where you wanted to go?'

'One of the keys from Hilary's desk,' wheezed Athur Wallington.

Harry pulled the keys from his pocket. He walked up to the gate, stuffing the gun into his trouser pocket and fumbled with the padlock. 'They don't fit.'

'What?' said Jane.

'They don't fucking fit,' he shouted, looking back along the tunnel anxiously. 'They must have changed the fucking lock, after Ellen and I were down here.'

Jane examined the lock. It was a bronze colour with a shiny silver shackle. 'It's new.'

'Stand back,' said Harry from behind her. He had pulled the gun from his pocket and was pointing it at the lock.

'Harry don't be an idiot. The bullet will ricochet back. It could go anywhere,' Jane pleaded.

'Do you have any better ideas?' said Harry.

'I saw an old sledge hammer, back along the tunnel. Give me your torch.'

'We don't have time,' said Harry.

'Yes we do. It wasn't very far,' she said holding out her hand.

Harry handed her the torch.

She turned and ran back down the tunnel.

Harry, Arthur Wallington and Jackson waited in silence until Jane had returned.

'The lift,' she said, panting. 'I heard it hit the bottom of the shaft. Whoever was in it, will be in the tunnel. Hurry,' she said handing the heavy mallet to Harry.

He walked across to the gate and hit the padlock as hard as he could. Nothing happened. He hit it again. Still nothing.

'Try it again Harry. Hurry,' said Jane looking back along the tunnel anxiously.

With the third blow, the lock burst and Harry tore the chain from the gates and flung them open.

They moved as quickly as they could, still hampered by Arthur Wallington but within a few minutes had found the steel door. Harry fumbled for the key.

'Stop right there,' called out a voice from the darkness behind them.

Harry had inserted the key and was about to turn it.

'Step away from the door, Stammers.'

Harry turned the key and reached for the handle.

The gunshot rang out and there was a thud. Jackson stumbled backwards and fell, his torch skittering across the tunnel floor and smashing against the tunnel wall.

Jane had flung herself to the ground.

Harry had already heaved the door open. He dodged behind it, pulling Arthur Wallington with him. With the old man out of the line of fire, Harry leant around the door, gun in hand. Jane was laying on the floor beside the unmoving guard. She turned and looked at him.

'Here,' she said and tossed him the remaining torch.

'It is useless, Stammers. You are trapped. Give up now and I might not kill you.' called out the voice. Harry shone the torch into the darkness.

Arthur Wallington stepped out from behind the gate.

'Stephens, you bloody thug,' he called out with surprising force. 'This is none of your damn business.'

Another shot rang out, the bullet ricocheting off the steel door. Harry grabbed the old man by the arm and pulled him to safety.

'Harry,' whispered Jane. 'The gun, throw it to me.'

'No, way,' Harry whispered back.

'I saw the gun flash. He doesn't have a torch. Throw me the damned gun.'

Harry hesitated. He tossed her the gun. Jane caught it and began crawling forward. Harry stepped into the room, pulling Arthur Wallington behind him. He flashed the torch from side to side. Ellen was cowering on the floor in a corner with her hands over her face. She was covered in black grime.

Harry knelt down beside her. 'Ellen,' he said softly.

'Harry?' she said with a tiny voice.

They heard a gun shot and the sound of another bullet hitting the door. Then another shot rang out and there was silence.

'Here,' said Harry, handing the torch to Arthur Wallington. Harry peered out from behind the door, into the darkness. There was no light in the tunnel at all. Harry's heart was in his mouth. 'Jane?' he called out, softly.

There was silence.

'Jane?' he called out.

'It's alright,' she called back. 'I think I got him.'

'Are you sure? Is he dead?'

'I don't know. I wasn't going after him in the pitch black.'

She got up and stumbled towards him.

'Jesus Christ. I thought he'd shot you,' Harry said, hugging her tightly.

'Is she in there?' Jane replied, handing him the gun.

He grinned but she could barely see him.

When Harry and Jane entered, they found Ellen on her knees. Harry helped her to her feet and held her. She was trembling.

'Ellen,' said Harry, his voice breaking. 'Are you alright?'

'A damn fool question, if ever there was one,' said Jane.

'Jane?' said Ellen, shakily.

Jane stepped into the light reflected off the walls by the torch in Arthur Wallington's hand.

'Ellen,' she said grinning. 'Thank God.'

Jane stepped forward and embraced Ellen, who began to cry. 'I thought that was it,' she said. 'I thought I was going to die down here.'

'Shh,' said Jane, stroking her hair.

Harry glanced at the old man who had slumped to his knees. 'She wasn't dead,' he was mumbling. 'Dear God, she wasn't dead.'

Jane and Ellen turned.

Arthur Wallington was kneeling in front of the remains of Martha Watts. She was a grotesque tangle of clothing and bone. Her head had slumped forward. Harry could see her curly hair and the brown leathery looking skin of her legs.

He walked across to the old man and knelt down beside him.

'She wasn't dead. I'm so sorry Martha. So terribly, terribly sorry,' he said between sobs.

Arthur Wallington had dropped the torch. Harry retrieved it and, with the torch in his hand, examined the wall beside the remains of Martha Watts. He caught his breath. On the wall, in small, bright red letters, Martha had written 'TELL MUM I LOVE HER'. Harry could see the lipstick. It was still in her skeletal hand.

Harry bowed his head and closed his eyes. He thought of the face in the photographs that Elsie Sidthorpe had shown him. He thought of the huts at Bletchley Park, where Elsie had worked with Martha and the thousands of women who had worked there. He thought of John Watts and the pride with which he had received the news that his sister had done such important work during the war. He thought of the young face he'd seen in the tube train window.

'Unfortunately, we were too late to tell your mother,' he whispered. 'But I am sure she knew. Perhaps you have been able to tell her yourself.' Then he helped a still weeping Arthur Wallington to his feet. 'Come on,' he said, taking the old man's arm.

Harry examined the guard's body. There was a red bullet wound in the centre of his chest. His eyes were staring. 'He's dead,' he said, quietly.

Ellen walked across to him and put her hand on his shoulder. 'Can we go now?' she said. 'I think I'm done here.'

Jane was holding a still weeping Arthur Wallington. 'I thought she was dead. I thought I had killed her. I would've gone to the police,' he spluttered.

'Then why didn't you?' Jane said gently.

'Hilary. My wife. She would not hear of it. She insisted that I return to the tunnels to hide the body.'

'You brought her here from the staff room?' Jane asked.

'Yes. I dragged her here. I thought she was dead.'

'Come on, let's get out of here,' Harry said, taking the gun from his pocket.

'I don't think so,' said a voice out of the darkness. 'Drop the gun, Mr Stammers.'

An elderly woman stepped into the torch light. Hilary Banks-Wallington was holding a silver pistol. She was pointing it directly at him.

Harry looked at her aghast.

'Hilary?' said Arthur Wallington.

A tall man stepped into the light, beside his mother.

'She said drop the gun,' said Max Banks.

Harry stared at them both and then slowly dropped the gun onto the floor.

'Now kick it away,' said Max Banks.

Harry flicked the gun away with the side of his foot. It went spinning across the tunnel floor.

'You have caused us no end of trouble Mr Stammers. It is time, we brought this saga to a close. You,' said Hilary Banks-Wallington, pointing the silver pistol at Jane. 'Help him to drag the security guard into the room.'

Jane and Harry did not move.

'Mr Stammers, either you and your friends will do exactly as you are told or we will shoot them, one at a time.' Do you understand?'

Jane took hold of Harry's arm and pulled him toward the dead guard. They dragged the body into the room.

'Now all of you,' she said pointing the gun at Ellen. 'Inside.'

Ellen backed away towards the door, with Harry beside her. 'No,' she gasped. 'I won't go back in there.'

Hilary Banks-Wallington stepped towards her husband. 'And you Arthur.'

The old man stared at her. His eyes were full of tears. 'She wasn't dead,' he said, through clenched teeth. 'If I'd gone to the police she would have been found. She might still be alive.'

'What utter rubbish,' said Hilary Banks-Wallington, defiantly.

'She wasn't dead,' he shouted. 'Don't you understand? All those years. A whole lifetime, living as a murderer. Thinking that I had killed her.'

'What are you talking about?'

'She wrote a message on the wall. To her mother. She died here, Hilary. Alone in the darkness,' Arthur Wallington spluttered, tears rolling down his face.

Hilary Banks-Wallington took another step towards him. 'You told me that she was dead. You couldn't even get that right,' she spat.

'If I had handed myself in, Martha could have been saved.'

Hilary Banks-Wallington starred at him and then laughed. 'Saved? She was nothing but a common slut. She means nothing to me. Now inside. All of you,' she said, waving the pistol.

 'No.' He said it simply as a statement of fact. 'Not this time,' and he swept his arm up and brought down his walking stick with all the force he could manage.

It struck his wife across her wrist with a loud crack. She gave out a piercing shriek and sank to her knees, the silver pistol spinning from her hand.

Max Banks grabbed his father's arm and wrestled the walking stick from his hand. He flung it aside and turned towards the gun that had spun from his mother's grasp.

Harry looked into the darkness and caught sight of the gun that he'd kicked away. He erupted from the doorway and dived. His hand closed around the barrel. He flipped the weapon as he turned onto his back. Max Banks was kneeling with his mother's gun in his hand. Harry pointed the gun and pulled the trigger, the gun recoiling in his hand. There was a deafening bang that made Harry's ears ring. Max Banks, fell sideways and remained still.

Harry scrambled to his feet as Jane and Ellen emerged from the doorway. Arthur Wallington was stood over his wife.

'She was alive, damn you. She was alive, do you hear me? If I had gone to the police, she might still be alive.'

CHAPTER FIFTY-THREE

Wednesday, 15th November 1944

Martha Watts drifts between consciousness and unconsciousness, so that the boundary between the two appears to her to be uncertain. At times she is aware of an all pervading darkness surrounding her and a complete and total silence. At other times her mind flits from scene to scene. She is in her bedroom, playing with her dolls or running through the fields at her aunt's house, chased by Gypsy, her aunt's beautiful English Setter. She laughs out loud and screams with delight as she tumbles into the long grass, the dog barking and licking her face.

At other times she dreams, if dreaming it is, that she is in her bed in her little room at home. She tosses and turns so that her bed sheet is wrapped around her head and she cannot breathe. Then the darkness comes, with a smell of stale canvas across her face and she struggles and cries out in frustration, tearing at the sheet wrapped around her.

Always she drifts away again, back to the field or the playground at school or the beach, with the sun shining and the sound of the waves lapping on the shore as she makes another sand castle with her mother. But at all times she returns to the empty darkness and the smell of stale canvass.

Sometimes, in the darkness, she can hear a faint rumbling like distant thunder and the sky above her field is filled with pouring rain, soaking her though to the skin. She lays in the wet grass and rolls herself into a ball, closing her eyes tightly so that all of the light is gone.

Once, when the rumbling came, she sees herself looking in through the window of a train, her pale, expressionless face peering through the glass. 'I am here' she calls out. 'I am here'. The lights of the train flash past her. Once, twice, three times and then the darkness. Always the darkness.

Once, and only once, she remembers the man. He puts a bag on her face that takes away the light. She reaches up to her throat and manages to untie the string that holds it in place. But when she removes it, the light does not return.

Martha sits, blinking in the darkness and thinks of Elsie in the bar at the Galleon and the other girls at the Park. She thinks of her mother in the Anderson shelter at the bottom of her garden waiting for her and worrying. She thinks of their walks in the park and holidays at the seaside. She bends down and picks up a handful of sand, letting the grains run out between her fingers. When she opens her fingers, there is a long, thin pebble there. She uses it to write a message in the sand.

Then the rumble of thunder comes, with a momentary flash of light and Martha is falling. She feels a sharp pain in the side of her head and the darkness begins to fade. Martha opens her eyes and sees that she falling into a pool of white light.

CHAPTER FIFTY-FOUR

Sunday, 4 th July 2004

Harry Stammers emerged from the stair well, clutching the arm of an ambulance woman. He surveyed the scene in the upper lobby, while he tried to catch his breath. It was a mass of men and women in uniforms.

The ambulance woman, looked at him anxiously. 'Are you alright?'

'Sure.'

To his right, Harry could see an unconscious Max Banks on a stretcher. It had taken two firemen and three paramedics to bring him up safely from the tunnels below.

He shook his head. He couldn't decide whether he was relieved or disappointed that the politician had survived the gun shot. Banks would certainly have fired first had Harry failed to use the firearm. But it was an odd feeling that came from the knowledge that he had shot a man. He wasn't altogether sure how he was going to feel if Banks died, even though the shot had been justified.

'Are you sure you're alright?'

'Sure, I'm sure. Could we get something to drink, do you think?'

The ambulance woman nodded. 'Come on.'

Hilary Banks-Wallington looked up as they passed her. She had been strapped to an evacuation chair for the ascent and was being guarded by two police officers, both of them armed. For two paces Harry ignored the words that were forming in his mind and the desire to turn and to hurl them at her. Then he stopped and turned, slowly. She was staring at him. He had never seen such hatred. It blazed in her eyes with an intensity that seemed to suck the air from his lungs. He wanted to tell her that she was as guilty as her husband. That if there was any justice in the world, then she was going to spend what was left of her miserable life behind bars. But the words died on his lips and, when it came to it, he said nothing.

A still weeping Arthur Wallington was being led across the upper lobby by a police woman. He looked impossibly frail and Harry wondered how he was going to survive the days ahead. When Wallington caught his eye, Harry looked away. In truth, he had little sympathy for the man who had dragged Martha Watts to her death, whether Wallington had known it or not.

Harry followed the ambulance woman to the staff room where, to his great relief, he found Jane and Ellen drinking cups of tea. 'Thank God,' he said, hugging them each in turn. 'That you are both safe.'

'I thought I'd never see you again,' Ellen said, her voice breaking.

'Oh, you are going to see plenty more of me,' he said, grinning broadly.

Ellen laughed through the tears that had filled her eyes.

Over her shoulder, Harry saw the staff room door open and a policeman in uniform enter. 'Mr Stammers, we'd like to have a brief word with you. Would you come with me please?'

Ellen turned and looked at the policeman and then back at Harry. 'Don't worry. I'm fine and we're not going anywhere without you,' she said.

Harry turned to Jane.

'Go on. I'll look after her.'

Harry kissed Ellen on the cheek and followed the policeman out into the hallway. 'Will this take long?'

'No, just a few minutes.'

Harry followed the policeman into the control room.

'Take a seat, Mr Stammers.'

Harry sat down, glancing as he did, at a grey haired man in a suit who was stood, watching him from the far corner of the room.

'I am Detective Inspector Ryan,' said the policeman. 'And this is Mr Smith,' he said, nodding at the suited man.

The man called Smith said nothing.

'Is there any news of Mike?' Harry asked, looking at each of them in turn.

'Yes, as a matter of fact there is. Mikkel Eglund was picked up earlier this evening,' said the detective inspector.

'Is he alright?'

'He is alive and right now that makes him a very lucky man.'

'Lucky?'

'Yes. He had two bullet wounds, one of which had passed through his left shoulder.'

'Shit,' said Harry.

'Indeed. He told us that he was a shot by a man in a black BMW.'

'Stephens,' said Harry.

'The same man who you say exchanged shots with Miss Mears in the tunnel?'

'Yes, that's right.'

'Which is odd, because we can find no trace of him at all, although the search is of course ongoing,' said the detective inspector.

Harry looked at the him blankly. 'Well the guard, Jackson, certainly didn't shoot himself in the chest.'

The two men exchanged glances and Smith nodded. 'What, exactly do you know about this Stephens?' he asked.

Harry looked at Smith and considered the question. What did he really know? 'Other than that he worked for Max Banks?'

Smith nodded again.

'Very little. I know that he was following me and that he threatened Ellen. I believe that he broke into my flat and stole the log book...'

'Log book?' Smith interrupted. He seemed surprised.

'To the shelter. It's on the back seat of the Jaguar, parked outside. Along with Martha's diary.'

Smith said nothing.

'Go on,' said the detective inspector.

'I know that he kidnapped Ellen and brought her here. That he was trying to stop us.'

'This man who used the name Stephens. He used it with you personally?' Smith said.

Harry hesitated. 'Well, no. Come to think of it, I don't think I ever heard him actually use that name in person. It was Arthur Wallington who told us his name.'

'He told you this earlier today?'

'Yes, that's right. Why do you ask?'

Smith said nothing.

'We will of course be interviewing the Banks-Wallingtons, at length,' said the detective inspector. 'However, at this stage we have reason to believe that this man you call Stephens was using a false name.'

'So what is his real name?' Harry asked.

'We were rather hoping that you might be able to throw some light on that?' said the detective inspector.

'I'm afraid not,' Harry replied, glancing from one man to the other.

There was an uncomfortable pause.

'When you were here on July 2nd, you discovered a woman's purse which contained a train ticket from Bletchley to London,' said the detective inspector.

'Yes, that's right.'

'And it was this ticket that convinced you that Martha Watts had been here in 1944?'

'Yes.'

'Did you find anything else?' Smith asked.

'On July 2nd?' Harry asked.

'Yes.'

The map? He had given it little thought since they had taken it from the locker room. 'Just some coins and a couple of bank notes in the purse. It didn't amount to much.' He hesitated. 'Oh, and an old map.'

'A map?' said the detective inspector.

'Yes. Of the tunnels,' Harry said, running his hand through his hair.

The two men exchanged glances. 'We will want to see these items, of course,' said the policeman.

'Sure. No problem,' Harry replied.

'And you found nothing else?' said Smith.

The key. He wasn't even sure what had become of it. 'No, nothing.'

'You are quite sure?'

Something was telling Harry to keep the key's existence to himself. A voice in the back of his head.

'I'm certain of it, Mr Smith.'

'And today, when you entered the room in which Miss Carmichael had been imprisoned,' Smith added, 'did you find anything else? Apart, that is, from the remains of Martha Watts?'

There was something faintly menacing about the way that Smith was questioning him and Harry didn't much like it. 'Like what?' he replied, evasively.

Smith hesitated. 'Like anything, Mr Stammers.'

'Yes. I found Ellen. She was my one and only concern. Apart from that, I was rather too busy trying to stay alive.'

The two men looked at each other. The man called Smith shook his head so slightly that it was almost imperceptible.

'Well thank you Mr Stammers,' said the detective inspector. 'We will of course want to take detailed statements from you all, in due course, but that will do for now.'

'No problem,' said Harry, casually.

The man called Smith stood up and walked across to the door. Harry caught his eye as he left the room. There was something familiar about him. Something nagging in the back of his mind. But as he crossed the corridor to the staff room, all he could think of was Ellen. At that moment, that she was safe was all that mattered.

CHAPTER FIFTY-FIVE

Harry stood at the graveside and watched the coffin being lowered into the ground.

'We now commit her body to the ground,' said the priest. 'Earth to earth, ashes to ashes, dust to dust, in the sure and certain hope of the resurrection to eternal life… '

After a few moments silence, Harry turned to John Watts and shook his hand.

'Thank you Harry. I never thought we would ever be able to lay her to rest.'

Harry nodded solemnly. 'It is very good to see you up and about John,' he said.

John Watts smiled. 'Oh, I wasn't ready to join my sister just yet. I have a reunion to attend, on her behalf.'

'You will be able to make it to Bletchley Park?' said Harry.

'I wouldn't miss it for the world,' said John Watts, beaming.

'That is good news.'

Ellen Carmichael squeezed Harry's hand, as he turned away. 'I spoke to Marcus, earlier today,' she whispered in his ear. 'I meant to tell you.'

'Did you?'

'Yes. He's awake and able to sit up. He said that they've told him that he's making remarkable progress.'

'He's not the only one,' Harry said and they both looked at Mikkel Eglund, who caught Harry's eye and grinned.

'I still can't believe that he's out,' said Ellen.

They walked over to Mike who was seated in a wheelchair.

'Hey hey, you two.'

'Alright, Mike?' said Harry.

'Never felt better,' replied the Norwegian.

Harry turned to Ellen. 'Tell me. How can a man get a hole blown clean through him, one side to the other, and still be grinning?'

'Beats me,' she said, bending down to kiss Mike on the cheek. 'He is our own little miracle.'

'Are you going to Tomasz's funeral?' said Mike.

'I think so,' Harry said. He paused for a moment. 'I know he tried to kill me and damn near succeeded killing Marcus in my place, but I don't believe that he was acting out of choice.'

'Neither do I,' said Mike. 'Is there any news of Stephens?'

'No. The police say that there was no trace of him at Belsize Park and they are still saying that they have been unable to trace his real name. Either Banks is keeping his mouth shut, or he didn't know his true identity,' said Harry.

'Man, that is crazy,' said Mike.

'Come on, Harry,' Ellen said, pulling his arm. 'Gran is looking tired. We ought to get her home.'

'I hope that you are not planning on driving off into the sunset, without giving me a hug,' said a voice from behind them.

'Jane,' said Harry grinning.

'Not you, dimwit. I meant her,' said Jane, walking across to Ellen. They both giggled and embraced.

'I hear that you two might be getting it together,' said Harry, nodding towards Mike.

'We might,' said Jane. 'Then again, we might not. He'll need to be fighting fit to keep up with me,' she said.

'No arguments there,' said Harry. 'Take your time Mike. She is not for the faint hearted.'

Jane pinched him.

'Come on,' said Ellen pulling his arm.

They walked across to Elsie Sidthorpe who was talking to the priest.

'Thank you Father, for your words of comfort.'

'Not at all Mrs Sidthorpe. Mr Stammers. Miss Carmichael,' he said nodding at each of them in turn.

'Thank you Father,' said Ellen.

They stood in silence for a moment, looking across the graveyard as people began to file away.

'Well I guess that's it,' said Harry. 'After all these years. She is finally at peace.'

Elsie Sidthorpe turned towards them. He eyes were full of tears.

'Gran, don't cry,' said Ellen, wrapping her arms around her.

'I knew you could do it, Harry,' she said, turning towards him. 'The day I received your letter from Bletchley Park. I knew that something good was going to come of it.'

'Which reminds me. I have something for you,' he said, pulling an envelope from his pocket and handing it to her.

'What's this?' she said opening the envelope slowly.

'It is your medal. For your service at the Park. You were due to be awarded it at the reunion, but today is a special day and it seemed appropriate that you should have it.'

Elsie Sidthorpe opened the envelope and held the medal in her hand. 'Would you mind, Dear,' she said, stepping forward.

Ellen took her arm and walked her to the grave side. They stood in silence for a moment, their heads bowed, each with their own thoughts. And then Elsie looked up and said out loud:

'I count myself in nothing else so happy as in a soul remembering my good friends,' and she dropped the medal into the grave.

As Harry, Ellen and Elsie Sidthorpe walked away, along the path to the waiting car, a man stepped out from behind a tree. He wore a long, grey coat and had a shaved head, but his beard was gone. He stood in silence and watched them get into the blue Saab and the car pull away. He spat on the ground. 'I'll be seeing you, Stammers,' said the man formerly known as Stephens.

Postscript

Quite where the story in *The Shelter* came from is, frankly, something of a mystery to me. I certainly didn't set out to write a book. Rather, there had been an idea floating around my head for some time, about a woman behind a wall in a London Underground tunnel. I had no idea who she was or how she got there (behind the wall or in my head). She was just there.

Thinking about her, trapped in the darkness, I began to wonder about how she would know whether she was alive or dead (a theme explored in Chapter 53). It was this single idea, of the trapped woman, that provided the seed for Martha Watts and *The Shelter*.

Martha Watts, Harry Stammers, Ellen Carmichael and all of the other people who appear in *The Shelter* are entirely fictitious. Any resemblance to real persons, living or dead, is coincidental and unintended.

The same cannot be said for the places and some of the historical references in the book. With the exception of 'Carmichael Interiors' (which is not on Barnet High Street - or wasn't, the last time I looked) and the Watts's house in Gospel Oak (Roderick Road does exist but there is no number seventy-six and no Mr Watts living there), most of the other locations in the book exist in reality or are at least based on real places.

Two places, in particular, are worthy of a little further discussion, as they will hopefully be of interest to anyone who has read *The Shelter*.

London's Deep Level Air Raid Shelters

In December 1940, having failed to prevent the general public using the platforms on London's Underground system as bomb shelters, the Government's Ministry of Home Security decided that it would construct a number of dedicated, deep level air raid shelters.

Originally, ten were planned to be built below existing stations on the London Underground, but in 1941 work on the shelter at St Paul's was abandoned, for fear of the tunnels undermining the foundations of the Cathedral above. Shortly afterwards, work on the shelter at Oval was also abandoned due to repeated flooding (this provided the inspiration for the book's abandoned tunnel at Belsize Park which, as far as I am aware, does not exist in fact).

Eight shelters were constructed in all:- at Clapham South; Clapham Common; Clapham North; Stockwell; Goodge Street; Camden Town; Chancery Lane; and of course, at Belsize Park. They were completed in 1942 but, mindful of the great cost of maintaining them once opened, the Cabinet decided to hold them in reserve for use in the event of intensified bombing.

Such an intensification came in June 1944, when Germany deployed the V1 'Doodlebug' in its attacks on London. This was followed, in September of the same year, by deployment of the V2 rocket. The arrival of these 'flying bombs' prompted the Government to open a number of the deep level shelters to the public for the first time. The shelter at Belsize Park opened on 23rd July 1944.

Construction of the shelters had been undertaken by five contractors, all with experience of tunnelling in London: - Kinnear, Moodie and Co., Charles Brand and Son Ltd., John Cochrane and Sons Ltd., Edmund Nuttall, Sons and Company Ltd., and Balfour, Beaty and Company Ltd. With regard to electrical installations (undertaken in the book by the fictional Banks Electrical Company Ltd. or 'BELCO') a number of companies were employed including the Hewittic Electric Company Ltd. (later part of the GEC Group) which made the mercury rectifiers, used to convert mains alternating current to the direct current required by the lift machinery.

Each of the shelters consisted of two 1,400ft parallel, inter-connected tunnels. The diameter was 16ft where cast iron was used for the lining, and 16ft 6 inches where the lining was reinforced concrete. The tunnels were, in fact, divided into two decks:- an upper and a lower deck, with a foul air duct running above the upper deck and below the lower deck. In *The Shelter*, these details are omitted for the sake of simplicity, so that there is only one floor.

Sleeping accommodation was provided in the form of metal bunks (as in the book). The shelters were designed to accommodate 12,000 people but, by the time they opened, the capacity had been reduced and each shelter was equipped with approximately 8,000 bunks.

Each of the shelters had two pairs of shafts sited some distance from each other so that if one was blocked as a result of bombing, escape could be made via the other. An additional means of escape was provided by way of a smoke proof access shaft to the host Underground station.

Each pair of shafts was arranged so that one shaft was used for ventilation and the other for the lift and stairs. In the latter case, each shaft had two sets of interlaced spiral stairs:- one to the upper and the other to the lower deck. In *The Shelter*, because there is only one level, so there is only one spiral stair case.

The lifts were, in fact, principally for the transportation of equipment and supplies. Shelterers would have used the stairs (in the book, Martha and the others shelterers descend in the lift, but returning to dispose of Martha's body, Arthur Wallington elects to use the stairs).

At 9 cwt., the lifts are somewhat smaller in reality than is implied in the book. Whether there are hatches in the ceilings of the lift cars is unknown to the author. In any event, it seems unlikely that in reality there would be sufficient space for a person to climb down the outside of the car in order to abseil to the bottom of the lift shaft (and I certainly don't advocate anyone trying it).

Entrances to the two main shaft pairs, at all of the shelters consisted of a circular, reinforced, concrete 'pillbox' and a square, brick-built, ventilation tower. There were usually small, brick built extensions to the side of the main door. The control and staff rooms, mentioned in *The Shelter*, are fictional.

At Belsize Park, the two shelter entrance buildings are still present and visible at street level. The northern entrance is situated between numbers 212 and 210, Haverstock Hill, London NW3 (this entrance is not mentioned in the book) and the other is on the corner of Haverstock Hill and Downside Crescent. This entrance is used on the book's front cover. It is used reluctantly by Martha Watts on the evening of Friday, 10 November 1944 and, somewhat more enthusiastically, by Harry Stammers some sixty years later. To my knowledge, the door to this building does not have a combination lock.

All of the shelters are provided with ventilation, sanitation, nurses' and wardens' posts, canteens and other facilities.

In *The Shelter*, Arthur Wallington invents an argument between two shelterers in order to create a diversion so that he can remove a page from the shelter log book. The warden uses the telephone to call his colleague, Joe, who is stationed at the top of the lift shaft. In reality, the wardens' posts were fitted with three telephones: - one connected to the national system, one to the Board system and the third providing connections within the shelter. There would certainly have been a telephone at the top of the staircase.

I have found no evidence that log books were kept in fact, although it seems likely that some kind of record was made by the wardens. If that is not the case, then it should have been!

London Bus Routes in 1944

'The Shelter' begins with a young woman in a knee length woollen coat (who we later discover to be the Bletchley Park log reader Martha Watts) stepping off a trolley bus in Haverstock Hill. As far as I am aware, there was, in reality, no trolleybus service serving Haverstock Hill in 1944.

Today, bus routes 168, C11 and N5 use the bus stop on Haverstock Hill, immediately to the north of Downside Crescent. The modern route 168 runs between Old Kent Road and Hampstead Heath, stopping at Belsize Park and Euston Stations. However, to my knowledge, this route was not in operation during 1944.

It is worth noting that throughout the War services were severely curtailed and many sections of route were withdrawn completely, especially during blackout hours. The time of the last buses, trams and trolleybuses were also much earlier than they are today.

10th November 1944

Having stepped from the trolleybus platform into the darkness of wartime Haverstock Hill, Martha is caught in an air raid, as she begins to walk back toward Roderick Road. The route described in *The Shelter* is three quarters of a mile and would have taken Martha between ten and fifteen minutes.

Martha has no intention of spending the night in the shelter and is arguing with the warden, when they hear a blast in the distance. An old man standing nearby tells her:- "Aldgate, I reckon". It is difficult to be certain about the precise dates and exact locations of V1 and V2 rocket strikes on London at the time but contemporaneous press reports suggest that a V2 did indeed strike Aldgate on 10th November, killing nineteen people.

Minutes earlier, a woman with a child tells her:- "You don't even hear them coming. One hit Islington a few nights back". Unlike the V1 'Doodlebug', the V2 flew faster than sound and arrived before anyone could hear it coming. On 5th November 1944, press reports suggest that thirty two people perished at Islington as a result of a V2 strike.

The date November 10th 1944 is also significant because, prior to this, the Government had been denying the existence of the Nazi's new, supersonic, flying weapon. But on 9th November 1944 the Germans announced that they were stepping up attacks on London using their V2 rocket, forcing

Prime Minister, Sir Winston Churchill, to make a statement in the House of Commons acknowledging the V2's existence.

More than 1,400 V2 rockets were fired at Britain in all. The attacks on London ended on 27th March 1945, when the last of the V2 mobile launch units retreated into Germany under the onslaught of the advancing Allies.

Bletchley Park

It is ironic, given the secrecy that until recently surrounded the work of the code breakers at Bletchley Park, that I probably don't need to deal with the major part of the Park's history here, as so much has been written on the subject elsewhere. It was as recently as the 1970's that the work of Bletchley Park gradually began to be revealed to the general public and not until more recent times that the full story has begun to be fully appreciated.

Prompted by a lifelong interest in radio and electronics, my personal involvement with Bletchley Park began in 2007. I had, until then, been a frustrated radio amateur, having managed to convince myself, as a young man, that I wasn't clever enough to pass the examinations necessary to obtain an operators's licence. It was my good friend, David Hodges (his amateur radio call sign is G6IXH), who told me about the training provided by the Milton Keynes Amateur Radio Society (MKARS), which was then based in an old wooden hut at one end of Bletchley Park's B-block. I arrived there, one Monday evening and was immediately both intrigued and appalled, in equal measure, by the rotting huts and semi-derelict buildings. Thanks to David and the trainers at MKARS (Andrew Thomas G8GNI and Frank Jackson M0JSZ), I have since taken two of the three possible amateur radio exams at Bletchley Park and presently operate under the call sign 2E0VPX.

I have spent many hours in B-block and in Hut 1 talking to visitors and learning about the wonderful work undertaken at Bletchley, by the thousands of men and women who worked there during the war.

Today (2012), Bletchley Park is much as it is described in *The Shelter*. The Park's archive, where Harry Stammers works (in the book), is located in a building at the centre of the Park, up a flight of metal steps, the Park's administrative and management staff are based in a bungalow at the top of the site and, sadly, many of the huts are still semi-derelict. Fortunately, the Bletchley Park Trust has been successful in securing funding for extensive renovation and work is due to begin, in earnest, in 2013. Unfortunately, my personal involvement at Bletchley Park largely ceased in January 2013, with the eviction of MKARS from the site due to the impending building works. That, I suppose, is progress.

The Central Party

In *The Shelter*, Martha Watts and Elsie Sidthorpe are members of a group known as 'The Central Party' which, in 1942, moves from Beaumanor Hall to Bletchley Park. In Chapter 6 of *The Shelter*, we learn that the Central Party was made up of a number of army men and A.T.S. (Auxiliary Territorial Service) women and later, a group of men from the United States Army (Elsie Sidthorpe tells Harry that "I cannot remember when they joined us, exactly, but there were quite a lot of them and they were devilishly handsome. Although, to be frank, I could not abide their ghastly accents.")

When it came to writing the book, I had it mind that Martha and Elsie would have been recruited from the Auxiliary Territorial Service, as many of the women at Beaumanor Hall (and indeed, Bletchley Park) were. In 1939, Beaumanor (which is near Loughborough, in Leicestershire) had been occupied by the 'VI Intelligence School' (part of the intelligence effort to intercept and interpret enemy communications). It later became one of the most important of the 'Y Stations' (the 'Y Stations' intercepted enemy radio transmissions and relayed them, for decryption and analysis at Bletchley Park or 'Station X').

The VI Intelligence School moved to the Government Codes and Cyphers School (the forerunner of today's Government Communications Headquarters or 'GCHQ', based at Cheltenham) at Bletchley Park in May 1942.

In his book 'The Hut Six Story'(1), Gordon Welchman, describes the   log readers at Beaumanor moving to Bletchley Park in 1942, where he says that they became known as the 'Central Party'. Welchman says that the Central Party worked in a separate hut but had such an intimate knowledge of German radio nets and the structure of the German communication system, that they quickly became an integral part of the Hut 6 organisation.

In *The Shelter*, Harry Stammers tells John Watts that his sister had been engaged in "enormously important work".

The work of the Central Party was indeed important. It was the integration of knowledge from signals intelligence with the decodes from cryptography, which the Central Party supported, which enabled a complete picture to be built up of the enemy's plans, movements and orders.

Security

In *The Shelter*, following the disappearance of Martha Watts, Elsie Sidthorpe is told by a security officer at Bletchley Park to accept the explanation given about the disappearance of her friend and to ask no further questions. As a consequence, Elsie has remained silent for sixty years about her suspicions that Martha Watts was not killed in an air raid on 10th November 1944.

Today, in an age of instant communication via the internet, smart phones, Twitter and the like, it seems improbable that a young woman would have, or could have kept such a secret for any length of time, let alone for sixty years. However, in 1944, the authorities at Bletchley Park were extremely concerned about security and all staff were required to sign the Official Secrets Act. A strict requirement was imposed never to ask or to talk about the work of others. This level of secrecy was accepted as necessary, within wider society, as a vital part of the war effort. As a consequence, those who worked at

Bletchley Park often told their parents, spouses and children little more than that they worked for the Government or, indeed, remained totally silent. In some cases, relatives are still not aware today of what their mother or father, grandmother or grandfather really did during the war.

I had, perhaps, one of my most moving experiences at Bletchley Park when I met an elderly woman who came into Hut 1, with her family, one Sunday afternoon in 2009. She was in a wheelchair and was almost blind. But, as she entered the Hut, she heard the morse code that was being demonstrated to visitors by one of my amateur radio colleagues. Her family had only recently learned that she had worked at Bletchley Park during the war and were astonished when she announced to everyone in the Hut that she could still understand the morse code, despite the fact that she hadn't practiced it in over fifty years. We offered to test her skills and to everyone's amazement, she was able to read morse, at the first attempt and to a reasonably high level of accuracy and speed. She even tapped out a few words, with a surprisingly steady hand, in reply. Her granddaughter burst into tears and her great grandson, who can have been no more than twelve or thirteen years old, left the Hut with a look of awe on his face, very proud of his great grandmother, as indeed he was right to be.

So here's to the women that Martha Watts and Elsie Sidthorpe represent in *The Shelter* and to all the men and women who worked at Bletchley Park during the War. Like the little boy in Hut 1 on that day in 2009, we should all be very proud of their achievements.

References

(1) Welchman, Gordon, The Hut Six Story, M&M Baldwin, 2011

Sources

(2) W.T.Halcrow & Partners, Deep Tunnel Air Raid Shelters, undated

(3) Subterranea Britanica, The Deep Level Shelters, www.subbrit.org.uk

(4) Underground History, Deep Level Shelters, www.underground-history.co.uk

(5) Halcrow, Our history - Deep Level Air Raid Shelters, www.halcrow.com

(6) Lee Saunders, Secret Weapons, www.leesaunders.co.uk

(7) Lee Saunders, The First V2 Attack on London? www.leesaunders.co.uk

Acknowledgement

I would like, firstly, to thank my wonderful wife Patricia for encouraging me to write the book in the first place and, subsequently, for never losing faith in my ability to finish it. Thank you darling - I really couldn't have done it without you. Thanks also to Bridget Mellett who read the first draft during a wonderful holiday in the New Forest and whose enthusiasm for the book (she really couldn't put it down) helped to convince me that perhaps I could write after all. Thank you too to my good friends Nicky Belton and Antonella Bednarek who were my very first readers and who gave me lots of helpful feedback. Thank you everyone.

Printed in Great Britain
by Amazon